RABETTE RUN

RABETTE RUN

NICK RIPPINGTON

Cabrilon Books

Published by Cabrilon Books

ISBN 978-0-9933323-4-0

Typesetting services by BOOKOW.COM

For Liz and Livvy - my world

ACKNOWLEDGMENTS

You have plenty of time to think when taking an underground train home from Central London late at night, as I do regularly from work most days. That was when the germ of an idea for Rabette Run began and after that it grew and grew.

At the root of it is how ordinary people can have their lives changed so drastically by extraordinary events completely out of their control. As it involves certain mental health issues - Obsessive, Compulsive disorder; Post-traumatic stress; anxiety - at times it was a bit close to home and in danger of inadvertently upsetting people who will be familiar with these things.

Hopefully that isn't the case and I have been able to treat these issues sympathetically while producing an entertaining and thought-provoking story.

Thanks to everyone who has helped me on my author path, especially my editor Emma Mitchell, my cover designer Jane Dixon-Smith and Steve Passiouras, whose Bookow formatting website is such a joy to work with.

I hope you enjoy it and, if you do, please leave a review on Amazon, Goodreads or any other suitable place. They are an independent author's lifeblood.

Thanks.

PROLOGUE

HE was sneaking a glance at his daughter in the rear-view mirror, listening to her talk about college and friends, when their blue family estate was broadsided by the Jeep.

Time suspended before a tsunami of shattered glass crashed in and he lost control of the steering wheel. The airbag deployed and the seat belt cut painfully into his shoulder as it absorbed the strain of his 15-stone bulk before boomeranging him back into place. What was left of the windscreen retreated as his body reacted like the lash of a whip and, in his confusion, he experienced that eureka moment... 'Ahhh, whiplash!'

As the car skidded across the road he was dazzled by a kaleidoscope of bright lights – neon advertising boards, shop windows and street lamps. When his eyes adjusted it was as if he was watching everything in slow motion: A couple he had noticed walking hand in hand moments earlier ran in different directions, while a newspaper seller deserted his pitch, money pouch flapping against his pounding legs. Further along, a dapper-looking bloke in tweeds seemed in two minds which way to flee before settling on the safety of the Underground steps.

The visions tumbled from his mind as the car completed its 360-degree spin and he finally locked eyes on his assailant. Marooned in the stationary Jeep, the dark-haired woman stared through the windscreen vacantly, a thick stream of blood meandering down her face from a garish wound above her eyebrow. Devoid of expression, it seemed the shock had vacuumed all thought from her brain.

As soon as she appeared, she was gone, the car continuing to spin. Facing the pavement again, the driver's attention was captured by what he thought was a bundle of blankets and rags in a shop doorway. With alarm he noticed startled eyes staring out from a face swamped in facial hair. 'Get out of the fucking way!' the driver mouthed as he realised one of London's street dwellers was totally oblivious to the approaching danger.

The car made jarring contact with the kerb and suddenly it was the driver who was spinning, like a sock in a washing machine. His head bumped against the ceiling, his left arm smashed against the twisted metal of the door and his right leg sent jolts of electrifying pain through his nervous system.

Finally, the fairground ride from hell came to an abrupt halt, the car thudding against something hard. The heap of tangled metal that was once a solid and protective shell settled slowly back in an upright position, bouncing like one of those gangster rides with hydraulic suspension that featured in American movies. This wasn't America, though, this was twenty-first century Britain and he wasn't a teen gangster, just an ordinary Joe going about his boring, routine business.

New sounds invaded the void left by the disintegrated windows: horns blowing, tyres screeching, glass crunching, people screaming. His ears slowly acclimatising to the noise, he then detected an unfamiliar ticking and saw steam pouring from the bent and buckled bonnet. Performing calculations in his head, he tried to work out how much this entire calamity might cost him. What would the insurance company say? Was there any possibility the vehicle wasn't a write-off and did his policy contain the use of a courtesy car? How the hell was he going to get to work? What the hell was he going to tell his wife?

Shit, his daughter!

'You OK back there, honey?'

There was a pause during which his heart skipped a beat.

Then...

'Yeah, I think so. I've a... pain in my tummy.'

Superficial damage. Nothing serious. Thank God. Relief flooded through him.

'You?' she asked.

'My leg's killing me but otherwise...'

His thoughts were interrupted by another sound. Looking to his left, he was surprised to see the passenger window still intact. Outside, a man in a navy-blue uniform and cap gesticulated wildly, but it was hard to make out what he was saying. The driver felt as if his head was submerged in that slime kids found all the rage.

Still, at least he was conscious enough to interpret the police officer's manic, hand-waving gestures and detect the urgency in them. Shaking his head to free himself from the gloop, he felt needles of pain attack his nervous system as he shifted sideways, utilising every muscle necessary to reach out and press the button which released the window.

The car's electrics made an uncomfortable, whirring sound as the glass slid down a few centimetres then stopped. Jammed. He continued pushing the button, but the internal workings were badly damaged. He watched as a gloved hand slipped through the gap at the top of the door and exerted pressure. There was another crunching noise and the window dropped to around halfway, the brute force almost certainly rendering the mechanism irreparable. Not thinking straight, his first reaction was one of anger and his mind made calculations about how much compensation he should claim once he was back on his feet.

The police constable battled gamely to get his point across amid a deafening ensemble of alarm bells and sirens. 'We need to get you out of there, sir. No need to panic, but we have to make you safe before we can get the paramedics to check you over.'

'Sounds serious, Dad,' said his girl.

'Thanks, Sherlock, always the optimist.'

'What was that?' The officer's face seemed blurred as the driver tried to focus.

'Sorry, it's my ears...' he shouted, the frenzied effort to make himself heard betraying his underlying fear. 'I can't... Is the car going to explode?'

'Umm, I sincerely hope not, sir, but there is a lot of fuel around, the engine's smoking... It's best to err on the side of caution. We need to get you a safe distance away in the unlikely event that things escalate. The fire brigade will be here in two ticks and they'll bring it under control in no time. Until then...'

'Not sure I can move to be honest, son. I think my leg's trapped.'

'Ahhh.' The policeman nodded. 'Can you have a look around – see what the problem is? You might be able to free it. On second thoughts, hold on, I'll come around to your side and see what I can do.'

Appearing at the driver's window, he then brushed aside fragments of glass and leaned through, peering into the gloom of the footwell. 'O... K,' he said slowly. He wasn't very good at disguising his feelings. It was serious. 'We have a bit of a problem. A lump of metal appears to have wedged itself in your leg. I'm guessing it will take special tools to get you out of there.'

Shit! The Jaws of Life. Only the other day he had been watching a TV programme about the fire service and the equipment they used to cut people free from road traffic accident wrecks. The jaws had saved many lives, but the name alone was enough to send a shudder rippling through his damaged body. The sirens in the distance were getting louder as they announced their urgency to the world. Blue spinning lights roamed the darkness of the car's interior, before a more permanent red glow encroached on the shadows. Was it getting hot?

'Ahhh...' said the officer.

There were snapping sounds followed by a crackle. Random memories of an old advert for cereal entered the driver's head: *snap, crackle, pop*. Twisting as best he could, the driver realised the noise was being created by flames eating into the car's paintwork. 'No!' he muttered through clenched teeth. Damn, he'd just forked out a small fortune on a touch-up job after some local punk had dug a thick groove right along the passenger's side with a coin or a key.

'Uh oh!' said his daughter, looking over her shoulder. 'They're going to get us out of here, aren't they, Dad? I'm scared.'

'Stay calm,' he replied, wishing he could practice what he was preaching. 'I'm sure it will be fine. The fire brigade is on their way and will be here shortly.'

'Ahh, they're here,' the policeman announced on cue, relief evident in his tone.

Moments later the driver heard a new voice, the accent pure Cockney. 'Stay calm, sir, and we'll have you out in no time.'

The driver twisted in the direction of the person speaking and another wave of pain rolled through him. On the periphery of his vision he could make out a tall man with a pointed jaw in a fire brigade uniform.

'What seems to be the trouble, eh? Let the dog see the rabbit.' The fireman leaned inside. 'Rrrr...igh...t,' he said before shouting some instructions to the rest of his crew.

Suddenly, the car was plunged into darkness. The driver guessed it was being buried in that foam the fire services used to bring a blaze under control. It felt strangely comforting to know they weren't going to be burnt alive. Another sound, a screeching, grating noise soon invaded the car's interior, setting his teeth on edge.

'Cool!' muttered his daughter as sparks sprayed through the roof. Moments later the metal was peeled back like the lid on a tin of tuna, bright lights invading the space, making them cry out and shield their eyes.

'Sorry, mate, it's got to be done,' advised the fire officer. 'Once we're inside, we can hopefully remove the obstacle that's holding you in place and get you out of there. Second thoughts, the best thing we can do, looking at it now, would be to remove the door, together with your good self. It should be easier to cut you free elsewhere, rather than in the midst of this, um, chaos. When we get somewhere a bit less volatile the medical people can assess the problem and hopefully free your leg from the door.'

As he said this, for the first time the driver realised that up until now the darkness of the footwell had prevented him taking a closer look at his injury. Shielding his eyes from the glare, he glanced downwards. A thick metal shard was protruding from his leg and a dark, sticky substance soaked his trousers. The limb looked like a theatrical prosthesis in a zombie apocalypse movie, the foot at a right angle to the rest of the limb.

He experienced an unfamiliar dizziness and passed out.

GLOVED hands grasped the limp body and gently carried it to the stretcher. The patient felt a needle entering the soft tissue in his arm and after that remembered little, sliding into unconsciousness as he murmured her name. The paramedic whispered to one of the fireman.

'What did he say? Sounded like a name? Jane, was it? I think he said something about a daughter. Was there anyone with him?'

'Nope,' replied the fireman. 'He was all on his lonesome.'

A colleague arrived at the paramedic's shoulder. 'Right, best get him to intensive care, lickety spit,' said the new arrival. 'I hate to be the prophet of doom, but it will be touch and go if he survives the night.'

ONE

I RECEIVE a broad hint that this isn't going to be an ordinary day when I realise I'm wearing the wrong shoes.

They're stylish brown suede affairs with tassels, no doubt hand-stitched with loving care in Italy. I remember years ago my father referred to them as penny loafers and, believe me, these ones must have cost a pretty penny.

After putting my briefcase on the floor, I drop to my haunches to take a closer look. The aromatic smell of leather immediately hits me in the back of the throat and confirms my suspicion that these are definitely expensive shoes. In fact, I would go so far as to say they're exactly the kind of shoes you should be wearing to a meeting which will decide your family's future.

My only issue with them is I'm pretty sure they're not mine.

I can't for the life of me remember buying them, and they're an awfully long way removed from my usual brand. My daughter, Jamie, ribs me constantly for buying footwear from bargain outlets only to find it falls apart within a couple of months. A false economy, she explains, though despite her soaring IQ I doubt she knows the meaning of the word *economy*.

If I'd obtained them on my annual pilgrimage to spruce up my sorry looking wardrobe in the summer sales, I'm pretty sure I would have remembered. Of course, there is a possibility my wife brought them for me as a gift while I was recovering in hospital and forgot to hand them over. I only came across them when I was searching for a suitable umbrella to combat the incoming showers and absent-mindedly mistook them for my regular pair. I should go back and ask my wife about them but there really isn't time.

The only other explanation I can think of is they were left behind by the idiot Marcus, Jamie's on-off boyfriend, who prides himself on his sartorial elegance. Surely by now, though, he would have noticed there was something missing from his impressive designer clothing collection.

Should I change them? I'm reluctant to do so because they're comfortable, and they fit perfectly. I lift a foot and look underneath. There is a number – 39. That decides it. By my calculations they're fine.

Stretching to my full 6ft, I realise the muttering and cursing has started and that I'm patting myself down anxiously. My right hand dives into the left inside pocket of my jacket and I count: One, two, three. Three pens. Red, blue, black. Everything's as it should be.

I guess you're wondering why I'm so overcome with nerves that I'm physically shaking and distraught to the point of tears. It's because I can recognise when I'm seconds away from a full-scale meltdown. Seeking to wrestle back control I tell myself that this is just a normal day, a working day like any other. I'm just leaving the house as I do every morning and heading for the same destination I have done for the last 15 years. For the time being, I'll ignore the elephant in the room. It's far too early to go there yet. For heaven's sake, I haven't even left my own doorstep.

Though the shoes have thrown me off kilter, my real anxiety stems from the fact I was a full minute and a half late leaving the house. Ninety seconds might seem like nothing to 'normal' people but such fine margins can throw my internal scheduling so far out that by the end of the day I'm a babbling wreck, my stewed brain desperately seeking to account for lost hours. It could be worse, though. At least 90 is divisible by three, which must count for something.

My timetable is carefully drawn up to factor in things beyond my control. The stopping, the turning back, the indecision, the confusion... My life needs a simple road map which must be adhered to meticulously, otherwise chaos reigns. Any little thing that pushes me out of sync causes the tension to seep slowly, like sludge, through my body until it finally takes over, turning me into a muttering, cursing ball of self-loathing. It can get to the stage where I hate everything and everyone, most of all myself and what I've become.

Mental, isn't it? Some "medical experts" would diagnose it as OCD – Obsessive, Compulsive Disorder – wrap it up in a nice bow and file it under Loony Habits.

Too.

Fucking.

Easy.

See, I'm swearing, which would persuade others involved in the dark arts of psychoanalysis to concur that I have a mild form of Tourette's syndrome, a condition which can lead sufferers to curse involuntarily. Not so. My swearing is simply a natural reaction to the fact that I can become as wound up and taut as one of those balls people construct from rubber bands.

I look at the three tiny white objects in my hand and, though they appear so insignificant, I'm relying on their power to overcome the monster growing inside me. I unbuckle my briefcase and grab the water bottle, unscrew the top, pop the chalky white medication onto my tongue and wash it down. Can I feel the pills taking effect immediately or is it just the psychological impact of going through the motions that makes me feel suddenly calm?

I sigh and study the threatening clouds above. The black mackintosh hangs loose from my sagging shoulders, so I pull the belt across. One, two... My God I'm out of condition. There was a time when I could comfortably reach the third hole without having to breathe in like some gone-to-seed supermodel trying to convince herself she's still got a pop at *Vogue*.

Three! It's tight, but I can live with it, the alternative's too awful to contemplate. I guess the bloated feeling comes from the fact my stomach is still digesting the three Weetabix I crammed in for breakfast, along with the strong coffee with three sugars I downed after a sleep-interrupted night. Can you see a pattern emerging?

There certainly has been plenty to keep me awake over the last month. It's been a real doozy. Rufus Wagner, my boss, made an announcement just over a month ago that threw me into a right state. He called us into his office – me, Ben and Hayes – and told us that the business was "downsizing" and, as a result, the three graphic artists in the specialist magazine department would be reduced to one.

It will be a straight shoot-out between the three of us as to who will stay and, the way I see it, the others have the ammunition to blow me out of the water. In a straight-down-the-line, toe-to-toe, show-us-your-skills matrix fight I reckon I can take Ben easily enough. He's a kid straight out of college and can't boast the on-the-job experience I possess. But if he has a joker to play, it's the fact his tender age marks him out as "one for the future"... and, more to the point, he's the cheap option.

Hayes is different: Cocky, cheerful and convivial, the man is a bon viveur who loves to regale us all with his latest tales of single-life debauchery during the daily meeting. People who only have short spells in his company find him entertaining and talented and imagine him to be a real team player. For those of us condemned to spending long hours working with him – like me – it soon becomes evident that a more bitchy, nasty and downright malicious person is unlikely to exist anywhere.

Hayes has another distinct advantage over boring old me. He's gay. This means any attempt at pointing out his personality flaws will immediately place you in the category of "homophobe". While his sexuality isn't identified as an attribute on the matrix, he'll have no qualms about using it to his advantage and contacting Human Resources if the fight cuts up rough.

The opposition itself is enough to cope with, let alone the growing list of black smudges against my name. I've been warned twice about my tardiness lately, while my most recent project received a morale crushing thumbs down from my editor. I've also been forced to take rather a lot of time off in the last few months due to one thing and another, my most recent absence because of the accident.

I can see Wagner now, flirting with his MILF of a secretary Sandra as he asks her, 'Where does Rab stand on the Bradford Factor, Sandy honey? Just bring the files in, bend over my desk and point out his rating with your long, slender fingers while I take in barely a word and focus on your pert bottom.'

Did I mention my boss is a perv? Still, I guess misogynistic tendencies figure high up in the list of requirements when your editor of one of the last lads' mags still in existence, *Boys and Their Toys*. In fact, maybe I can use the fact Randy Rufus is a notorious womaniser in a positive way. I've noticed the way he makes a beeline for Cherry at social get-togethers. If he removes me permanently from the picture, he'll no longer be able to flirt with my better half.

Taking time off immediately after the "restructuring" announcement can't have helped my cause, but the accident wasn't my fault. Come to think of it, Randy Rufus has to bear some of the blame because it was shortly after he told us he was throwing our futures up in the air that it happened. If I'd been concentrating rather than replaying the work scenario time and again in my head I might have avoided the other vehicle entirely.

When the collision took place I was in a daze, trying to figure out how to explain to Cherry that we would have to cancel Christmas this year, together with the new laminated flooring for the hallway and the surprise shopping trip to New York for Jamie. The plan had been to let her choose her own presents from one of the big department stores like Macey's. After all, she was going to be 18 – all grown up – and what teenage girl wouldn't jump at the chance to take an all-expenses-paid bite out of the Big Apple? She'd done extraordinarily well in her exams and we felt it only right to give her something equally extraordinary as a reward. So far, she didn't have a clue about the plan which, in a way, was fortunate.

Cherry isn't going to be happy, though. She rarely is these days. I have the feeling she expects more from me, that I should be acting the same way I did when I romanced her into bed and then into marriage all those years ago. In the main, my wife is pretty supportive of my condition, a tough-as-teak crutch to lean on. Deep down, though, I suspect she feels I use it to wriggle out of my obligations as a husband and father. To be fair, she may have a point. It's easy to highlight my "illness" in order to avoid the annoying family chores other men have to cope with. Mind you, when I do use it as a get-out-of-jail-free card it suits her purposes admirably. It means she can paint me as the bad guy and find solace in piling purchases on the joint credit card.

To talk about how the condition affects my life in isolation would be the equivalent of an artist painting only half a picture, omitting to colour in the broad outlines. Truth is it impacts on all our lives and the knock-on effect for family and friends is glaringly apparent.

The most annoying thing about the voices in my head is I know they're talking rot. When they tell me the consequence of not doing something is that a member of my family might be harmed in some way I know they're blowing hot air up my backside, dispersing malicious nonsense with the confident foresight I won't challenge them. They're right, because the truth is: I'm too scared to try, like a believer receiving electrical impulses from a benevolent God. It's not worth attempting to make sense of it because all it will do is leave you turning circles in the wind until your mind flips out, too.

I interrupt this jumbled train of thought to look back at the three-bedroom house where we live, a stone's throw from Clapham Common because Cherry insisted it was the place to be, the right catchment area for the good schools, conveniently ignoring the fact that it was well out of our price range. Every month is a battle to keep the costs down – a battle we would never win without credit cards – and I wonder how the hell we'll handle the mortgage payments if the worst-case scenario comes true.

Cherry's money from her part-time job as a primary school assistant won't go anywhere near meeting our obligations and it will fall on me to go out into the world again and apply for new posts. Finding that elusive job at my age will be no easy task. Let's face it, having just turned 40 I'm a long way down the road to the scrapheap. Yes, the government introduced legislation preventing employers discriminating against someone because of their age but that doesn't mean it's effective. You can write anything down on a scrap of paper and declare it to be law, but it won't silence those voices – the ones that whisper inside the head of a prospective boss: "Forget this bloke, he's past his sell-by date. He'll cost you too much and will probably break down at the first sign of hard work. It's far better to go for some young, impressionable guy who will come cheap and give more miles to the gallon in a bid to prove himself in the real world."

I can't really disagree with the sentiments and, believe me, I know all about listening to the voices.

'Let's go!' one commands on cue and I wave a pointless farewell in the vague direction of the house, knowing no one will be watching. They will all be consumed by the mad morning rush. Besides, they know how long it takes me to kick myself into gear.

My watch tells me I'm now a full three minutes behind schedule. I check the time with my mobile phone, then remove a small pocket watch from my mac to get a third opinion. They all confirm the original prognosis.

Finally, with briefcase in one hand, umbrella in the other and dazzling new Italian shoes on my feet, I turn away from the house and head off for central London.

'Gate!' the voice orders, and I turn obediently. Open, shut... open, shut... open, shut. There. No one will be hurt today.

TWO

AH YES, the elephant in the room. There's no avoiding it now. It's there, looming large in front of me, waiting to trample me underfoot.

The Tube.

This is my ultimate nemesis, the one thing above all others that will turn my legs to jelly, shrivel my heart and dissolve my brain to mush. People think it's claustrophobia that causes my irrational angst, the madness of thousands of commuters cramming into carriages like matches in a box needing just one spark to set the whole thing off. That does play a part, but it's too simplistic an explanation.

It's about a complete lack of control, your inability to influence anything that happens. You're hundreds of metres below ground and some greater authority is about to dictate your immediate future. Of course, there is a driver, a timetable, people in the background sitting at computer screens guiding you all the way. There are fallback situations, complex algorithms written to avoid every possibility of something going wrong. And yet...

The way I see it, only one small part of the operation has to misfire to set in motion a whole chain of events. Once that happens, it can gather a momentum all of its own. Above ground, in a car, you at least have some say about what's going to happen. Beneath the surface you're putting everything in the hands of others and, what's worse, you don't even know who those others are, what their motivation is, what kind of sleep they had the night before, if some emotional crisis at home has sent them reaching for the bottle, whether they're a hair's breadth away from a heart attack or some inadvertent muscle spasm which will cause them to flick the wrong switch.

Then there are your fellow passengers: What makes them tick? You can't help but sweep the carriage with your eyes, study every bag and try to envisage its contents. If someone looks a bit overweight is it because they have several pounds of explosive strapped to their chest ready to detonate at some pre-arranged time in a carefully selected place? If they're looking around furtively is it because they're trying to select a victim for an opportunistic robbery? On top of all that there is the scenario that frightens us most of all, the prospect of an encounter with "The Nutter".

Everyone talks about "The Nutter on the bus" but generally it's possible to move away, go downstairs and jump off at traffic lights or the next stop, knowing another will be along any minute. When you're a mile below civilisation, though, with a crush of bodies wedging you in place, there is no escape from the vacant gaze, the manic attempts to engage you in conversation, the roaming eyes that seem to act independently of each other, the hand in the pocket that could be playing with a knife, its owner biding his or her time before plunging it into your side.

With all these thoughts circling my brain you're quite within your rights to ask me, 'Why not just drive, take the bus or order a taxi?'

Not. That. Simple. The bus doesn't go anywhere near my destination, unfortunately, while I don't really get on with cab drivers or, rather, I'm not No.1 on their Christmas card list. They tend to balk at my little foibles, the winding up and down of the windows and shouting 'Go' at the top of my voice as they approach a light which is turning from yellow to red. It's not at every light, mind you, just every third one.

As for the driving issue, well I touched on that earlier. A yummy mummy in an urban Jeep straddled two lanes, not sure which one would suit her purposes best. In my mind's eye I envisage most of her driving experience has involved ferrying Jocasta and Moon Boy the 100 yards up the road to the local school from their cosy, suburban home. This time, having travelled further afield, she seemed oblivious to the fact that her top-of-the-range Safari vehicle was equipped with indicators. While I suppose there isn't much call for them in the wilds of the Masai Mara, in central London they simply are a must.

The collision was inevitable. Thump. The car span in the road a couple of times, was broadsided by another unsuspecting driver, flew through the air and smashed into the shop. I had no time to do anything, powerless to prevent the impending disaster. I guess I must have been a bit concussed because I don't recall the immediate aftermath other than someone shining a bright light in my eye and declaring, 'It's touch and go but he should live'.

The accident changed many things. At the time I was planning the best way to drop the bombshell on my wife that I could be out of work soon, but concussion put an end to that. Since being discharged from hospital, the more I've put it off the harder it has become to break the news. This morning at the breakfast table didn't seem the right time or place to upset the applecart along with the cornflakes.

Anyway, I should know more today. We are all due to have personal interviews with Randy and I'm up first, being the senior member of the graphics team. I'd been prepping myself to fight my corner from first light, hence the lack of sleep, and now believed I had it all mapped out carefully in my head. Being first wasn't ideal but if I could drop a few timely incendiary devices in here and there, I might be able to stand back and watch them detonate around Hayes, knocking the cocky bastard off his haughty pedestal.

Feeling around in my pocket, I retrieve my mobile phone, noting it's 9.15. Despite having lurked around outside my house for far longer than was necessary and then having had to backtrack a few times to touch lampposts, I'm still on schedule. My interview is at 11.15 and because the deadline has passed for this month's edition, we have been told we needn't turn up at our normal start time, which is some consolation at least.

It will take me around half an hour to get to where I need to be, Old Street, but I want to make sure I have ample time to factor in delays. If

I arrive early all the better, I can find a nearby coffee shop and revise my 'pitch' once more.

I cross over the small section of common between my street and the Tube station, touch the third lamppost on the right and then look up at that imposing sign, a red circle with a blue strip across the front, the universal logo for the London Underground. Across the middle it reads Clapham Common.

A free newspaper is thrust in my direction by one of the people milling around outside and, after shaking my head in response, I plunge into the forbidding void. A person pushes past me without a second thought while another stops dead in their tracks right in front of me, forcing me to alter direction rapidly before colliding into someone else from behind. 'Hey!' a voice protests as I impede another person's progress in turn.

Looking back over my shoulder, I then mouth a silent apology to a blockheaded man in donkey jacket and heavy work boots, his head shaved in a military style. He just glares. With no wish to expand on our rather frosty first introduction I move further into the belly of the beast.

It's only when I reach the barriers that I remember I haven't bought a ticket. Commuters in a rush to get to their place of work barge into me and there is a Keystone Cops moment where five or six of them, dressed neatly for the city, collide like dominoes.

'Oi, you in front... get a move on!' someone shouts in a Cockney accent. I turn and push against the tide. There is a ticket machine to my right, a queue forming in front of it. To get there I must intersect the path of customers pouring in the other direction. 'Hey, that's my bloody foot mun!' The words are delivered in a male Welsh accent. I look up at a burly figure with curly brown hair dressed in a red rugby shirt. He is clenching his fists and snarling at me like some sort of crazed animal. The missing link? Or maybe just The Nutter.

My attempts to placate him with a smile fall flat, my inane grin causing his expression to darken. He seems about to inflict serious physical harm on me until a pretty crimson-haired girl in a white ski jacket puts her arm on his elbow and guides him away. 'He's not worth it,' she whispers to him and, however much I want to take umbrage, I can only agree with the sentiment.

Reaching the ticket machine, I then watch the scenario play out in front of me. It doesn't seem difficult. Press the screen, select your ticket, insert your credit card, tap in your pin number and voila, your ticket appears in the little tray at the bottom of the machine. Two others attempt it without incident, but I should know better than to take my condition for granted.

When I reach the front of the queue, I read the instructions carefully, ignoring the groans and moans from those behind me. I can either purchase an Oyster Card, top up my existing one or buy a temporary travel card. As I have no intention of repeating this exercise in the near future my finger hovers over the travel card option and I'm about to press it when I realise I have no clue how long I'll be dependent on public transport. At the last moment I choose the Oyster option, but suffer one of my jerky spasms, my finger acting as if it has a mind of its own, requesting the travel card three times.

The machine politely informs me I've ordered three peak-day travel cards and demands I hand over £24. I respond by pressing the cancel button, not once but three times. The machine takes an age to think about this then performs its own equivalent of a mental breakdown, fuzzy lines crossing it before some code number flashes on screen. Ridiculous. I swear and my fist connects with hard metal. A hand touches my shoulder. I swivel and lock eyes with a uniformed member of the London Transport Police.

'I don't think hitting inanimate objects is going to help, sir,' he advises calmly. Behind him there is a rumble of agreement punctuated by a few unprintable insults clearly aimed in my direction. Christ, I haven't even got past first base and the Tube network has beaten me.

THANKFULLY, the policeman is one of the more amiable human beings I've encountered today. He understands my dilemma and calms me down, talking to me as he might address a young child performing a tantrum after being denied their favourite sweets. Guiding me away from the trouble spot he stands me in front of a window and inquires what I want. When I tell him I need an Oyster Card, he explains my plight to a grey-haired woman who hands one over, requesting I tap my debit card on the reader. Moments later I have my reward for five minutes of almost intolerable stress – a small, stiff, blue card.

'There you go, sir,' says my new policeman pal. 'Just press it against the yellow pad on the right of the barriers and you're on your way.' I thank him and offer an embarrassing little wave as I walk away, like a lover parting company after a brief encounter.

Mercifully, the early rush has eased and nowhere near as many people are battling to be first on the platform. Negotiating the barriers, I reach the top of the escalator and stop, eliciting a "tut" from the person behind me. I ignore them, tap the top step three times with my left foot then clamber on board. 'Idiot,' someone mutters.

It's as I begin my descent that a nagging feeling pecks like an irritated bird at my brain. I look down at the new shoes and it comes to me. My briefcase! Hell. I must have left it by the ticket machine when everything was going Pete Tong. I know I can't do without it because it contains my portfolio, CV and record of achievements and, though they should be rubber-stamped on Randy's brain by now, I don't want to take any chances. After all, a general reminder of some of my better work might go some way to pushing aside more recent memories, like my failed attempt at a glamour centre spread a few weeks ago. What made things worse was on that occasion Hayes had ridden in like a knight in shining armour to save the day.

Reaching the bottom of the escalator I'm about to turn back and retrace my steps when I see the briefcase travelling in my direction under the arm of the girl with the crimson hair. She waves and mouths, 'This yours?' and I stick my thumb up, an inane grin stuck to my face. The realisation of how immature the gesture must look sends the blood rushing to my face and I feel a burning sensation accost my cheeks. She indicates the bottom of the escalator and, highly conscious my complexion is the colour of her hair, I move across to meet her.

'Hi!' she says, in a cheery, welcoming manner which puts me at my ease straight away.

'Hey,' I reciprocate.

'Wow, I'm glad I caught you,' she says. 'I was worried you might have got on the train without this. I suspect it's pretty important.'

'My life's work.' I give the briefcase three affectionate taps as she hands it over.

'Winter,' she says, thrusting her hand in my direction, palm out.

'Oh, um yes.' I wipe my sweaty hands down the side of my mac. 'Emerson.' I grasp her hand. 'Sorry, is Winter your first name?'

She nods.

'Well, this is very kind of you, bringing my briefcase down here for me. I thought you were...'

Confusion furrows her brow then a light goes on behind her eyes.

'Ahhhh,' she says. 'I recognise you. You're that bloke who got my little brother all hot under the collar. Jeez, don't worry about him he's a yokel, not used to the big city. He lives in the wilds of South Wales, farmer he is, but he's come up here for the rugby. I'm only here to make sure he gets the Tube OK. He's lovely really, but he's got a flamin' temper. He could start a fight in a chapel, him...'

'Sorry, Winter. It was my fault. I'm not used to the Underground it, um, flusters me. I normally drive.'

'The Tube?' Her eyebrows arch. 'Oh, there's nothing to it. Look, now I've paid to get down here I might as well get my money's worth. You could say, ah, the world's my oyster.' She laughs, throwing back her red hair and shaking it. I'm sure I recognise her from somewhere and wonder whether she might have been a model in one of our photo shoots. She certainly has the looks and the figure, curves in all the right places combining with green eyes that sparkle.

'Excuse me for asking, but have I seen you somewhere before?' I say, risking the fact she'll think it a cheesy chat-up line. 'I mean, um, are you famous?'

Hell, I'm making things worse.

She touches my arm and sends a jolt of electricity racing through me. We both jump then laugh. 'That was strange,' she says. 'Must be static, perhaps from this dress.'

Below the jacket she is wearing a thigh-length, woollen blue dress which highlights her shapely legs but doesn't seem appropriate given the time of year. 'People do say I have an electric personality,' she says. 'As to your question, I don't know. I guess you may have seen me around on a poster or something. Sometimes I'm lucky enough to feature on billboards. Where are we going, by the way?'

She points at the display boards hanging above us on the platform.

'Old Street,' I say. 'I've got a pretty important meeting and I can't be late.'

'Oh, right. Where do you work?'

'I'm a graphic artist... with a magazine.'

'Really?' Her face lights up. 'Which one? I've done some mag work.'

I'm a bit embarrassed to reveal the sordid truth. *Boys and Their Toys* is hardly on an equal footing with the likes of *Cosmopolitan* and *GQ*.

'You probably don't know it,' I say. 'It's a bit niche. Anyway, I'm guessing from what you said you're a model: what kind of work have you done?'

'Oh, you know, mainly travel brochures and stuff,' she says. 'Anyway, there should be a train along soon, let's get you to Old Street. Seems like there have been enough delays already what with you leaving your case behind and the, um, kerfuffle at the ticket machine. You seem a magnet for trouble so I'm going to make it my mission to keep you on the straight and narrow, so you get to your important meeting.'

THREE

I GET the feeling Winter isn't the type to take 'no' for an answer and whatever the reason for her generosity, she presents a nice distraction from the gloomy thought processes infecting my brain.

'I can't be late,' I say, checking the time on my various gadgets. 'It's just gone a quarter to 10. I've an hour and a half to make my destination.'

'Easy peasy,' she says. 'I reckon it will take 40 minutes at the most to get to Old Street, provided there are no further, um, distractions.'

A smile creeps across my lips. Distraction could be my middle name. 'Problem?'

Realising the explanation will take too long I just shake my head.

The platform is fairly crowded despite the fact most of the rush-hour traffic headed into the City some time earlier. Winter follows me along to the third pillar and we stand waiting for the next train. The electronic board informs us that it's heading for High Barnet via Bank and is due in two minutes.

'So...' she says. 'Tell me a bit about yourself.'

Generally, I'm a very private person, but I sense a level of empathy in this woman that makes me feel justified in sharing my unexceptional life story with her. Soon I'm talking about Cherry and Jamie and how our comfortable existence is being threatened by developments at work. She nods her sympathy but insists I look ahead with confidence and optimism.

'Let's face it, your skills can be used by all sorts of media,' she says. 'Just because you work in magazines doesn't make you a one-trick pony. Think of all the industries that employ graphic artists.'

'I'm not getting any younger,' I point out, the words registering as I say them. Here I am, the wrong side of 40, chatting up a girl barely half my age. At least, that's how it must look to my fellow travellers.

'Blow that!' she says. 'Young isn't everything. You've got experience. Give me an older man with knowledge of the ways of the world any time rather than some young pup who doesn't know his arse from his elbow.' She laughs then abruptly puts her hand to her mouth. 'Oh shit! That sounded like a come on. Sorry, it wasn't meant to be. Whatever must you think?'

'I'm pretty sure your intentions were innocent,' I say, joining in the merriment. It feels strange, though. Here I am in one of the most intimidating places I can envisage, laughing and joking with a beautiful young woman, seemingly without a care in the world.

'Here it is!' she says as we hear the low rumble of a train approaching. Leaning out, she then gazes down the tunnel. I reach out instinctively and pull her back towards me.

'Hey!'

Too late, I realise I've overreacted. People who stand too close to the edge make me nervous.

'Sorry!' I interject. 'I didn't mean to manhandle you like that it's just, well, you were a bit close and I didn't want you to, I don't know, maybe over-balance and...' I leave the sentence unfinished.

'Ahhh, you're very sweet, thank you!' she says, giving me the big smile again. 'I can tell you're a caring person. I promise I won't do it again.'

There is a whoosh as carriages whizz past us rammed full of people hanging from overhead straps. One, two... the train begins to slow, and I realise I've made a misjudgement so start walking back along the platform.

'Hey, Em, where are you going?' shouts Winter in confusion. I keep on walking, pushing through the crowd. A growing protest of mumbles and swear words greet my progress. In front of me now, the train screeches to a halt. I look up and count again. One, two, three. I've got it right this time.

Winter's shoulder-length hair has been blown across her face by the back draught from the train. It's like one of those moments on a modelling shoot where, out of shot, someone turns on a wind machine. I feel a strange tingle inside which I haven't experienced for some time. I tell myself it isn't anything sexual just professional admiration but decide it's best not to dwell on the moment.

People behind and to the side of us are jostling for position and once again my inner child takes over, seizing me in an icy grip as if I'm about to take a leap into the unknown. I wait with anxiety for the double doors in front of me to slide back. When they do, it's as if a dam has been breached, a torrent of travellers thrusting themselves forward to exit the train, pushing me aside and leaving me flustered and frozen in their wake.

'Come on!'

I blink and return to reality as Winter grabs me by the hand and drags me onto the train.

'Wait!' I say, pulling away from her and stepping off.

'Bloody hell!' grumbles a uniformed man hauling a huge kitbag towards the doors.

'Sorry!'

'You will be,' he replies angrily.

I step on then off again as the chorus of curses and shouts rises. The doors start to close, and I see Winter's face through the window, drained of colour, yelling something I can't hear above the hubbub. With a last, desperate lunge I push myself between the closing doors and thrust out my hand to hold them in place. They push back again, and I squeeze through, getting an admonishment from the train driver over the intercom. "This train is ready to depart. Please don't impede the doors it can be dangerous. I repeat, mind the closing doors..." There is a whoosh and a shudder, and I stagger against someone as the train begins to move.

A hand grabs me, familiar in its slender delicacy, and I look down to see nails coated in a strange combination of red, white and blue. 'This way, Em, quick, someone's just got off. If we hurry...'

I'm yanked through the carriage and pushed down into the comfort of a seat. Across the way the squaddie from earlier looks stone-faced at me and I read the word 'dick-head' on his mumbling lips. I don't react. Well, what can I do against a bloke who could probably bench press me and another like me without breaking sweat?

'There,' says Winter, bouncing down into the seat beside me. 'Care to tell me what that was all about?'

'Sorry,' I apologise for the umpteenth time that morning. 'It's a "thing" I do.'

'Ooh how exciting. Is it OCD?'

'Sort of.' I nod. 'I think these days they call it being "on the spectrum".' I make quote marks in the air with my fingers.

'A friend of mine's like that,' says Winter. 'Excessively tidy... I mean, to a ridiculous degree. Spends all her time...'

'I'm not tidy,' I say, 'Quite the opposite, in fact. I think sometimes that can be confused with OCD when actually it's just plain fussiness.'

'Ahhh.' She chuckles. 'So, all this time I've been worried about my mate's health when really she's just a nagging fusspot.'

'I don't know,' I say. 'I don't know her.'

'Tell me about how your condition affects you personally then,' she says. 'Really, I'm interested.'

'It's hardly glamorous,' I say. 'I'm not really sure if I can tell you... I might have to kill you.'

She laughs but I sense the soldier opposite doesn't take kindly to the remark. His thoughts are written in every line of his craggy face. 'You think you can kill? Listen, mate, you can't. I'm the one who does the killing around here.' I put my head down to avoid his piercing gaze.

'Getting off the train and on again when it's about to depart,' says Winter. 'That's going a bit far though, isn't it? What possessed you?'

'It's not like I can control it, otherwise I would cut it out altogether,' I snap. 'Look, I know it sounds stupid but something inside tells me to do it and threatens consequences if I don't. It's all bullshit but somehow, I can't explain that to my body. It won't take the risk.'

'Well, I guess it's never boring in your world then,' she says.

The train pulls into another station and a few seats become available. A man wearing an expensive-looking electric blue designer suit, paired with a white shirt ironed within an inch of its life and a black pencil-thin tie with some sort of pin attached, sits down opposite. An elderly, rather plump woman with a hat decorated with an assortment of apples, bananas, grapes and pears takes the seat next to me, restricting my room and making me feel trapped. Once she has made herself comfortable, I expect her to remove the rather flamboyant headwear, but she leaves it in place. Her arrival seems to send the temperature soaring in the carriage, but I guess it's just my internal barometer reacting to an invasion of my personal space. She smells of lavender.

A skinny black kid with earphones and a rucksack stands directly in front of me, bouncing up and down on the toes of his Converse trainers in time to whatever tune is playing in his head. As he holds onto the bar above him with sinewy arms the drumbeat leaks out, tapping irritatingly on my skull. Looking past him, I see the bloke in the designer suit studying me. When he realises I've clocked him, he picks up the paper discarded by a previous passenger and gives the impression he's reading, though I have my doubts.

Strange.

There is a nudge to my ribs. 'You OK?' says Winter. 'You zoned out there for a moment. Is that part of the condition or have I upset you? I hope not.'

'No, no... of course not,' I say.

'You know, talking about your, um...'

'Quirk?'

'Yeah that.'

'It's fine.'

The train lurches into another station and this time the kid moves towards the exit and I can see Mr Designer Suit more clearly. His dark hair nestles perfectly on his head and I suspect some kind of gel is keeping it in place. He fascinates and scares me in equal measure. I want to know more about him, but something tells me I won't like what I learn.

The soldier, meanwhile, is chewing gum in a forceful, regimented fashion as if it isn't something he enjoys but simply another duty to perform. The kit bag at his side is bulging and I wonder if he is on his way to some exotic country to meet new people... and kill them. The old woman is squeezing into me now, her thigh pinching my leg, but I'm not sure what the etiquette is in this situation. Should I ask her to move or would that offend her sensibilities? I'd hate to be thought of as fattist.

She digs into a bag and comes out with a small compact. Opening it, she then stares into the mirror and applies powder to her face. Strangely, though, the mirror seems to be angled in my direction. Managing to shift slightly and squeeze my hand into my trouser pocket I pull out my key ring and count the three keys on it. While doing so, I can't help reading the legend on it, a reminder to myself that there's no need to scrutinise everyone around me so carefully.

'I'm not paranoid,' it says. *'Everyone IS out to get me.'*

It was a birthday present from Jamie a few years back when she was barely a teen. I chuckle and look to my right, only to find that my totally relaxed travelling partner has, in fact, dozed off.

Winter's red hair spills onto my shoulder and, though in other circumstances I might have fretted about hairs from a strange female being discovered on my coat collar, in this instance it seems perfectly innocent. In a strange way, it makes me think of my Jamie as a youngster growing up, how on long journeys when Mum was driving, she insisted I sit in the back so she could snuggle up to me. I look around and see a bloke with a top hat perched on his lap. He gives me a knowing look and winks.

Without warning, the train pulls abruptly to a halt and my nerves take a hike. The lights dim for a second then come back on and I can see the darkness of the tunnel outside the opposite window. I feel the blood coursing through me as my stress levels shoot up. I fear being stuck here for life.

By contrast, Winter doesn't stir.

In the brief time the train has been at a standstill the soldier seems to have disappeared without me noticing. Designer suit man is still there, though, his unwavering gaze directed at me. Farther along the carriage I notice someone else I hadn't registered before, the transport policeman who was so helpful to me at Clapham Common.

'Sorry for the delay,' says the driver over the intercom. 'We're just being held at a red signal. Some slight problem up ahead. As soon as it has been sorted, we'll be on the move.'

The lights dim again, and I close my eyes, muttering a silent prayer.

FOUR

A COMMOTION further along the carriage brings me out of my daydream. When I look up, a man is standing directly in front of me, manic eyes staring out from between greasy curtains of lank, mousy hair. He is dressed in little more than rags and weeks of facial stubble hide his cheeks and chin. With barely a couple of feet between us, I can smell his pungent, rancid breath, which makes me think of the decaying, dead fox I'd seen in the street a couple of nights earlier, maggots feasting on its broken flesh.

I lean away but he follows me, his eyes zeroing in even though I'm pretending I haven't noticed, focusing on something farther along the carriage.

'I'm very sorry to disturb your journey, ladies and gentlemen,' he says in the fashion of a poor actor reading straight from a prepared script. 'I realise you all have busy lives to lead but a small donation will help me pay for a warm drink, food and some accommodation for the night. It's extremely cold outside in the evenings as I'm sure you're aware and I've fallen on hard times. I just need to make £20 by the end of the day to get me off the streets.'

Looking down, I notice his feet aren't restricted by shoes or socks. They're charcoal grey with black stains, the nails long and diseased. I imagine this no-shoe trick is a way to elicit sympathy from his captive audience. Without thinking, my hand gives an inadvertent wave as if I'm swatting away a fly.

'Oh, there's always one,' he says. 'One who thinks they're better than me... that I'm an inconvenience like shit they can scrape off their expensive Italian designer shoes. I know you though... It wouldn't take much for you to end up just like me.'

Others look directly at me now and, as if to shame me, the woman with the fruity hat digs into her purse. She pulls out a £5 note and hands it to the beggar. He thanks her in the way a humble servant might address one of their superiors in a TV drama set in the early 20th century. Looking at me, she tuts and returns to fumbling in her bag.

'See?' he says, turning back to me. 'Not everyone's like you, you selfish prick!' Without warning, his forehead crashes into my nose. My hand flies to my face and I feel warm liquid pulsing through my fingers. When I look up again my assailant is nowhere to be seen.

'Hell, Em! What happened?'

Winter is awake. She pulls my hand away and gasps. 'How the hell did you do that?'

She reaches into her bag and hands me a pack of tissues. I rip it open and dab at my wound.

'I didn't do it, it was a homeless guy,' I say. 'He wasn't a fan of mine, for some reason.'

'Look, there's a cop!' She waves her hands in the direction of the transport policeman. I swear for a second he smirks, then turns away and walks to the far end of the carriage. The train lurches and Winter falls into me.

'Sorry for the delay, we have now got the all-clear,' announces the driver from a nearby speaker. 'This is a Northern Line train to High Barnet. The next stop is Oval.'

I dab at my nose and pray that by the time I reach Old Street a black eye won't have formed. That would be all I need with the big interview due in under an hour. Time is getting tight but as long as there are no more interruptions, I'm still on schedule. How can I explain away my injury, though? My nose already feels badly swollen.

'Take a rest, Em,' says Winter. 'I'm going to find that cop. This animal can't be allowed to get away with what he's done.'

'It's OK,' I say. 'Really. I don't want to cause a fuss. What's done is done.'

'No,' she says. 'I can't just ignore what happened. What if he attacks someone else? The man's a menace and has to be dealt with.'

She gets up, murmurs 'excuse me' to passengers standing in the carriage, then disappears from view.

Returning my attention to my fellow travellers, for the first time I notice a man cradling a trilby hat sitting in the seat the soldier had previously occupied. He looks like a throwback to the 60s with his long, greying hair which kisses his shoulders. The semblance of a goatee is in the process of forming on his chin and he has livened up this poor excuse for facial hair by applying purple dye. Small piggy eyes enlarged by rimless spectacles scan the carriage before they fix me in their sights. Slowly, he points upwards.

My eyes follow the direction of his finger and what I see sends tendrils shooting along my spine. Prickles of sweat break out on my forehead and I realise I'm struggling to breathe. Inside my chest, my heart thumps rapidly and I scan the carriage to see if anyone else has noticed the strange message inscribed on the carriage ceiling. Everyone is trapped in their own little world, though, plugged into headphones or hiding behind books and newspapers.

Or are they faking it? No one seems to be watching me anymore whereas I sensed I was the star attraction earlier and that there were enemies everywhere: The man in the electric blue suit, the woman in the fruity hat and the soldier, not to mention the tramp that assaulted me.

I think about finding Winter so she can bear witness to what I've seen but am reluctant to draw her into my nightmare. There is the risk my mind is playing tricks again and I don't want her to look upon me as a charity case. Instead, I pinch myself sharply on the leg and gasp at the self-inflicted pain. It's necessary, though. I have to make sure this isn't a new phase of my condition brought about in response to a different environment. After surveying my surroundings once more, I glance upwards.

The message is still there, scratched into the very fabric of the Tube carriage by some sharp metal implement. There are just three words but they have knocked my world from its axis.

"Run Rabette Run!"

FIVE

I LOOK right then left along the carriage, urgently seeking an escape route. My eyes fall on something that sends ripples of fear through my body. One of my routes to safety is blocked, the soldier's bulky frame looming large, the heavy bag at his feet. I seem to recall it's known as a Bergen – a vital piece of kit marines carry hundreds of miles on their backs as a testament to how tough they are. Even at peak condition, I would be no match for him.

His thousand-yard stare cuts right through me as I wonder again what might be in the bag. Guns? Knives? It could contain all manner of handy equipment for the man-about-town killing machine.

Looking across the carriage I'm surprised to see the man with the purple goatee has disappeared, but I catch Designer Suit sneaking another look at me over his newspaper. Is he part of the conspiracy, too? Or am I just in the grip of paranoia, brought on by the new pills I've been prescribed by my doctor to help control my condition. I've only been trialling them for a few days to see how I get on and realise they could be responsible for this whole charade.

Calmed by these thoughts I look at the ceiling again, more deliberately this time, expecting to see a hotchpotch of meaningless scribbles where I'd imagined that alarming message to be. No such luck. The words are still visible, unmistakable in their menace.

"*Run Rabette Run*".

The next seconds fly past in a blur. Tucking my briefcase under one arm and holding my umbrella in the other hand, I begin barging, poking, squeezing and thumping my way to the opposite end of the carriage from the soldier. In no time I'm slamming into the door which connects one section of the train to the next, pushing down on the handle as I do so. I pause only briefly in response to a voice I recognise.

'Steady on, fella,' advises the policeman.

I want to stop, to apologise to him as an act of common courtesy. He has, after all, been one of the few friendly faces I've encountered today. A voice in my head overrules me, though, insisting I leap into the next carriage without delay.

It's just as packed though and I hear grunts and groans and the occasional shout as I continue to move forward. I feel a pain in my back, the sort of agony only a well-directed punch to the kidneys can produce, and whip around half expecting to see the soldier, but whoever was responsible has quickly melted into the background.

Then something strange catches my eye. Of all the people I expect to see, I haven't bargained on the woman in the fruity hat giving pursuit. Passengers behind me look alarmed, stepping aside as she barrels towards me through the partition between the carriages. Her face is a dark shade of puce, her breathing laboured, and in my jumbled mind I'm thinking that if she's a hired assassin, she probably doesn't have a particularly good success rate. All the known stereotypes tell me that to make a living in the dark arts you have to be able to operate in the shadows and blend into the background. You also have to be extremely fit. This hefty old bird doesn't measure up for any of the criteria. She would probably get away with her choice of camouflage in the middle of the Amazon rainforest, but on a packed Tube train in central London she stands out like a nudist in an Eskimo colony.

With no time to hesitate, I push on. Angry faces mesh into one another as I accidentally tread on toes and elbow people aside. By now the grumbles have become the human equivalent of white noise, their voices drowned beneath a teeth-jarring screech of brakes, and I feel an overwhelming sense of relief as we enter a station. By chance, I'm standing directly in front of a set of doors and, glancing over my shoulder, I see the old woman gaining. I have to make a split-second decision.

Fight or flight.

I can wait for the train to stop and hope she won't catch me in time or push on to the next set of doors and risk missing the opportunity of getting off altogether. I make an instant decision, put down my briefcase and throw my umbrella into her path, watching in fascination as she treads on it and momentum takes over, sending her face down to the floor. She lets out a shriek as all around her passengers desperate not to get caught up in the melee react by falling onto those unsuspecting fellow travellers lucky enough to have seats.

I hear a familiar voice. 'So sorry, so sorry! Look, here let me help you to your feet. Is this your bag? Oh, how terrible! You seem to have an awful rip in your tights and you're bleeding. You need to be checked over by medical experts. Let me help you off the train and we can call an ambulance. No, not that way, back this way. It will be quicker.'

The transport cop is once again my guardian angel. Has he come to my rescue deliberately, having watched the drama unfold on this Tube ride of terror?

"Shhhhhh." The doors slide apart and I stare at the wall opposite. It announces that I've arrived at Oval, home of the famous international cricket ground. It's not much good to me, though. There are no other connecting Underground lines here and I guess I'll just have to lose my-self in the crowd and find another way to reach my destination. The good thing is I'm just three stops from Clapham Common, a numeric coincidence which appeases the panicked voice inside me.

The train disgorges me onto the platform, and I pick up the pace, following other passengers in the direction of the escalators. Clambering on, I choose the left-hand side, taking the steps three at a time until I reach the top. With no time to search for my Oyster Card I follow a man with a walking stick through an open gate before racing out onto the street with the curses of a station attendant ringing in my ears. Risking a backward glance to see if anyone is following from the train, it seems I'm in the clear for now.

What to do? I'm a complete ignoramus when it comes to the London public transport system. Will it be safe to return to the Tube platform after a while and get the next available train?

A shudder runs through me and it takes me a few seconds to register that it's my mobile phone vibrating inside my coat pocket. I pull it out and look at the screen. The caller ID has been withheld. Tentatively I push the answer button and put the phone to my ear, expecting to hear someone tell me that I was recently in a car accident and could be owed compensation. For once, it's actually true.

As soon as I hear the crisp tone of the male voice on the line, I realise it's not a cold call. 'Go to the bus stop 100 yards to your left and board the 333,' the voice instructs. I'm not sure I recognise the softly spoken caller but take a shot in the dark.

'Hayes?'

'Listen. You're in great danger. Consider me a concerned citizen giving you a friendly warning. Suspect everyone, trust no one.'

'Hayes, if this is your idea of a joke...'

There is a click like an old-fashioned telephone receiver being replaced on its cradle before those annoyingly loud three-tone bleeps cut in to indicate the line is dead. Looking around suspiciously, my eyes lock on a stooped figure in a tweed jacket standing at the entrance to the station, just a few yards from a traditional red public telephone box. Until that moment I hadn't realised there were any of them left in London. Could the figure be my mystery caller? The build is right for Hayes but... no, it's not him. This person is carrying a trilby hat and, bloody hell, it's the character with the purple goatee from the Tube!

I walk towards him, determined to get a closer look. Too late, he spots me and moves at speed in the opposite direction, a classic indication of guilt. As I break into a trot, he also picks up the pace and within seconds I'm sprinting full out, only to have to double back when I realise I've passed the third lamp post between myself and the Tube station without touching it. When I swivel around again, I lose my bearings for a second, finally spotting my quarry crossing the road ahead of me. I can't let him get away, so jump out amid the busy morning traffic, determined to cut off his escape.

My mind wrapped up in the pursuit, I'm startled back to reality by the blaring of a car horn. Putting my hand out, I make contact with the hood of a slick metallic blue BMW whose driver doesn't seem happy that I'm using his bodywork as an armrest. He glares at me from behind the wheel and when I put my hand up by way of apology, he acknowledges my gesture with a V sign.

Continuing the pursuit, I make it to the other side of the road without further mishap and feel panic creeping through my body as I realise the man I've been chasing has disappeared. It seems he's taken full advantage of my 30-second distraction. Could Hayes really be giving me grief? Might he have employed some kind of private eye to fuck me over? It seems unrealistic, and yet...

Hayes knows where I live, he knows I'm without a car and he knows what time my interview is. He also knows how much emphasis Randy places on punctuality. If I'm late, it will give my vindictive colleague the small advantage he needs.

'You're not paranoid, everyone is out to get you!'

The words on the key ring spring to mind again and drag me back to normality. Going to all this trouble is way over the top even for my favourite drama queen, and the sheer practicalities don't add up. Scratching a message onto the ceiling of a random Tube carriage is extremely hit and miss and, even if Hayes has somehow contrived to organise it, how did he know which train I would board and which carriage I would be in? He would need to be watching me all the time and, even then, writing a message and ensuring I see it represents an organisational feat of epic proportions. It's the sort of trick only a professional illusionist could pull off.

My thought processes are running away with me and I'm in danger of a full-scale breakdown. For health reasons, it's probably best I give up the chase. I'm just about to retrace my steps when I catch a glimpse of a trilby hat reflecting off a mirror in a window display. My target has dived into a shop doorway for cover, unaware that the mirror is handily placed to betray his whereabouts. Not letting him out of my sight, I break into a run again, camouflaging myself among the newly arrived commuters who have flooded out of the station exit on this side of the road. His head darts back and forth jerkily in a bid to find me amid the crowds and it's only when I'm 200 yards away he sees me.

Crash! As he attempts to escape again, he collides with a pedestrian heading in the opposite direction and lands on his backside. The pavement is slick with rain that must have fallen while I was on the Underground and as he tries to push himself up his brogues slide away from under him on the wet surface. I seize the opportunity and pounce, grabbing his shoulder and holding him down. His head turns in my direction.

It's definitely him, the man from the train. If there were doubts before, one look at the goatee, the piggy eyes and the rimless spectacles confirm it. He tries to pull away, but I hold him fast.

'It was you, wasn't it?' I demand.

He looks at me blankly.

'Don't act dumb. It was you who made the call.'

'What call?'

'Come off it, I saw you calling me from that phone box over there.'

'I wasn't calling you, I was phoning my wife. I had to remind her...'

'Don't lie to me!'

Someone taps me on the shoulder, and I swivel around. My God, but this is too much of a coincidence. It's the transport cop.

'You again,' he says. 'Are you going to be trouble all day? I suggest you unhand this person immediately.'

'But...'

'But what?'

The man on the ground speaks. 'He's a madman. He keeps wittering on about some phone call I'm supposed to have made. Go on, officer, I'd lock him up if I was you. He's a danger to everyone, including himself I wouldn't wonder.'

'Yeah, all right,' says the cop in an attempt at appeasement. He turns to me. 'Sir, if you don't let go of the man like he asks I might be forced to take him up on his suggestion. I've no desire to arrest you but to all these witnesses standing around it might appear a simple case of common assault and they'll be expecting me to do something about it.'

Sighing, I reluctantly let the man go. He brushes gravel from his trousers then swears quietly under his breath as he sees the rip below the knee. He looks at me as if I'm personally responsible, though the truth is he slipped without any assistance from me. With a final groan and a muttered 'thank you officer' he departs, limping along the pavement.

Watching him go, he resembles a down-on-his-luck college lecturer who smoked too much weed during his time at uni; harmless, but I'm sure it's just an act. Anger bubbles up inside me at a missed opportunity. I feel sure he made the call. If he didn't, why did he run? And why has he been spying on me from a concealed shop entrance? Unfortunately, I'm unlikely to get the answer to those questions any time soon. The cop has a firm grip of my elbow.

Having now put a crowded pavement of pedestrians between us, the man with the purple goatee steps out into the road then turns in my direction. Transfixed, I read his lips, a 'superpower' I've acquired since having to communicate with a hearing-impaired cousin. 'Your bus!' he mouths.

Caught off balance, I look in the direction he is pointing and see the Number 333 pulling into the rank opposite, the very bus I'd been told to board, a secret shared by only myself and the mystery caller.

SIX

I'VE seconds to decide whether to follow the man with the goatee or brave the traffic and catch the bus. It all adds up so there is no contest. The bus is number 333.

I wriggle free from the cop, ignoring his protests as I charge into the road. Sensibly he thinks better of giving chase, watching in stunned silence as I play matador with the city's cars, buses, taxis and lorries. With a last desperate leap, I thrust my aching body in front of the red London double-decker and signal frantically for the driver to open the doors. He isn't pleased about the human obstruction but has two options – wait or run me down.

'You're crazy!' he shouts as the doors open and he glares at me from his cab.

'Probably,' I say. 'Thanks for stopping, you're a lifesaver.'

He nods. 'If I'd been any quicker out of the blocks, they would be scraping you off the road,' he moans.

He jerks his thumb towards the back of the bus, and I stumble down the aisle to take a seat, brushing my Oyster Card on the reader as I pass. The other passengers give me odd looks and a wide berth. It doesn't bother me anymore, though. I'm becoming a seasoned veteran at this public transport lark.

Sinking down into an empty seat, I let my mind wander over what has happened since I stepped out of the house this morning. Reaching inside my pocket, I pull out my phone and check for missed calls. As I do, I note it's 10.20. It seems hard to believe it's barely an hour since I walked away from 15 Pepys Drive, Clapham Common.

Suddenly it dawns on me I haven't a clue where I am or in which direction the bus is heading. Yes, I'm at Oval, but how far is that from Old Street and are we even travelling the right way? My knowledge of south London isn't great, despite the fact I've lived in the area for the majority of my adult life.

I went to a college of further education out at Twickenham, cutting the apron strings and leaving the quiet surroundings of the small leafy village in Buckinghamshire where I was brought up. My father, God rest his soul, had chosen that quiet retreat so that he had somewhere to which he could escape after a week spent whiling away countless hours in front of a computer terminal in the city.

I inherited the creative side of my personality from my mum, Joan, who spent much of my childhood helping me make things out of egg boxes, fashion imposing constructions from moulding clay and draw wonderful pictures of the wildlife outside our windows. Later on, I took to designing my own futuristic comics, borrowing ideas from the Marvel and DC American superhero mags. It was a good grounding for adult life.

I don't really remember how my condition manifested itself in those early days. My mother probably thought it was a phase I was going through while I'm not sure my father would have noticed there was an issue at all. He was far too busy coping with the dilemmas of the real world.

That was my father, Laurent Rabette.

He always seemed a cold fish, even to me, but I never doubted he loved me in his own way. The more I think about it, though, the less sure I am he wanted kids. The impression grew as I got older that my birth had been a concession to my mother, who feared she would rot away through loneliness in such a remote place. Any chance of me having a sibling died with Father's realisation that it was impossible to live by the old adage, 'Children should be seen and not heard'.

Still, he made a comfortable home for us and I never really wanted for anything growing up. It's a shame we lost him so early because I never really got the chance to tell him how I loved and admired him, despite his unusual ways.

From what I can recall he was a bit of a mathematical genius and I often wish some of his attributes had rubbed off on me, even though I accept I'm pretty damn good with every equation involving the number 3, which tends to dictate the course of my entire life. As you have already seen I have an obligation to touch every third lamp post, get on and off transport three times, even dissect my "calming" tablets into three reasonably equal pieces so that I can take them when required.

When I was first given these new pills, I read the instructions on the label and my stress levels soared. I had to take one a day and if I didn't stick strictly to the dosage, I would suffer particularly unpleasant consequences. The medical advice battled with my own inner voice, though, which was telling me I couldn't take just the one or worse disasters would befall me. Then I hit on the solution: I would divide each pill into three roughly equal parts.

This was no simple task, as I'm sure you can appreciate bearing in mind these pills are about half a centimetre in circumference. Taking a blunt kitchen knife to them would end up with bits of the medication flying off in all directions so, after thinking long and hard about it, I came up with the solution: razor blades and a magnifying glass. I'm not sure how the New Zealander Ernest Rutherford first split the atom, but I wouldn't mind betting that he tried something like this.

Holding the magnifying glass to my eye, I took the blade and slowly and carefully carved a Y-shaped incision into each pill. Then, when I was satisfied I had divided them up into roughly equal measures, I traced over one of the pills with a pencil and a piece of tissue paper to make a template. I continued cutting the original pills on the draining board, slowly drawing the blade backwards and forwards, until my three pieces fell apart with minimum waste. Taking my template, I made copies then put it over the next pill and went to work with the razor blade again. Repeat 30 times and you're set up for the month.

Unfortunately, this morning I started a new batch of pills and had little time to divide them so carefully. My efforts at the sink during breakfast time were lax and I hope when I have a bit more time this evening, I'll be in a better position to do a proper job.

My obsession with the number 3 is why I'm now heading for an unknown destination on a red London bus. I touch the shoulder of the person in front of me, her head shrouded in one of those patterned scarves to protect her from the excesses of the weather. I'm surprised she hasn't removed it since she came on board.

'Excuse me,' I say, leaning forward. 'I wondered whether you could tell me the destination of this bus.'

'Of course,' replies a familiar voice. 'We're on our way to Elephant and Castle. Now, are you going to explain to me why you left me behind, Em?'

Winter turns to face me, a beaming smile splitting her rosy red lips. I'm rendered speechless, my mouth open in shock.

SEVEN

'YOU disappeared!' The words come flooding out. 'How the hell did you get here and how long have you been sitting there? I'm sure you weren't there when I got on.'

'Yes, I was,' she says, laughing. 'I boarded just before you did. I saw you playing your crazy game of chicken with the traffic…'

'Sure, but how did you know I'd even got off the Tube? You thought I was heading for Old Street. It's all very confusing.'

'Not really,' she says. 'I could hardly miss you charging hell for leather down the carriage, now could I? What's a girl supposed to do? I'd only got on the train in the first place to help you conquer your fears and get you to your meeting on time, and there I was neglecting my duties. We pulled into Oval and when the doors opened, I saw you flying across the platform like your life depended on it. It was as if a ghost was chasing you or something.'

'Someone was chasing me. That woman.'

'Which woman?'

'You know the one. That rather portly lady with the hat on her head made from imitation fruit.'

'Her? Seriously? Why the hell would she be chasing you? I know you're a bit of a catch but…'

'Ha ha,' I say, my voice edged with sarcasm. 'Not like that.'

She punches my arm. 'I'm joking, silly! God, you're so easy to wind up sometimes – talk about paranoid.'

I'm enjoying every moment of this vivacious girl's company again, but the question has to be asked.

'Why are you here, Winter?'

'It's the good Samaritan in me,' she says. 'I was worried about you. You seemed to be in a bit of a panic and if something happened to you, I wouldn't be able to forgive myself. Plus, you left this behind again.'

She turns to face me, and I see she's holding my briefcase. Unbelievable! I remember now putting it down on the train so that I could impede the old woman with my umbrella.

'I followed you off the train, intrigued to see what you were doing really, and when you ran across the road, almost getting yourself killed, I knew I'd made the right choice,' she continues. 'You're as mad as a box of frogs, I'll grant you, but I find it endearingly mysterious and I'm a girl who loves adventure!'

'I was chasing that bloke – the one in the hat with the goatee,' I explain.

She shakes her head. 'Don't remember him,' she says. 'Anyway, I watched you sprint across the road, then run back and throw yourself in front of the bus, arms waving like some kind of manic puppet. I thought that if I climbed on board, it would do you a favour and stop the driver taking off without you. See, that's another one you owe me. It's OK, you can thank me later.'

She smiles radiantly and my ego swells at the thought this beautiful young woman is paying an old buffoon like me so much attention. Perhaps I remind her of her father or something.

'I wanted to surprise you,' she says. 'I tried to catch your eye, but you were so wrapped up in your own little world that you didn't even acknowledge me when you got on the bus. It was an amazing coincidence that you sat in the seat behind me. When I counted the seats, though, I noticed you were nine rows back. Divisible by 3, right?'

'I guess I'm predictable in that way.'

'Or maybe I'm a clever girl, not just a pretty face,' she says, striking a pose, head resting on the back of her hand, long eyelashes fluttering wildly. 'Anyway, perhaps you'd like some peace and quiet. I get the feeling my presence makes you feel uneasy. I can see you don't seem sure of me, Em. Don't worry, I can get off at the next stop, Elephant and Castle, it's no biggie. I'll get the Underground back to the common from there. Come to think of it, you might want to follow my lead. You can resume your journey to Old Street. That old bird in the fancy hat should be long gone and I don't think this bus goes anywhere near there. I believe it terminates in a couple of stops, in fact.'

'Perhaps I should... I don't know.'

'Oh God!' Her slender fingers shoot to her gaping mouth. 'I bet you think I'm a stalker! I'm not, honestly, just a girl with a day to spare and a penchant for helping lost causes. You should see the menagerie of rescue animals I've got at home: 3 dogs, two cats, a rabbit, three guinea pigs and a python.' She giggles and I can't help laughing, too.

'You like a bit of risk in your life then?' I say. 'You really have a python? That's scary!'

'Not at all. Ponchus is a sweetie. He was found on Wimbledon Common. When the story appeared in the local newspaper about this house-trained snake turning up, I made inquiries. After no one came forward to claim him, I got in touch with some people I knew from when I did work experience at the RSPCA, and they let me have him.'

'Well, I'm flattered that you put me in the same category as Ponchus and see me as a wounded animal,' I say. 'You're right, though. I need to get to Old Street, and I don't fancy venturing underground again on my own.'

I peer out as the rain starts again, pattering against the window. The glass is rapidly steaming up as morning does a passable impression of night. I can just about see the sign for the Underground looming in the distance as cars and lorries circle the Elephant and Castle roundabout like skaters on an ice rink.

'Here we go,' says Winter. 'Next stop is ours.' She pushes a buzzer on a metal pole and the bus starts pulling to the kerb. 'Shall we?' she says, rising from her seat.

It's as I reach down for my briefcase and take a final look out of the window that I see it. The butterflies begin circulating in my stomach and I slump back into my seat. Written in the condensation on the window, letters dripping with menace, are the words: *'Get off now and you're dead.'*

EIGHT

'COME on, Em, we'll miss our stop.'

'I can't!'

'What are you talking about? We've just discussed this...'

'Look!'

She studies my face as if I really am crazy then stares past me to the window. 'Oh, come on!' she says. 'Seriously? That's been scrawled there by some kid. Why should it refer to you?'

'Count!' I urge her as the bus disgorges passengers. 'You see? Six words, divisible by three. A bit too much of a coincidence, don't you think?'

'No, I don't!' she says. 'Wow, you really are in a bad way, aren't you? Anyway, it's not six words it's seven – You're is really two words: you are. I think you need a doctor, Em, to review your medication. This is getting out of hand.'

Suddenly, despite the murky atmosphere, the full picture becomes abundantly clear.

'My God, it's you, isn't it?' I say. 'You've been winding me up all along ...thought you would have a laugh at a loony's expense. Did your brother put you up to this after what happened at the station?'

She pulls back from me, frowning.

'Wh...what are you talking about?' She's a good actress, I'll give her that. 'Oh no.' The penny drops. 'Seriously? Jeez, Em, if you think I'm responsible for all your problems then you really are The Nutter on the bus. I got on seconds before you, didn't I? When would I have had the time to scrawl that on the window?'

Perhaps I'm grasping at straws, but it seems logical to me that the woman who has been at my side all along is the most likely candidate to be messing with my head. I have to follow my thought processes and establish the truth without being distracted by a pretty face.

'Look at it from my point of view: You appear out of the blue one morning, latch onto me, question me about my mental, umm, frailties, then... hell, I don't know. You know what my problem is, though, you've just explained as much. You grill me about my fixation with the number 3 then this strangely appears!'

'If I understand you correctly, Em, what you're saying is rather hurtful.'

For the first time I'm aware of her vulnerability. She looks like she might cry at any moment, making her either an incredibly good actress or someone who is genuinely having trouble getting her head around my weird logic.

'Let's just calm this down a minute,' she says, the words catching in her throat. 'I guess I can see where you're coming from, but why? What would be in it for me? I don't even know you! And the issue remains... I would never have had time to write that remark on the window in the few seconds before you boarded the bus.'

'No?' I have to test her, despite the tears forming on her bottom eye-lids. 'I was delayed, wasn't I?'

Even as I say it, though, I can feel my argument drifting into the mists of confusion. I stutter out the rest of the sentence. 'I got talking to the bus driver because he took issue with the way I ran in front of him.'

'Oh, stop this!' she says, her eyes reddening as she finally loses her temper. 'You can get off or not. What do I care?'

'Sorry,' I say. 'Go if you want but I'm staying...'

The bus lurches forward and suddenly we are pulling out into the traffic again.

'Great,' Winter says, sitting back down and flashing me a look that could freeze blood. 'Now I've missed my stop. Don't worry though, I won't bother you anymore. You obviously think I've got a screw loose and have set out with the express intention of fucking up your life. I feel sorry for you, Emerson, I really do. You don't want my help so, fine, you won't have it.'

Turning her back to me she then picks up a newspaper left on the seat by a previous passenger. I feel like a total bastard.

'Sorry,' I mutter but she has zoned out or, at least, is pretending not to hear. I look at the window, the words that have changed my thinking now almost illegible as they leak down the pane. Something else attracts my attention, though. There is a blue, pulsing light on the other side of the glass. Its source is behind us somewhere and I twist around in an effort to get a clearer view. The back window is too far away from me to see through, so I move across to an empty seat on the other side of the aisle and wipe the condensation away. Pressing my face against the cold glass what I see makes my throat constrict and my head shake involuntarily.

Standing on the sidewalk is the man in the electric blue designer suit from the Underground. He is leaning through the window of a police patrol car and having a one-sided conversation with the driver, as if he is issuing instructions. I can't see the reaction of the man behind the wheel, but I have a strange sense that this all somehow relates to me. The man in the suit is stretching out his hand and pointing in our direction. A shudder rolls through me again and I physically jump from my seat.

My phone.

I snatch it from my pocket and press the answer button.

'Where are you?' It's Cherry.

'On the way to work, darling,' I reply without letting designer suit man out of my sights. 'What is it?'

'Well, you can't be on the Tube Rab or you wouldn't be able to answer your phone.'

'Well done, Sherlock,' I say. 'You're right. There was a problem with the trains so I'm now on a bus.'

'I'm just ringing to remind you about your doctor's appointment tonight...It's important. You have to get that poorly tummy sorted before it gets any worse. It's not been right since the accident, you know. It may be some kind of infection.'

Just as she says this, I feel an involuntary spasm pass through my midriff. My insides haven't been right since the crash, but the local quack puts it down to digestion problems. I've been trying to sort it with off-the-shelf remedies, but nothing seems to work. My biggest fear is there might be some invasive and uncomfortable tests leading to an operation at the end of it all. I've been pinning my hopes on training myself to eat properly and hoping it eventually goes away, but it's not working. Tonight, I intended to seek a second opinion.

A bleeping sound tells me the phone has gone dead. Either I've lost the signal or Cherry has got fed up waiting for an answer and hung up. Remembering my circumstances, I refocus on the scenario playing out beyond the glass. Why would the police and the man in the suit target me?

'You're not paranoid. Everyone IS out to get you.'

Whenever I say the slogan to myself, I always hear it in Jamie's voice, I guess because she bought me the key ring in the first place. Thinking logically, there could be any number of reasons why the police are here and who they're looking for. This bus isn't the only moving vehicle on the roads.

As I replace the phone in my pocket, I let my other hand drift down to the troublesome spot in my stomach. Undoing a button, I reach inside my mac to rub the area giving me the most grief. Shocked, I pull my hand away instantly. It's red hot! Nervously I look down and pull the coat aside. Through my white shirt I can actually see a small patch of discoloured skin. It seems to be glowing, throbbing. I gulp. What is this new hell?

There's no time to dwell on the problem. Sirens fill the air and I'm suddenly frightened. I need to do something fast. I get up from my seat and move towards the front of the bus, feeling as if my progress is being monitored by every passenger.

'Hey!' the driver says as I push past a couple of people standing in the aisle. I stare at his soulless eyes in the mirror. There's something strange but familiar about them, and I can't recall them from our earlier encounter. I prepare for a reprimand for standing too far forward on the bus. Instead I'm in for another shock.

'You Rabette?' says the driver.

I look at him in the mirror and nod.

'Instructions are to get you to Liverpool Street, whatever it takes. Sit tight and enjoy the ride.'

'Instructions?' I ask. 'From whom?'

Before he can answer, I'm thrown off balance as the bus gathers speed, sending the passengers pinballing around too. There's an assortment of gasps and screams as we tear through the London traffic and swerve to avoid a large lorry which was blocking our path. The sirens are deafening now, other patrol cars joining in the macabre symphony. Grimly I cling to a pole, my other hand prodding nervously at the tender spot in my stomach.

'You're determined to leave something behind, aren't you?' Winter's suddenly right there beside me. 'Even though you want to get rid of me it's strange you keep leaving a little trail for me to follow, like bread-crumbs to attract the ducks in the park. I can't help following either. Maybe I'm quackers too.'

She forces out a chuckle tinged with bitterness.

'I'm sorry, Winter, really I am,' I say. 'But not now, eh? I've got to get away from here.'

'Not going to get much done without your case,' she says, raising it to eye level. 'If you don't want it, I'm sure my brother would consider it a jolly nice present. He's looking for a cushy office job rather than spending his days sloshing around in pigs swill.'

I give her a resigned shrug. 'You've got me,' I say. 'I can see I'm not going to get far without you.'

The bus changes direction again, shaking up the passengers once more. A high-pitched scream pierces the air. 'Christ almighty, what's the god-damn hurry?' shouts a voice from behind me. I turn to see an American tourist the size of a house sitting at the back of the bus munching crisps. How do I know he's American? The accent is one thing but the fact he wears a Stetson hat and a stars and stripes cravat is a real giveaway. JR Ewing from the 80s TV show *Dallas* springs to mind and I realise I'm showing my age. Mention JR to Winter and I doubt she'd have a clue who I meant.

'Hey, hang on, you missed the last stop!' shouts another irate passenger. The mood is turning ugly and I have the feeling those on board are blaming me. I scan the faces, but most of them appear scared more than anything. There's an old couple whispering to my left and I overhear the words 'terrorist' and 'kidnap'. It gets me thinking, too. The driver says he's helping me but what if he's doing the opposite?

Maybe the man in the designer suit's sole objective is to stop our driver before he does untold damage in the business district of the city. I've been so fixated with my own problems that I've failed to see the bigger picture. Even though the driver mentioned me by name and there was the writing on the window, maybe my condition is to blame for that, just like Winter suspects. My brain is poised to explode trying to apportion reason to the rising chaos.

The bus slews again and a huge puddle sploshes across the windows on the left-hand side. We strike a kerb and there are more screams as we balance precariously on two wheels for a moment.

'He carries on like this, we aren't going anywhere other than the morgue,' I tell Winter.

She nods. 'What can we do?'

'I'm going back up front. Maybe I can find out what this guy is aiming to prove and calm him down.'

'Be careful,' she says. 'He seems a bit unstable. Mind you, he must know something about you. He called you by your name, like he knows you. You don't recognise him?'

'I've never seen him before in my life!'

'Well, good luck anyway,' says Winter.

I push past passengers clinging to the poles in the aisle for dear life. They don't protest at my intrusion this time, preferring to conserve their energy, self-preservation at the top of their agenda. Scrambling to the front, I then address the back of the driver's head.

'Mate, what's your problem?' I say. 'You're doing a great job scaring the living daylights out of your passengers. It's madness!'

'You think so?' He takes his eyes off the road and turns his head in my direction. I almost fall to the ground in shock. The person behind the wheel isn't the driver who had 'welcomed' me onto the bus earlier, but the military buzz cut, the chiselled jaw and the steely gaze are all extremely familiar. It's the soldier who gave me filthy looks and mouthed obscenities at me on the Tube.

'You! How...?'

'Just following orders, soldier,' he says. 'Must admit I thought you were a bit of an arsehole on the train, but the higher ups tell me you're a VIP and I've got to get you away from those guys out there. I don't ask why: Orders is orders.'

'But what happened to the original driver?'

'Him? He made a hasty exit at the last stop, with a bit of encouragement, if you get my drift.' He waves a gun around.

My mouth falls open, rendered speechless by the new turn of events. 'My God, you didn't...?'

'Nah, don't be silly, he's not dead. It's not in my remit to kill innocent civilians if I can help it. I just encouraged him to take a walk.'

'Are you working on your own?'

He shakes his head. 'Nah, course not,' he says. 'I enlisted a friend to help out... you guys should meet. If he's a friend of mine, he's a friend of yours, too. Ain't that right, Franklin?'

'Sure is, Tank.' A familiar American voice chimes in from behind me and a giant hairy hand clamps my shoulder. It's the bloke who was munching crisps on the back seat. 'Your mission is now of international concern, buddy.'

'What mission?'

The question falls on deaf ears, my new American ally taking his opportunity to address the other passengers.

'We're going to ask you kindly to hang on to anything you can grasp, ladies and gen'le people,' he announces. 'It's time to sit back and enjoy the goddamned ride.'

NINE

THE BUS falls silent and I sense the passengers are saying prayers in their head, begging their Gods to ensure they escape with their lives. Despite the reassurances from the soldier and his American pal, I certainly don't feel like I'm in safe hands. Traffic is slowing in front and I peer through the rain-speckled windscreen in an attempt to identify the problem. The familiar brick archway of the famous London landmark Tower Bridge looms large in front of me. That's all we need. If my mystery pursuers are intent on doing me harm this has to be their chance.

'Take the wheel, Rabette!' orders the soldier, his voice resonating through the silent apprehension. 'You're driving the bus.'

'What?' I'm shocked. 'You're joking! I've never driven one of these before. I'm not sure I can, particularly across Tower Bridge. It's so narrow.'

'Well, it's that or die my friend,' he says with a shrug. In that moment, things suddenly become very clear to me.

'You wrote that message on the window!' I say. 'And you were responsible for the warning on the Tube as well.'

I'm not sure it makes me feel any safer knowing my guardian angel wears army fatigues and is capable of putting people to sleep with a single blow. If anything, it has the opposite effect. I'm petrified.

'Don't know what you're talking about,' he says.

I guess he is trained to resist interrogators with far more dangerous tools at their disposal than a briefcase.

'Now, haul ass over here and take the wheel.'

Passing up the chance to remind him the only job I'm really suited to is based around computer programmes and colouring pens, I move forward into the chair he's vacated. The bus has stopped at the entrance to the bridge and as I slide into the seat, I can see the murky depths of the Thames ahead. A large warship is steaming up the river, and I realise with alarm this is the cause of the delay. The bridge is up! It could take 10 minutes for us to get moving again, and the reflection of the blue flashing lights in the windscreen, together with the increasing volume of the sirens, tells me our pursuers are closing the gap rapidly.

'Pass that bag, Rabette,' growls the soldier. This is someone used to dishing out orders rather than making polite requests. I lean in the direction he's pointing and put my hand through the straps of his holdall. I attempt to lift it, but it won't budge.

'Come on, we haven't got all day,' he says. 'You do want to get out of this alive, don't you?'

'You think these people are trying to kill me?'

'You'd better believe it, soldier,' he says. 'I haven't got time to go into it now. All I can say is it all centres around that.'

He is pointing at my midriff and I subconsciously pat the pockets of my mac, wondering if I might be concealing secret documents without knowing it.

'No, not the coat ... oh, never mind, out of the way.' He grabs me under the armpits and roughly hauls me from the seat. 'Hey, Franklin, some help here please.'

'On it, pardner,' says the Yank, pushing past me and grabbing the bag. Placing it at his feet, he says, 'Let's see what goodies you've packed for our little picnic, Tank.' He pulls back the zip and when I see the contents I stumble backwards, gasping for air. The thing is overflowing with deadly ordnance of every shape and size.

'Here!' shouts Franklin, throwing an automatic weapon in Tank's direction. He catches it expertly in one hand, pulls it down in front of him and performs a series of dexterous moves impossible to follow with the naked eye. The mechanical sounds that accompany his actions tell me this lethal "toy" is now fully loaded and ready to discharge. I just hope he isn't going to let rip in the confines of a jam-packed bus.

The traffic ahead starts moving slowly and the soldier known as Tank inclines his head, indicating I should get back behind the wheel. I'm not going to argue with him considering what he is now holding in his hands. Slipping back into my seat, I'm about to put the bus into gear when I realise I don't have a clue what I'm supposed to do. The passengers sense my unease and a low rumble grows.

In the mirror I see the haunting image of a young black mother hugging two young girls to her side, fear etched in every contour of her face. Her lips don't move but I know what she is thinking. *Please, mister, whatever you do, remember there are women and children on this bus, old people and young, all with families who want them home in one piece. Don't do anything stupid, I beg you.*

I look helplessly at the gear stick then try to shift it, but it's stuck fast. 'What the hell!' says Tank. 'Don't tell me you can't even drive a flamin' bus.'

'That's what I was trying to tell you!' I protest like a child arguing with a parent over school dinners. The last vestiges of calm and control are rapidly draining from my body. 'I'm a soddin' graphic designer not Emerson Fittipaldi.'

As soon as the words tumble out of my mouth, a vision shoots into my brain – my father watching his hero on TV, the Brazilian racing driver from whom I got my name. I feel my eyes welling up.

'Oh, for fuck's sake, are you blubbing, you snowflake?' barks Tank, raising the gun and pointing it in my face. 'Start that business and I'll drill a nice king-sized hole in your head.'

As I brush a tear from my cheek with one hand, I raise the other in a submissive gesture aimed at warding off my gung-ho 'bodyguard'. He drops the murderous weapon to his side as quickly as he's raised it, as if his brain has belatedly informed him it's folly to wave a loaded gun at the person you're supposed to be protecting.

'You see what happens, Rabette?' he says, turning the blame on me. 'You're getting me wound up, and I can't think straight when I'm wound up.'

Suddenly the sirens, ear-shredding in their intensity, change pitch, slowing down as they're replaced by an out-of-tune wail that sets my teeth on edge. It's the same sort of musical torture I experience when listening to those odious Scottish musical instruments, the bagpipes. The bus lights up like Blackpool during the illuminations, searchlights circling the interior.

'Here they come, y'all,' says Franklin, holding a pair of spherical objects in his hand. 'Shall we do this?'

'Too right!' says Tank and the two of them charge down the aisle like a latter-day Butch Cassidy and the Sundance Kid, the rest of us gawping in their wake. I realise that if they're here to protect me the least I can do is fulfil my part of the bargain. After crunching the gear lever around and pressing my foot to the floor, I manage to persuade the huge monstrosity to lurch forward.

'Hey, steady bud!' shouts Franklin, 'You don't want me to drop these do ya?'

He holds up the objects so I can see them in the mirror. Grenades. I recognise this particular type from an army feature I'd designed at work. Before I'm able to respond, he turns back to face the pulsating lights behind us, pushing open the emergency door at the back and shouting, 'Geronimo!'

Launching one of the items airborne like an All-Star outfielder at a baseball match, it sails in a high arc just as a crackly voice on a megaphone announces, 'Please put your hands on your heads. There needn't be any trouble. We just want to speak to Mr Rabette, please, Mr...'

Kaboom!

The massive explosion is accompanied by a blinding, bright flash, the combination pummelling my senses. My vision is shrouded in a sea of white, my ears assaulted by a tinny, ringing sensation. Time seems to pause for a moment before resuming at double speed. People are diving for cover as glass and loose bits of mangled metal fly everywhere, threatening to rip holes in any human flesh with which they come into contact. Tank and Franklin are sprawled on the floor, hands covering their ears, staring out of the back door of the bus and waiting for the fog to clear. An old man who has been sitting near the back moans, and the woman beside him cries as she fusses over him. 'His leg!' she shouts to anyone prepared to listen. 'It's gone straight into his leg. Help us! Help! We need a doctor!'

Shaking myself from my paralysed state I realise similar appeals are going up everywhere. Passengers lucky enough to avoid the flying debris are attending those who haven't been so lucky, the whole surreal episode being played out to a background of moans and groans. One of the little girls I had noticed earlier is lying across a seat, her hair matted with dust, as her mother dabs at a cut on her arm with a tissue from a small pack she has liberated from her coat pocket. The scene resembles something you might see on a late-night TV documentary focusing on the aftermath of a natural disaster.

As I look around, I'm becoming increasingly aware something is missing. The picture isn't right. Then I understand. It isn't something that's missing, it's someone.

Where the hell is Winter?

TEN

AN uncomfortable feeling of nausea nestles in my stomach as I search desperately for the girl who has helped me through plenty of personal crises. Now the roles have switched, and I'm worried about her. I feel obliged to return the favour and seek her out, so I leave the cab. Ducking down, I then move along the aisle in a crouching, crab-like manner, checking the spaces behind the seats. The man-made fog is clearing slowly, particles in the air losing their battle with gravity and sinking to form a layer of dust on the floor.

I study the passengers' faces and realise they resemble those refugees from war zones you see on the news, or survivors of a terrorist atrocity. Unfortunately, none of those I see is Winter.

'What the hell do you think you're doing, Rabette?' says Tank. I figure with a mouth like his he'll be the last in line when they hand out clandestine operations.

'I can't find her,' I mutter, my mind in a daze.

'Who?'

'Winter. She isn't here.'

'Your red head? Yeah, I saw her. She decided to give the fireworks a miss and exited stage left, via the front doors. You probably didn't notice, seeing as you were too busy keeping an eye on me and my friend here. Shame, you were punching well above your weight there: Good-looking piece.'

He turns to Franklin, who slaps the hand he's raised in the air. These blokes are treating the worst day of my life as if it's an afternoon game of volleyball on the beach. I shudder at their cold-hearted indifference and lack of empathy with those who have been injured or, heaven forbid, killed as a consequence of their actions.

'Well, did you see where she went?'

'Sure, because I had nothing better to do than watch your bit-on-the-side skidaddle,' says Franklin.

'She isn't my...'

'Look, if she's got any sense, she'll have gone that way,' says Tank, pointing across Tower Bridge. 'I reckon she was keen to make her exit before the manure hit the fan or, should I say, the grenade hit the van.' He chuckles and gives Franklin another high five before brushing chalky sediment from his close-cropped hair.

'I'm interested, anyway,' he says. 'How well do you know her? Is this some kind of blind date?'

I shake my head. 'You've got the whole thing wrong. We only met at Clapham Common Underground station this morning. I was going to ...' A thought dawns on me and I pull up my sleeve to stare at my watch. 'Christ it's quarter to 11. I'm never going to make it now.'

'Make what? You do realise this ain't no ordinary day in paradise?' He steps forward until he looms a good six inches above me, invading my personal space. 'You,' he prods me in the chest with a finger as inflexible as a metal rod, 'Are... a... wanted... man.'

'But why?' I protest. 'What am I wanted for: using too many garish colours on a fashion spread? For Christ's sake, I'm an ordinary bloke with a family, a wife and daughter, a job. I don't know about any of this cloak and dagger shit, I'm a graphic artist by trade.'

'Shit!'

'What?'

'Well, I just hope... never mind, forget it. We can't afford any negative thoughts right now. We've got to get out of here, as those celebrities say on that TV show. The blast may have stalled them, but I wouldn't be surprised if reinforcements turn up at any moment. If I was you, I would follow in your young lady friend's footsteps.'

He gives me a sly look, expecting me to argue with his description of our relationship but I refuse to give him the satisfaction.

'OK,' I say, but how do I get to Old Street? I don't know which way I'm going and, anyway...' I look down at the clothes I'm wearing, which were pristine when I left for the office that morning. They're caked in all sorts of muck. '...I can hardly turn up for my interview like this.'

Tank looks over at Franklin, who seems to be in deep thought. 'How do I put this?' he says, appearing to address the American. Then he swings back abruptly in my direction and pokes me hard in the shoulder. 'Forget about Old Street!' he shouts in my face, spittle running from his bottom lip and down his chin. 'You need to get to Liverpool Street now, and as fast as you can. Arrangements have been made.'

'What arrangements?'

'Getaway arrangements.'

As if on cue, we hear more sirens in the distance.

'At least tell me where I'm going and who I'm getting away from,' I say tentatively, staring back down the bus as if the answers might lie there, nestling in the dust.

'That's need-to-know,' says Tank, fixing his eyes on the ceiling. 'As for who you're getting away from, it's them.' He nods in the direction of the back door.

'The police?' I say. 'What, I'm on the run? But I've never done as much as earn a parking ticket in the past, what on earth...?'

'Oh, they saw you coming, didn't they? Those aren't proper coppers. They might look like it, but this lot are real clever. They can take over anything or anyone at a moment's notice. But you should know all about that... If you could recall anything, of course. I guess amnesia's wiped your brain of everything. Hopefully some of it will come back soon, but we haven't got time to shoot the breeze. We'll hold them at bay for as long as we can.' He nods at Franklin, who acknowledges him with a cheery grin. 'You get yourself to Liverpool Street.'

'You don't want me to drive?'

'For heaven's... no, I don't want you to soddin' drive. It's too late for that. I reckon this bus is fucked anyway and by the looks of things we're gonna have to make our last stand here.'

He shoves me back towards the front of the bus and I stumble, almost falling face down in the dust. Gathering myself, I try to hide my true feelings from the other passengers. They appear to have partnered up with people who were complete strangers to them when the journey began. Some are just whispering while others squeeze each other tightly as they watch me pass, trapped in my straightjacket of pure, undiluted, fear.

'Oh, for pity's sake, he's forgotten it again,' I hear Tank say as I lean across to press the button which opens the doors. 'Pass it to him would you, kid?'

I turn to see a young Asian boy approach, my briefcase in his hand. Whereas once it was in pristine condition, as good as when Cherry had given it to me for my birthday a few months back, the black leather is now scuffed and scratched, like it has been thrown over a cliff and rolled end over end to the bottom. I take it and thank him. He doesn't say a word, just scuttles back quickly to where his mother sits, her hand to her mouth, choking back the tension as she watches her boy walk away from the strange man.

'Off you pop then,' says Tank.

The doors whoosh open, but something isn't right. I push the button again and again and Tank watches with an expression of incredulity on his face as the doors open and close twice more. Before he can admonish me, I leap from the driver's seat, take a deep breath and plunge into the unknown.

Outside, huge cloud of dirty smoke hover above my head and before I set off the voyeur's instinct kicks in and, like a rubbernecker taking some inane pleasure from getting a glimpse of a motorway pile-up, I stare back at the carnage. First responders triggered into action by nearby fire stations and hospitals are gathered around prone bodies on the floor, checking for signs of life, the apocalyptic vision enhanced by the protective suits and breathing apparatus they wear. There is a whole leg, severed at the point where it was once attached to someone's body, lying in the middle of the road beneath the remains of a mangled vehicle, though the damage is so severe I can't identify the mode of transport.

Slowly, the thick mists of destruction begin to separate, leaving a path through which I'm able to see the whole panorama laid out in front of me. There is a police patrol car on its side, the light on its roof lazily twirling like that of a lighthouse stranded at sea, its windscreen smashed and a body hanging through the space like a discarded child's doll. Lying underneath is another leg, and I quickly arrive at the conclusion this one is still attached to a body crushed beneath the scrapheap of mangled metal.

Stretching off into the distance there is a whole vista of carnage where drivers have been too late to avoid the trouble in front of them. The victims of collateral damage – cars, taxis, lorries, bicycles – are strewn across the street at random angles to each other, cutting off the route for the emergency vehicles stacked up behind. I know the noise is probably deafening, car horns blaring, flames roaring and people screaming with the ringtones of hundreds of unanswered mobile phones providing a modern-day soundtrack to it all, but I feel as if I'm submerged in a bathtub full of water and I wonder if my ear drums are intact.

Standing there, dazed, I ask myself the question: Is this all my doing? Is this catalogue of mayhem with its glossary of innocent victims all wrapped up in this mystery that surrounds me and which I cannot understand? Why am I being pursued by "enemy forces" and who has decided I need to be rescued at all costs? Have some of these innocent people been sacrificed just so that I – ordinary, nondescript, stressed-out, run-of-the-mill graphic designer, husband and father Emerson Rabette – can live? The many unanswered questions send my stress levels rising towards critical.

Reaching into my coat pocket, I search for the small bottle of pills, feeling panic take a grip when I realise they aren't where I left them. I know it's too early to be thinking about a top up – I only took my first of the day less than two hours ago – but it doesn't help me maintain my equilibrium knowing I might have dropped them somewhere on the madcap journey. I don't remember putting them in my briefcase, but my main hope is that I've done so instinctively. I look at the tattered, torn and dusty case at my side and wonder for a moment how I can reasonably expect to give a good impression at my upcoming interview when I bear a striking resemblance to a tramp dragged straight out of cardboard city. Then I remember Tank's words. 'Forget Old Street.'

Looking up from my fumbling, I register movement which doesn't fit with the overall picture. Whereas before everything has been seemingly constructed in a haphazard fashion I now see groups of individuals, dressed in brown overcoats and hats like some kind of warehouse workers' convention, carefully using large brushes to move machinery, glass, bodies and body parts to the side of the road. I watch this strange activity in frozen fascination until it hits me with a jolt what they're doing. Their aim is to clear a path through the mishmash, but who is the intended beneficiary?

Pretty soon, the answer presents itself, causing me such shock and confusion I almost faint, coming dangerously close to falling over the parapet into the Thames. I adjust rapidly, though, as through the clearing smoke, a tall, regal white horse emerges, heading in my direction.

This beautiful steed is a strange enough sight on its own and couldn't have looked more out of place if it had been put there by advertisers trying to cash in on the shock factor. Yet even as I stand, mouth open, staring at this ridiculous, random vision emerging from the gates of Armageddon, I catch sight of something even more stupefying.

Sitting side-saddle astride the horse, like some ancient queen trotting self-importantly through the massed ranks of her down-at-heel subjects, is the plump woman from the Tube, staring out from beneath her fruit-encrusted hat.

11

'THIS can't be happening,' I mutter.

'Oh, it is, all right.' Tank's voice comes from behind me. 'She's definitely here and she's coming for you. It's out of our hands now. We can't afford any more civilian casualties, so it's over to you. I suggest you get moving!'

He leans down from the bus and points towards the other side of the bridge. Checking my bearings, I note the Tower of London to my left and the famous Bridge Hotel on my right. I start trotting at first then, once my legs have got used to the idea, break out into a full-scale run. As I pick up speed, I shout warnings to the hordes of tourists and office workers making their way across the famous landmark.

'You don't want to be going that way – it's mayhem. See the smoke? Please move out of my way!' People turn around, their expressions registering every point on the scale from fear to anger. Voices of protest join in with the cacophony of craziness I'm trying to leave behind.

'Hey, mister, that ain't very polite!'

'Oh my, you've knocked off my hat.'

'*Sacre bleu!*'

'Watch it ya fackin' twat, I'll knock ya block off!'

Above the general hullaballoo, though, a new, more sinister sound is rhythmically tapping into my brain, the relentless percussion of horseshoes on tarmac. It increases in pace and volume the faster I run. Damn! I've missed the third lamp post and have to turn around. I swivel quickly and push against the tide, more voices joining in the protest movement.

The horse is now on the bridge and making good progress. It easily side-steps some of the queuing traffic as its rider fiddles in the large bag slung over her shoulder. I have to blink to make sure I'm not seeing things as she withdraws a brown, leather whip. Rather than beat the horse with it, she points it in my direction and mouths the word 'Stop!'

It's a surreal moment and I stand frozen to the spot, shutting my eyes and willing the image to disappear. When I open them, she is tapping the whip menacingly against her side. I thrust my hand out, touch the lamp post and skid as I change direction sharply, landing on one knee amid a sea of legs.

Pushing myself up like a sprinter leaving the blocks, I then start running again, my briefcase swinging loosely from my arm. It catches a teenager amidships and he howls as he goes down, more collateral damage in my quest to escape this relentless pursuer. Behind me the hooves resume their repetitive rhythm, gaining velocity like a train given the all-clear after being held at a red light.

"Click-clack, click-clack-click, clickety-clackety-clickety..."

The horse breaks into a gallop and pedestrians scream as it cuts across in front of a white van and heads straight for the pavement. Over my shoulder I watch as the woman in the fruity hat lifts the whip above her head and brings it crashing down on an unsuspecting bystander who clatters to the floor, holding her cheek as blood pours from an ugly wound. Another couple, in the wrong place at the wrong time, come off second best as the horse barrels into them.

Reaching the end of the bridge I then bolt along the pavement, people in front of me falling against the stone wall or into the road, preferring to confront the traffic rather than the rampaging animal advancing at speed towards them.

Another lamppost. Second? Third? I've lost count but touch it, anyway, hoping I've got the right one. The distance between myself and the charging beast is shrinking at an alarming rate: It's 100 yards behind, then 80, then 60. I desperately cast around for a means of escape and think about pulling someone from one of the static cars in the queue heading back south of the river. I decide against it because somewhere off into the distance the lights are red and effectively blocking any possible route to safety. I have a better chance on foot, though I'll be infinitely worse off if it comes to a collision between my bulky frame and the hundreds of pounds of muscular horseflesh bearing down on me. The velocity of the animal alone would be enough to knock me into next week, and this is a thoroughbred, not an underfed old nag rescued from the knackers' yard.

As the final metres between us are eaten up, the psycho on horseback raises her whip for the killer strike. At the last moment I veer off down the steps to my left, knocking people out of the way. I hear a female voice shout "Whooah!" and realise my pursuers have overshot the exit. Grateful for the brief respite I hit the bottom of the steps and see a tunnel to my right with directions for St Catherine's Dock and Wapping. Alternatively, I can go left and head for Tower Hill Underground station. I vaguely recall that you can take a Circle Line train from there to Liverpool Street. If I can find my way there, maybe I can get some answers to the myriad questions saturating my brain.

As I turn, I know instantly that I've made the wrong move.

The narrow footpath in front of me is blocked by a solid mass of tourists. They all seem excited about something in the grounds of the Tower. I lean over the stone wall in an attempt to see what all the fuss is about. Below me there is a sea of red, gently rolling in the breeze. No, not a sea, it's a field; a field of poppies. The sight is breathtaking.

I snap back to reality in response to the sound of hooves on concrete and see the white horse approaching along the path under the bridge. It's an elegant and awe-inspiring sight, inducing admiration and fear in equal measure. I turn and run, the station entrance in my sights. People shout and push me angrily as I rip a meandering course through the human traffic. There is no time to delay. I repeat to myself, 'I can make it, I can make it, I...'

A blast of hot, steamy breath hits my neck and I know the horse is right behind me. The woman on its back cackles like a witch from one of those fairytale stories I used to read Jamie when she was younger. 'Zer is no escape, boy!' she shouts with the hint of an eastern European accent as she thumps the leather whip against a hand enclosed in a white glove. In my peripheral vision I'm aware of the crowd parting, eager to watch some live entertainment.

Stepping back a few paces to consider my options, I feel the stone wall against my back and realise I have no alternative. Behind me I hear the old crone say, 'No escape, my pretty!'

We'll see about that.

Without hesitation I throw the briefcase through the air and follow it over the parapet, gasping as the air rushes past me. As I swallow-dive towards certain death, I can hear the woman cursing while my brain runs flashbacks of those days in school swimming lessons when I used to dive from the high board.

Around me the poppies, shimmering as the sun makes a belated appearance through the clouds, seem to stiffen, bracing themselves for the impact of my falling body. Briefly, I think of blood on a battlefield, figures bereft of life entwined together in a tableau of mud and barbed wire. Then I reflect on the carnage I left behind earlier on a busy street in London and wonder if I'm destined to become yet another victim of a war I don't understand. As the flowers rush up to meet me, I close my eyes and shut out all sound, concentrating on turning my body in such a way that I can best absorb the impact.

12

'OH, my goodness, Doc, thank God. He's still with us. He's coming around.'

'It could be just the body's initial reaction to the drugs, don't get your hopes up, he could...'

'No. No. I tell you. I saw his eyes move.'

'Involuntary muscle reflex.'

'Can you hear me, Em? Can you...'

For a moment I think the voice belongs to Cherry and expect to find myself lying alongside her in bed having dreamt the whole thing. My brief injection of optimism is crushed, though, when I open my eyes to find Winter peering down at me, her head enshrined in golden light.

'Hey!' I protest, 'you're blinding me. What the hell?'

'Em... thank God,' says Winter. 'You're alive. We saw you jump the wall. Are you OK?'

'I don't know. Everything feels all right, I...'

'You've had a pretty miraculous escape if you ask me,' intones an unfamiliar voice. A man in green overalls appears in my blurry field of vision. He's got a torch in his hand and has been shining it directly into my eyes.

'Did I hear Winter say you're a doctor? Am I in hospital?'

'Yes and no,' says the man. 'What I mean is, yes, I'm a doctor but, no, we're nowhere as grand as a hospital. We've managed to get you somewhere safe for the moment, but you only passed out for a few minutes. From what I can gather there is still danger around.'

'This is Joel,' announces Winter rather proudly. 'He's my plastic surgeon!'

'Oh, um, right.' I'm confused about how a man more accustomed to performing nips and tucks is in any position to apply splints and mend broken bones. How is he going to assess my injuries and give me the necessary treatment to get me back on my feet?

'When you were talking earlier, before I opened my eyes, you mentioned drugs?'

Dr Joel pushes a pair of glasses back on his nose, the type those alleged brainboxes wear in TV commercials when they explain why you should buy one toothpaste in preference to another. 'I gave you something to ease the pain,' he says. 'Best if you don't ask too many questions about it.' He taps his nose. 'It's used mostly for, um, recreational purposes.'

'Are you telling me you've dosed me up with something illegal? I'm in enough trouble as it is! What is it: cocaine?'

'Now come on, Em, don't get overexcited,' says Winter in her friend's defence. 'The good thing is you're alive after such a huge tumble and that Joel here is willing to help. It's rather fortunate I ran into him.'

'Where did you go?' I ask Winter. 'One minute you were on the bus ...'

'Yeah, well, you were being pretty horrid to me, so I figured you didn't want my help. You seemed to be getting rather chummy with that soldier and his American buddy and, quite frankly, those blokes scared me. When I saw all those guns and other lethal stuff in the black bag that soldier was carrying, well, I didn't want to be there anymore. I'm a pacifist. Hate weapons. You can't blame me, can you?'

'I guess not,' I say. 'I thought you might have said goodbye, though.'

'Ahhh.' She squeezes my cheek. It's either spiteful or affectionate, depending on your threshold for pain. '...So you do care! Did you miss me, buddy? I guess I'm like a bad penny, always turning up when you least expect it.'

I smile. It's a phrase my mother used often, God rest her soul, and something about Winter reminds me of her. Perhaps that's the reason I'm warming to her after our relatively short time together. When I first clapped eyes on her I thought her extremely good looking with a body to kill for, but it's the hidden depths to her personality I find most mysterious and alluring.

Also, of course, I'm flattered. This young woman must have no end of offers from people wishing to spend time in her company yet for some reason she has chosen to be with me. After all we have gone through already this morning I would expect her to give me the widest berth possible.

Memory clicks back into place and I sit up abruptly.

'Steady,' says the doc.

'Where is she?' I demand.

'Where is who?' he asks, pushing me gently back down.

'The woman on the horse; the one with the hat. She's the one who forced me to jump down here.'

'A woman on a horse? I didn't see one, did you, Winter? You would think she might stand out in the crowd. Maybe the drugs...'

'I didn't, but that doesn't mean Emerson is hallucinating,' says Winter. 'You haven't been with us all morning, Joel. A load of crazy shit has been going on and if Em says he saw a woman on a horse, then I have no reason to doubt him.'

He raises his eyebrows, the subtext being, 'You're crazier than he is'.

Behind those glasses, which emphasise the deep brown of his irises, I can imagine his mind ticking over. To him I'm an oddball, delusional and probably in need of a straightjacket. Brushing his hand through blond, wavy, film-star hair, he stretches out his gangly frame. 'Let's talk about this back at my office... It's not too far from here.'

I lever myself into a sitting position, then bite my lip and push on again, the pain rolling through me in waves. Winter grabs one arm and the doc the other and I manage to stand on unsteady legs.

'No,' I say in answer to his suggestion, rather more bluntly than intended. 'Sorry but I can't do that. I have to be somewhere. I've missed my interview, but I've been told the answer to this mystery lies at Liverpool Street.'

'Who told you this, those dodgy characters Winter has been telling me about: the soldier and the big American?' asks the doctor. 'They don't sound very reliable. Anyway, just look at yourself. You've had a horrendous fall and can hardly stand. I suspect you're suffering from concussion, too.'

Looking over the top of his glasses, his eyes perform an inventory of my body parts. I follow his gaze downward to see that one leg of my trousers is torn at the knee, while the other has been shorn right off. There is a jagged edge where the finest cotton material had once been. I almost faint when I see the metal stem sticking out of my calf, as if some tribesman had targeted me with a poisoned arrow. After a delayed reaction, I howl.

'Ooh yes, I hadn't noticed that,' says the doctor. 'That's nasty! It's one of those artificial ceramic poppies they've planted in the grounds.'

Without hesitation he leans over and tugs it out. A stream of blood gushes from the open wound like water flowing from a breached dam. My teeth bite down hard on my tongue as I try to absorb the pain.

'Are you crazy?' I gasp, struggling to breathe properly in response to the shock. 'Call yourself a medical man? I'm pretty sure you weren't supposed to do that.'

'Got any plasters?' he asks Winter.

'Of course,' she says, emptying her bag across the grass. 'I come prepared for every eventuality.'

Fearing I might faint, the doctor talks to me in an effort to keep me from losing consciousness. 'Where are we, do you know, Emerson?'

'No, um I thought I was in the grounds of the Tower of London, but this doesn't look familiar.'

'We moved you. Winter and I carried you here to a more secluded spot. You were only out for a couple of minutes. I thought a fall like that would have killed you, but you're obviously a lot more resilient than I took you for. Now, hold still and I'll just put this over the wound. You'll be right as rain in no time.'

'Good,' I say, 'I really need to get going. I have to get to the bottom of all this.'

'What about the job interview?' says Winter.

Shit! I dig out my phone. The least I owe Randy is a call to apologise. The meeting that will decide my future is due to start in five minutes. I need to dream up one of my best excuses. Pressing his number on my speed dial I get through to secretary Sandy on the first ring. She sounds shocked when I tell her who's speaking.

'You should be here,' she says. 'He's expecting you.'

'A bit of a problem I'm afraid,' I say. 'I've had a fall and I'm on the way to hospital.'

'Oh dear, Emerson, that's terrible.' Despite her words she doesn't sound very sympathetic. 'I'll put you through to him and you can explain it all.'

'Couldn't you just...'

'That you, Rab?'

Fuck!

'Uh, yeah... sorry, Ran... uh, Rufus I, um, I've been in an accident.'

'Really? Now that's funny,' he says, '...Because I've just had my little TV on in the office, passing the time while I waited for you to turn up. I couldn't believe my eyes to tell you the truth, son. I didn't think you had it in you.'

What is the man babbling about? 'Sorry, Rufus, I don't follow.'

'You're all over the news, me old son. Apparently, the police want to question you about some terrorist attack on a London bus. A grenade was thrown, no less. I'm sure it was your mug they flashed on screen, but they called you something else... suggested you were a master criminal – unless, of course, you have a doppelganger. Anyway, I don't know what trouble you're in, mate, but I can see why our meeting might have dropped to the bottom of your agenda.'

'No, certainly not, R...'

Winter snatches the phone and hurls it against the nearest wall. It pings off ancient stone and small pieces of circuitry bounce across the floor. I hobble over and stare at it. The modern gadget has proved no match for masonry that has survived for thousands of years. The phone's screen is cracked beyond repair, while the battery has landed 50 yards away. 'What the hell did you do that for?' I exclaim.

'Sorry,' she says, biting her lower lip like a naughty schoolgirl caught flouting uniform rules. 'It suddenly occurred to me that the easiest way for anyone to track you is through that. They can triangulate your phone signal and narrow down your whereabouts. I've seen it on those TV programmes where celebrities are hunted down by the authorities.'

'Well, fine!' I shout. 'Now I've no form of contact with the people who matter most to me and it's all because you saw a reality TV show. My boss is going to think I deliberately hung up on him.'

'Calm down and think about it,' says Winter. 'Who are these hidden enemies going to be watching for clues as to your whereabouts, dummy? It's pretty obvious.'

I look at her blankly.

'I suspect your calls are being traced, Em. We've seen the resources these people have available to them. They've probably bugged the phones of your loved ones, friends and work colleagues. Did you ever think how they knew you were on that bus, for instance? You took a call from your wife, I recall. It wouldn't have taken them long. It could be the same with work. They want to track you down and finish off what they started, so it's best to have minimal contact.'

I'm starting to think Winter knows far more about this sort of thing than a fashion model should.

13

THE doc keeps me hidden from sight while Winter hails a taxi. I can understand their reasoning. I look a real mess and no self-respecting London cabbie is going to consider me fare potential. Feeling edgy, I peer through the crowd of tourists, keeping my eyes peeled for a white horse. Weirdly, it seems to have disappeared without a trace.

'How the hell do you lose a horse?' I ask myself.

'What's that buddy?'

Too late, I realise I've voiced my concerns out loud.

'Are you American too?' I ask, changing the subject.

'Canadian actually,' says Dr Joel. 'I've been in this country for a few years though. We've got a couple of clinics. You Brits lap up the old facelifts, boob jobs and the like.'

'What have you done for Winter?' I ask. 'She looks pretty good.'

'That would be telling... hey, wait up, buddy, where are you going?'

I've torn away from him to march up to a bus stop and touch it. The Number 633 stops here, meaning I have to make contact with the post four times. When the doc catches up with me, he gives me a curious look.

'What's that all about?'

'I don't know if it's got a name. I just know sometimes I have to do certain things. I try to fight the urges but when I do my stress levels go through the roof. Better to go with the flow.'

'Hey, you two!' Winter signals wildly from the side of the road. Pushing through the crowds using Dr Joel as a human crutch we reach her and the two of them shovel me into the back of a black cab.

'What's this, treacle?' the driver asks in a real apples-and-pears Cockney accent as Winter climbs in beside him.

'Friends of mine,' she says. 'You don't mind, do you? One of them has just had a nasty accident and we need to get him some medical attention.'

He looks me up and down in the rear-view mirror and a strange feeling comes over me.

'Ain't I seen you before, me old cock sparrer?' he asks. I shake my head, though a creeping sense of déjà vu filters into my brain. 'Yeah, I have,' he persists. 'I know I have. Maybe yous remember me like this.' He reaches into the space between him and Winter and emerges with a top hat. 'I was wearing this earlier. I've got to go to me pal's wedding in the city, so I thought I would get some fares in first, you know, had to get some readies to satisfy the beer monster.' He laughs. 'It'll be a right old knees up, I suspect. I might even get to play the old Joanna.'

I faintly remember a bloke holding a top hat on the Tube. 'Sorry, I haven't a clue what you're talking about!' I laugh.

'Not a Cockney then?'

'I'm from a little village outside London, in Buckinghamshire. Name of Silverbirch. D'you know it?'

'Can't say I do. Ain't that strange, though? I had a bloke in the cab earlier this morning saying he was from that exact same place. Spooky. Hey, maybe you know him! I imagine it's a small village.'

'I left there more than 20 years ago,' I say. 'Just after my dad died. What did this person look like?'

'Elderly geezer, whispy grey hair with a bit of stubble. Said that back in the day he worked in the City, but didn't miss it. Think he lives abroad somewhere now.'

'Right, well if he is a lot older than me I wouldn't...'

'Mad on motors he was. We talked about Formula One and swapped stories. Back in the day, before things went downhill and I ended up on the cabs, I used to follow the circuit everywhere: Monza, Monte Carlo, you name it... saw all the greats: Lauda, James Hunt, our Jackie.'

'Stewart?'

'That's right. Into your grand prixes are you?' I smile. He actually says it just like that – Prickses.

'My father used to be. He was a big fan of...'

'Emerson Fittipaldi,' says the cabbie, stunning me into silence. 'That's who this bloke was into. Could tell you anything there was to know about him. All the stats, how many races he won, how many times he spun off. Amazing.'

I freeze. These are exactly the sort of things Rabette Senior would reel off while relaxing in his armchair on a Sunday afternoon as he watched the cars speed around the track. I lunge forward towards the partition separating the passengers from the driver, reach out and grab him by the shoulder. 'Are you winding me up?' I demand. 'If so, it's not very funny.'

The cab swerves and Dr Joel and Winter act swiftly to pull me back into my seat before there's an accident. 'Fuckin' ell, you got a right nutter there,' says the cabbie. 'I knew I should have kicked you out as soon as I seen him, the flippin' tramp.'

Winter is whispering to me, 'Calm down, Em. Take it easy. You're getting all stressed out and it's affecting your behaviour. I can't blame you, mind, if people are accusing you of being a terrorist and hunting you all over London. The best thing is to keep our heads down and not attract any attention if we are to get away, though.'

She raises her voice so the cabbie can hear. 'My friend is very sorry,' she says. 'He's had a frightful day and suffered a serious fall earlier in which he bumped his head rather badly. I assure you he's not normally like this. We need to get him to my friend's clinic.'

Joel joins in on cue. 'Yes, nasty case of concussion, I think. He's a bit delirious. Sorry about that, buddy.'

I shake Winter off but am beginning to calm down. The whole scenario seems so unreal. It's as if people are deliberately messing with my head, but perhaps the fall had a bigger effect than I first thought.

'This bloke,' I say calmly. 'Did you get a name?'

The cabbie blows out huffily. 'Oh, being polite now, are we? Nah, he wasn't in here long. He was heading for the same place as you mind,

Liverpool Street. Still, strangest thing, he said he was so much a fan of that Fittipaldi that he named his son after him. Odd name for a boy though, Emerson... don't you think?'

Winter's eyes flash me a warning and I bite my tongue. She takes over my side of the conversation.

'I quite like it. It's better than some of those silly names Hollywood celebs give their kids nowadays, you know, like Seedless Grape or Prince Dandelion?'

He laughs which, for Winter, signals mission accomplished. She has defused a potentially explosive situation.

'Here we are,' he announces, pulling into the kerb next to one of the entrances for Liverpool Street station. Outside there is a large sign with the telltale symbol of two red lines interspersed with a zigzag, indicating it serves mainline trains. Winter gets out first then opens the back door. 'There's £10 on the meter, can any of you help out? That's all I've got to my name.'

I put my hand in my pocket and pull out a small black leather bag, like a child's purse. 'Strange,' I say, holding it up for her to see. 'I don't seem to be able to locate my wallet, but somehow this has appeared from nowhere.'

'Oh, Em, what on earth? Have you got kids at home and somehow picked up the wrong thing? You can be so endearingly daft at times.'

Her tone sounds a bit condescending and I decide the question isn't worth an answer. Instead, I pull open the strings on the pouch and tip the contents into my hand. There is an assortment of small change, a child's coat button and, small mercies, a fiver.

'Look, don't worry, let me stand for this one,' offers Dr Joel nobly, pulling a thick brown leather wallet from the inside pocket of his green coat. When he opens it, I sneak a peek. It's jam-packed with all denominations, including quite a few £50 notes, the brown colour an instant giveaway. He passes £20 through the partition between the back and front of the cab. The cabbie looks for change, but Joel interrupts him.

'Don't worry, sir, you're out celebrating this afternoon, why don't you have a beer on me? That will just about stand you one at London prices.'

'You're a Gent, guv,' says the cabbie. 'Always said you colonials was all right. Won't never hear a bad word against you in this cab.' He leans into the footwell next to him, lifts the top hat and places it on his head. 'Tip my hat to you I do, sir,' he says, starting to sound more like Dick Van Dyke in the film *Mary Poppins* than an actual cockney. With that Dr Joel is helped out of the car by Winter, who then manoeuvres me rather painfully from the back seat.

'Jeez,' I say, 'I've gone stiff.'

Winter casts a cheeky look in my direction and the temperature shoots up as if I'm having the male equivalent of a hot flush.

'Now,' says Dr Joel, 'I've got to get back to work. I hope you feel all right from here on in, Mr Rabette, and there are no ill effects from the, ah, medication I gave you earlier.' He shakes my hand and heads in the direction of the Underground. Winter stays by my side. I'm still embarrassed and the feeling is enhanced by the fact I seem to have developed an erection.

'Right,' she says, 'We're here. Liverpool Street. What the hell are we supposed do now?'

As she looks around for clues, I spot a newspaper seller sitting at the side of the road, bundled up against the elements, and it seems a good chance to break away and regain my composure for a minute. There is something familiar about the vendor and I wonder if he ever operates out of Old Street.

Recalling the conversation with my boss I walk towards the vendor, hoping to snatch a glance at the headlines. I need to know whether Randy was playing a silly trick on me when he told me I was public enemy No. 1. It's only as I approach that I realise how improperly dressed I am. Hell, the vendor looks like someone out of a fashion catalogue in comparison. I can hear his sales pitch clearly above the general mishmash of noise generated by a major transport hub.

'Read all about it: Tiger escapes zoo, nationwide hunt ensues.' Relieved to find I'm not the top item on the agenda, I retrieve the little purse from my pocket and count out coins. 'Blinkin' 'eck, Bunny, you're a bit out of date, aint ya?' he says as I try to hand him the money. 'They're all free now, these papers. You, of all people, should know that. Say, what's yer ugly mug doing around here, anyhow? This ain't your usual turf.'

I stared at him blankly. 'You know me?'

'Oh, come on, leave it out! Forgotten your own moniker now, have you? You're Bunny you are, to all of us unfortunate enough to know you.'

His face is definitely familiar but the fog in my head won't clear.

'Don't worry, I get it,' he says. 'You're out to impress that good-looking piece of blart, no doubt, ain't ya? Too hoity toity for the likes of us now.' He turns to another customer. 'How d'you like that, says he don't know me, and after all I done for him in the past?'

The new customer raises his head and the atmosphere changes in the blink of an eye. The last time I saw him he was giving instructions to the occupants of a patrol car, moments before the world exploded. It's the man in the electric blue suit!

I snatch a paper from the seller's hand and dash in Winter's direction. From behind me there's a loud peep which revives memories of old cop shows my dad used to watch.

'Stop that man!' For the first time I hear my pursuer's voice and detect the hint of a foreign accent. Who exactly is chasing me? Whatever the organisation, they seem to have the entire Met Police Force at their beck and call, and before long there are officers advancing from everywhere.

'Em, what's up?' says Winter. I grab her hand, my other arm weighed down with the briefcase. 'Hurry,' I say. 'We need to get out of here!'

I lead her into the bowels of the station, and we look around for a departures board with no real idea of where we are meant to be going. 'Let's make a decision,' she says, her eyes scanning the mainline platforms. 'Through here.' She tugs me in the direction of Platform 2.

'No way!' I say, breaking her grip. Turning back, I spot a cabal of cops advancing through the human traffic. Twisting this way and that,

I desperately search for inspiration, some kind of sign to make everything right. On cue the message board above one of the platforms clicks around. 'That's it!' I shout. 'Quick, this is the one!'

'Don't we need a ticket?' asks Winter.

In response, I hurdle the barrier and skid along the platform, the stylish Italian loafers struggling to get a grip. I'm shocked to see how battered they now look.

'Why this train?' Winter arrives alongside me, breathing heavily. 'Is it something the soldier told you?'

I shake my head and look into her eyes, my mind slipping again, imagining her in a different context. How the hell can I feel so turned on amid everything that's happening? At this moment I need to focus on just one thing: Escape.

'Look at the sign!' I say.

She scans the boards, costing us precious seconds as behind us the guard slams doors and puts the whistle to his mouth. 'No time,' I say, grabbing her by the hand and hurtling towards the one door that remains open. She doesn't argue, just chases after me as I sprint further down the length of the train.

The guard, having signalled to the driver he's OK to depart, looks up in shock as he sees a wild character dressed in tattered rags heading straight for him, a beautiful girl hanging from his arm. He is about to say something when I barrel into him, knocking him on the seat of his pants. With no time to help him up, and his curses still ringing in my ears, I jump onto the step of a carriage, lean inside the open window and push the handle down to release the door. Manoeuvring myself into the carriage, I then yank Winter in after me before going through the usual rigmarole with the door...open, shut, open, shut, open, shut.

The train starts gathering pace and I lean out of the window, feeling intense satisfaction as I spot Designer Suit man arriving at the barrier. He thumps it hard with his fist then looks to the roof of the concourse in despair. It's almost as if he is imploring the thing to fall in and impede our progress. On this occasion he's out of luck. Briefly, at least, we have escaped.

14

WE slump into seats and try to ignore the dirty looks we are getting from our fellow passengers. I'm getting used to it now, though I lean over and say to Winter, 'I can't carry on dressed in rags. I need more suitable clothes. Walking around looking like this is attracting attention.'

'I noticed you have a few admirers,' she says, chuckling. 'Maybe they think this is how the man about London town is dressing these days. Hey, you could set up your own fashion chain! I'd model for you.'

'It's not funny!' I respond, though I have to admit to myself it is a bit. 'This whole thing is a nightmare. I'm supposed to be sat in my office, telling my boss why I want to keep my stupid job.'

'Sounds like you don't.'

'The important thing is not whether I like it but that I need it. I have so many financial commitments my family will suffer if I end up out on my ear. It doesn't look like I'm going to be able to do anything about that now though. I might as well get used to walking around in rags.'

She sighs. 'OK, look... this is hardly the time to feel sorry for yourself, is it? We have to get to the bottom of this, find out why we're in this position. Where is this train heading, by the way?'

'Colchester.'

'Nice. And you're sure this is the right one? How do you know?'

'By paying attention to the electronic platform board. It told me to get on this train.'

'Oh.' Doubt passes across her face. 'Like those "words" that made you get off the Tube and that message written in condensation on the bus window? That all worked out well, didn't it? Your "intuition" nearly got us killed.'

'It didn't though, did it? We're still here and we're alive.'

'So, what did this message say?'

I think about my answer. It sounds ridiculous as I mull it over in my mind, but I have no doubt about what actually happened. Then again, maybe this is all part of a nervous breakdown I'm experiencing. A nagging feeling in the back of my mind tells me something similar happened to me a good few years ago, but my thoughts are so scattergun I can't recall the details.

'Look, this will sound strange but... well, I heard the board clicking around to announce the destination of the next train. It was above platform 12...'

'Which happens to be divisible by three. Convenient.'

I ignore the blatant sarcasm and plough on with my explanation. 'I looked at the board and the stations the train stopped at on the way to Colchester were listed there. The third one down said "Rabette".'

She bursts out laughing, attracting more venomous looks from our fellow passengers. 'You're kidding!'

'I swear to the Almighty that someone somewhere is getting messages to me when I need them. I know it sounds mad, it even does to me but, well, that's what happened.'

We are interrupted by the guard. His face is devoid of emotion, like a robot's. 'Can I see your tickets please?' he asks.

'I, um... we didn't have time to get any before we boarded the train. We were in a real hurry.'

'Yes, sir. Shame. It means you're eligible for the £80 fine the rail company dishes out to fare dodgers.'

'Sure. Right. Do I look like a fare dodger to you?' I say, before realising my mistake. He gives my torn clothes a long, meaningful look. 'OK, fair enough. I've had a really bad day. I'm a graphic artist with a reputable company but, well, I had a nasty fall and...'

'...All your clothes ripped themselves to pieces before you dived into mud puddles and your shoes fell apart. Yes, sir, I believe you. You don't have to draw me a picture, Mr Artist.'

Sarcasm is the lowest form of wit. Another of Mother's phrases comes to the forefront of my mind.

'Look,' interrupts Winter. 'You're only doing your job, I know. Is there anything we can do to make all this go away?' she gives him a wink.

'Rules is rules, Miss. I'm afraid I'm not open to bribery of any description.'

'Really?' she says. 'I'm sure those scrooges with the train company don't pay you anything like what you're worth. Maybe a little perk would go a long way.'

I can't believe what I'm hearing. Is Winter offering him some kind of sexual inducement in lieu of the train fare? This just isn't right. All this is my fault, yet she is willing to put her body on the line to get us out of the mess. I shake my head in her direction, but she ignores me and starts tracing the shape of a heart gently on the ticket collector's hand. Aghast, I look out of the window and try to think how I can stop this seedy exchange taking place. I see my briefcase reflected in the glass, all battered, scraped and covered in dust, and it comes to me in a flash.

The other day at work, when I was packing up my stuff to leave for the evening, Ben announced our syndicate had managed a small lottery win. It was only 25 quid and rather than split it between the six staff who made up our group, we put names in a hat to see who would take it home. I was lucky enough to come out on top. When Ben handed the notes over, I absent-mindedly scooped them into my case, meaning to take them out when I got home and transfer them to my wallet. My best intentions were thwarted by the accident.

'Listen,' I say. 'How much will tickets cost to Colchester? If we pay now, are we good?'

'Hmm,' says the ticket collector. 'I'm not sure that's a better offer than your friend is proposing.'

'How about this for an offer then?' I say, my temper rising. 'You disappear and do whatever it is you're planning to do with my "friend" and I get hold of your bosses to explain the bribe you accepted in lieu of two unpaid fares. Does that sound more acceptable?'

He looks at me then shakes his head, his expression indicating he considers his surrender an opportunity missed. 'Not necessary, sir,' he says. 'I don't know what sort of person you think I am but I was only having a laugh. I would never enter into such an, um, arrangement, I can assure you. I was just being polite to the young lady in an effort to try to solve her, um, conundrum.'

'Sure you were. So... how much is it for two tickets?'

'Colchester? £12 each.'

'Perfect,' I say. '£24 in all, then.'

'And divisible by three,' Winter points out. She tosses her hair back and smiles, then mouths the words 'Thank you!'

Pulling the battered case onto the table in front of me, I then try to open it, but it seems jammed. I didn't lock it, so this is another strange development, perhaps caused by the battering it has taken over the last couple of hours. I smile at the conductor in an attempt to hide my embarrassment. Both he and Winter are watching me intently and as I study the case more closely, I twig why I can't open it. It isn't mine!

Somehow, during all the dramas of the morning, I've picked up the wrong briefcase. It's the same size and colour as mine, although its dark brown exterior has faded away under the onslaught it has been forced to endure. It has the same plastic handle and weighs the same in my hand; the only difference is that between the two clasps you have to slide back in order to open it there is a tumbler, one of those combination locks, which you must twist until you come up with the right four-digit code. Only then will it give up its secrets.

The ticket collector is becoming agitated at what he perceives are delaying tactics on my part, but I have no option other than to continue with the charade. Glancing at the table I notice the paper I picked up at the station. A roaring tiger stares out at me and underneath is the story:

"*A dangerous white tiger escaped from Colchester Zoo in the early hours of yesterday morning, causing widespread panic across the East of England.*"

'Sorry to interrupt your daydreaming, sir, but are you going to pay me or am I going to have to alert the transport police and have you thrown off the train?' asks the guard.

'Sorry,' I say. I'm just about to try to blag it and put in a series of random numbers when something catches my eye at the bottom of the story. "*Anyone seeing the tiger shouldn't approach it. Instead they should contact the special wildlife squad on 0203-548-6363.*"

Why not? It's a punt but I'm out of options. I raise the case so that I can see the tumblers clearly then move them into position… 6-3-6-3. As I take a calming breath I push against the clasps and, to my huge shock and relief, they move. Triumphantly I sit the case back on the table and open it.

Glancing down, what I see in front of me rips the breath from my lungs. On the left-hand side are bank notes piled into different denominations and held together by currency straps of different shades. There's a lot more than my £25 lottery winnings in here, that's clear.

'Shiiiit!' says the guard, unable to subdue his amazement. 'You two rob a bank?'

It's delivered as a joke, but his eyes give away the true sentiments behind the outburst. He is petrified, which perhaps has more to do with the heavy looking black pistol which is sitting alongside the money than anything else.

15

'IT'S a prop,' I assure him. 'I'm using it for a project at work.' He sighs with relief, but I can see he is still mulling things over in his head. The gun looks pretty real. 'We're doing an article about the latest *James Bond* film in one of our magazines,' I add for good measure.

'Aaah,' he says. 'Doesn't Bond carry a Walter PPK? That's a Glock if I'm not mistaken.'

Trust me to find the one ticket collector on the entire rail network with an encyclopaedic knowledge of guns.

'Yeah, um, I just needed a general shape to work off. I'll be able to tinker with it later. Now, is there a problem? Here, how about this.' I peel six £20 notes from a bundle and put them in his hand. 'That should keep the wolf from the door.'

His eyes grow wide. 'Certainly will, thanks very much, sir.' He holds it up to the light. 'It is legal tender is it? Looks real, but it would have been cheaper to pay the fine wouldn't it?' A nervous chuckle escapes his lips.

'Maybe, but then the police would have to become involved.' I give him a dark look. I have no idea from where I have attained my new acting skills, but I figure it won't hurt for him to feel wary of us. I have the distinct impression he thinks I'm a gangster and Winter is my moll.

'What's your name?' I ask as he tucks his booty into his inside jacket pocket.

'Raymond, sir,' he says. 'Friends call me Ray.' A new air of respect has crept into his voice.

'OK, Ray, listen up. I'm not your friend. In fact, we never met. You didn't see anything in that case because you didn't see us. Got it? Someone may come around asking awkward questions and it's in your best interests to keep your mouth shut.'

He's about to salute me then thinks better of it. 'Not a problem, sir,' he says. 'You people have a nice trip. We'll be in Colchester in just under an hour... say, that sounds low.'

He leans forward and looks out of the window as a familiar noise intrudes on the peace of the rural countryside now surrounding us. Looking at Winter, I make a rotating motion with my finger. 'Helicopter,' I mouth, pointing upwards.

Moving to the window, I peer out to see a large whirlybird skimming the fields. It's adorned with camouflage paint, the kind associated with the military, and seems to be playing some weird game of hide and seek with the train. One minute it's visible the next it has disappeared. It dawns on me that it has been dodging from one side of the train to the other, looking for something or, more likely, someone. I thought of the man with the Expensive Suit and did the sums. Had he called in the cavalry?

'Is there any way you can stop the train?' I ask the guard.

He shakes his head. 'You're joking,' he says. 'We were 10 minutes late leaving Liverpool Street and the driver is expected to make up the time. He'll get a rollicking if there are any more delays.'

'Can you speak to him directly?' I ask.

'Yes, there's an intercom I can use but...'

'I don't think I made myself clear.' I take three £50 notes from the pile, my hand hovering close to the gun. I hope the subliminal message gets through. As I peel off the currency, I make a rough calculation in my head. There must be upward of £2,000 in the case. I wave the newly liberated notes in his face. 'This says you can get this train to stop. We only need a few minutes.'

'See what I can do,' he says, grabbing the money before I can withdraw the offer. 'Wait here.'

After he's gone, Winter leans across the table towards me. 'Ooh, I like you coming over all tough, Em,' she says, but I detect an underlying note of concern in her tone. 'Do you really think that thing is after us?'

'Not you... all the indications are that I'm the target,' I say. 'They seem to have plenty of resources, and you saw that bloke in the suit back there. My boss says the media is branding me a terrorist, so that gives these people carte blanche to stop me in whichever way they wish. Also, that bloke in the blue suit seems to be taking it personally. He looked furious about missing the opportunity to grab me at the station. I've got a feeling these people will stop at nothing and if that's the case it might be time we parted company... for your safety as much as anything.'

On cue, the window next to me shatters and I duck below the level of the table. Winter joins me. Around us, passengers start screaming, their fear evident as they grab their belongings and search for somewhere safe to hide.

'Shit!' says Winter through clenched teeth. 'Shit, shit, shit! Maybe you're right. What the hell have you got me into, Em?'

I laugh. 'That's funny,' I say. 'I seem to recall you were the one who approached me! Come to think of it, nothing like this happened to me until you showed up. Maybe it's all about you, not me...perhaps it's you they're after.'

'Maybe,' she says, 'But I'm not the one having messages directed at them from Tube train ceilings, platform announcement boards and the condensation on bus windows.'

Touché. Struggling for a response I do what I often do in such circumstances: lose my temper. 'Hell, I don't know, Winter! It's not beyond the realms of possibility that you're the one leading me into some kind of elaborate trap. Those three incidents you mention: you have been with me for every one of them.'

'Oh, come on!' Her face takes on a look I haven't seen before. Though it could be a trick of the light, shadows and sunlight mixing under the table, I'm pretty sure she's genuinely furious. 'We've been through this over and over. Surely you would have seen me leaving that message on the bus, and as for the platform announcement: I was urging you to get on another train! I was running alongside you when that electronic board changed, and I only have your word for it that it happened at all. I didn't see it.'

She takes a breath, but still has things to get off her chest. '...And, by the way, I'm not the one with a gun in my soddin' briefcase, together with a pile of cash.'

'I've no idea where that came from,' I insist. 'Someone must have switched cases.' Then the truth dawns. 'Tank! That soldier on the bus. He gave me the case when I was coming after you.' Then another thought comes to me, the memory of waking in the grounds of the Tower of London. '...And what about your pal, Dr Joel, eh? Tell me about him. It was very convenient he turned up when he did, and he didn't seem much of an expert in the field of medicine. Maybe he switched the cases then you sent him off to fiddle with the train announcements.'

'Bloody hell, Em!' This time Winter completely loses it, spittle shooting from her mouth and spraying my face. 'I thought you were just a bit quirky when I first met you... that you needed a hand. Now I can see your totally doolally!' She makes a twirling movement with her finger next to her head. 'What the hell have I done? I'm going to ring my brother, see if he can get me out of this mess before it's too late.'

'Oh yeah, that's just who you need!' I say, turning on full rant mode in response. 'A thicko Welsh farmer with a rugby obsession and a hot temper. I'm sure he'll do the trick.'

From nowhere she produces a short-armed rabbit punch, like she's some sort of martial arts expert. In the small space under the table there is no room for me to get out of the way and it connects hard with my mouth. I put my hand to my face and am stunned to feel a damp patch on my top lip. Blood. 'What the...?'

She goes quiet.

Eventually, she says, 'Sorry,' moving to touch the damaged area. I flinch away. 'You did deserve it, though. You may not think much of my brother, but you only met him for five seconds or so this morning.

You have no right to talk about him that way. He's a real sweetie, and he always looks after me. I don't think he would be very pleased if he saw the way you have treated his big sister today.'

We fall silent, immersed in our own thoughts, brooding as the air around us fills with the sound of churning rotor blades, louder now as the craft passes by the shattered window. Another volley of automatic fire explodes the upholstery in the exact place where I'd been sitting a few moments earlier and I let out an involuntary yelp. As I do so, I hear a squeal of brakes and the train starts slowing down. For a moment the helicopter noise recedes.

'This must be our stop,' I say.

16

CRAWLING from beneath the table, we make sure to stay low and avoid being framed in the broken window. I pull the briefcase down and look inside again. There is a strange assortment of things I hadn't noticed earlier but we have no time to take an inventory. Instead, I remove the Glock and tuck it into the waistband of my ruined trousers before closing the case and picking it up. Still in a crouch, I move into the aisle, beckoning for Winter to follow.

The other passengers have scattered, most of them moving to other carriages. Those that remain in our coach are frozen, quivering in their seats, the shock having drained their faces of colour. They shrink further back as we pass. Perhaps they've seen the money and the gun. As if that isn't enough to raise their suspicions about us, the fact that not only are we acting furtively but also a helicopter gunship has blasted out our window, will have done the trick.

In a funny way, finding myself public enemy No.1 has helped restore my self-esteem. Since Randy made his announcement and the ensuing accident I have been on the defensive, my mind filled with negative impulses. Now, puffing my chest out and swinging the bag in one hand, I make sure the gun is visible to our fellow passengers. The guard, walking towards our carriage, scampers back in the other direction when he sees us approaching.

When I reach the area between carriages I look out over fields of tall, swaying yellow grass. I can see some of it has been flattened and figure the helicopter must be hovering just out of view. 'Here's what we do,' I say, taking control. 'We sneak out of this door and immediately throw ourselves under the train.'

'Good idea,' she says. 'A joint suicide.'

I ignore the gallows humour. 'The train will be stationary, and we can use it as cover to hide from that thing.' I raise my eyebrows skywards.

'What if the train starts up again, though?' says Winter.

'We'll have to take our chances. I don't see any other avenues of escape open to us. If we stay low and keep off the rails, we should be OK whatever happens.'

'You can't say that for definite, though.'

I make a slight nodding gesture with my head, conceding the point. 'No, but I don't see an alternative. These people have been instructed to shoot to kill. You saw what happened in that carriage back there. If we had remained seated...'

'All right,' she says. 'I've followed you this far, but what is the plan after that?'

'We find somewhere we can regroup and assess our situation. I want to take a good look inside this.' I lift the case. 'I need to see exactly what I've got.'

'But it's not yours, Em,' she says.

'Don't you think I know that?' I'm raising my voice again and have to make a conscious effort to keep it in check. 'It's a bit of a coincidence though, don't you think? I've ended up with this case when we seem to be under attack from all angles. It's as if I'm meant to have it... like in one of those computer games where you pick up things to help you on the way to achieving your objective.'

'Well, if you're Super Mario I guess that makes me Sonic the bloody Hedgehog,' she says. I look at her, totally bemused by her response. Then, like a balloon bursting, the tension pops and we both begin to laugh.

'Seriously, though,' says Winter, puffing out her cheeks and brushing tears of laughter away. 'Who the hell are you, Em? This isn't the normal everyday life of a graphic artist is it?'

'I'm asking myself the same question. This is insane. Either they've got the wrong bloke or... hell, I don't know. Anyway, you agree we have to do something, right? I'm not hearing an alternative plan.'

She shrugs and that's all the encouragement I need. Before she has time to change her mind, I yank the window down. Thinking about it, I pull it shut again and perform the task twice more, earning an admonishing glance from my companion. Ignoring her, I put my hand out and reach down for the handle. With the force of my weight on it, the door flies open, and I jump down in one swift movement, pulling Winter behind me.

We land with a crunch, rolling down a gravel bank and ending up at the foot of a wooden fence. Looking down, I see blood where the scab from my earlier leg wound has been removed by the rough terrain. I dab at it, wincing, but Winter is already up and moving. 'Come on!' she says. 'There isn't time to sit around admiring your war wounds. We need to get going before the train starts up again.'

Taking the lead, she scrambles on elbows and knees back to the top of the bank before disappearing from view. Admiring her fitness, I suspect it comes from many hours on the treadmill in the gym and feel strangely in awe of her. I have a gym membership which costs me upwards of £60 a month but if I use it once in that time, I consider it an achievement. The concession to middle-class living is another thing that will have to go when I strip away all the perks to adjust to my new jobless existence.

I put the thought to one side and follow Winter's lead, forcing my way up the bank, my ears filtering sounds as I listen for the helicopter. When I arrive back at the train, I can see she has already crawled through to the other side.

'Winter, take this!' I say, throwing the briefcase in her direction. She has to crawl back under to retrieve it as I lower myself flat to the ground. The brakes hiss and for a brief moment I pause, knowing the train could move at any moment. There is no time for hesitation. A smell of burning fuel invades my nostrils, not unpleasant, and I use elbows and knees to manoeuvre myself across the sleepers. Hot liquid scolds the back of my neck and I yelp. It dribbles down underneath my collar.

'You OK?' asks Winter.

'Think so,' I say. 'Just hot water, or oil or something, dripping on me from the train.'

The next moment her hand is in mine and she's pulling me clear the other side. Immediately we scramble down the hill to the bottom and lie flat in the long grass, struggling for breath. A screeching sound makes us instinctively turn in the direction of the train as it begins to slowly creep along the tracks.

'We made it just in time,' I say.

'Lucky for you!' says Winter, smiling down at me.

For the first time I notice a small red fleck in her left eye, abandoned in a sea of green, long dark lashes framing the pretty picture. Her waves of bright red hair, translucent where the re-emerging sun shines through, frame her face and I imagine how soft her cheeks must feel, one cute dimple interrupting the smooth flow of flawless skin. Without thinking I put my hand up to touch that cheek and confirm my suspicions. 'You're beautiful,' I say.

'Why thank you, kind sir.' She leans across me until the sun disappears and I'm bathed in shadow, my nose detecting the sweet mixture of vanilla and honey.

As I shut my eyes the world explodes.

17

WE bolt upright, banging heads as the air fills with smoke. At a spot around half a mile away, a fireball is painting hellish patterns in the sky.

'The train,' I say, unable to disguise my disbelief. It's hard to equate that the raging inferno we are now witnessing had been transporting us through the peaceful Essex countryside just moments earlier. Clasping each other's hands seems a logical move, an automatic reaction satisfying the need to feel some living, breathing thing close to you at a time of excessive stress. It tells us we're alive and in the moment. Hundreds of our fellow passengers might not be so lucky.

Our private thoughts are interrupted by the low thumping noise of rotor blades and we watch as the helicopter turns in our direction. Ducking low, we then attempt to hide ourselves in the long grass. The noise drills ominous patterns into my skull as the bird passes above us. I feel the air displaced, my hair drawn up, and get the sense of being pinned to the ground by a force too strong to resist.

Beside me, Winter is lying flat on her stomach. We look wide eyed at each other, shocked into silence, wondering if we will ever speak again. For what seems an age, the chopper hangs there, a few hundred yards off to our left, the people inside trying to establish if anyone has survived the blast. We can hear the grass shifting in the down-draught.

Looking up, our pursuers are so close I can see the pilot talking into his headphones. I try to read his lips but he's too far away. I suspect he is informing his bosses about the success of his mission.

A figure behind him moves forward into sight, admiring the carnage the chopper has left in its slipstream. It's the man in the electric blue suit.

He sits back so that someone else can get a look at his handiwork and this time my nemesis, the woman in the fruity hat, edges forward. I recognise her because even though she is no longer wearing her headwear, evil is etched deep in the crags of her face. I note with surprise and alarm that without the hat she is completely bald.

I don't share what I've seen with my companion. If we get out of this alive, I'll tell her later, but for the moment I fear any little mumble on our part might be detected by those on board the chopper. They seem to have the uncanny knack of tracking us down and possess every resource at their disposal. It isn't beyond the realms of possibility they have some kind of device on board capable of detecting human conversation at long distances.

Having taken a good look around, the woman I'd last seen astride a white horse in the centre of London sits back and disappears from view. The helicopter's rotors increase in speed, the noise level rises and the craft banks, lifts and turns in the general direction of London.

'THAT was a lucky escape,' I say, feeling able to breathe properly at last.

'What now then, Em?' whispers Winter.

'We need to get as far away from here as possible,' I say. 'They're a bit too thorough for my liking. I wouldn't mind betting a few people turn up on foot pretty soon to search the area and confirm they've achieved their objective. Maybe they'll arrive in the form of first responders – fire engines, ambulances and police cars – the way they did at Tower Bridge. It's impossible to know who we can trust.'

'They want to make sure you're dead and they aren't leaving anything to chance.' It's a matter-of-fact statement. I note she is no longer saying 'we'.

'Looks that way,' I agree.

'I can't believe this is the work of legitimate government agencies, really I can't. All those poor people dead, and they're treated purely as collateral damage. They must want you pretty badly, Em. The question is: "why"?'

'I don't know.'

My head is thumping from the intolerable stress I have been put under. 'I've got to figure it out. I can't believe that my graphic design skills are that much in demand.'

My half-hearted attempt at a smile would fool no one. Standing up, I stretch in an effort to ease the aches and pains now manifesting themselves in my back and wonder if I'm set for another spell on sick leave from work. It seems ridiculous in the circumstances that I still can't let go of the day job. What is happening to me is earth-shattering, game-changing stuff and my life will probably never be the same again. There is a danger that the very act of returning home will put my wife and daughter at risk. Who is to say there isn't someone waiting at the house on Clapham Common right now with a bullet reserved especially for me? Damn, maybe they've already kidnapped my family and are planning to use them as a bargaining chip if I surface again. If they know anything about me, they'll have worked out by now I'd trade my freedom for the lives of the two people who mean the most to me.

For the first time since the whole saga began, I'm starting to anticipate the next move of my pursuers. It makes me wonder whether at some time in the distant past I have played this game before and been brainwashed into forgetting all about it. I recall the soldier expressing shock when I mentioned my family on the bus and, accompanied by a wave of nausea, the thought springs to mind that he believed they'd already been taken. It's probably written down in some manual somewhere, point number 3 in the everyman's guide to clandestine warfare: *"Kidnap the family and hold them as insurance"*.

If that's the case, I have to find a way to strike back at my enemies, even though I have no idea who they are or how they can be found. Only the briefcase holds clues to what my next step should be.

Winter is watching me in reflective silence. I lean down and put my hand out to haul her to her feet. 'Come on,' I say, 'we can't stay here. Let's see if we can find somewhere to hide out and study the contents of this.' I nod at the case.

'OK,' she says. 'Go careful with that gun, though, I don't want it going off accidentally. I'm too young to die. Is the safety on?'

It's a good question. 'How the hell should I know?' I say. 'We'll just have to take our chances.'

'No,' she says. 'It's too dangerous. Hand it over.'

I stand back and look at her, perplexed.

'My brother has guns on the farm,' she explains. 'I reckon I can work it out. I've seen him do it often enough and we used to do a lot of target practice together, shooting at cans and stuff.'

I remove the firearm from the back of my tattered pants and pass it across. She hefts it in her hands, looks along the barrel, then pulls it down to her waist and makes a few quick adjustments. 'There,' she says, holding it out to show off her handiwork. 'All done. Perhaps I should hang on to this for the time being.'

'Be my guest,' I say, relieved the responsibility has been taken out of my hands. I've never fired a gun and I have a sneaking suspicion Winter knows a lot more about them than she is letting on. If we ever get cornered, I figure it's best she shoots our way out.

As if we have a telepathic understanding, we simultaneously start walking through grass which is well above our waists. Neither of us talks for a while, our eyes continually drawn to the blaze in the distance, wondering when the rescue crews will turn up. At least in the long grass we can immediately drop to our knees if we see something to trouble us. Mind you that doesn't take into account...

'Dogs!' I hiss and Winter looks at me, a silent question passing behind her eyes. 'Listen'. I hold my hand to my ear. 'I can hear barking. Shit!'

'Might be time for a little jog then,' she says, gripping the gun tightly. With no idea where we are heading or from which direction our pursuers are coming, we change pace. Her movements are graceful and athletic, her legs adopting a comfortable rhythm instantly. She is wearing modern blue jeans with strategically placed holes in them which my daughter informs me are 'distressed' and all the rage. Protruding from them, her knees lift her effortlessly clear of the cloying grass. It's odd, because I can't recall her changing out of the blue woollen dress she had on when I met her. Perhaps I was unconscious at the Tower for longer than I thought.

I'm struggling to keep up already, stumbling like a drunk in a nightclub as I look around vainly trying to gauge from which direction the hunters will come.

'Over here, quick!' she says, pointing to a wooden copse and changing direction in one slick movement. For a second I'm daydreaming, happy to watch her glide across the ground until the barking re-enters my head, louder and more urgent, and I realise this isn't the best time to take a mental break.

Bursting into the copse I tumble over a tree stump and Winter leans down and helps me up. Blood seeps from a graze in my knee, clearly visible through my tattered pants. My breath is coming in a rush now, my chest heaving, a further indication of how unfit I am. I gave up smoking six years ago, but I realise now I should never have started.

'Listen!' says Winter as I bend over, hands on my knees, and greedily suck air into my lungs.

'What is it?' I croak, barely able to get the words out. 'Yes, I can still hear the dogs.'

'Not them,' she snaps. 'Can you hear something else?'

I listen more attentively until another sound registers on my consciousness. It's faint, but it's definitely there, the delicate tinkling of water over rocks. 'River?'

'Probably a stream. If we can make it there, it might throw the dogs off the scent.'

'Is that even true?' I ask.

She shrugs. 'It always seems to work in the films. Come on.'

I follow her deeper into the woods, gnarled tree branches grabbing at what is left of my torn and tattered clothes. Reaching an incline, I slip in a puddle made from the rain which fell earlier in the day, landing on my backside this time. I hear laughter and look up to see Winter in fits of giggles. Looking down at my feet I realise the beautiful Italian loafers

I was so mesmerised by earlier in the day are now being held together by mud alone. I sigh. Easy come, easy go. Winter once again pulls me to my feet.

'These shoes were new on today, would you believe?' I say.

'Yeah, well I don't suppose they were made to stand up to a sprint around the streets of London, followed by a cross country jog through the woods. Which way now?'

I listen. The water seems to be away to our left. 'Over here somewhere, I think.' I begin jogging again, the barking getting louder, interspersed with the chatter of wild birds in the branches above us, excitedly discussing the strange goings-on in their normally quiet location.

'They sound close,' says Winter, reading my mind. 'What if they have trackers, too, familiar with the area?'

That famous scene from the film *Butch Cassidy and the Sundance Kid*, one of my father's favourites, springs to my mind. I loved it as a kid. Butch and Sundance had been trailed for days by a native American tracker and were forced to jump off a cliff to escape. I hope we won't end up in a similar situation. 'You be Sundance, I'll be Butch,' I say to lighten the mood.

'What?'

I keep forgetting how young my accomplice is, the analogy totally lost on her. 'Never mind,' I say, feeling deflated and old. Not for the first time I question why a beautiful young woman like this has chosen to be my companion on this mind-bending day of all days.

Reaching a fork in the forest path, the yipping, sniffing and snarling of the hounds seems so close I imagine I'll catch sight of the lead attack dog at any moment.

'Hell!' says Winter.

I toss my head from side to side in a panic, trying to choose a path and second guess our pursuers. Then I see it, and my mind is made up for me.

'This way!' I grab her hand and leap over twisted vines before slipping down a slaloming mud slope to where a small, sun-dappled stream winds sleepily through the woods. Without taking the time to remove my shoes I plunge in, tugging my companion behind me.

'Hey,' she complains, 'These are expensive trainers. I was going to remove them first.'

'Yeah, I'm sure those dogs would love chewing on them... and the rest of you for that matter,' I say, head down as I splash through the shallows.

'How the hell did you decide which way to go? I didn't see or hear anything.'

'You didn't see the symbol?'

'What symbol?'

'There was something carved into a tree, three wavy lines and what looked like a silhouette above them. Below it was an arrow, pointing in this direction.'

She shakes her head in disbelief.

'Three lines, you say. I get it. To be totally honest with you, I didn't notice a thing.'

'I guess it's the condition, but things like that leap out at me. Maybe there is a bit of wishful thinking, too. What I saw was like some kind of logo. It looked familiar. And it pointed us to the stream, didn't it?'

She wears a puzzled expression, and I have the feeling she is wondering if the elevated levels of stress are causing my overworked brain to hallucinate. I know what I saw though, and once my mind focused it was as plain as the lifelines on my hand. What's more, like a lover's note chiselled in the bark, beneath the three lines and the arrow my initials had been carved: ER. There couldn't have been a clearer signal that I was on the right track.

Now it's Winter's turn to take control, tugging my hand and pulling me to the far side of the stream, into the shadows. 'Get down!' she says as we come to a barrier of overhanging bows. The water is deeper here and we are both up to our waists in it. She ducks down even further, submerging her shoulders so that only the top of her crimson head is visible to me. Casting around, I see the first of the hunters emerging through undergrowth, straining against the muscular demands of two fierce-looking dogs. Quickly I sink to my knees so the water is up to my shoulders, gasping at the drop in temperature. There is no time to waste, though, and I pull a stray branch across to hide us from sight, hoping it will be enough.

We are silent, frozen to the spot for what seems like minutes as the snuffling dogs pass by on the other side. At one stage one of them stops, snarls and looks straight across the stream at us. For a horrible moment I fear our cover has been blown until a large river bird, a heron or a crane, lifts off to our left and flies low along the contours of the stream. Peering through the gap in the branch I see the hunter tug at the dog and they carry on down the trail.

My body aches in the cramped space and I'm about to break from our cover and stretch out when Winter tugs me back. I look at her and she puts her fingers to my mouth to stop me speaking, then points back across the river. Materialising from the woods, two more men yomp along the mud path, shotguns held against their chests like mothers nursing babies. There is no softness in their faces, though. They have all the demeanour of experienced killers, used to tracking their prey across all terrains.

Next to me there's a clicking sound, and I jerk around. Winter's teeth are chattering, and it makes me reflect again on how cold this country stream is. We have to get moving soon or there is a danger we'll suffer hypothermia. When the men carry on along the opposite path and disappear back into the woods on the far side, we wait for as long as is physically possible before raising ourselves slowly and quietly to our feet. Pushing aside the branch, I then pull Winter up the bank and instinctively wrap my arms around her, rubbing to get the circulation moving again. She gives me a grateful look and returns the favour, hunkering close. The tender moment seems totally out of keeping with our nightmare circumstances. We stand there for a moment, enjoying contact with a fellow human being, our minds reflecting on how the passengers on that train weren't so lucky.

Eventually, I lean my head to the side indicating we should make a move and she nods. Without a word passing between us we scramble up the rest of the bank, using the branches to aid our progress.

<h1 style="text-align:center">18</h1>

I ESTIMATE we have been walking for a good hour, though I'm finding it more and more difficult to keep track of time. My watch has stopped working due to the traumas to which it has been subjected, I've lost the pocket device and my mobile phone lies smashed outside the Tower of London. At one stage I ask Winter whether she has any idea, but she shakes her head and flashes a blank screen in my direction.

'My battery died,' she says. 'It's either run out because I didn't have time to charge it this morning or more likely the phone was damaged in the stream. I forgot to take it out of my jeans pocket when we submerged ourselves to avoid those hunters. The ads said this model was state-of-the-art and supposed to be water-resistant, but I don't know whether they're designed to resist freezing temperatures, too. It might be all right in a heated swimming pool, but I don't suppose anyone put it through the same endurance test as we've just done.'

'I wonder where they went,' I say, my mind switching to other concerns. 'I can't hear the dogs any more, which is a good thing at least. I don't think we are in any sort of condition to outrun them.'

'I'm dead on my feet,' Winter says. 'If we don't find somewhere to rest soon, I think I'll expire on the spot.'

'Where the hell are we, anyway?' I ask. 'We seem to have been walking through these fields forever. No buildings, no towns, just fields. It's as if we're the only two people left alive. Well, apart from those who seem intent on tracking us down and doing us harm.'

'You've seen too many horror films,' says Winter with a chuckle. 'I don't think we've been plunged into some dystopian world. We're somewhere in rural Essex I would imagine. Or maybe Suffolk. If we keep walking, I'm sure we'll find civilisation soon. I'm hungry, what about you?'

I haven't thought about it until now, but I put my hand to my stomach and when I make contact, the burning sensation causes me to double up in agony.

'What's wrong, Em?'

'I'm not sure,' I say, pulling at what remains of my shirt until it comes free from my trousers. I close my eyes and bite back the pain. Not only does my gut feel the way it might had I consumed a dozen of the hottest red chillies known to man, but when I touch it with my hand, I feel a blister forming. Unreal. Daring to open my eyes again I gaze down at the troublesome area and feel like screaming at the sight which greets me. The whole area on the right side of my body is a translucent orange colour and is visibly glowing. 'What is that?' I say, my cracked voice betraying my fear.

'A bruise?' volunteers Winter. 'Your body's taken quite a pounding over the last few hours. Perhaps it happened when we slid down the gravel after jumping from the train, or maybe you struck a tree branch as we ran along that stream. Sometimes you don't realise what damage you've done to yourself on the spur of the moment. It's only later, after you've had time to think about things, that the pain registers. Something to do with the way the body reacts to adrenaline and shock, I believe.'

'Thanks, Dr Winter,' I say rather stroppily, 'but this is different, surely. I've had a few problems with my stomach of late. When I spoke to my wife earlier, she reminded me I was meant to have a doctor's appointment this afternoon.'

'Perhaps you should cancel.'

'Ha ha.'

'Oh, don't get grumpy with me,' she says, finding a second wind and marching on ahead. 'It's hardly my fault. I'm sorry about your aches and pains and all that, and it does look like you should get that seen to, but I can't see many doctor's surgeries around here.'

We look around, just to confirm her observation. There are fields stretching as far as the horizon nestling under a cold, blue sky interspersed with white clouds and faint wisps of smoke which remind us that somewhere behind us a passenger train had been reduced to scrap metal. 'All we can do is soldier on and see if we can find somewhere to rest up.'

Finally, after walking for another half an hour, we crest a small rise and a farm comes into view. There is a tractor in the yard, and I hear the clucking of chickens. The environment must be pretty familiar to a girl who grew up in the Welsh countryside, but Winter gives no indication that's the case.

'We can't just go marching in there,' she says. 'Anyone seeing us for the first time would think us escaped criminals or, at least, on the run from someone.'

'They'd be right,' I say. 'What should we do?'

'Let's find a building far away from the house. Perhaps there's a hayloft or somewhere we can hide out, just until we've had a chance to rest up. I bet they've got food though. I could kill for some nice farmer's eggs right now.'

'Over there,' I say, pointing into the distance. 'That might do the trick.'

A collection of rundown outbuildings stands some distance behind the farmhouse which hasn't seen a fresh lick of paint for many a year. There is some rusty machinery outside which has seen better days and the doors are buckled and broken. We make our way across the fields as quickly as we can. 'Not quite The Savoy,' I say as we reach our destination.

'No, but then again I'm not sure the way you're dressed they would let us into The Savoy,' Winter says, drawing attention again to my ripped and ragged clothes. 'I can't imagine the maître d' telling you that you scrub up nicely.'

I punch her playfully on the arm then trip and almost fall headlong onto the mucky, rutted track we are following. 'Hell!' I say, raising a foot. The sole has now parted company from one of my Italian loafers and is flapping about like an ill-fitting toupee on a vain windsurfer. They're completely beyond repair and I pray they aren't a gift from Cherry. She'll be pretty cheesed off at how I've treated them.

Then I laugh. What on earth am I thinking? Here I am, fearing a ticking off from my wife when out here somewhere a highly skilled team of killers is intent on tracking me down and ending my life. Surely in the circumstances Cherry will understand I have far more pressing concerns than keeping a pair of shoes pristine.

The intruding thoughts get me thinking of my family again and hoping they're safe. I'd love to contact them, to hear friendly voices and tell them about the ridiculous situation I've found myself in and that I love them whatever happens. I need to warn them that, because of me, they may become targets too and should make plans to get away as soon as possible. How, though? I've broken my phone and, as stupid as it may sound, even if I could find a public one, I wouldn't have a clue of Cherry or Jamie's numbers.

That's modern-day living for you. In the dim and distant past, phone numbers of those near and dear to you would be stored in a little pocket of your mind or in an address book to be taken out and used when needed. Now, with built-in phonebooks on your mobile and other means of communication through *WhatsApp* and messenger, there is really no need to memorise useful numbers.

Well, not until you find yourself a fugitive in a countrywide manhunt and have lost or broken the very device that could summon help – in that case you're stuffed.

'Will you stop mourning the death of those shoes!' Winter says, snapping me back to the present. 'Anyway, what does the 39 mean? It can't be the shoe size. You must be close to 6ft and 39 equates to size 5 or 6 feet in English money. If that was the case, you would be toppling over all the time.'

'I've had my moments,' I point out. 'I suppose 39 might be the price?'

'You don't know how much they cost?' Winter looks at me with incredulity. 'They're your shoes!'

'Yes, well no. I mean I don't know where they came from,' I admit. 'I just looked down as I was leaving for work this morning and saw them on my feet.'

'Oh... my... God! You know what, Mr Rabette? You are something else! You put on shoes and you don't even know where they come from or who they belong to?'

I shrug.

'It must be a pile of laughs in your house in the morning. Do you ever walk out in your wife's coat or carrying your daughter's handbag?'

I think about the question and it directs my train of thought elsewhere. 'Hang on a minute!' I say. 'How do you know I've got a daughter? I don't remember telling you...'

Looking her in the eye I think I detect a moment of uncertainty, but she quickly answers my concern. 'You mentioned her when we first met, remember? You told me all about them. Jamie isn't it? You were also mumbling about "your girl" when you came around after your fall at the Tower.'

'Oh right,' I say. 'The Jamie I was talking about could be a boy though.'

'Not the way you talked about her. Anyway, boys are nearly always called James or Jim. Jamie is the preferred choice for girls – I don't know what it is short for.'

'It isn't. It's just Jamie. We both liked it.'

We arrive at the outbuildings and take a look around. In the distance there is the throbbing of an engine, some heavy farm machinery in operation. I study the door to one of the buildings.

'This seems a bit pointless,' I say, raising a padlock to show Winter. The whole crumbling stone outhouse seems ready for demolition. The wooden shutters in the windows are in various states of disrepair and there are holes in the masonry that a pretty large animal could crawl through. I can't see the need for additional security when anyone with an ounce of nous could gain entry whenever they chose.

There is a scraping sound and I turn to see Winter forcing aside one of the shutters. She climbs up and starts pushing her way through, only to get stuck halfway. 'Give us a shove,' she says.

'Are you sure? You could hurt yourself.'

What I mean is does she really want me applying my hands to her bottom? She brushes aside my reluctance.

'It's OK in here,' she says. 'It's pretty empty. There's just a bit of hay, adequate to break my fall, a pile of old magazines and, well, nothing much. I doubt anyone's been in here for ages.'

'Sounds ideal.'

'Get on with it, will you?' she prompts. I grab both calves and try to manoeuvre her through the gap but it's impossible to get enough force behind my effort. 'That's no good!' she says. 'Push my arse. Now! I'm bloody stuck. Or perhaps you would rather leave me like this, exposed to the elements or who knows bloody what?'

I swallow back my protests, take a short run-up and shove. She disappears through the hole and I hear an expletive as she lands.

'Everything all right?' I ask.

'Peachy!' she shouts. 'I wish I'd remembered that gun was in my hoodie, though. I landed on it and it wasn't a very pleasant sensation.'

'Thank God it didn't go off,' I say.

'Yeah. Lucky I knew how to put the safety on.' It sounds like a barb directed straight at me, but I let it pass. 'Your turn,' she says.

'OK, but who will push me if I get stuck?' I ask.

'You'll be OK. You may be a bit podgy around the midriff, but I reckon you're smaller than me in certain places,' she giggles.

'This will be the final indignity,' I grumble. 'All I'll need is to get stuck and then be found that way by our pursuers. I'm sure I could just force the padlock off and enter by the front door. It looks pretty flimsy and the screws around the lock don't look capable of resisting a bit of brute force.'

'Yeah, fine,' says Winter, meaning the complete opposite. 'Then if someone turns up nosing around, they're going to notice the padlock missing and we'll be sitting ducks. Swallow your pride and get on with it.'

'Here goes then,' I say, slotting the briefcase through the window before walking back a few paces. Taking a run at the wall I scramble up and into the hole and with a certain amount of wriggling and twisting, I'm through.

'There,' said Winter. 'I told you it wouldn't be a problem.' I turn to look for the briefcase, then hear a guffaw from my companion. 'Scratch that,' she says. 'Perhaps it wasn't quite so clear cut.'

Immediately I place my hand on my backside to find a bit of material flapping around, leaving my cheeks completely exposed. 'Oh for…' I rip my mac off and wrap it around my waist. 'I thought you said it would be OK?'

'Look, you're here and in one piece, aren't you?' she laughs again but I refuse to rise to the bait. Instead I bend to retrieve the briefcase, only for another wave of pain to cross my stomach, doubling me up.

'Hey, you OK?' Winter says, getting to her feet and putting her arm around my back.

'No, it's agony!' I explain.

'Look, sit down and let's try to ease things a bit for you. Perhaps some rest will help, and the pain will settle down.' She turns me around slowly. 'Wait here.'

Quickly gathering an armful of hay that has been stacked haphazardly in the far corner, she then brings it over and places it below me. 'Sit on this.' She lowers me gently down before stripping my shirt away. 'This is, well, bizarre!' she points out.

'It shouldn't be glowing like that, should it?' I ask rhetorically. 'I mean, it's as if I'm radioactive or something.'

'We need some expert medical advice,' she says. 'I wish Joel was here. Oh well, looks like we'll have to find a local doctor or a nearby hospital. I think it's a risk we need to take. You can't go on like this. If the bad guys don't get you this – thing – will.'

'Thanks for the optimism,' I say, lying back and attempting to fill my lungs with oxygen as the pain slowly leaves my body. 'It's easing now, thanks to you. I'm grateful.'

'No problem,' she says. 'Now, while you're lying there all comfy, I think we should have a look at what's in this thing.'

Pulling the case towards her she surveys the tumblers. 'What did you say the code was again?'

I tell her and she whizzes the dials around with the speed of an ace safe cracker, pushing the lid open and peering inside. She removes the money and puts it in one pile then starts to pull out other objects. There is a key on a fob with a BMW logo on it, a small screen which I recognise as a portable satellite navigation system, a lighter and a postcard.

'Funny,' she says, reflecting on the random nature of the items. She hands the postcard to me. I stare at a large container ship with the name *Esprit d'Orleon III*. On the top right is the word Felixstowe and scrawled across the back are those familiar words 'Wish You Were Here'.

'What do you think it means?' asks Winter, looking over my shoulder.

'I think we're supposed to go to Felixstowe and find this boat. Following the signs hasn't turned out to be a bad policy so far, has it? I mean, we're still alive, despite all that has happened and we haven't been caught by police, dogs, women on horseback... that's got to mean that whoever is leaving these messages is on our side.'

'I guess you could look at it that way,' says Winter. 'Or you could say it was because we did certain things that the whole situation escalated. For example, we stayed on a hijacked bus and you ended up getting chased around the Tower of London, almost throwing yourself to your death to get away. Then we got on a train that later blew up, just in case you had forgotten, and we only boarded it because we saw one of your "signs".'

I grunt, not prepared to concede the point. 'How would the alternatives have turned out?'

'Well, that we'll never know but, perhaps, if you'd just stayed on the Tube this morning you might be enjoying a hearty celebratory lunch somewhere near Old Street having persuaded your boss you deserve to keep your job.'

'Fair point. It wouldn't have been so much fun, would it?'

She smiles, and we settle back onto the hay.

'I'm cold,' she mumbles, and I take the hint, wrapping an arm around her.

'This doesn't mean anything, by the way,' I add quickly, the sight of Cherry and Jamie springing uninvited into my vision.

'No, of course not. You're a happily married man, and I'm not a home wrecker.'

'I'm glad we understand each other,' I say. 'It's funny, though. I really don't know anything about you. You appeared out of nowhere, returning my briefcase at the Tube station and, since then, well, we've been through a hell of a lot more than the average couple on their first 'date'. In fact, the only thing I've gleaned is that you do magazine modelling work and that you have a brother who lives in Wales.'

She nestles her head into my shoulder, crimson hair tickling my chin. 'I guess it's time I gave you a bit of a personal history lesson then,' she says, wriggling to get comfortable. 'I grew up in west Wales, out towards Pembrokeshire. My parents ran a farm, but I was never interested in that sort of thing. I went to the local school, did OK in my exams then moved to the big city – Swansea – for college. I was going to do something really boring like a secretarial course, but they had photographers' classes there, too. I met this boy, Shaun, who was taking one of them and he persuaded me to model for him. We ended up going out together. He was a bit of a lad, came over from Ulster on the ferry and was looking to make a name for himself on the Mainland.'

I sense my eyes closing, lulled by the gentle lilt of her voice. The Welsh tones are flowing over me in waves, pleasantly soothing. They have the same effect as someone singing a lullaby.

'Hey, don't fall asleep on me now, Em, will you?' she says, nudging me in the ribs. 'You were the one who wanted to know this stuff.' She gazes at me intently and once again I see the small patch of red in her eye and wonder how amazing it is that this blemish enhances her features instead of detracting from them, bestowing on her something unique and special.

'Of course not,' I say. 'I'm fascinated.'

'OK, well... I suppose Shaun became more important to me than my secretarial classes. We had a lot in common. We both enjoyed the rugby – though of course he was an Ireland fan and I was a Wales fanatic – and we also liked the same music, you know rock stuff like U2 and Oasis, and went to gigs together and the cinema. Just a normal boy-girl relationship.'

Her words make me recall what young love feels like and the early days of my courtship of Cherry, a cinema trip in particular when we went to see one of those *Halloween* films in which Jamie Lee Curtis was the star. It's no big leap to think that played a subconscious part in helping us choose our daughter's name.

'Anyway, Shaun's work started to get noticed up in the big smoke and I did too,' she continues. 'He persuaded me to build up a portfolio and pretty soon I'd established a small client base, doing modelling work for a few clothing catalogues. I probably did a couple of photoshoots for you guys, too, maybe you remember them, maybe you don't, but I think you said I looked familiar when we first met?'

I nod, fighting the sleep that seems about to consume me.

'Anyway, we moved to an area of North London – Kilburn – and he soon fell in with a bunch of Irish mates, who were more intent on drinking and enjoying the "craic" than hard graft. I outgrew him as the phrase goes. I was getting more work than him and resented the fact that while I was busting a gut, no pun intended,' she gently rubs my stomach, '...he was lazing around with his mates and not contributing to the bills etc. When we split up it was inevitable, I guess. We had naturally grown apart. I had enough money by then to move to a place of my own and ended up in Balham, just down the road from you. I've no regrets. Shaun and I had a good time while it lasted but I guess we all have to grow up at some stage.'

'It's a bummer, though, isn't it?' I say. 'I'm sure Cherry and I would be getting on better if all the growing up hadn't intervened like, you know, having a kid – not that I regret Jamie's birth in any way at all. She means the absolute world to both of us, but at some point all your own thoughts and feelings – the things you used to enjoy as individuals – go by the wayside, taken over by someone who needs all your attention.'

'I can imagine,' she acknowledges. 'I've never considered kids myself. My brother is getting married soon and his future wife already has a bun in the oven. Talk about starting early.'

'How old is he?'

'24.'

'You say he's younger...'

'Ahh, I wondered when we might get on to my age. Don't you know that's a rude question to ask a lady?'

'Sorry but...'

'Only joking,' she says. 'I'm 26. I guess I'll be too old soon for this modelling lark. They get rid of you as soon as you start to sag a bit and need the odd nip and tuck. It's hardly a job for life.'

'Don't be daft!' I say. 'You're still young, immensely beautiful and have a pretty dazzling body.'

'Not that, as a married man, you're interested.'

Without warning her lips connect with mine. She pushes against me, her hand reaching up to caress the hair at the back of my neck, sending tingles through my entire body. Her other hand continues to weave circles on my stomach and in an instant, I've forgotten the pain. Her hand drifts down and I feel my body responding...

'Stop! I really can't,' I say.

'That's not the message I'm getting,' she says, chuckling, as her hand lightly brushes the bulge in my trousers.

'No...I'm sorry. It wouldn't be right.'

'It's me that should be sorry,' she says. 'It's just, I don't know, this last day with you... We've been through so much and we don't know what awaits us tomorrow.' She stops mid-sentence, pushes herself up so her eyes are level with mine and gives me a chaste peck on the cheek. 'I do like you, Em, you know that, don't you? There is something that's drawn me to you. I can't explain it, but you feel it too, don't you? When I saw you trying to fight all those angry commuters off this morning, well maybe it alerted a maternal instinct I didn't know I possessed. And despite everything that's happened, and I'm not for a second saying I wouldn't swap right now for getting my mundane, everyday life back, I'm glad I met you. Now, message understood, OK? And for the record, I admire your loyalty. Shall we try to get some sleep?'

'Thanks,' I say. '...For being so understanding and, well, for everything. What about the door? Should we set up some kind of boobytrap or something?'

'We could lodge your briefcase over the top, I guess, but other than that...'

'You're right. We're going to have to take our chances.'

Without saying another word, she slips from under my arm, gets up and looks around the barn floor. Eventually she finds a sturdy wooden pole, lifts it and walks to the door where she jams it through the handle. It's by no means foolproof but might give us vital escape time if someone tries to get in.

'It's hardly going to stop an army,' she says, once again reading my thoughts. 'It could delay them by a fraction of a second, though, and they might make enough noise to wake us up.'

'What then?' I say.

'Well...we've always got this, haven't we?' she lifts the gun and waves it in front of my nose.

19

'EM! You awake?'

A nudge in the ribs ensures I am.

'What?' I wipe sleep from my eyes.

'Can you hear that?'

I sit bolt upright and tune in to my surroundings. It's pitch-black in the outhouse, the light that was sneaking through the cracks earlier having completely disappeared. I feel like I've slept for hours and am much better for it. My stomach has calmed down and I can think more clearly. I listen carefully but there's nothing.

'What am I supposed to be hearing?' I ask.

'Just listen,' hisses Winter. I can feel the tension in her body as she pushes up against me. I shuffle into a sitting position and she does the same. We fall silent again.

Then I hear it: A deep, throaty growl.

'Dog?'

She shakes her head. 'Seriously?'

I don't think it is either, but the sound seems out of place in the midst of the Essex-Suffolk countryside.

'I know what it sounds like and it isn't a family pet. Remember the article on the front of that newspaper you got in Liverpool Street?'

'You're not serious?' I say. 'Perhaps that's fed your imagination. You might have even dreamed about it. You can do that when you're over-tired.'

I can't see her face properly but sense she isn't happy with my answer. Her next words confirm my suspicions. 'What would be your conclusion then, Mr Clever Clogs? Or don't you have one?'

'Well, we're on a farm. We know there are chickens. Couldn't it be a common-or-garden fox or something? I mean…' I'm interrupted by a rumbling roar that seems closer than ever.

'Hell!'

'Exactly! That isn't a cute little foxy now, is it? What should we do?'

I clamber to my feet, aches and pains I hadn't noticed before kicking in at every point of me. Yesterday's activities have certainly taken their toll on a body unfamiliar with strenuous physical activity. There is a smell of hay mingled with something not quite so pleasant and it occurs to me lots of wild animals probably use this place as a sanctuary during bad weather.

Crossing to the window through which we gained entry, I peer out. I can see lights on in the farmhouse away in the distance but not much else. The darkness and silence is a world away from what I've become used to in a major city where the traffic can be unrelenting 24/7, both motorised and human.

'See anything?' asks Winter.

I turn and shake my head. 'Not a sausage. I think…'

Without warning I'm hit with the force of a truck, except instead of being man-made this behemoth is all fur and teeth. I howl as something akin to a knife penetrates my left arm and instinctively punch out with the other one, a move triggered by self-preservation. The blow isn't flush, but it knocks my attacker off balance. For a moment I sense its hold on me release as it flies into the confined space where we have made our temporary home. Landing softly on what I can only surmise are four gigantic paws, it's pure white body seems to glow in the dark and I realise Winter has removed the lighter in the briefcase and spun the wheel to illuminate the confined space.

Black stripes cross the beast's torso in parallel lines, like a living, breathing barcode; a barcode with huge white fangs, claws as sharp as stilettos and dark eyes that glisten menacingly in the reflective flame. I'm locked in a staring contest with a monstrous, living, breathing white tiger.

From deep inside my memory I've conjured the image of the TV wildlife guru David Attenborough explaining that in this situation you must show no fear. He may have been talking about sharks or snakes for all I know, but I puff out my chest, steady my breathing and prepare for the next attack. Where is Winter? I thought she was somewhere to my right but can't risk a look. That would present our uninvited dinner guest with all the invitation he needs to launch himself at the first course.

'Steady,' I say, hands out in front of me as if I have a wooden chair to protect me like a trained lion tamer in a travelling circus. The difference is the lions you see in those circumstances are generally lazy and disinterested having been overfed before entering the ring. Who knows when this meat-eating predator enjoyed its last meal? On the run and having been brought up in a captive environment where food is provided at regular intervals, this big cat might not have had a decent bite for some time. I know how he feels, hungry and a long way from home, keen to satisfy the demands of an empty stomach.

Why hasn't it gone for the chickens, though, or perhaps searched out some well-nourished pigs in one of the barns? This is a farm, for God's sake, it should be like an all-you-can-eat buffet for our furry friend. Instead it sees me leaning through a window into the cold night air and decides I would make the perfect snack. The fact that I'm resisting has only served to make this wild predator more frustrated and annoyed.

It prowls now, its tongue passing across its lips with anticipation. As it looks out from beneath long bushy eyebrows, I can't help thinking of Shere Khan, the tiger from one of Jamie's all-time favourite films, *Jungle Book*. Khan was the baddie and spoke in a posh English accent and our young hero, a boy named Mowgli, had to fight the man-eater off at the climax with the help of some friendly vultures. Mowgli was a skinny wretch, much smaller than me, but used cunning to outwit the tiger in typical Disney style. Our white tiger is toying with me, just as Khan did with Mowgli, and it's only a matter of time until he leaps in for the kill.

Wait a minute! Just as I'm about to dismiss the *Jungle Book* analogy I'm forced to backtrack. I urgently whisper from the corner of my mouth, 'Lighter!'

Winter is perplexed by my outburst. 'What?' she hisses back.

'Chuck me the bloody lighter!' I say a bit louder, prompting the tiger to circle its head as if trying to shake off a crick in its neck. It lets out a deafening roar and I grasp the opportunity to look in Winter's direction. She has finally caught on and as she prepares to throw the small, silver implement I know I'll have to guess where it's heading in the darkness. The flame goes out, she lets go and I reach out, fumble then catch it. As I strike it quickly, I turn to see the tiger spring-loaded on its back legs, primed for launch. The moment it takes off I do too, throwing myself through the musty air of the barn and landing on the hay we had earlier been using as bedding.

Falling awkwardly on my ankle, I squeal but have no time to consider my latest injury. The tiger crashes down on the crates and topples backwards in my direction. I make a quick calculation that the weight of the animal, over 500lbs of pure killing machine, will crush me into submission if it lands on me so roll as quickly as I can out of its way as it thumps down on its back, snarling and snapping, hoping to get lucky and sink its teeth into some part of my anatomy.

It rights itself in seconds, and I realise I've run out of room. Turning the wheel of the petrol lighter, I put it to the straw bed next to the big cat. The flame goes out. Damn! The next thing the ferocious beast pounces and almost knocks me senseless as I fight for breath underneath its muscle-bound body. I see my reflection in its eyes and feel a huge goblet of drool land on my chin as it opens its mouth to its full extent and roars again. I'm out of fight and my conqueror has won. All that's left is for it to enjoy the feast of the victor.

Whoooooosh!

I don't realise it at that instant but it's probably the sweetest sound I've ever heard. The heavyweight jungle hunter springs from me and yelps like a scolded kitten as a fast, steady stream of water catches it amidships. It scrambles away to the far corner of the outhouse and sits there, cowed and frightened, as a hand reaches down and pulls me to my feet.

'Get the door open!' orders Winter, holding the hose in front of her between two rock-steady hands. 'We've got to make a break for it. I don't know where this water is coming from and how long it will last.'

'What about the gun?'

'Sorry,' she says. 'Whatever the tiger's intention was for us, I'm not sure I could shoot such a beautiful animal. You know they're an endangered species, don't you?'

'Yeah, and so are we right now. Give it to me, quick!'

'No!' she says. 'Can't do that, sorry. Concentrate on getting that door open will you and let's make a run for it. I'll only use the Glock if it's the last resort.'

Just my luck, I think, being stuck in a life-or-death situation with a tree-hugging wildlife lover. Still, her earlier quick thinking saved my life. I lean down and pick up the lighter, curse it for failing me in my hour of need, then slip it into my pocket. Walking back a few paces I remove the makeshift barrier Winter installed earlier that evening and rest it against the wall then throw myself at the door, shoulder first, and burst through as the latch snaps, rendering the padlock redundant. Landing in a heap on the ground, I push myself to my feet. 'Come on!' I shout.

Winter manoeuvres the hose between some crates so that it's still firing in the tiger's direction, keeping it trapped in the corner until it works out a way to get clear or, alternatively, the flow of water stops.

'Do you think we should warn someone?' she asks as she exits the building. 'I feel sorry for it, being trapped out here in the English countryside without any food or anything. It's probably scared.'

'I can relate to that,' I say. 'Not sure about the tiger, though. I can't say it seemed that petrified when it was taking a chunk out of my arm.' We both look down and see that blood is still flowing, having already covered my entire sleeve. Winter rips the material away. 'Hell, you really are keen to get me naked,' I joke, but if she sees the funny side, she does a brilliant job of masking her expression. Instead, she tears the sleeve from my other arm to balance things up, then wraps the material around the area where the teeth had entered.

'That will have to do for now, but you'll need tetanus and rabies shots as soon as possible. We'll definitely want a professional to look at it. We can't afford for it to get infected. I'd wash out the cut if I could but the only source of water we seem to have is in there.' She points back in the direction of the tiger. 'I suppose we could ask at the farmhouse but I'm not sure how they might react to us turning up in the early hours of the morning and we can't afford to attract unnecessary attention. I certainly don't fancy going back in there. Do you?'

She indicates the barn and I shake my head. Having completed the tourniquet, she gives me the thumbs up like a girl scout who has just earned her war-wound dressing badge. 'We'd better make tracks,' she says.

'Winter.' I put my hand out to stop her just as she is about to set off across the fields.

'What?'

'Isn't there someone waiting for you?' I ask. 'Someone expecting you to phone home and tell them everything is fine but that you've been caught up in this ridiculous adventure with some stranger you met at a Tube station? What about your brother?'

She gives me an earnest look. 'Right now, I don't see I have a choice,' she says. 'I live on my own and my brother is the only real person I care about. Our parents died some years ago, and we have looked after each other ever since. Besides, my phone doesn't work, remember?'

I shrug my shoulders. 'What I'm saying is that maybe it's time we went our separate ways. I'm sure the farmer would let you use his landline, a woman alone and in distress.'

'Don't take this the wrong way, Em, but I don't want my brother dragged into this mess,' she says. 'You're in this up to your eyes and, though you insist you know nothing about the reasons for it, just by being at your side over these fateful few hours has put me well and truly on the radar of your enemies, too. The only way I can see we're getting out of this alive is if we stick together and try to figure it out between us.'

As she finishes her speech, I'm alerted to a new noise. I look back but the tiger is still in place, licking its paws now like a child's pet pussycat. It's almost purring to itself, accepting that for the moment it must bide its time and chill out.

This new noise is dirtier, lower, constant. It's not been designed by nature, but in a factory. The longer we stay rooted to the spot, the louder it becomes. Edging to the corner of the outbuilding, we stay low and look around it to see what has interrupted the peaceful status quo of the countryside.

Open-mouthed, we both stare at the new invader, neither of us able to get the word out first. In the end we say it together, the look of disbelief passing from one to the other.

'Tank!'

20

THE vehicle heading rapidly across the fields in our direction is a Challenger II series, the main battle tank used by the British army. I'd read an article at the magazine recently about how they were in much demand by the forces out in Afghanistan and Iraq.

Its main weapon is a 120mm gun known as the Charm, which sticks out in front in all its phallic glory while its caterpillar tracks churn up the field at speed. I know whoever is inside this machine of wanton destruction is scouring the land, looking for targets. I'm pretty certain we are those targets. What are our options now?

We can head off in the opposite direction, of course, but that will send us back towards the railway track and the hunters who are probably still combing the local woodlands searching for us. To head towards the tank is a suicide mission and to stay put makes us a convenient supper for the white tiger as soon as the water runs out. We are trapped and I've reached the end of my tether.

'What now?' asks Winter.

'You do what you want,' I say, needlessly snapping at my only ally. I start walking in the direction of the tank, my hands raised high in the air.

'What are you doing, Em!' shouts Winter, trying to pull me back to the cover of the outhouse. I won't budge, though, my anger feeding my strength. The day has been a fiasco from start to finish and I'm not built for the action-man lifestyle. If this final, defiant gesture costs me my life, well, at least it might protect my loved ones at home who are being put through a petrifying experience which is none of their own making.

For a moment I spare a thought for my colleagues Ben and Hayes. With me out of the way it will be a straight fight between the two of them and I guess they would both prefer the odds at 50/50. Finally, there is Winter. I turn and look over my shoulder at her as she stands rooted to the spot, unsure how she should react.

'Go!' I shout, pointing in the opposite direction. 'Go now and don't look back. Get to the nearest phone, ring your brother and see if he'll come and collect you. You've done more than enough for me but now you need to accept this isn't your fight.'

'Please, Em, there's still time,' she says, deep furrows of anguish stretching across her forehead as her eyes plead with me to change my mind. 'If we set off in that direction, east, we can outrun that blundering thing and find somewhere to hide out – you know, in the same way we shook off the dogs?'

'That's not a dog,' I needlessly point out as the Challenger bears down on my position. I can picture the commander inside this metal killing machine, ordering his minions to input the co-ordinates for the first strike. 'It's got thermal imaging on board so hiding behind a few trees won't do any good. Then, with that massive gun, it's just going to blast away at us until you and I are dead. Do you understand?'

I turn and walk back to her and for a moment I see a glimmer of hope in her eyes. In moments I shatter it. Holding her arms at her sides and looking into her eyes, the intensity of my stare emphasises the points my words have been unable to communicate properly. Then I do something hurtful and horrible, but with the overall intention of doing good. I shove her to the ground. Striding back in the direction from which I came, I refuse to glance back, feeling guilty yet convinced that she'll be grateful for my actions when she considers them in the cold light of day.

I take an inventory of what clothes I have left and realise there is nothing white to hand so rip the tourniquet from my arm. It has a large red splurge across the middle but will have to do. Waving it in the direction of the tank, I hope they understand I'm trying to surrender. The turret swivels in my direction, the gun levels and I realise this must be how Dr

Who feels when he comes face to face with one of those Daleks in the TV sci-fi series. The tank rumbles on, but its pace slows, and I wonder if it's just taking its time to savour the kill. When there are just around 100 feet between us it grinds to a halt and I'm looking straight down the barrel, a black, hollow void of nothingness ready to dispense death at the touch of a button.

I wonder who is at the other end of that button, perhaps the man with the designer suit, the woman with the fruity hat or even my old pal Hayes, though that is taking my paranoia a step too far. For all the accusations I've levelled at him, for all my suspicions about his secret agendas and use of underhand office politics to make him look big and me small, I don't see any way he could have mustered such powerful forces against me.

Suddenly, from deep within the metal beast, there is a clanking sound and, without warning, a lid lifts on top of it. Whoever my enemy is, they're about to reveal themselves before claiming their kill.

Finally, a head breaks the surface, the face peering down. Protective goggles shield the eyes but can't disguise the familiar scowl. 'Bloody hell, Rabette!' shouts the man I know as Tank. 'We haven't got all day. I've orders to fulfil, and you're needed. Don't know what you think you're doing, lolloping around the countryside. Hop on board, would you? There's a good soldier.'

21

SCARCELY able to believe my luck, I don't need a second invitation. I move around to the side of the tank and the soldier climbs down to offer me his hand and haul me on board the mighty metal killing machine. I cast my eyes back across the field looking for Winter. I want her to know she's safe to join me, but she's nowhere to be seen. Damn! She must have taken my advice, turned back and found somewhere to hide.

'Where's that briefcase, soldier?' asks Tank.

I realise with alarm that I've left it in the outbuilding and anyone attempting to retrieve it will be risking life and limb. The tiger is sure to be wound up beyond belief by now. I explain the situation.

'Well, there's a surprise!' says the soldier, shaking his bullet head to show I've disappointed him again. 'Seems to me you incite trouble wherever you go. You're a real jinx, Rabette.'

I shrug.

'Let's clear everything out of the way here, so the dog can see the rabbit, or is it Rabette?' His voice echoes as he shouts down into the deadly tin can, his words bouncing around the walls. 'Fire in the hole!'

Before I have time to consider the implications, a ball of flame shoots from the huge gun, leaving a raging inferno where the stone building had once been. I can't see the white tiger escaping the blast and I hope Winter has headed in a different direction. Sheets of flame rise into the night sky and I see people running from the farmhouse to take a closer look at the scene of destruction.

'Bloody hell, was that necessary?' I demand of Tank. 'What about the case?'

He turns and grasps me by the rags hanging loosely around my neck. His hand is super-strong, forcing me to choke and splutter in response to the obstruction blocking my windpipe.

'You questioning my orders, soldier?' he asks. 'It has to be done. We can't have that case falling into enemy hands now, can we?'

It takes an immense effort to shake my head slightly in acknowledgement.

'Glad we agree,' he says. 'Now get down there and retrieve your bloody handbag. There are things inside we're going to need.'

I'm stunned. Not only is he ordering me into a blazing inferno without any safety gear, but he actually believes the case might have survived his hasty overreaction. For my own health, though, I decide it's safer to risk life and limb in the fire than face his wrath.

Climbing down off the tank, I know the tiger could be anywhere right now but am strangely more frightened of the human wrecking ball I'm leaving behind. Thankfully, there is no sign of the escaped zoo exhibit as the smoke clears and I head in the direction of the flames. Part of me hopes it has got away. While just a short while ago I was pleading with Winter to shoot it, now the danger has passed, I reflect on the beauty of the creature I encountered.

Stepping gingerly into smoking rubble, I scan the area where the out-house once stood. The fire has dried out the ground and there are pieces of rubber everywhere, the only signs left that the hose existed. By contrast, the battered suitcase sits proudly on a rocky plinth, still in one piece and seemingly unaffected by the destruction around it.

OK, it's covered in dust and flecked with burn marks and it's important I reach it before the flames do. They're pretty close and will soon be licking at its edges. With seconds to act I count to three in my head and swing my foot like a Premier League striker, kicking the case clear of the danger zone then running after it, the scorched earth burning into the soles of my shoeless feet. Kneeling, I apply the combination, lift the lid and peer inside.

With alarm I realise that Winter still has the gun while I spent some of the money bribing the ticket collector on the train and hope that won't incur the wrath of Tank. The GPS tracker and the car key are in the same place I originally found them, inserted in small pockets in the lid, and the postcard has survived the ordeal, too.

Just as I'm about to turn back and climb on board the tank, I notice something shining on the floor, reflecting the flames. Stooping, I pick up a pendant, the bit where it attaches itself to a garment bent out of shape. I recognise the symbol immediately and turn it over in my hand, studying it for further clues. It's the three wavy lines with the strange emblem on top which I'd seen carved into a forest tree. It strikes me that the symbol above the lines might be the top half of a person though I'm unsure what they're supposed to be doing or who they represent. Are they stuck in quicksand? It's a bit like the hieroglyphics they used in ancient Egypt.

A strange feeling of unease grips my stomach, the shivery sensation unrelated to the medical problem irritating my digestive system. Perhaps this is what they mean by gut instinct.

The pendant has to be Winter's. There is no other logical explanation. She must have kept it covered up while in my company then dropped it on making her hasty retreat. It begs another question: Why has she lied to me? She claimed to know nothing about the symbol and had no idea what it might mean when I described what I'd seen in the woods. Her denial made me question my own sanity, wondering whether the signs I was seeing were merely hallucinations conjured up by a troubled mind. Maybe at some stage I had caught a glimpse of Winter's pin and confused things inside my head while undergoing the trauma of the manhunt.

If what I saw back there was real, however, then it suggests that, rather than being an innocent cast adrift in this storm of confusion, Winter knows an awful lot more than she has been letting on.

'Hey, daydreamer!' Tank's growl interrupts my thoughts. 'We gotta be making tracks, if you'll pardon the pun. The patrols will be out looking for you and I promised to have my ride back by morning. The Mrs has to do the weekly shop.' He lets rip a guttural laugh and when I turn to face him, he taps the side of the tank affectionately. Then, as if reading my mind, he says, 'I know she's a tasty bit of blart, but you have to forget your girlfriend for now. There is someone far more important waiting to see you...and The Commander don't like to be kept waiting.'

<h1 style="text-align:center">22</h1>

INSIDE the iron shell it's sweltering. I've swapped wading through a freezing stream in November for sweating buckets in a mobile, all-terrain sauna. I look around to see if there is any liquid refreshment available and simultaneously take a closer inventory of my surroundings.

In all, there are four of us inside the Challenger. Two other uniformed soldiers have spent the entire journey in front of computer screens, pressing buttons and pushing levers as we trundle from the latest scene of destruction left in my wake. I count the crew as three and me, though, so I know I've done the right thing agreeing to take part in this magical mystery tour. It all adds up.

Tank is studying a big screen illuminated in glowing green as he navigates our way across the fields. It's easy to see how he has earned his nickname. He doesn't seem too bothered about adhering to the niceties of countryside etiquette. Any fences that stand in the way are just bulldozed as he heads on relentlessly towards his appointment. When he says The Commander isn't one for tardiness, I can see Tank is focused on following his orders to the letter. Nothing is going to prevent him from making sure I arrive for my appointment with his boss at the designated time.

'Here,' he says as if the tank itself has some kind of detector alerting him to the fact I'm watching his every move. He holds out a bottle of water and I get up to collect it before leaning over his shoulder.

'Thanks.' I unscrew the cap and take a long and grateful gulp. Immediately, I'm feeling better.

'Dehydration's a bitch, ain't it?' he says. 'We had to be wary of that in the 'Stan. It was as big an enemy as the Taliban.' He stretches the word out, emphasising each syllable.

'You served in Afghanistan?'

He nods. 'Just the two tours. Then when I got home, I landed this little number. Not bad, eh? They gave me my own company car and everything.' He pats the console in front of him gently, as if the 60 tons of metal under his command is a family pet.

'I don't understand, though,' I say. 'Are you regular army and, if so, who are the guys chasing me?'

He touches his finger to his nose. 'Sorry, soldier, that's NTK.'

I shake my head, baffled.

'Need to Know,' he explains. 'They haven't told me anything other than it's my job to keep you out of trouble and I must give up my life to defend you if necessary. I've done my best to achieve those goals over the last few hours, even if you seem hell-bent on self-destruction.'

'That's not fair,' I say. 'I've eluded these people even though they don't give up easily – and for most of the time I've done it without your help.'

'Hmm, if you say so, but you can be a bit careless.' He points to the briefcase. 'You keep leaving that behind which ain't clever, is it? Still, luckily you have me here to remind you about it. Ah, looks like we've got ourselves a welcome party.'

I can see from the screen we are approaching a vast building, some kind of stately home, with large ornate white gates bookended by two soldiers armed with rifles. There is a camera on top of the gates moving left and right, scanning the terrain around us, on the lookout for potential intruders. Behind the gates is a long, wide driveway which I estimate stretches for almost a quarter of a mile with, at the end of it, a circular area where a selection of expensive-looking cars is parked.

'My God, who are we meeting: the prime minister?'

'No,' says Tank, 'Someone far more important, given your circumstances.'

I think he might be joking but he maintains the same grave expression, as if he has been carved from stone. What does he mean? Who is more important than the head of the country's government? Was I about to meet royalty? The mystery both perplexes and excites me.

Our armoured vehicle shudders to a halt and my soldier friend climbs up the rungs of the ladder, throwing back the turret when he reaches the top. He barks a few orders, salutes then steps back inside. On the screen, I see the gates open electronically. 'Fancy a drive?' he asks me, but I decline. A family hatchback is my limit when it comes to motor vehicles, and even they can get me in trouble. I've had a little go at the wheel of a London double-decker bus now, but that was hardly a resounding success and fortunately my efforts were curtailed swiftly. I have a feeling this beast can do far more damage than the 333 to Elephant and Castle.

For one horrifying moment, I imagine losing control of the mighty armoured behemoth and crashing through the resplendent mansion, battering its magnificent stonework and laying waste to a lovingly nurtured throwback from the Victorian era, which undoubtedly costs a small fortune to maintain and upgrade.

I study my surroundings. To my left there is a strikingly beautiful array of natural colours highlighted in the large arc lights that illuminate the grounds. As my eyes adjust to the scene, I realise they're the leaves of different trees someone has taken great care to import from around the world. There are Japanese maples, Chinese spindles and Persian Ironwood, interspersed with North American pines reaching for the heavens.

Spanning across the awe-inspiring vista laid out in front of me, I come to the other side of the drive. Here I spot something familiar, a large garden maze, together with a collection of glass houses, a 300ft pergola and a clock in the shape of Big Ben constructed entirely of flowers. Whoever owns this place has spent a great deal of time, trouble and money maintaining these exquisite gardens. I wonder if it's open to public scrutiny, but the presence of the soldiers suggests otherwise. Even though he has created something to be admired by all, I would wager the owner is fanatical about his privacy.

To create such a setting purely for your own enjoyment must be the work of a self-centred narcissist and I conjure up images of one of those evil villains in the *James Bond* spy films. I imagine being invited into a drawing room to find menacing sharks swimming beneath a glass floor. 'Ahhh, Mr Rabette,' says my host as he strokes a white cat. 'I've been dying to meet you.' Before I can respond he pulls a lever and I'm fed to the strategically starved fish.

'Oi, dream boy, snap out of it,' says Tank. 'Let's not keep The Commander waiting. I'm sure you'll have a lot to say to each other.' My armoured taxi grinds to a halt and he waves me to the ladder. 'Age before beauty,' he quips, laughing at his own joke. I don't want to defuse his good mood by telling him it's an out-dated cliché, like most of the things he says.

Clambering out, I then take a moment to study the huge property more closely. It has three floors with about eight large windows on each level. Of course, this is just the one side of the house and I can scarcely get to grips with how large it must be in its entirety. How many bedrooms, bathrooms, dining rooms and living rooms are concealed within its walls? I can't help but compare it to my own three-bedroom terraced townhouse in Clapham and how we were forced to break open our piggy banks just to put a deposit on it. I try to do the maths but can't hazard a guess as to how much this place has set the owner back. He must be one rich cookie.

Sitting atop the tank, I see below me the liveried uniforms of the servants, who appear to have gathered to specifically welcome me to this stately extravagance in the middle of nowhere. As I begin to manoeuvre myself towards the ground, a hand comes up to guide me. One small jump and I hit terra firma.

'Lovely to meet you, sir, and if I may say, "Well done".' The servant's tone is patronising in the extreme. 'It's not easy getting out of one of those things and we're glad you made it.' I nod. 'If you would care to follow me, I'll take you to your host. He's been waiting such a long time for this moment.' Talk about impatience, I thought. We only left the farmhouse just over half an hour ago.

'You're not coming?' I shout up to Tank, who is poking his head from the top of his "company car" like a prairie dog leaving its burrow to sniff the air, alert for signs of unwelcome predators.

'No, Rabette, this is your moment,' he says. 'You two need time alone and I need to stay alert.'

'NTK?'

He nods, and at that moment I realise I could never be a soldier. I'm too inquisitive by nature. I also couldn't stay locked up in one of those sardine cans for any period of time.

I follow the man dressed like an old-fashioned British butler as we pass through giant double doors into a luxuriant foyer. Its centre piece is a fountain and behind it a meandering wide staircase disappears into the distance. What secrets lie hidden up there, just beyond the boundaries of my vision? I wonder. Instinctively wiping my feet, I wince at the feel of brushed matting on skin and remember I'm now completely shoeless. Crossing polished marble floors, we pass silently along corridors lined with glorious paintings and portraits of noble characters from the past, with their twirling moustaches and gold-encrusted uniforms. Each intersection seems to be guarded by a marble bust immortalising some character or other from British history at a time when we ruled large swathes of the world.

'Sorry, sir, but there's no time for tourist activities,' says the butler, furnishing me with his best Jeeves impression. Who is servant here and who is master? Being in the employ of someone who can afford a place like this almost certainly means you're well recompensed, commanding a bigger salary than, say, a graphic artist plying his trade in the city of London. The irony of a man dressed spick-and-span in tails and blemish-free trousers guiding along a guest in rags is lost on neither of us.

Changing direction, we head down another corridor. I look at the walls and what I see nearly sends me sprawling face-first into the chequered pattern on the solid stone floor. The pictures have changed.

While they're still in ornate, decorous frames the subject matter is to-tally different and chills me to the bone.

The pictures on the walls are of me at various stages of my development from a curly haired, rosy-cheeked youngster sitting on the floor holding a stuffed toy lamb, through a first school picture resplendent in uniform with shorts and long grey socks, to senior school where I'm proudly pos-ing with a curly yellow mop of a fringe that hangs down over one eye. It's my nod to popular culture because it makes me resemble a pop star who was big in the charts at that time.

My heartbeat quickens and I feel faint. The butler turns and instructs, 'Not that way, this way please', noticing I'm heading back in the direc-tion from which we came. A voice that has been subdued until now is shouting at me, the words echoing through my head.

'What about the threes? What about the threes? You've forgotten, haven't you?' I must go back to the very beginning of the hallway and count meticulously, touching every third coloured stone tile on the floor, then moving across to the paintings and placing my hand on every third picture frame.

I hear the butler tut and look up to see him studying his watch, an expression of discomfort creeping across his face. I'm reminded of the white rabbit in *Alice in Wonderland* and almost expect him to announce that we're late for a very important date.

At the sixth frame I stop dead in my tracks. There is a family portrait I've never seen: my mother, my father and me. Anyone would think it had been taken to mark the sombre occasion of a funeral or that the person on the other side of the camera has delivered the worst possible news before imploring their subjects to say: 'Cheese!'

I stop, touch the frame and let my fingers wander over the faces of my mother and father. Waves of intense sadness flow through me and I feel water amassing at my tear ducts. What is this torture? It seems so long ago since I've thought of them, and I chastise myself silently for letting them slip my memory so easily.

'Cheer up, son, it may never happen,' I hear my father say, and it makes me smile.

Until I realise the voice isn't solely inside my head.

I stagger and slide to the ground, the butler and two other servants racing quickly to grab me and prevent me dashing my head against the floor. They look down on me with expressions of concern, though I can't focus on exactly what they're saying. My mind is elsewhere, drowning in a whirlpool of conflicting emotions and untrustworthy memories. Shielding my eyes from a bright light hovering over me I see shady faces looking down, like scribbled pencil cartoons with no discernible outlines.

Then they part and another familiar face materialises, this one as comfortable and familiar as an old jumper.

'Hello, Emerson,' says my father.

23

IS this a vision before me, brought on by a bump to the head? Or is my condition kicking in as it's prone to do at times of stress? I haven't taken my pills for some time, having lost them somewhere as I fled London, and the longer I go without medication the worse my stress is liable to become. It's possible this is just the beginning of a meltdown. I shut my eyes in an effort to scare the spectre away with sheer willpower. Unfortunately, it won't stop talking.

'I appreciate this is a huge shock, son,' the apparition says. 'I can't tell you how long I've waited for this moment, how much I've wanted to see you, to let you know I'm OK and that everything you and your mother were told by the authorities was a lie. But to do so would have been to put all of you – not to mention those dependent on you – in real danger.'

When I open my eyes he is standing there, just a few feet away.

My father, Laurent Rabette.

He must be in his 70s now but doesn't look any different. There are a few more wrinkles on his face and the skin is mottled and worn while a deep crevasse I don't recall travels from one side of his forehead to the other. Besides all that, he still has the earnest dark brown eyes I remember, hard and fast barriers to what lies behind them. I always suspected they hid a wealth of secrets. He still has all his hair, too, though where once it was thick and black it's now tinged with flecks of silver. Any question that this person might be a doppelganger or fake disappear when I see the purple splurge behind his right ear, a random design fault in his skin which would be almost impossible to replicate accurately.

What is completely different is his clothing. I recall him wearing country tweeds mostly, or comfortable slacks and nobbly, colourless cardigans when he was gardening. Now, he looks resplendent in a dark blue military jacket with silver buttons and epaulettes on the shoulder, a couple of ribbons dangling from the pocket. It's as if he is about to head out for a fancy-dress party, though the father I knew was the last person you would expect to see at something so gauche. To be frank, he was the most solemn and serious man I ever met.

'Lift him, please, and bring him to the Banqueting Hall,' instructs the father I haven't seen for almost 25 years. In response, the servants put their hands beneath me and hoist me up. I'm then transported through a set of heavy oak doors while he continues to issue precise orders, a man used to being firmly in control.

'Get some blankets, there,' he says, the slight French inflection in his voice coming through as he speaks. 'A pillow for his head, too, that's it. It would be better if we could take him upstairs and let him sleep but that will have to wait. There isn't time right now. We need a full debrief. Are you going to be warm enough, son?' It's the sort of question a father asks a son, but when the boy is in his early years not when he has just travelled the wrong side of his fortieth birthday.

Before I can answer I'm lowered onto a large ornate chaise lounge, a pillow cushioning my head. Someone drapes a blanket across me. 'Thank you, team,' says my father and the staff drift away, the butler leaving last with a gracious bow to his boss, the elaborate performance totally out of context in this day and age. He pulls the doors closed behind him.

I'm feeling slightly better now and am anxious to get to the bottom of this crazy saga. I don't want my father to see me as an invalid, or to give him the impression I've struggled to cope without him. There are important issues to discuss and, swinging my legs around, I attempt to rise to my feet. Only then do I realise I'm unable to move.

It's as if I'm being held down and I imagine a pair of ageing, wrinkled hands exerting pressure on my shoulders. 'Don't,' my father says. 'Please son, you must conserve your energy. We wouldn't want you to have a relapse, would we? Best to give it a bit of time to regain your, um, balance and whatnot. Shame. You've always been a bit of a sickly child, but the good news is we have drugs here to replace the ones you lost on your travels.'

How did he know? The mystery grows deeper.

'In a way that's how this all started,' he says. '...your illness, I mean.'

'What do you mean?' I say. 'How what started?'

'This, um, business you've sadly become caught up in.'

He waves his arms around as if giving me the customers' tour of the factory floor. I establish it's nothing more than an empty room, his voice echoing off the high ceilings and plain green pastel walls. In my dream state, it seems he is there in spirit but not in person – even though I can see him quite clearly from where I lie.

'When you're feeling more yourself, I'll start at the beginning,' he says. 'I can't tell you how wonderful it is to see you, though, even though I can understand the circumstances are quite upsetting. I expect you've been driven to your wits end by everything that's happened. It's fortunate for all of us you could read the signs we left. Any other scenario and I don't know what would have happened. Can I get you anything: A glass of whisky, perhaps?'

'Maybe some water and, well, I'm pretty hungry. I've been on the go all day and I haven't eaten since breakfast.'

'*Sacre bleu*! That's no good,' he says, acting the concerned parent. 'We must sort this out straight away.' He lifts some sort of communication device to his lips and says, 'Food for our guest, please.'

Moments later a servant dressed in a French maid's uniform enters the room carrying a glass of water on a silver salver. Putting it down on the large banqueting table in the centre of the room, she then removes a small box from the pocket of her uniform, opens it and takes out something small, round and white. She pops it into the water, allowing it to bubble up before bringing the glass across to me.

'Try this,' says my father. 'It should aid your recovery.'

'I don't know.' Hesitantly, I take the glass from the servant's hand.

'I insist, it will help you tackle the stress. You forget I know all about your condition…since you were a child, I've closely monitored it. It has a part to play in all this, but I can't tell you any more until I'm sure you're fit and well enough to hear it. Nothing I have to say is for the faint hearted.'

Shortly afterwards, the servants come in and lift me on shaking legs to the banqueting table where I'm presented with a plate well stocked with medium rare steak, French fries, tomatoes and mushrooms. My father stands at the other end of the table, raising a glass of wine in my direction. 'To you, son,' he says. 'You've turned out rather well if I say so myself.'

This is high praise indeed from a man who once looked upon me as just another piece of furniture in the room. He seems to have shaken off some of his chilly disposition in the intervening years and I have to admit I prefer the new, more open version.

'I know exactly what you're thinking,' he says. 'This can't be my father; he is being far too friendly.'

It really is uncanny the way the old man seems to be able to read my mind. I nod.

'You must understand, I had a lot to worry about and a lot of secrets to protect when I "died",' he says. 'In fact, you could say dying was the best thing that ever happened to me… accepting the inevitable drawback of having to cut off all communication with my family. It had to be done, though. You've seen what they're like and how persistent they are when you have something they want.'

'Who are they?' I say. 'I take it you mean the man in the electric blue suit and the woman with the elaborate hat?'

'We'll come to that in a minute.'

Suddenly, I can't hold back any longer. I need to give him some idea of the pain he caused to us, his family. 'Mother was absolutely distraught when she heard about the skiing accident in the Alps,' I say. 'She never fully recovered, and I believe that when she died a few years later it was from a broken heart. It meant I lost both parents before my twentieth birthday. Do you know how that feels? How tough it makes life?'

He shakes his head slowly. 'I'm sure it's quite terrible,' he says.

'What's worse, none of it makes any sense to me,' I continue. 'It never has. I'm sure the psychological damage caused by losing you both still affects me every day. I sometimes find myself crying for no reason, even now. I've put it down to the condition, but I'm not sure that's true. Look at it from my point of view; one minute you were heading off on a team-building trip with the bank, the next there was a knock at the door and a glum-looking policeman was standing in front of us. Mother invited this officer into the front room, and he told her you were missing, and they believed you had fallen into a crevasse. All attempts to find you had failed. Damn, we had a funeral without a body and a wake where Mum physically collapsed on the floor, having drained herself of tears. I don't think until that moment I truly realised how much you meant to her.'

'...And you?'

'Oh, come on, Father, what do you expect?' I say. 'To me you were always a cold fish. I used to tell my school friends you were a robot just so they would think me a bit intriguing and different. You were unapproachable at the best of times. Yes, now and then there were signs of a human being concealed within that frosty exterior – moments like the small displays of excitement you showed when you were watching the Grand Prix – but other than that, if someone had told me you were a computer in a human shell I don't think I would have batted an eyelid.'

'That bad, Emerson?' he says thoughtfully, his mind flashing back to that period when our lives intertwined. 'I guess that's fair. What you don't realise is the amount of pressure I was under. I was looking over my shoulder, expecting a stranger to knock at the door any day and cart me off to some dark place where he would put a bullet in my head.'

'But why, Father? What do you mean? You were just a banker!'

'A lie, I'm afraid, and one of many.' His eyes focus on his shoes, the expression one of shame. 'I was a good mathematician, certainly, but I wasn't using my skill for the benefit of any financial institution. I was working for a top-secret government agency which did everything from code breaking to developing weapons.'

I shake my head, finding it difficult to take it all in, but now he's started there's no stopping him. It's as if a plug has been removed and the torrent of words is so strong he can't fit it back in the hole.

'All our troubles began one day at the agency when I intercepted a message sent from a relatively unknown department within the European Union to a government think-tank. When I deciphered it, I learned the prototype for a new bomb was to be tested in a major European city. I alerted my superior and we put plans in motion to try to prevent the attack. The matter was handed to MI6, they mobilised their network of spies and phone chatter directed them towards Madrid. Putting boots on the ground and interrogating suspected terrorists, they managed to track down the bomber and intercept him before he could do any harm. Comprende?'

I nod, though it's like sitting at his feet as a youngster while he reads me a fairy tale.

'Anyway, things took a complex turn when the man went into huge convulsions and dropped dead before we could discover who he worked for and what he planned to do,' my father says. 'We thought we would never get to the bottom of it, never find the bomb, but in the autopsy all became clear. The medical examiner found something highly unusual inside the corpse. Blood tests revealed a strange and highly volatile set of chemicals in his system. On their own they were harmless but if mixed together with another agent, they could cause a vigorous chemical reaction.'

'You're saying *he* was a bomb?' I look at him with incredulity.

'Well done, Emerson, yes,' he says. 'Of course, the matter needed closer investigation and I was called in because of my knowledge of chemistry, among other things. I needed to establish what it all meant, *n'est pas?* This man's body obviously couldn't handle what had been injected into him, and the lethal concoction had killed him. Was he supposed to die after delivering a bomb so that he couldn't be interrogated? And how was he to receive the other vital ingredient that would set off the whole chain reaction? Surely it was easier to strap the explosives to him like a normal suicide bomber. That would kill two birds with one stone. Then, I thought, maybe he didn't even know he was being used to deliver a bomb at all. Imagine. Creating a human bomb that wouldn't be activated until the last moment has its advantages. In this way you can avoid all discovery at checkpoints, customs searches and the like and he's not going to reveal the secret, because he is totally unaware of what has happened to him.'

'What was your part in all this?'

'Aaah.' My father takes a sip of his wine. 'Well, I looked at the data, studied the formulas, did some equations and solved the problem – I did my job in other words. Having worked out what the whole thing was designed to achieve, I took to the lab and together with my assistant we replicated the process the terrorists had followed then added a couple of missing ingredients to the formula and did our own set of experiments. In doing so, we made the whole thing less volatile and answered the original conundrum.'

I look at him quizzically. My head is spinning from trying to follow his train of thought and a thudding pain has invaded my frontal lobe. This is a man who barely muttered more than a few words to me in the first 14 years of my life. Now he is in his element, talking about what he obviously knows and loves best... his work.

'My partner and I worked out that the chemicals weren't designed to kill the bomber until the detonation itself,' he says. 'Mistakes had been made in its development and that's why the trial run had failed. In "customising" their work, we had remedied those mistakes. Put simply, young man, we'd managed to perfect the first, working, human bomb.'

24

THE room plunges into silence as I sit there staring at him, too stunned to speak. When I eventually find my voice, I say, 'Are you telling me you found out how to turn a human being into an explosive – someone you could blow up at the push of a button? Wow. They call that spontaneous combustion, don't they?'

It was something I'd read about, but I'm pretty cynical. If I haven't seen something with my own eyes, I doubt whether it can actually happen.

'Perhaps *spontaneous* isn't quite the right word because it can be controlled,' says my father. 'Obviously, it's not quite as simple as I've just made out but I'm trying to give you the overall picture.'

I can't let the matter rest. I have so many questions swirling around in my head I don't know where to start. Words start tumbling from my mouth randomly like a one-armed bandit dispensing a jackpot.

'Why would you want to do that? And how the hell did you test it without the whole thing literally blowing up in your faces? Did you have volunteers?'

'One question at a time please, Emerson,' he says. 'It's complicated I know, but I'll try to break it down for you.'

There's the Laurent Rabette I know, the one who used to come across as slightly condescending when showing me how to do my homework or explaining the best strategies in a game of Monopoly.

'How do scientists normally test things?' he continues, though I know it's a rhetorical question. 'In a controlled environment, of course. We have special labs for this sort of thing where everything is conducted behind reinforced glass, and for the bigger explosions we go off to some spot in the wilderness far from anywhere like, you know, Salisbury Plain, where the army carries out special manoeuvres.'

'Surely you need living subjects to test these theories though?'

'Well, we use animals, of course...'

'But how can you be sure that will work? The chemicals might not react the same way in a rat as they would in a human being.'

'Oh, come on, Emerson!' He dispenses the kind of look which tells me he can't quite believe I'm his own flesh and blood. 'How do we test anything? We work by exactly the same principles as the big cosmetic companies, who test their eye shadows, nail varnish and other products on animals before marketing them to humans. The top pharmaceutical firms work in the same way.'

I refuse to let his superior tone faze me. He has foregone the right to play the know-it-all father where I'm concerned.

'In this case, though, there has to be more at stake,' I say. 'You can only be sure it will work if you test it on real, live human beings. What are these chemicals anyway? What would cause a human being to explode? Wouldn't you need some kind of trigger, a switch?'

'Look, it's complicated and you're tired,' he says. 'I can sit here for days trying to explain it all to you but without a scientific degree you would find it impossible to understand.'

My father is at his patronising best now, but he's known me from childhood and has a good idea how my brain works. Maths, equations and chemical reactions all went over my head as a kid. I was an artist, pure and simple, making the most of attributes I inherited from my mother.

'That's enough questions for now,' my father says. 'The servants have made up a room for you. Take the opportunity to rest before you move on. We need to get you out of the country.'

'Why?' I ask, surprised at this latest development. 'Surely I'll be OK here? I refuse to go anywhere before I know Cherry and Jamie are safe.'

'I assure you they've been taken care of,' says my father. 'My people have guaranteed their safety.'

'Your people?' He sounds like a Mafia boss and I don't care for the way he has suggested he's 'taken care' of my girls.

'Look, Emerson, you know we're the good guys, don't you?'

'Really?' I say. 'And how am I supposed to know that? I haven't seen you in years. When you left us – supposedly having died in a freak skiing accident – we were devastated and yet until now you have never given us a clue you survived. How does that make you a "good guy"? For all I know, you could have been working with the enemy all this time. You created a human bomb, for Christ's sake. No good can come from that.'

He acknowledges my statement with a nod. 'You're right, of course you're right. I realise that now. At the time, though, the problem was so intriguing I guess I let my curiosity get the better of me. I took my findings to my bosses, but didn't know at the time that my assistant had been coerced by a different paymaster.'

'You mean he was a traitor?' I say, shocked. 'Who is he?'

'His name is Melrose, Alexander Melrose,' he replies. 'I believe you bumped into him at some stage on your travels yesterday morning. He has long, straggly hair and a beard which, I believe, he dyes purple these days as part of his "disguise", though I would recognise him anywhere. They have a name for that style of beard these days.'

'A goatee.'

'That's right. So, you have met him?'

'Yes, but it seems very odd,' I say. 'I mean, he gave me every impression he was trying to help me. He told me which bus to get on and advised me to trust no one.'

'It's a double bluff,' says my father. 'From what I've been told getting on that bus nearly led you into a trap and delivered you up to the enemy. It was only the quick thinking of Tank to commandeer that vehicle that extricated you from that mess.'

I sigh. 'I didn't really think of it that way. And what about the people who were waiting for me... do they work for this Melrose character?'

'Describe them.'

'I mentioned them earlier: a man in a shiny blue suit with immaculate, slicked back black hair. I thought he was special branch or something. He had some sort of rapport going on with the police.'

'That makes sense,' says my father. 'I think you're talking about Martin Aston, former commissioner of the Metropolitan Police. He was drummed out in disgrace for doing favours for some particularly nasty criminal elements while also turning a blind eye to some dodgy newspaper practices. He goes where the money is and is a ringleader in a conspiracy designed to grab the reins of power not just in this country but all over Europe. We're talking about a full-scale revolution and you'd be surprised at how far these tentacles reach. Anyone else?'

I don't have to consider the question for long. 'This one is really weird,' I say. 'I thought my mind was playing tricks at first. There was this woman, elderly, plump, wearing a hat decorated with artificial fruit. She chased me on a white horse and proved to be a top-notch rider. I was lucky to escape. Then later, I saw her in the helicopter that shot up our train. She wasn't wearing the hat then and was completely bald. For goodness sake, who is she?'

My father dashes his fist into his palm and curses. For the first time in our discussion he seems rattled. 'The Female Cossack,' he says, nodding. 'I wondered when she might raise her ugly head. She's a real charmer and no mistake, originates from the Steppes of Southern Russia; a fantastic horse rider and lethal swordswoman. Pretty good with a whip, too, I've heard. People think she is just an urban myth, but I know better. If you escaped her, you've done very well. Around here we call her Lady Ascot because she has been spotted in that vicinity in the past. I came up against her once and never want to again. She's the reason I had to "disappear".'

'This must be some kind of joke,' I say. 'At any moment I'm going to wake up. I can understand why you wouldn't be putting the welcome mat out for these people, but what has all this got to do with me? Surely, they don't think I know anything about this formula? You've pretty much proved I'm a complete ignoramus when it comes to science or maths. If they've done their homework on me, they will know that. So, what aren't you telling me?'

'They want to use you as leverage against me.'

Though he says this in persuasive tones, my father can't look me in the eye. He shakes his head slowly then turns and walks away. I want to call him back to finish his story, but an overwhelming weariness has started to consume me. Even so, our conversation up until now has provided me with one vital piece of information. As I flop my head onto the table at least I'm sure of one thing.

My father is lying to me...and I need to find out why.

25

WHEN I wake some time later there is a blinding bright light shining directly into my left eye. I flinch from it and a voice says, 'He'll live.' I look up to see the face of my old friend, the plastic surgeon Dr Joel.

'Not those bloody lights again,' I say. 'This is déjà vu. What are you bloody doing here? I thought you had waists to nip and wrinkles to tuck.'

'Ha ha, yes.' The feigned amusement doesn't reach his eyes. 'You're at Ramsden Hall, the big stately home in Essex to which you were brought by tank two days ago,' he explains.

'You're not a plastic surgeon, are you? That's a lie.'

'Not at all,' he says. 'On the contrary I'm one of the finest in Harley Street. I just have this little, um, sideline going on. In fact, the plastic surgery is a great cover story.'

'You work with my father.' The truth dawns and I wonder how many more people are employed by The Commander, as Tank calls him.

'For him, dear boy, I work for him,' he says in an attempt at a posh English accent. 'We have our little dealings together at times, yes, and he pays me well.'

He lifts my hand and checks the pulse, then signals to someone else in the room to bring around a blood pressure machine. 'We're just going to give you a little check-up and then you can be on your way.'

A woman in a white gown steps into my line of vision and when I catch sight of the bright crimson hair I gasp.

'Winter!'

'Hi, Em,' she says nonchalantly, as if we parted two minutes ago.

'You're in this, too?' I say. 'Hell, I'm such a fool. I thought you were lost or that you'd found your way back to your brother.'

'A necessary deception,' she says in a voice completely devoid of Welsh inflection. 'I had to go and make a report. By the way, he's not my brother. He's just another one of us.'

I look at her as if she's talking a foreign language. 'And just who exactly is us?' I ask.

She looks over and Dr Joel gives her an almost imperceptible nod. 'We're called Department 3,' she explains. 'We were formed some time ago, during all the Islamic Fundamentalist stuff going on in Afghanistan, Iraq and Syria. Originally, we were to get to the bottom of the Isis and Al-Qaida plots, monitor their computers and cell phone transmissions and the like. A lot of Brits went out there to wage Jihad as you'll recall so there could be no resting on the job. It was while we were checking up on certain known activists in Europe that we uncovered something new – what we now call the European Plot. It started with the Madrid transmission, something I believe your father may have told you about, and it has grown out of all proportion since then.'

'And throughout the time we were together fighting for our lives... you knew my father was behind it all along?'

'Certainly,' she says. 'He's been a kind of surrogate father to me too. He rescued me from an orphanage in Eastern Europe and put me with foster parents in Wales to grow up, hence the accent I lapse into when the need arises. I owe your father so much, you wouldn't believe.'

My father, the man with the social conscience. The image doesn't sit right with the person I know. 'So, your brother...?'

'My stepbrother, I guess you could say. We aren't related by blood, but we grew up together and I love him to pieces.'

'And Department 3? How did all that come about, and how did you get involved?'

'Long story,' interrupts Dr Joel, squeezing air out of a syringe and pushing the needle into my upper arm. 'I'm sure Winter will expand on this later, when we have more time.'

'Owww!' A shooting pain engulfs my arm. I'm used to injections, but the size of this needle suggests it would be more suited to piercing the hide of the white tiger we encountered on our travels. Then I have a thought. 'How long have I been asleep?'

'It's Wednesday morning, Em,' says Winter, her smile lighting up our bland white-walled surroundings. 'You've been asleep for around 16 hours. It's still very early, though, about 4a.m., but that's fine. You definitely needed to recharge your batteries. The sedative in your steak did the trick, no doubt about it. You will be able to continue your journey today.'

'My journey?' I raise an eyebrow. 'I need to see my family, or at least talk to them, before anything else. They haven't heard from me for two days.'

'And that's good because it can only go badly for them if we don't complete our mission. I assure you they're quite safe. Your father must have told you as much.'

I wasn't sure I believed her, considering her track record for deceiving me in the past, but I can't see I have an option.

'Where am I going then?' I ask. 'What's the mission?'

I push myself up and stare into her eyes. The red mark is more prominent now, the overhead light reflecting off her iris.

'Abroad,' she says, picking up the postcard with the container ship on the front. 'And this is how we're going to travel. We need to get you to France, to our main research facility. Next stop is Felixstowe where it's arranged for us to hide on this vessel. Your father will be waiting for you when we reach our destination.'

'He left before us?'

At this she and Dr Joel laugh in unison as if I've told them the funniest joke in the world. I fear the punchline is me and feel aggrieved that I'm being ridiculed by these two intelligent young people.

'When you had dinner last night, did your father touch you at any stage?' asks Winter, 'Give you a hug, perhaps?'

She leans over the bed so that the crimson locks fall around her face and her eyes sparkle. I'm lost in those eyes for a minute but recover quickly.

'Well, no, but he's never been very affectionate in a huggy-feely sort of way. He's...'

'A hologram,' says Dr Joel. 'That's what you saw. Good wasn't it? We've perfected the art over the last few years. I'm glad it worked so well, we haven't had a live, um, guinea pig to try it out on before.'

I don't know how I feel about the description. It's hardly flattering, but my annoyance is tempered by a desire to know more. 'You mean that wasn't my father in the room last night?'

'Winter asked you whether he made physical contact?' says the Doctor.

I shrug. 'I don't remember. He first saw me in the corridor but, no, I don't think so. We were in that long banqueting hall. Anything he needed he asked the servants to fetch. Then, during dinner, he didn't eat anything, just sipped at a glass of wine.'

'Ah yes, his favourite,' says Dr Joel. 'Chateau Troisieme, he developed it himself. They say the French are the wine experts but he sure picks things up quickly, your old man. I suppose it's a logical progression. If you're good at mixing chemicals together and getting the desired result, then you can be equally good at producing a fine wine. You didn't see him pour it though? Or offer you a glass?'

'No... He said after what I'd been through it probably wasn't a good idea... particularly given the fact I'd mislaid my drugs.'

'Wow, he'll be thrilled to know he fooled his own son into thinking he was there in the room. Of course, it would be far too risky for The Commander, as we call him, to stay here for any length of time. He was over doing some business dealings in London the day this all started but that was a rare journey away from his secret hideaway across the Channel.'

'The taxi!' Suddenly something else makes sense.

'Yeah, bit of an oversight that. Unfortunately, Winter and I couldn't prevent that nattering cabby spilling the beans. We won't be using him again... completely blew the old man's cover, and to his son as well! It's such a key factor in your father's work that we keep up the pretence he died.'

'What exactly happened?' I ask. 'How did he fake his death? He was a bit frugal with the facts last night.'

Winter leans forward. 'I guess it can't hurt to fill you in. Do you remember your father going on that skiing trip when you were 15?'

'I was surprised,' I say. 'I didn't even realise he could ski!'

'He was actually attending a multi-agency conference at Chamonix in the French Alps. Your father was very excited. He'd cracked the code and couldn't wait to demonstrate his achievement. What he didn't know was that some of the people at the conference weren't who they said they were. The whole thing had been infiltrated by members of those behind the European plot. They knew about his discovery and intended to kidnap him and steal his plans. Obviously, anyone in control of a weapon as deadly as the human bomb could literally hold the world to ransom.'

'These people... their ultimate goal is money?'

'Power, pure and simple,' says Winter. 'Certain right-wing factions across Europe formed an alliance, fed up as they were with all the cross-border immigration from inside Europe and further afield. They wanted a halt to the number of refugees from war-torn countries in Africa and the Middle East entering their countries and threatening to "weaken" the blood line. They claimed it was an unbearable strain on resources and were annoyed their voices weren't being heard. You only have to look at the rise of certain groups in this country to get an idea of what was happening.'

'But surely those groups couldn't suddenly wield all this power? There have been extreme political parties dating back through history in this country, but they've always had such small support bases that they've eventually fragmented. To pull off something like this would take an incredible consensus.'

Dr Joel interrupts. 'That might be true of your normal right-wing loonies, but the people we are talking about are far more stealthy and influential. Reluctant to show their true colours they've piggy backed on these groups, allowing them to stir up fear so that they can then ride to the rescue... a compromise arrangement. These 'influencers' have their roots in the old establishments: we're talking banks, newspapers, multi-nationals, the civil service, the police and the armed forces. They've been used to getting their way for so long and are frightened to death someone new will come in and upset the old order – an order that they're determined to keep in place. Most of these organisations can cross borders with impunity so it has been easy for the conspiracy to spread.'

'Why do they need these "bombs", though? Why bother if they have some of the country's biggest powerbrokers in their ranks? Who are they going to attack?'

'It's all about misdirection,' says the doctor. 'Out of chaos comes order. The big institutions have always relied on spreading a climate of fear to get the general public to toe the line. Imagine the after-effect of dropping a few human bombs in strategic places – well-populated city centres and the like. You can blame it on left-wing terrorists, religious fanatics... anyone you want really. Then you offer yourselves up as a solution. It's the sort of tactic that proved so successful in winning the Brexit vote. Frighten enough people and feed their prejudices... and once you've lit the blue touchpaper stand back and watch the bastard explode.'

I whistle loudly.

'Brexit was democracy in action, surely,' I say. 'This is something else, one hell of a conspiracy theory. You could be talking about anyone in a position of power. Who are the good guys and who are the bad guys?'

Suddenly I'm overwhelmed with another blast of *déjà vu*. I believe I'd asked my father the very same question the previous night.

'Not everyone is completely power crazy,' says Dr Joel, who gives me the impression he is quietly building his own little empire. 'There are plenty of good people in these organisations. It's like everywhere. I'm sure there are good and bad people in your place of work.'

I think about Ben and Hayes, one a good mate, the other consumed wholly by self-interest.

'You're right,' I say. 'Separating them, though...'

'There is a list,' interrupts Winter. 'We managed to get someone on the inside to supply us with names, the whole shebang. We can't trust MI5 and MI6 in its entirety, of course, because some of the old top brass there are part of the establishment. As you point out, though, it's hard to detect who is on which side... and while it means we always have to be on our guard, it also makes it easy to infiltrate them. We think the battle lines are drawn up now, the black hats on one side and the white hats on the other. There may be a couple of people who occupy that grey area – hell, even in this building there could be a situation where someone is working for the other side – but we'll take our chances. And while The Commander's safe...'

'You mean my father.'

'Yes,' says Winter. 'A truly great man... his integrity is beyond question. I certainly don't know where I would be without him. While he is safe, I don't think we have anything to worry about.'

As she says this, I remember the pin I found on the floor of the burning ruin which had once been a farm building.

Smoke and mirrors, I think. Games of deception. Is Winter one of those people who occupy the grey areas?

26

FROM fearing I was being interred in a madhouse, everything is now starting to make a strange sort of sense. After the huge confusion that has raged in my head over the last two days, not knowing who are my enemies and who are my friends, I'm able to start putting people into the right boxes. Better than that, I can finally discard the rags I've been wearing and put on some decent fresh, clean clothes.

Admittedly, designer tracksuits and running shoes aren't my usual attire, but they're infinitely better than trousers ripped above the knee, a filthy mac and a shirt covered in mud and blood, its sleeves torn away. It's as if the Italian loafers that caused me so much confusion and joy when they'd mysteriously appeared on my feet a few mornings ago never existed.

I'm sitting down to breakfast in the main hall when the image of my father appears.

'Hello, Emerson,' he says, addressing me in a heavily stained lab coat rather than the pristine military uniform he wore the night before. I nod a greeting, though what I really want to do is have a go at him about his latest deception, the fact he appeared to me as a hologram and that he ordered someone to slip a sedative into my food.

Winter's words have had an effect on me, however. She described my father as a truly great man whose integrity was beyond question and it has struck a chord with me. That's how I've always wanted to think of him. Perhaps I should accept his explanation for why he left us. It must have been tough and lonely without his family to support him. I pray for the day when we'll be together again as father and son, out in the open rather than sneaking around in clandestine circles.

'I'm sorry I didn't tell you about the hologram thing but I wasn't sure how much more you could handle and didn't want to freak you out,' he says, immediately addressing my concerns even though I haven't voiced them. 'I know all about your condition, son, remember? I know what triggers it and what helps, and there is no doubt one of the best things to counter it is food and a settled night's sleep, which I provided. I learn from the doctor that you're now up to speed with Department 3 and all its workings, plus the European Plot and some of their leading players. What else can I tell you?'

'Well, how about what happened to you?' I say. 'I think I deserve the full story now about the Chamonix Conference and how you uncovered your enemies and made your escape?'

'It was down to a mixture of luck and some very brave people who put their own lives on the line,' he says, his expression wistful as he casts his mind back. 'There was a rest day before the main presentations. I was off to the slopes to try my hand at skiing when I got a call from the Department. They'd cracked some digital code flying through the ether, and discovered my life was in danger. Whoever was behind the "chatter" knew all about my formula and was planning to kidnap me but my people weren't 100 per cent sure how or where the attempt would be made. One phrase was repeated three times and they assumed this was a key part of the plot.'

'What was it?' I will him to go on, intrigued by the story of how my father, the bombmaker, escaped the shadowy forces lined up against him.

'The Female Cossack,' he says. 'It was her. I'd never heard of this woman before but even so, the name sent a chill through my bones. There I was in the French Alps, in fear for my life. I walked on, not knowing which way to turn or who to look out for. There were plenty of people milling about – it was a busy holiday season after all. I remember climbing aboard the ski lift and heading for the top of the mountain then noticing this elderly woman sitting in front of me with one of those fur hats which do up under the chin like the Russians wear. She seemed too old and out of condition to be attempting one of the French ski runs. More fool me for going with the stereotypes.'

'It was her?'

'The Cossack? Yes,' he says, his lips drawn thinly together as if he is fighting an internal battle with himself over whether to tell the full story. Finally, he makes a decision.

'Carrying my skis under my arm, I headed for the slopes, unaware that she was following me. As I bent down to put them on, I caught a reflection in the blades. This elderly woman had produced a gun from her pocket and was approaching me. I didn't know what to do. I wasn't used to this espionage lark and it was terrifying.'

Even as he thinks about the moment, I can see the anxiety in his face, his eyes wide and unblinking, the ageing skin around them bleached of colour. His voice rumbles on in monotone.

'Fortunately, my people swung into action like a well-oiled machine,' he says. 'I hadn't really noticed them but some guys from special branch had been keeping a close eye on me. One of them stepped in front of the Cossack just as another threw himself upon me, hiding me from sight. There was a moment of hesitation on her part before a gunshot cracked, the echo reverberating around the mountains. One of those poor guys paid for his bravery with his life – but the other took advantage of the Cossack's hesitation, dragging me to some kind of snowmobile contraption and whisking me away from danger.'

My father looks to the ceiling for a moment, his thoughts no doubt on the agent who sacrificed himself on his behalf. 'What I didn't know at the time was that another person, dressed in identical clothing to me, was heading off down the slopes,' he says. 'Later, I was watching the TV news in a mountain hideaway set up by the Department when I heard that a skier lost his life on the black run. He disappeared down a crevasse and all they managed to recover was his hat. Of course, it was the same hat I'd been wearing.'

'That hat was among the possessions they handed over to Mum on the doorstep,' I say. 'A fawn woollen hat with three wavy stripes along the bottom.'

Then it dawns on me. Could it have been the same symbol I'd seen carved into a tree in the forest and which I found on a pin in a burnt-out farm building? His story happened a long time ago, though, and I decide to keep my counsel and let him carry on.

'A few days later I was whisked off to another place, somewhere in central France, a laboratory where I could continue my experiments,' he explains. 'I was told that I could make no contact with my family and from that moment on, Laurent Rabette ceased to exist. Giving up everything I loved was a terrifying prospect but the idea of my family being tracked down and murdered by the enemy was worse. The knowledge I'd survived was restricted to a chosen few. Not even my work partner, who had fallen under suspicion as the person who tipped off the plotters about my movements, was told. My bosses left him in place, though, intending to keep an eye on him in the hope they might learn more about the conspirators.'

'When did you morph from mild-mannered scientist to Commander?' I ask.

'It's just a term, Emerson, like the President of the United States is called Commander in Chief of the Armed Forces. It's not like he pursues any active role in that regard. They did give me some nice bling for my arm to mark my rank. Silly, if you ask me, but they said I put my life on the line for my country and deserved to be recognised with some kind of promotion. Who I command, though, I have no idea, and it's a slim reward if you can't let anyone know about your achievements, even your family.'

'What about this place?' I ask. 'You're treated like a lord here, even to the extent there are family pictures on the walls.'

'Indeed, but they were only put up a few days ago, to ease you into the situation and let you know you could trust us. This is a government facility and they want you to know you're on the right side and to remind you who you're doing all this for.'

Another question occurs to me.

'What about Dr Joel? What part does he play in all this? Is he a real doctor, because he certainly has some strange ways about him?'

'Is that what he calls himself in civvy street?' says the father I've never really known, cracking a broad smile for possibly the first time I can remember. 'The doc's a funny geezer, mad Billy Joel fan, but I assure you it's not his real name. It's probably safer if you keep calling him that, though. He's been very useful, altering people's faces when they've needed to "disappear". It may be something you can take advantage of in the future.'

I'm about to object, not wanting Dr Joel within half a mile of me with his knives and scalpels, when the door bursts open and Tank charges into the room.

'Sorry, sah,' he says, saluting the hologram. 'Some enemy fighter planes have been detected on radar, coming our way.'

'How the hell...?'

'Not sure, sah, it's as if they have some sort of sixth sense or, well, there could be a mole. If you ask me it's the only feasible explanation...'

'God help us,' says my father. 'Not another one, surely.'

Tank approaches me and I notice he is far more polite in the presence of my father. 'I think you'd better come with us, Mr Rabette. We need to get you safely out of their reach and onto that boat so that the two of you can be reunited again.'

My father nods in my direction. 'Go with him, son. He'll make sure you get to where you need to go. He's one of the best.'

'And where is that?' I ask, but my father's image fades away in front of my eyes. Tank grabs me by the arm and guides me towards the door.

'Plenty of time for questions when you see each other face to face,' he says.

As we make our exit the room shakes and dust and lumps of plaster fall on us from the ceiling. I notice they travel straight through the area my father's image had occupied barely a minute earlier. Hurrying now, I hear the tinkle of glass behind us, then a crash. Turning, I see the ornate crystal chandelier that had adorned the centre of the ceiling now lying shattered in the exact spot where I was standing before Tank intervened.

'We gotta make tracks,' says the soldier. 'I don't know what sort of hardware they've managed to get their mitts on this time, but it looks capable of putting quite a sizeable hole in this place... and us, too.'

Bursting through double doors, we are then greeted by scenes of pandemonium. 'My ride's out front,' says Tank, making his way towards the huge double-door entrance to the Mansion. I pull free of his grip.

'Wait here!' I shout. He looks puzzled. 'We have to find Winter. I can't leave without her; it wouldn't be right. She got me this far, I need her help getting the rest of the way.'

'This is no time for bloody romance, soldier!' he curses. 'It's every man and woman for themselves. She's been trained by the best. She'll be fine.'

Ignoring his protests, I head off down another corridor until I arrive at a pair of double doors with the word infirmary marked on them. I burst through and see Dr Joel in the process of gathering as much equipment as he can, scales, boxes of test tubes and jars of chemicals which he is cramming into giant wheely bins. 'Where is she?' I demand.

'Back there.' He indicates the door to the storeroom with his head. I race over and burst through.

'Winter!'

She's on her knees dragging something from a cupboard.

'Hey, lucky you're here,' she says. 'You nearly forgot this again!' Turning with a big grin on her face she then waves the briefcase in my direction.

'Quick,' I say. 'We have to go... now!'

'Sure you want me tagging along?' she asks. 'I thought your troubles only began when I appeared on the scene. I seem to recall you suggesting that I'm either the enemy or a jinx.'

I can't help but smile, only to have the humour shaken from my face as a massive explosion rips through the lab, throwing me to the ground amid an avalanche of jars, bottles and other scientific equipment. I feel like the assistant to a knife thrower might as sharp objects bury themselves in the linoleum around me. Shutting my eyes, I'm then aware of a soft, feminine hand grabbing mine and pulling me to my feet.

'I guess there's a plan?' says Winter, her questioning green eyes staring at me as I manage to prise mine open again.

'I think so. Tank came for me and was leading me towards the front door when the shit hit the fan.'

My words are greeted by a quizzical look. 'Hang on,' she says. 'The front doors are in the opposite direction. You didn't come back just for me, did you?'

'I lost you once,' I say before I realise the words are out of my mouth and what they mean. 'I don't want to let you out of my sight again.'

'My hero!' She links my arm and kisses me on the cheek. 'Now, how about we get the hell out of here before we end up resembling one of those limb-challenged statues lining the hallways?'

27

AS we leave the building, we immediately look to the skies. There is a distant rumble coming from somewhere behind the house which is buried beneath huge clouds of smoke. Flames lick the early morning sky, reflected in the dark pools of Winter's eyes. It's as if she has seen these exact scenes before and they're imprinted on her irises. The streaks of fire eerily resemble the fleck of red I noticed earlier when I stared into those eyes. As we silently question each other about our next move, the rumble grows louder rising in intensity until it becomes a shriek.

'No time for sightseeing, love birds,' says Tank from behind us. 'Quick, unless you want to end up as skeletons in the rubble of yet another English stately ruin.' He stands at the end of the maze, beckoning us to enter.

'Oh, come on!' I say, shaking my head. 'There has to be a better way.'

Looking back over my shoulder I see a jet buzz the buildings and drop its payload. The bomb smashes into the east wing with a deafening roar, shearing the tower clean off.

'Shit!' exclaims Winter, 'Hope the doc will be all right.'

I can find no words to ease her concern.

'Tornado,' Tank states almost proudly as he enters the maze at a crouch, the aircraft roaring low above our heads. 'We used them in Iraq, brilliant for honing in on specific targets. Hopefully it won't be able to track us in here and we can get back to Bertha soon enough.'

'Bertha?'

'Sorry,' he says. 'It's the name I gave my tank, God knows why. Anyway, it's on the other side of here, now we just need to find our way out. Any ideas?'

'What?' I'm stunned. 'You've led us in here without the faintest idea of how we get to the other side?'

'I was told you were the brains of this operation,' says Tank. 'I'm just the muscle. The tank's just the other side of the maze so, naturally, it's the quickest way to go. You want to take point, soldier?'

The low rumble begins again, the aircraft coming in for another pass. I've never thought of myself as leadership material but if my father qualifies as a Commander, perhaps it's in my blood. 'This way!' I say, waving my hand and leading onwards. We pass two entry points on the right, but I wave us forward as if I've done the whole thing many times before.

'You're sure?' asks Winter.

'Leave him be, honey,' whispers Tank, jogging alongside her in my slipstream.

At the third entrance on the right I abruptly turn then count my steps. When I reach 12, there is another entrance, this time on the left, and I take it. The throaty growl of the Tornado tells me it's approaching fast. In contrast, we are eerily silent as we stalk along inside the impenetrable walls of our green prison. I measure off seven steps to the next turn, ignore it, eight more steps to the next, making a grand total of 15, and take it. There is no logic to my movements, but it's almost as if I have a satellite navigation system built into my DNA, based on multiples of three.

Another nine steps and we are clear and running, Bertha standing proudly in front of us. Tank mounts first then leans back to haul us up. Just before descending we watch the Tornado dive extra low over the maze and drop its payload. In seconds the whole green construction has become a towering wall of flame.

'That was close,' says Winter, leading the way into the belly of the beast.

'Too close,' I say. 'Why would they target the maze unless...?'

The question hangs in the air to be replaced by an all-too-familiar drawl.

'Here he is then, the bloody troublemaker!' The American we know as Franklin is folded into a corner of the vehicle, concertinaed like Alice after she'd consumed the *EatMe* cake in Wonderland and outgrown her surroundings. He chuckles. 'Keep turning up don'tchya?'

'Yeah,' I reply, 'and I could say the same about you. The funny thing is you always seem to be in the thick of it when the trouble starts.'

'Just think of me as a magnet.' He grins.

'Fine,' I say, '...And who exactly are you, Mr Magnet?'

'Jim Franklin.' He sticks out his hand. 'CIA.'

I ignore the gesture. 'What part does the CIA have to play in all this?' I ask. He looks at me as if Winter and I are dumb and dumber and I'm the latter half of the equation, but I won't be dissuaded from my line of questioning. 'I thought this was purely a European matter. How do the Americans fit into this charade?'

He lowers the large hand that had been offered to me and uses it to steady himself as the tank judders into motion. 'You haven't heard of the *special relationship*?' He is one of those annoying types who insist on answering a question with a question.

'Of course.'

'Well, your PM asked POTUS, that's President of The United States to you, if we could send in some resources to back him up, so here I am.'

'You're the resources? Whoopee do! Typical of the Americans to send one lone cowboy then insist they're saving our bacon.'

'Hey, show some respect,' he says. 'I've got a pretty good record and I pulled you out of the molasses back on our London bus tour, didn't I?'

'That's not quite how I would describe it,' I say. 'Part of me thinks you actually made matters worse. It was once we got off the bus after you'd wrecked it by going all gung-ho that my real problems began. I don't recall you coming to my rescue when I was being chased around the streets of central London by a crazy woman on a horse.'

His sneer suggests my complaints have no validity. 'Well, I'm here now, boy, and I've sworn to help you complete your mission.'

'And what is that, exactly?' I say.

'Your mission? Hell, how am I supposed to know? You ain't been briefed? I thought that was why we were here.'

I shrug. 'What exactly can you do to help then?'

'Oh, you'll find me useful in plenty of ways, believe me,' he looks me in the eye. 'How's the belly ache, by the way?'

I look down and it suddenly hits me. I've been pain free since I woke. The horrendous stomach pains have gone as has the translucent light that had so disturbed me, shining as it did through my skin. At this very moment everything seems fine and, anyway, I have far more pressing things to worry about, like RAF attack jets trying to blow me to smithereens.

'My stomach's fine, thanks,' I answer. 'How did you...?'

He dips his hand into his pocket. 'Perhaps you're missing this,' he says and, like a conjuror, pulls out something concealed in his fist. I half expect him to ask me which hand the penny is in, but when he has my full attention, he opens his fingers to reveal a small, white item the size and shape of a piece of chalk. At the top of it, an orange light blinks on and off.

'What is that?' I ask.

'A goddamn bug... what you Brits might call a homing deeevice,' he says, deliberately extending the first syllable of the second word. 'It was injected into you at some point, but whoever put it there didn't realise your body was going to react against it in the way it did. I reckon these little beauties have been installed in plenty of people over the years, and very rarely has a body rejected it. Fair kudos to you, Rabette... your body's a better agent than you are.' He laughs.

'How did it get there? I mean, I haven't done anything...'

'No injections or anything? No check-ups?'

It came to me in a flash. 'The accident!'

'What accident?' asks Winter, joining in the conversation.

'It's kind of the reason we met. I was in a car accident. That's why I was taking the Tube the other morning.'

'Aaaah,' she says. 'I don't know anything about that. I was just told to link up with you at Clapham Common.'

My mouth drops open in shock and I stare at her for seconds, my brain having trouble processing this latest revelation.

Finally, I break the silence. 'So that "chance" encounter was all part of this. My God, is there any tiny slither of my life that hasn't been organised by someone else? How did you know where to go and when? Who told you?'

'We've monitored your progress since the smash,' Franklin says. 'You don't think we could leave you out there in the big wide world without keeping an eye on you? We knew you might be a target and the crash, well, we weren't sure whether that might be a deliberate attack? Let's just say we overheard a phone call to your wife a few days later and alerted these guys to the danger you might be in.'

'Sorry, take a step back,' I say. 'Did the CIA bug my phone?'

'Look, don't worry your little head about that now. Back pedal a bit. The accident: What happened?'

I let my mind rewind. 'As far as I recall I was with Jamie in the car and some jerk ran us off the road. The emergency services were great, though. They gave me something for the pain, knocked me out then got me out of there. I woke in hospital some time later, and after a few days observation they let me go home.'

'They inject something into your arm, did they? Told you it was a sedative?'

'Yes... hell, there were plenty of injections. You should have seen the state of me. I guess I probably looked worse than I was but...'

'It must have been when you were out cold that they pumped this little beauty into you. Still, we've found it in time.'

'In time? Look outside. They obviously know where I am so I would say it's served its purpose, wouldn't you? And by the looks of it that thing's still active. Are you mad bringing it with us?'

'Just clever,' he says, showing us his chubby-cheeked profile, his finger nestling under his chin. 'In 10 minutes' it will be on the back of a lorry travelling at a rate of knots in the opposite direction to us. I'm not just a pretty face.'

'We'd better hit the road, or we'll be blown up where we sit,' says Tank. 'I thought the Tornado might follow us, but we've got away with it for the moment. No doubt the orders will change soon but in the meantime, hopefully we'll have got rid of that thing and dodged a bullet.'

I can't help thinking that the poor lorry driver destined to be the recipient of this tracking device might not be so lucky.

28

WE ditch the device at a truck stop near the main approach road to Stansted Airport while the driver is away from his cab. I feel guilty about signing his death warrant, a person I've never met, but Tank insists there is no room for sentiment "in this game". Hardly a game, I think, when people are losing their lives just because they happen to be in the wrong place at the wrong time, but I keep my opinions to myself.

Later, Tank brings our all-terrain hunk of metal to a halt in the square of a small Suffolk town. I'm sure we must be attracting strange looks, but Tank points out that the army performs regular manoeuvres in these parts.

'This is where we say au revoir,' he announces, and we briefly shake hands.

'I'm sure I'll bump into y'all sometime,' adds Franklin with a wink. Something makes me hope this isn't the case. We have things to thank him for, admittedly, but I have no wish to become best buddies with a person who has made a career out of monitoring other people's private phone calls.

'Where exactly are we going?' asks Winter. It's a question I haven't thought about until now. Everything prior to this moment has been about escape and losing our trackers. Now we have a mission and a destination to aim for, though I'm not sure what the reward will be should we succeed.

'There's a car park behind that rank of shops where you'll find a BMW3 Series,' says Tank. I can't hide my smile when he announces the car's make, particularly the number associated with it. 'You should have the key already. Drive to the port at Felixstowe and find the *Pride of Orleans* or whatever the damned boat is called. The money inside that briefcase is in case you need to bribe the captain or something. The Commander's reimbursed the cash you frittered away on that railway ticket collector, a real waste considering what happened afterwards.'

He smirks as if he's told a funny. For poor Raymond's family it will be no laughing matter. The callous talk makes me feel sick and reminds me that, despite all the social niceties he has been refining, we are in the presence of an unscrupulous killing machine.

'Right, we'd better get going before someone realises we've laid them a false trail,' I say, suddenly keen to put as much distance between myself and the soldier as possible. 'Come on, Winter.'

'Sure thing, sah,' she says, saluting playfully. I'm amazed at her capacity for good cheer considering all we've been through.

Finding the car quickly, Winter points the key and the locks spring open. She looks around for anyone taking more than a passing interest in what we are doing. 'Hey, can I drive?' I say nervously. I've never been a good passenger.

'Don't think so,' she replies. 'You seem to be a bit of a magnet for bad drivers. Weren't you telling me just now about a recent traffic accident which put you in hospital?'

'That wasn't my fault!' I pout like a schoolboy.

'Come on,' she says, 'I'm a really good driver; Got my advanced test and everything. I used to go to all those car-of-the-year shows and what have you, and for doing a day's modelling some of the guys would let me take their products for a spin. Great fun!'

I'm reminded once again of how young and full of life she is.

'That's settled then,' she says when I don't reply. She presses a button and the car springs to life with a throaty growl. Resigned to my fate I walk around to the passenger's side and settle into my seat, pulling the belt across me, then releasing it and repeating the process twice more before clicking it into place. The digital clock on the dashboard reads 6a.m.

Most people won't have risen by now and here we are having spent a morning being bombed by a jet and driven around the south-east of England in a tank. I suddenly feel incredibly hungry and look down at my stomach, expecting to see an orange glow before remembering the tracker has been removed.

'Briefcase?' she says. I look at her dumbly.

She points at my feet and there it sits in the footwell, the dusty box of tricks that will guide us on the next leg of our journey. I lift it onto my lap then twirl the tumblers and it springs open.

'Pass me that sat-nav,' she orders.

I hand it over and she fits it into the bracket on the dashboard above the stereo system. Pressing a few buttons, a woman's computerised voice then responds.

'Your destination is Felixstowe,' we are advised. Winter taps the accelerator a couple of times to give my heart a flutter before we set off on what I hope is the final part of our 'adventure'.

On leaving the small town I spot a fast food drive-through on our side of the road. It says 24 hours on the sign and my tummy rumbles in response. 'You need food,' Winter says, the words delivered in the form of a statement rather than a question.

I nod and she turns into the car park. 'To be honest, I need the rest rooms. Shall we park up and go in?'

I shake my head. 'Let's just swap places and go through the drive-in. It's quicker so there's less chance of being spotted. We don't know where these European plotters have eyes. For all we know they could be monitoring the CCTV at every off-road service station.'

She gives me a funny look, her mouth curling up in a smirk.

'What?' I ask.

'Listen to James Bond,' she says. 'Three days into this situation and you know all about the spying game. You can't fool me though... you just want to get behind the wheel of this beast. Go on then, knock yourself out.'

'You know me too well.' I chuckle.

She tosses her head back and laughs, silky locks pouring over the back of the seat. 'OK,' she says. 'I'll have a cheese and bacon muffin and a black coffee, no sugar, if you don't mind. Have you got any...?' She doesn't finish the sentence, remembering the wads of cash in the brief-case.

Stepping out of the car she then wanders off towards the toilets and I switch seats and pull into the drive-through lane, stopping to study the menu at the ordering machine. It's the usual collection of cardboard burgers, overpriced nibbles and E-number saturated fizzy drinks. I press the button.

'Hello,' says a crackling male voice before announcing the name of the restaurant chain. 'Please can I take your order?'

I give it to him succinctly.

'Will that be all, Mr Rabette?'

Mouth open, I stare at the machine.

'Sure you don't want any sides, like maybe a new gun and a replacement mobile phone?'

'Hang on, who...?'

'I told you to trust no one,' the voice says and as he utters the words, it all comes back to me. The man in the Trilby hat with the purple goatee, the one I'd chased across the road after fleeing the Underground at The Oval. How the hell did my father's former partner manage this?

'You're Alexander Melrose,' I say. 'I know all about you and what your game is.'

I think about executing a quick getaway, but I'm blocked in, with cars both behind and in front of me.

'Your father's doing, no doubt,' says Melrose. 'How much longer is he going to pretend he's dead, by the way? The charade's gone on a bit too long. Oh yes, we know he walked away from that skiing incident. Does he think we're stupid? We've got eyes everywhere. I expect he calls me a traitor, doesn't he? Well, understand this, Emerson. I'm not the bad guy here. It's your father and those renegade soldiers, doctors and CIA cast-offs who have taken the wrong path. No doubt he has used his parental influence to condition you to his way of thinking, but I bet he hasn't told you anything resembling the truth.'

'How dare you...?'

'Think of it this way,' he continues. 'Don't you find it slightly odd that he turns up at this stage, during his son's hour of need, with some kind of sob story and a rather fanciful explanation about his "death"? I'm sure he made the Female Cossack story sound plausible but look at it in the cold light of day. Does it really sound very likely?'

The man in the car behind me honks his horn, impatient to get his early morning burger fix and hit the road again.

'Why should I trust you?' I say. 'What can you show me that will make me believe you're on the right side?'

'Sorry, sir,' the voice changes again, the crackly kid back on the line. 'Can you repeat that? Did you say a cheese and bacon muffin, coffee and a double cheeseburger.'

'Oh, come on!' I shout, reaching out and pressing the button on the machine. 'Put Melrose back on again.'

'Please, sir, my name is Timothy and there's no one here but me. Drive to window three please and collect your order.'

'Where's the other guy?' I demand. 'The one I was speaking to earlier.'

'I don't know what you mean, sir,' says Timothy. 'I've taken your order and now you need to move on. There is a large queue forming behind you.'

Just then there's a rattle on the handle that makes me jump. The door pops open and I reach across to see if the gun has been put back into the briefcase, but it isn't there.

'Sorry about that – queue for the hand dryers,' says Winter, leaning in. 'Why are you still sitting here and what do you need from the case?'

'Shit, I'm glad you're here. Something odd...' Suddenly I have a nasty thought. What if Melrose is right? What if everything I believe has been twisted, turned completely upside down? That might mean Winter isn't who she claims to be, either.

'What's that, Em?' she asks, climbing in behind the wheel as I shuffle across into the passenger's seat.

'Oh nothing,' I say casually. 'I'm just surprised they've run out of chicken burgers so early in the morning. It's not even 7a.m. yet.'

She looks at me as if I have two heads. 'Perhaps they haven't had the delivery. I don't suppose they get many orders for chicken this early in the day. I expect even now those burgermeisters are hidden away in that little hut, with their microphone's strapped to their ears, imagining themselves as members of some teen band, having a good chuckle at your expense. "Some stupid bloke's demanding chicken – at 7a.m."!' she mimics in a high-pitched voice, nudging me in the ribs and forcing a smile to my face.

'You're right,' I say. 'You know I'm an oddball though, that's why you love me.'

There is another blast from the horn behind us. 'I might love you, but someone doesn't,' says Winter. 'We'd better make tracks. Don't tell me ... I'm guessing we've got to go to window 3.'

The car purrs into life and we drive to our collection point. I'm still in a state of total confusion, though. Either the bad guys have managed to track me down already, or I have been working for them all along. I need time to think carefully about my options before I encounter Melrose again.

29

CONVINCED our being tracked is a thing of the past, Winter is confident enough to follow the major A roads in the direction of the container port at Felixstowe, Suffolk. Outside, the sky is getting lighter and the traffic increasing. 'We're making good time,' I say as a sign for Ipswich looms up in the foreground.

'Told you I was a good driver,' she says. 'At least, I haven't heard any complaints.'

I hold my hands up in mock surrender. 'You're doing fine,' I say in the seconds before I nearly punch myself in the face as she slams on the brakes. The windscreen rushes towards me, then retreats just as quickly. I have an awful feeling of déjà vu.

'What the hell?'

'Roadblock!' she exclaims. 'Just ahead. The traffic is nose to tail and there are cops walking up and down asking drivers questions and checking IDs.'

'Shit!' The first thing that springs to my mind is that Melrose engineered our conversation simply as a delaying tactic to enable him to get his chess pieces in position. 'What are you going to do?'

Winter looks around anxiously. We are blocked in between a white van and a large four-wheel drive. To both sides of us are fields, protected by sturdy barriers capable of doing serious damage to the car should we choose to drive at them. 'We'll have to get out,' she hisses. 'Ditch the car and continue on foot. Perhaps we could jump a train or something.'

'Been on any nice rail journeys lately?' I say, my question loaded with sarcasm. 'In any event, I can't see a railway line around here.'

'If you have any better ideas, I'm all ears,' she says. I think about getting the money out of the briefcase and putting it to use again, but I'm not convinced bribery will work in this case. Instinctively I open the glovebox then sit back in shock. It contains wigs – two of them – together with false passports. Grabbing them and pulling them out, I shake the headgear in Winter's direction. 'Unbelievable!' I exclaim, 'you guys think of everything.'

'I can't take credit for that,' says Winter. 'I had no idea they were there.'

'Yet it looks as though you posed in this wig for your passport photo,' I say, waving it in front of her. The woman in the picture has a black afro but still possesses those familiar green eyes with the red flash in them.

'Wow!' she says. She takes the wig from my lap, pulls it on and then starts primping and preening in the mirror. 'Photoshop, I guess. Still, I really like it, what do you think?'

'It's sure to attract attention, even if they don't recognise us in the first place,' I say. It seems likely the police will have a description of our car and have been advised that the occupants, a man and a woman, are extremely dangerous. Melrose managed to hack the machine at the burger restaurant in order to speak to me so organising this must have been child's play in comparison. The more I think about it, the more it seems like the end of the line.

I look at the other wig, an Elvis quiff. 'You've got to be kidding me!' I shout. 'How can...?'

'Do your best,' says Winter. 'Lots of people dress as their heroes. We'll have to blag it – you can claim you're an Elvis impersonator and I'll play the part of your assistant.'

'Uh...hu...hu,' I say with a joviality I don't feel.

Opening the passport, I note the person staring back at me from the thumbprint picture has the singer's luxuriant head of black hair but my face. The problem is that I know next to nothing about rock music of the fifties and sixties.

'Put it on…they're coming!' hisses Winter, grasping my knee. 'If all else fails we've got this.'

With her free hand she draws the pistol from her pocket. I shiver. Another life-threatening fire fight is the last thing I want and the thought of doing time for aiding and abetting a cop killer scares the life out of me.

There's a tap on the window and I jump. When I look out, a face is peering back at me. It screams ageing rock star wannabe suffering mid-life crisis. The quiff has flopped just a little bit and fallen over the right eye, suggesting I'm portraying Elvis during his drink and drugs phase. I wind down the window so that Elvis disappears and a young, blond police officer takes his place.

'Well now,' he says. 'People told me the king was still alive and there was I thinking they were telling porkies. Got a day off from the chip shop, have you?'

The joke is lost on me but Winter leans over and whispers, 'It's a Kirsty McColl song: "The guy who works down the chip shop thinks he's Elvis".' She turns her attention to the cop leaning through my window. 'You don't look old enough to remember it, officer. Funny.'

So, our friendly, neighbourhood bobby fancies himself as a comedian. At least he hasn't hauled me out of the car and slapped on the cuffs yet. He is still enjoying chatting up my sexy accomplice and pangs of jealousy stir within me.

'My mum was a big fan,' he says. 'So, what are you doing around these here parts?' His drawl is a poor attempt at imitating an American from the Deep South.

'We've got a gig in France,' says Winter. 'But we're in a bit of a rush. We have to catch a boat from Felixstowe and this delay is causing havoc with our schedule. Any idea how long this will take?'

'Sorry,' he says. 'All I know is there's some kind of security alert at the port. You may have to alter your plans.'

An older, more experienced looking officer appears beside him. He has three chevrons on his arm. I feel an indescribable relief flood through me and inwardly curse my condition for making me grasp at straws this way. Three chevrons is no guarantee of anything. 'What do we have here then?' the new arrival asks his colleague.

'Elvis impersonator, Sarge.'

'I bloody love Elvis,' says the sergeant. 'What's your name? I've seen loads of impersonators. I've even been to that annual competition down in Porthcawl, Wales, to find the best Elvis. Have you ever taken part in that, mate?'

I shake my head. 'Bloody hell, you should do,' he says. 'Anyone who is anyone in your profession goes down there to try to justify their existence and you look really good. What are you going to perform for us today?'

'Pardon?' I feel my face heat up. 'Look.' I hold my passport out in front of him. 'I think you'll find all my papers are in order.'

He gives it a brief glance, then chuckles. 'Gordon A.Trapp? Ha ha ... That's a good one.' He pulls open the door and starts singing, '...I'm Gordon A. Trapp, I can't walk out...' before leaning in and grabbing my arm. 'Come on then, let's be havin' you, Mr Trapp.'

'What are you doing?' I ask, psyching myself up to resist arrest. I wonder if at this very moment Winter is reaching for the gun. If she shoots him it will guarantee the entire Norfolk police force raining down on us.

'You do requests?' asks the older cop. I'm about to answer in the negative when Winter emerges from the driver's side. Here we go...

'It would be a pleasure, officer,' she says to my utter disbelief. 'I have to help though. He's been ordered by doctors to rest his voice between gigs. Now, what would you like?'

'Well, given his name, perhaps we could hear a rendition of *Suspicious Minds*, one of the King's very best. What do you reckon, Andy? Any favourites? I don't suppose you young 'uns even know the classics... still strung out on that bloody rap music. We might as well have a bit of fun, though. This traffic ain't going to be moving for some time so a little sideshow can't do any harm. Tell you what. If we like what we see, we'll bump you to the front of the queue... a bit like the A14 version of *X Factor*.'

I still recall my last miserable attempt at karaoke. It was at the work's Christmas party when Hayes nominated me to sing Culture Club's *Do You Really Want to Hurt Me?* I mumbled and mimed my way through it. At this moment I'm thinking arrest sounds the better option. I get out and hear the driver's side door clunk shut at the same time and fear Winter's about to shoot our way out of this predicament. As she walks up beside me the young copper smiles and the sergeant slaps his knee.

'Double whammy!' he shouts. 'Look who we got here... the white Diana Ross.'

People emerge from their cars, curious to see what's going on ahead and keen for anything that might alleviate the boredom. I jump when a hand falls on my shoulder, then breathe a sigh of relief when I realise Winter is standing next to me and my wig's still in place.

'We can do this!' she whispers.

'But I don't know any Elvis,' I hiss. 'They've got me bang to rights!'

'Not quite,' she says, turning to the younger policeman and giving him a stern look. 'We're just discussing our set list, sugar, if you don't mind.'

He steps back, suitably scolded. 'Right,' she says, returning her attention to me. 'I'll help you, but you've got to do this. We'll try *Suspicious Minds*, like the man said.'

'Appropriate,' I say. She gives me a look that suggests she thinks me an idiot. 'How does it go?'

'Oh, Em, just concentrate on wiggling your hips,' she tells me, turning up the collar on my tracksuit. 'Flick your head rapidly from one side to the other now and again and stare at your audience from below your eyebrows. Also, can you do a pose with one leg straight and the other kind of bent, with the opposite arm pointing to the air?'

'Sounds like John Travolta in *Saturday Night Fever*.'

'You've seen that? OK, that's good. Do that now and again and try to mime along with me.' She turns to the sergeant.

'We're ready,' she says. 'Like I said, he's under orders not to sing. He had a problem with his larynx which nearly wrecked his career – but like a brave soldier he has carried on, under strict instructions. Don't worry, though, I'll help him out and we'll see how it goes.'

'OK, Diana,' says the Sergeant as he clicks his fingers to an inner beat. '3-2-1,' he counts down and I find myself miming as Winter belts out, 'I'm caught in a trap...'

Swivelling my hips as best I can, I look into Winter's green eyes and then shoot my hand skywards, standing and holding my position for longer than necessary. There are wolf whistles and shouts of "all right" and "Elvis Lives" from the surrounding audience.

We carry on, Winter doing most of the singing and me mumbling along and throwing the odd pose as we enter the chorus, her singing about how we can't go ahead and build our dreams on suspicious minds. There is spontaneous applause around us, and we bow our heads to acknowledge the crowd's reaction. It feels surprisingly good, performing in public when all my life I've done my best to steer away from such self-aggrandising nonsense. I had started enjoying myself a little too much because the next moment I twist my head extravagantly... and the wig falls off!

'Hell, isn't that...?' the young cop exclaims.

'Step clear,' the sergeant orders his partner. 'You'd better put your hands on the roof of your car, mate.'

He looks in my direction, removing a pair of handcuffs from the belt at his waist.

'Don't think so,' says Winter, producing the gun and levelling it at his chest. 'Now, why don't you step back and let us drive on out of here?'

There are screams all around us as the other motorists realise the woman in the Diana Ross wig is waving a Glock in the air. 'Search them for weapons, Em,' she says.

I look at her, dumbfounded. 'What?'

'You heard me! Search them for weapons, for heaven's sake. We don't want them to go all trigger-happy and start shooting us down.'

I tentatively approach the sergeant, who has his hands in the air. As I bend to remove the truncheon at his waist, he whispers, 'Put faith in the numbers, son, you know it makes sense.' He angles his head in the direction of the chevrons on his sleeve. Underneath them is his police number -339 – and I know exactly what he is saying. Everything is divisible by 3, which turns the odds in my favour.

'Don't try to be a clever cowboy,' shouts Winter in her best Bonnie and Clyde growl. She stands, legs apart, and fires into the ground just inches from the sergeant's feet. There is a collective intake of breath from those surrounding us as if the air has been sucked from their lungs by some invisible force. Then I hear a child whimper and look at my partner. She remains ice cool.

'That's right, muthafuckers!' she shouts so that all the marooned travellers can hear. She wants people to be afraid and is achieving her objective. With her curly wig and her choice of insult she has the same intimidating effect as Samuel L Jackson's gangster character in the film *Pulp Fiction*. Unsure what she is going to do next, I relieve the cops of their truncheons and return to her side.

'Hey, you!' she says, waving the gun at the younger policeman. I can tell he is petrified. 'Yeah, that's right, numb nuts, I mean you. Come over here. You're taking a ride with us. Em, you'd better get behind the wheel. I'll sit in the back with the hostage.'

He hesitates briefly, looking in the direction of his sergeant for advice, and Winter responds by striding over and clubbing him around the head with the pistol. A nasty gash appears at his temple, oozing blood. I can't believe this girl I thought so friendly, kind and gentle earlier on in our journey is now displaying all the hallmarks of a psychotic criminal.

'Bloody hell, no need for that!' I exclaim but she waves my words away.

'You want to get out of here?' she says. 'How do you think we're going to do that by playing Mr and Mrs Nice Guy eh? I'm sorry Em but these bastards would do the same to you if they got the chance. I doubt if they're even real cops. They're more likely contract killers hired by those behind the European Plot.'

She marches the young officer to the car, shoves him into the back seat and leaps in after him. 'Come on, Em, drive!' she says.

Without further protest I hop in and push the ignition button, pulling out and around the parked traffic in front. I can see the sergeant on his radio, telling those at the blockade what has taken place. As I put my foot to the floor and the Beamer gathers pace, I see more law enforcement people dismantling the barricade to allow us safe passage. I guess the news of the hostage situation has drained their resistance. As the car speeds through the gap, Winter shouts, 'Yeeha!' and throws the Afro wig in the air. The constable is silent. He doesn't want to do anything to provoke more erratic behaviour from the crazy woman sitting next to him.

'It's OK,' I say, making eye contact with him in the mirror. 'We aren't going to hurt you. You were just our ticket out of there. When we find a convenient place, we'll release you.'

'I don't know, Em,' Winter interjects. 'This guy could ensure our safe passage all the way to Felixstowe and onto that boat. Perhaps we should keep him a while longer.'

I've had enough of the charade, though. We might be running for our lives, but we aren't dangerous, crazy kidnappers – at least, I'm not. Winter can see in my eyes that I'm unhappy with the turn of events.

'OK,' she says. 'I get it. You're a sensitive bloke. You're not trained to think in a certain way, you're just a civilian. My mission is to protect you and ensure you get where you need to be and bugger anyone who stands in our way. I'm starting to come around to your way of thinking, though. Maybe splitting up is the right thing to do.'

30

'SPLIT up? Why? What do you mean?'

'They're obviously tracking this car,' says Winter. 'I don't know how they've done it seeing as we got rid of that tracking device, but somehow they still know our every move. Well, let them track it. Hopefully, it will be too late by the time they realise you aren't in it.'

'That's dangerous for you, though, surely?' I argue. I watch her shrug in the rear-view mirror and feel protective of her. She has been selfless so far, doing everything in her power to keep me from danger, and although I now know she's just been doing her job, it doesn't make me feel any less indebted to her. 'No, I can't allow it,' I say. 'While you're with me...'

'...I'm as much a target as you are.' She finishes my sentence. 'With our little hostage here, though, I think we can both get out of this in one piece.'

Two police cars roar past us in the opposite direction, lights flashing and sirens shrieking. 'Look, let's get out of the "hot zone" and we'll discuss it then,' says Winter. 'I've a cunning plan forming.'

Opting for a country road to take us away from the main arterial route to Ipswich, eventually she instructs me to pull into a lay-by where we can use the overgrown trees as camouflage.

'Get out!' she instructs the young officer, dragging him by his arm. He stumbles and falls to the gravel.

'What now?' I ask. 'What are you going to do?'

'Just wait here,' she instructs.

I watch as she pulls the police officer to his feet, ramming the pistol into the side of his temple before ordering him to climb a country stile into a field. I shiver, suddenly alarmed at what her intentions might be. On the other side of the fence there is a small path through the woods and as I peer into the gloomy light of a winter morning, I see smoke coming from that direction, indicating there might be buildings further down the path. The thought comforts me in a small way, and I sit back and let the tension pour out of me in one long, relieving exhalation.

'Stressful isn't it, Mr Rabette? All this running...'

I look around, trying to work out what's going on. Who's talking to me? Have I put my phone on speaker? Then I remember I don't have a phone.

'Hello? Who's that?' I shout into the empty car, looking around in a bid to identify where the voice is coming from.

'Talk into the satnav,' it instructs.

What the hell? It takes me a while to process the information before realising the item from my briefcase has been rigged for two-way communication.

'Melrose!'

'Have you thought about what I told you?'

'There hasn't been much time. Some of your guys tracked us down to just outside Ipswich and held us in a roadblock. We've had to kidnap a police officer in order to escape. What do you want?'

'I want you to realise that we are on your side and give yourself up, Mr Rabette. It's the only way.'

'And why the hell should I do that? You've been trying to kill me for three days. You had the police chase me, that mad woman on horseback attempted to trample me down, my train blew up and a Tornado jet made a pretty good run at blasting me off the face of the earth. So explain. Why would you do that if you were on my side?'

'Very good question,' says Melrose. 'We have our reasons.'

'Well, you'd better share the secret pretty quick, or this conversation is over.'

'Your father, the great Laurent Rabette... always been there for you, has he?'

The question baffles me. 'What's that got to do with anything?'

'Everything. Now be honest.'

'Well, OK, no... not really. He was always a bit distant when I was a kid, but I understand why now.' I'm still trying to come to terms with the fact I'm talking to the satnav. 'How did...?'

'Never mind all that,' snaps Melrose. 'We need to get a move on. She could be back at any time. Listen, do you want to know what's really going on, or not?'

There is nothing I would like more, but how will I know if this man is telling the truth?

'I realise you're suspicious and I can't blame you,' he says. 'Here's someone you might believe though.'

There is a hiss and a couple of blips, then a voice that cuts my heart in two. 'Honey?' says Cherry, 'Are you OK?'

I feel a tear escape my eye and brush it from my cheek with the back of a hand. 'Cherry, darling, I'm fine. But what about you? Are you OK? Jamie?'

'We're fine,' she says, 'We've been treated well. Look, you must listen to what this man is telling you. He is one of the good guys, he's shown me proof. Do what he says. Your father isn't who he claims to be, OK? Your daughter is fine, but her future depends on the decisions you make right now.'

I wonder if she's talking under duress and it's vitally important I find out. Then I remember an old school habit to test her. Back when Cherry and I were in our teens, a gang of us used to go around together and, like most kids that age, we tended to have our own adult-proof code. Silly, but there we are. A member of our group would make a statement and if it was a complete lie, the others would agree wholeheartedly with it. I guess it was our first experience of irony. Daft as it seems, at this moment a bizarre kids' game could just save our lives.

How to phrase the question, though, so that she understands what I'm doing? I'll have to start with the code and hope she picks up on it while keeping her captors none the wiser.

'Why should I do what this man says?' I ask.

'Because we're worried about you, that's why,' she replies.

Time to drop the code. 'True that,' I say.

She hesitates and I feel sure she has picked up on the hidden meaning and remembered the old game.

'Tell you who I could really do with in this situation?' I say. 'Hayes. You know how he keeps his feet on the ground, refuses to panic and always gives good advice?'

I've laid the bait. Cherry knows full well how much I hate my colleague and don't trust him an inch. If she is being coerced in any way, she'll completely disagree with the sentence whereas if she is acting of her own volition, she'll say something to indicate she is in total agreement. I seem to be waiting an age for the response before I hear her take a deep breath.

'True that. Hayes would be perfect,' she says.

Relief and fear surge through me in equal measure – relief that my family are safe and well; fear that I'm playing for the wrong side. If I am to believe what Cherry is telling me, my father and Winter are actually the bad guys in this crazy war.

'That's enough chit-chat,' says Melrose. 'We haven't got long. The first thing you must do is get out of there, fast. If you wait for that girl's return, I can assure you of one thing... you're a dead man.'

31

NOW I know Cherry and Jamie are safe there's no time to waste. The engine roars to life and I shoot out onto the mud road. As the car skids and dovetails across rutted tracks deformed by the wheels of assorted farm vehicles, I look in the mirror. The policeman is running in my direction, waving the gun in his hand. For a moment I think he must have overpowered Winter, grabbed her weapon and escaped. Then I notice a few strands of crimson hair sprouting from beneath the cop's hat.

Winter! She must have stolen his uniform in order to disguise herself. Now she is hurtling after me on foot. I see desperation in her eyes and read my name on her lips, even though the racing engine blocks out the sound of her voice. For a moment I feel traitorous for leaving her behind, but then I notice the steely glint in her eyes as she levels the gun. Ducking down, I apply my foot firmly to the accelerator, the car levels up and I power off down the road. I don't know if she's fired, but no bullet pierces the back window or explodes the tyres.

My mind is a sea of conflicting emotions after my lucky escape. The family is safe, but I've just deserted the girl with whom I've spent the most electrifying 48 hours of my life. I can't think of any time I've felt more alive and if she is the enemy, she deserves an Oscar for the terrific acting role she has performed. I wonder whether she'd been on her way to finish me off, yet to think that means I'm taking the word of someone I hardly know over someone with whom I feel intimately acquainted.

'Don't think about her,' says Melrose. How does he interpret my thoughts like that? 'Believe me, she is your biggest nightmare. You should be anticipating the moment you're reunited with those who really love you. No question, you've done the right thing.'

Everything he is saying now seems logical, but my mind is shrouded in a fog of confusion and for a while I drift on autopilot. It's only when I arrive at a junction and see the sign for Felixstowe that I snap back into gear.

'OK, speak,' I instruct the satnav. 'We should be in the clear for the moment.'

'As you wish,' says Melrose. 'The reason I asked you the question about your father is entirely relevant. There is something you need to know, and it holds the key to your entire experience over the last few days. Before your father disappeared, do you remember being taken ill? You were about 13 or 14 I guess, and you complained of feeling light-headed then collapsed?'

'It rings a faint bell,' I say, sifting through the cobwebbed recesses of my brain. 'I can remember a hospital and an operation.'

'That's right. Tell me exactly what you remember,' he insists. 'I'll try to fill in the blanks.'

October 1989

IT was a crisp autumn day as I ran through the leaves, stooping now and then to pick up a conker that might serve me well in the playground battles ahead. The garden was a carpet of russet-brown which made crunching sounds underfoot as I ran. I was full of life, anticipating Christmas just around the corner and all the festive delights that would entail. Not only that but I'd just snaffled my first girlfriend, a little raven-headed beauty with chocolate brown eyes with the sweet-tasting name of Cherry. I'd met her at the youth club, and we had enjoyed a couple of 'dates', rendezvousing at the bus stop and going for a quick milkshake in the town and then the cinema. Still shy at the idea of it, I was keeping my relationship a secret for now, though I sensed my mother had a pretty good idea what was going on.

Looking over my shoulder, what I saw made me immediately stop what I was doing. My father was standing there, stock-still, watching me through the panoramic patio doors. The scenario seemed all wrong. He was always at work at this time of day and as a person known for his meticulous adherence to routine, it didn't seem right that he would just take the afternoon off. I felt the hairs on the back of my neck rise, frightened that something momentous was happening in my fledgling life that I was too naive to know anything about.

My thoughts were interrupted when I saw another conker, bigger, shinier and more attractive than any of those I'd collected so far. It was a perfect sphere, without blemish, and I just knew it would be a winner. I bent down to pick it up, and as my fist closed around it, I marvelled at its firmness. It was only as I tried to stand that I realised my knees wouldn't do my bidding. I squinted as a bright light shone through the horse chestnut tree above me, feeling as if I'd been transported into an alternative, slower world. I was surprised to see a trail of drool dropping from my bottom lip onto my T-shirt. My brain tried to grapple with the situation, but everything was twisted out of sync, my thoughts coming to me scattergun from every direction. I couldn't focus, couldn't breathe. Unable to control my limbs any longer I tumbled forward onto my knees and looked around, intending to shout for help but failing to convey the message to my lips.

Out of the corner of my eye I saw my father running across the lawn towards me. I expected to register concern on his face, but as usual it was a blank canvas. He leant down and lifted my eyelids so that he could make a closer inspection. His face swam in front of me as if submerged in rippling water, his lips moving. I used all my willpower to interpret the strange language he seemed to be speaking. 'Aah, Emershunson, donworrynowboy will be OK.'

Then everything went black.

I woke days later in unfamiliar surroundings. I'd been admitted to a private clinic, perhaps as some kind of perk of my father's job. It certainly bore no resemblance to the NHS hospital where I had my adenoids removed when I was seven. This was far more pristine with far fewer patients.

I was alone in a private room, the walls bright and white, as if they had been painted just days earlier. The nurses were different, too. Rather than wearing standard uniform they seemed to be dressed in lab coats. Back in the land of the living I was feeling much better and wondered what had caused my collapse. I tried to ask a couple of passing nurses, but they brushed my questions aside, saying the consultant would be around to see me.

An hour went by. They provided me with a reasonable lunch and as I tucked into roast beef and vegetables it dawned on me how hungry I was and wondered how long I'd gone without food.

I was just finishing pudding and was grateful for the ice cream as it soothed the sore throat I seemed to have contracted when the doors swung open and there he was, my father, flanked by a nurse on one side and a tall man in a lab coat on the other.

'How are you feeling, boy?' my father asked. It was always "boy", rarely Emerson.

'Fine thank you, Father,' I said. 'What happened to me? Am I OK now?'

'You just had a bit of a fainting episode,' he said, dismissing it with a wave of his hand. 'I can't say I know much about it but the doctor here will be able to fill you in.'

The other man moved forward. He was carrying a clipboard with the number 3 emblazoned on the back. 'You had a bit of a nasty turn, son,' he said, smiling as he adopted his most soothing bedside manner. He looked at the clipboard. 'Your blood sugar levels were very low, and it appears that you fainted in the back garden. This happens when you lose consciousness for a short period of time because your brain isn't getting enough oxygen. Very bad luck. Fortunately, you didn't bang your head and your dad brought you straight here.'

'Where am I?' The whole episode was all very confusing.

'You're in a specialist unit for youngsters like you who have certain, um, weaknesses, largely involving the brain. They can cause nasty things: seizures and the like. Still, we have these pills here that are going to help you overcome that.' He held a white bottle in my eyeline. I could see the tablets silhouetted inside.

'What are they?'

'Oh, they just help control your heart rate, blood pressure and stuff. They ensure you don't get too, um, excited because in your condition that's a definite no-no.'

'Does my condition have a name?' I was actually quite excited to explain to my school pals how there was something different and unique about me. Unfortunately, the doctor's smooth line of chat deserted him, and he looked at my father as if he wasn't medically trained to provide the answer. My father nodded in his direction and took up the baton.

'What you suffered was a bit of a stroke I'm afraid, boy. But provided you follow all the guidelines we set out for you everything will be OK. That means taking these tablets every single day without fail, exercising properly and trying to avoid stressful situations. You understand?'

Not really, I thought. My Auntie Sadie had been struck down by a stroke a few years earlier and had never properly recovered. Part of her face had crumpled, giving her a lopsided look and meaning that all her words were slurred and difficult to understand. The difference was Aunt Sadie was 85, and I was only just approaching my 14th birthday. I wanted to scream.

My father gently moved the doctor out of the way and took his place in my line of vision. 'This isn't an Aunt Sadie situation,' he said. 'Nothing like it. If you do everything the doctors tell you, then you should be able to live a completely normal life, finish school, go to work and in time get married and have your own children. Your condition is pretty rare, but it's eminently treatable, so there's no need to panic. Oh, and don't be concerned about that,' he said, pointing to my hands. For the first time I realised I was drumming out a rhythm on the steel frame of my bed with a bracelet that had been fitted to my wrist.

Tap, tap, tap... Tap, tap, tap... Tap, tap, tap.

The beat was steady and persistent, and I realised I'd been doing it ever since I'd recovered consciousness.

'Wh...what's happening?' I stuttered. 'Why am I doing that?'

'It's a slight side effect of everything that's happened to you,' my father said. 'You've got a mild form of something we call OCD: Obsessive, Compulsive Disorder. It's been developing in you since you were young, but you may not have noticed it before. Nothing to worry about, though. How would you like some more ice cream?'

Present Day

'YOU left hospital after that,' says Melrose in his slow, drawn-out way. 'Do you remember that? Can you recall the grounds of this hospital, for instance, and how long it took for you to get home?'

I thought about the question, faint memories pinging back into my mind. 'There were some nice gardens, though it was winter, and most things were under a blanket of snow,' I say. 'I don't recall anything particularly distinguishing because I went straight from the front entrance to the car.'

'You're sure?'

'Well, I recall looking back over my shoulder as the place receded from view. It was some sort of grandiose country hall – not as big as the place I was in earlier, but I would say three stories, red brick, plenty of windows. It was unlike any hospital I'd seen before. Oh, and there was this plaque.'

The air is still and for a moment I think the connection has been broken. Finally, Melrose, almost whispering, says, 'Yes?'

'It had a big number 3 on it, I vaguely recall. It said something like The 3 Institution.'

'Department.'

'Oh my God, I was there?'

'You were,' says Melrose, his voice betraying a note of excitement. 'And so was I, working with your father.'

'You were the doctor.'

'Yes, you've got me.'

I feel my temperature spike. 'What? You mean you have been asking me to remember all this stuff from God knows how long ago when you already know the answers? Why the hell would you do that?'

'Because it's not me who needs to remember, Emerson, it's you. Of course, you won't recall the operation, but I needed you to think back so that you would realise everything I'm about to tell you is the truth.'

'Which is?'

He ignores the question.

'First, let me tell you about your dad's work,' he says. 'He had become obsessed with this human bomb idea but knew the government would shut him down as soon as they found out what he was doing. I was young, impressionable... keen to learn from such an astute mind. He was my boss, the voice of experience, and I was in no position to question his instructions. He knew exactly how to manipulate me. He kept praising me, dragging me into his schemes, getting me more and more involved, knowing that the deeper I became embroiled the more difficult it would be to pull out. Pretty soon I was a co-conspirator in his little world. You won't recall your family's financial situation at the time, I shouldn't expect?'

'I was 14 for Christ's sake.' I feel the temperature inside me rising and it's as much as I can do to keep my feelings from boiling over. 'Who at that age knows how well off their family is for cash and, anyway, what has that got to do with anything?'

'Quite a lot, unfortunately,' says Melrose. 'I don't know if you realise but your dad was a gambler. Perhaps it's a trait in all of us scientists, that we think we can work out a method for everything, and he thought he could do the same with sport. A bit stupid really for such a clever man, but he seemed to forget all the principles of chaos theory, that as things go on little glitches will send everything spinning out of control. He was particularly big on following the fortunes on the Formula One circuit. You know all this, of course, because of your Christian name.'

I nod, forgetting I'm talking to a machine, though for some reason I have a feeling the man on the other end of the conversation is watching my every move. I glance around the Beamer again, trying to work out where the secret camera might reside.

'Emerson Fittipaldi had won the F1 championship twice and finished second twice, but in 1976 it all went wrong for him and for your father as well.'

'How so?'

'He backed Fittipaldi all the way, couldn't work out how it could go so wrong for such a brilliant driver and figured it was just a matter of time before he turned things around. He hadn't factored in James Hunt, though, an English guy who carried all before him that season. Laurent kept lumping money on Emerson to win the next race, and the more he suffered the higher the stakes he played for in an effort to cover his losses. He started sliding down the gambler's slippery slope.'

'Come off it! My father? He was extremely careful when it came to money and my mother would never have allowed him to fritter it away.'

'Of course, he didn't tell her the full magnitude of his problem,' says Melrose. 'Addicts are like that. She thought he was so well paid that it was just pennies in the grand scheme of things, but he had re-mortgaged the house and failed to keep up the payments. The banks were poised to foreclose.'

I fall silent. Although I find this scenario difficult to grasp it might explain something about my father's stand-offish nature, his bad moods and his reluctance to engage with his family.

'So, he struggled for money,' I say. 'How is that reflected in the grand scheme of things?'

'Come on, Emerson, I thought you were the bright guy,' says Melrose condescendingly. 'It's pretty clear, isn't it? Your father, up to his eyeballs in debt, needed a get-rich-quick scheme and, lo-and-behold, he was in the process of inventing something for which there would be a global demand, particularly among some of the world's most notorious terror organisations. There's nothing like a bit of debt to tempt you over to the bad side. We have established that for some time he was being paid to provide secrets to "the enemy". It was only titbits for years but may explain why he failed to engage with you like father and son. Then in the late 80s something happened to change all that.'

'The human bomb,' I say, the tumblers clicking into place.

'That's right,' says Melrose. 'He had a problem, though. He knew the government were on to him. His bosses, well, that's to say our bosses, were suspicious. So, he came up with a three-pronged plan. One, he needed to disappear, two, he had to make sure his family were looked after, and three, it was imperative he hid his invention until he could sell it on later.'

'So, he faked his own death.'

'At last we're on the same page.' He sighs, relaxing into his storytelling role. 'Yes, he faked his own death but, of course, that takes care of only two of his three main concerns. With the life insurance he had taken out, you and your mother would be catered for and you'd keep the house so there wasn't a problem. What about the bomb though?'

I shrug, once again casting my eyes around the car's interior for a concealed camera.

'Well, this is the clever bit,' says Melrose. 'He comes up with a plan to hide it in plain sight. He develops a prototype but leaves out some key, umm, ingredients, knowing he can extract what he needs or add what he wants at a later date. It's unstable, of course, and he doesn't want any mishaps, like the guy who died in Madrid, so he has developed a 'medication' to control the combustible elements and make sure that at no stage can anything go wrong. Then he heads off to the conference in Switzerland.'

I feel sweat prickling on my brow, my temperature rising, my eyes filling with water and starting to sting. I want to throw up, to stop the car and wander off into the wilderness. I'm pretty sure I know the answer to my next question but have to ask it, anyway.

'What did he do with his prototype?' I ask.

The silence in the Beamer is so tangible it's almost a solid mass, formed from the waves of fear and hatred pouring from me. I want to rip it apart, to put my fingers in my ears and scream until all the oxygen had been expelled from my lungs. Before I can do so, the answer I don't want to hear comes out loud, calm and crystal clear from the satnav.

'The prototype is you, Emerson,' says Melrose. 'You, old bean, are the human bomb.'

32

'NO!' I shout. 'That can't be possible. This is just one long, horrific, nightmare.'

'I can understand your concerns, but I'm afraid it's true.'

Melrose oozes sympathy but a small voice in my head is still warning me not to trust him.

'If you're so keen on helping me, why have you spent so long trying to kill me?' I ask. 'The tracking device...'

'Come on, Emerson,' he says, that condescending tone cutting in again. 'If we wanted to kill you, we could have done it at any stage. Yes, we were tracking you, so why do you think we didn't finish the job after blowing up the train? We knew exactly where you were, that you had jumped off and were "hiding out" in that field. And, by the way, don't worry... we had evacuated the train before it exploded – you don't think we would kill innocent people, do you?'

'I don't know what to think. If you knew where we were all the time, why didn't you...?'

'I would have thought that was pretty obvious,' he says. 'We wanted you to run, because we needed to flush out your father from under the rock he was hiding. We knew he would come to your rescue if he knew you were running for your life. It's what the whole thing was about, the chase across Tower Bridge, the train pursuit and the hunters in the woods. We monitored you right the way to your father's English base of operations, that stately home in Suffolk, only to find he had outwitted us. He wasn't there.'

His words are starting to make some kind of sense. I'd thought it strange we were still in one piece when Franklin had shown us the tracker. How long had we hidden at the farm without being disturbed, for instance?

'What now?' I ask.

'Well, the good news is we believe there's an antidote, an injection of various chemicals that can render you, um, less combustible.'

'Less?'

'Wrong word. It will completely sort you out. No problem. You will be able to live a normal life again, hopefully. Of course, this is experimental because quite honestly there had been no one to test it on until you came along. You're the only Guinea Pig, at least as far as we know, so it's a gamble... not much, but a bit, I'm afraid. The real problem is your father has it in his base in France, so we need to find it.'

'Well, that makes me feel so much better,' I say in a voice weighed down with sarcasm. I need time to myself to digest all the information Melrose has given me so, without thinking things through, I lean over and jab my finger hard on the button that disconnects the satnav. It falls out into my hand and I stare at it for a second, totally perplexed at how this everyday piece of motoring equipment has delivered such a devastating message.

Shit! Looking up I see the tailgate of a lorry looming large in the windscreen and slam my foot on the brake. Behind me there is a screech and a blaring horn. I look in the mirror to see a woman accompanied by two young children strapped into baby seats and admonish myself for failing to concentrate on the road. My God, knowing what I do now, I can't take any risks at all. If I am in a collision, it could trigger the bomb ticking inside me. It makes me realise how lucky I've been so far, what with the car accident I was involved in just a few weeks earlier. Taking a deep breath, I hold up my hand to apologise and get a V-sign in return.

Charming.

Bringing my nerves under control with three deep, drawn-out breaths, I search for road signs and see one straight ahead, an arrow pointing off to the left with the word *Felixstowe* printed below it, accompanied by the icon of a ship. Things are so confused now I can't be sure if I can see the light at the end of the tunnel or whether I'm heading straight into a trap. What else can I do, though? I have the postcard and the case, but if I'm to believe what I've just been told then the people who gave them to me are now my enemy. Even more baffling is what I'm supposed to think about the man in the blue designer suit and the Female Cossack, who have seemed hell-bent on my destruction since the first time I set eyes on them. If I am to believe Melrose, those two deadly characters are now my allies.

I decide the only person I can trust is myself. I can't put faith in Winter, Tank, his CIA sidekick Franklin, my father, my father's old partner or, by association, my wife Cherry.

I'm not paranoid, everyone IS out to get me.

If there is one thing I'm now sure about, it's that I have to confront my father face to face. I'm unsure of his exact location, but I know he has a retreat in France. It's a big country, though, with plenty of places to hide. Perhaps, then, I have to play the game. There is the chance I may be killed before I get to meet him, but that's a risk I must take. They say the mere act of crossing the road can be a gamble but when you're the human equivalent of a lorry-load of TNT, the jeopardy factor escalates one hundredfold.

With a degree of trepidation, I turn the car in the direction of the Suffolk container port, primed to begin the search for a boat called *Esprit d'Orleon III*.

33

AS tall cranes and rows of warehouses loom into view against the backdrop of the dull grey expanse of the English Channel, I know I can't go any further until I've collected my thoughts and stopped the world from spinning. As if in answer to my prayer I notice a small transport café hidden away behind some tall, empty buildings. A cup of tea and a few minutes contemplation could be just the thing I need to kick-start my stuttering mission.

As I enter, the chef is wiping his hands on a badly stained apron, no doubt transferring unhealthy bacteria from one to the other. He looks like he dines out on cardboard boxes full of the stodgy congealed pies he has on offer behind the plastic-fronted display cabinet.

'Hungry, chum?' he asks, leaning forward to reveal a stomach straining to escape his apron. 'What can I get ya?'

'Um, you're all right, I've already eaten.' I get my excuses in early. 'A cup of tea with milk would be just fine.'

'Suit yourself,' he says, transferring the germs from hand to head as he brushes chip-fat greasy, long black hair behind an ear. Wiping his hands again, this time on a tea towel the colour of coal dust, he walks to an industrial-sized teapot perched on a shelf behind the counter, removes a large, chipped china mug from a ring on the wall and splashes brown-stained liquid into it.

Bending over to reveal a posterior desperate to break free from the confines of jeans boasting an elasticated waistband, he then removes a plastic milk container from the fridge and tops up the tea until it spills over the sides. Picking up the mug with pudgy fingers, none of them able to fit inside the handle, he brings it across and crash lands it on the counter, spilling more tea over the side as he does so.

'8op to you, chum,' he says, holding out his hand as if he is offering me a supreme bargain. I scrabble around for change in my pockets, remember the small black purse and empty it into my hands, coming up with the exact money. Retrieving the beverage from the counter, I then walk to a table from which I can monitor the entire room, see out of the windows and keep an eye on the emergency exit in the back.

I consider my escape options. The back exit is an obvious one but if the enemy close in I'm sure they'll have that angle covered. A better alternative would be to sprint behind the counter and make my way through the kitchen to my right. The area is protected by one of those shelves café staff can lever up if they need to clear away used plates and cutlery and clean the tables.

Judging by the half-eaten, congealed mess on the plate that has been discarded on my table, which has been lovingly decorated with an assortment of artistic sauce stains, the Formica surfaces don't get wiped that often. This is probably because Mr Greasy Spoon seems to work alone, which is ideal if a quick exit strategy is required. I wouldn't want to attempt sidestepping the incredible bulk to be honest, but I doubt he's quick enough to obstruct someone charging through the gap without prior warning.

I lift the briefcase onto the table, input the code and raise the lid, looking over the top suspiciously at the couple of truckers on my right – the only other clientele in the café. They're more intent on studying the attributes of a young model in one of the red-top tabloid newspapers than paying attention to me. One does prise his attention away for a second to look in my direction, before writing me off as another boring office worker there to check ledgers and manifests. He might think differently if he gets to see the wads of money in my possession, but then again, he would probably assume I'm in charge of the payroll for one of the shifts on the dock.

Lifting the postcard, I tap it against my teeth and decide to take the plunge. Although recent experiences should have taught me differently, I just can't imagine these two drivers being wrapped up in any organised spying charade. My chair screeches as I pull it back and rise to my feet. The noise doesn't even register with the truckers, who are totally absorbed by their current pursuit.

'Don't fancy yours much,' I hear one of them say as the other reaches across the table to give him a friendly thump in the upper arm.

'Um, excuse me, gents,' I say politely. They both turn their attention to me, the one on the far side quickly closing the paper so that I'm unable to see the source of their amusement.

'What can we do for you, pal?' the other one asks, twisting in my direction, his massive forearms resting on the table as he places a large, tattooed fist under his chin.

'I wondered if you might know where I can find this ship?' I hand him the picture. He looks at it then passes it on to his mate.

'Funny you should say that,' chimes in the other. 'They were loading that vessel not that long ago. I had the feeling she was about to sail.'

'Oh, right,' I say. 'Any idea of the destination?'

'Sorry, pal, can't help you there,' says the man with the newspaper, who has tight ginger curls sitting on a square block of head. 'She's berthed about three-quarters of the way along, so if you have any business on board, I suggest you leave pretty sharpish.'

I return to my table, load things back into the briefcase and take out some money, placing it in the inside pocket of my jacket. I turn to the drivers again. 'So where's...?'

They appear in front of me like figures floating in a mist, even though I know they were sitting just feet from me a moment ago. I stumble forward, losing control of my legs. 'Woah!' I hear one of them say. 'You all right, pal? You don't look at all well. Can we...?'

'Tea!' I demand in my delirium.

'What? I think you'd be better off with a glass of water, what do you reckon, Ali?'

'No!' I say. 'Tea. Drugged.'

'Well, that's your own silly fault if you do drugs, I'm afraid,' says the driver. 'Let us...'

He starts to get up but moves no further. I slump forward into his arms. 'Drugged...' I mutter again as the mists consume everything.

34

I WAKE with my head wedged into the corner of a wooden container, my neck aching with a persistent, dull pain. I can hear a constant throbbing sound which seems to maintain rhythm with the banging inside my head. My feet are tucked up somewhere underneath me and my back screams in response to the contortions my spine is being put through. Just when I think I can take no more I feel the wood giving way behind me, accompanied by a series of cracks. Before I can stop myself, I'm falling backwards as the material that has been supporting me gives way.

Sprawled on the floor I'm immediately dazzled by light which floods my senses and hampers my vision. As I try to focus, a figure appears in front of me surrounded by an almost saintly glow. Ironic, really, when only recently someone was trying to warn me she was the devil.

'Winter,' I slur, my tongue feeling as dry as a piece of leather in my throat.

'Sorry, Em,' she says, crowbar in hand. 'It was the only way. I took the money from you and bribed the captain. We'll be in France before long. There's just enough time to explain a few things, so sit back, shut up and hear me out for a second. Can you do that?'

She is still wearing the police officer's uniform, which must have helped her extricate me from the café without someone raising the alarm. She leans over me and brushes a soft, cool hand across my forehead. 'Sorry I drugged you,' she says. 'Still, Tim carried out his task to perfection. You didn't suspect a thing.'

I remember the awful, weak brew I'd been handed in the cafe and put two and two together. I should have had my suspicions when I tasted the cafe proprietor's tea. 'He was one of yours?'

'Not *yours*, Em, *ours*. Yes, he's one of ours. Look, people have been taking advantage of you in your vulnerable state, haven't they: planting ideas that you might have got things wrong? The truth is, they – Melrose and Co – are the enemy and they only want you to turn yourself in so they can kill you.'

'Did you know?'

'Know what?'

'Don't play games, Winter. Did you know... I'm a bomb?'

'Sure, OK, I knew about it but was assured there's absolutely nothing to worry about. If it was that easy for you to blow up – if you were that combustible – don't you think it would have happened by now with everything we've been through? You didn't explode and take out a large chunk of London when you were in that car accident did you?' She chuckles.

'I'm a fuck... fuck... fucking human bomb!' I lose my temper completely. 'That's nothing to laugh about, is it?'

'Sorry, but you're not. What you are is a mix of chemicals that would be dangerous only if they came into contact with other, specific chemicals... and not everyday ones either. Jeez, it's a bit like one of those international diseases, you know –AIDS or Ebola? You can only get them through direct contact with bodily fluids. By the same token you can only become 'live' if somehow you come into direct contact with pharmaceuticals you don't find on the shelf at your local Boots. These chemicals aren't floating around in the atmosphere ready to latch onto you at the first opportunity. The way I understand it, they have to be deliberately administered to you.'

She looks in my eyes for signs I understand what she is telling me. 'Now, your father isn't going to do that but your new friend, Professor Melrose, will,' she says. 'That's after he has experimented on you first to find out exactly what chemicals are in your body, what concentrations of each and the like. It will take a few weeks before he eventually gets to the bottom of it all. When he does? Well, you'll be no use to him anymore so... booom!'

'Thanks. That puts my mind at ease,' I say sarcastically.

'Sorry, I'm forgetting you're a sensitive flower.'

'This Melrose seems pretty clued up though,' I say. 'He gave me more answers than my own father when it came to my condition. Give me one reason I should believe he's wrong and you're right.'

'Look, I didn't really want to have to do this, but it's the only way.' She reaches into the top pocket of her cop's uniform and pulls out a phone. Pressing a button on it, she thrusts the screen in my direction, holding it at arm's length. 'I'm so sorry,' she says.

As my eyes focus on what's in front of me, for the umpteenth time in three days my world implodes. 'Cherry,' I say, touching the screen as if the very movement of my hand might bring her physically within my grasp. I run my finger across the picture. It shows my wife standing in the doorway of a shop. I know it's her because she is wearing her distinctive spotted white coat, like Cruella DeVil in *101 Dalmatians*. She looks dangerous and incredibly sexy.

That isn't all that's wrapped around her though. She is in the embrace of a man and, though I can only see the man bun at the back of his head at first, when he turns slightly, I see the purple goatee. It's enough to persuade me that something is terribly wrong. The man enjoying a lover's tryst with my wife is Professor Alexander Melrose.

'This... you've manipulated this!' I say. 'Secret government agencies can do all sorts these days. Hell, you should see some of the things we get up to on the magazine to airbrush out blemishes on the models. This isn't real.'

'Suit yourself, but if it's true it would certainly put a different complexion on things, wouldn't it?' she says. 'If you look at it another way, there could be an ulterior, far more basic, reason for disposing of you... one that suits them both.'

'Oh, come on, really? You've got some of the world's greatest brains at your disposal. You're telling me they haven't mocked up this situation to get the response they want? I don't believe any of it.'

Despite my words, some things are becoming clearer in my own head. For almost two years Cherry and I have been living separate lives, so much so that last year she even chose to go on holiday without me, a trip to Boston with her older sister because I'd been too frugal to countenance time away for us both. It wasn't my fault. I hadn't told her, but I'd seen early warning signs that things at work were about to take a dramatic downturn and wanted to save as much cash as possible for what my pessimistic brain interpreted as the inevitable rainy day.

Melrose, though? I wouldn't have been surprised if it was my boss Randy Rufus Wagner who had got his grubby paws on my woman, but how did she even know this person? He looks a lot older than her for a start.

'He's clever,' Winter explains, anticipating my questions. 'He engineered a 'chance' meeting with her in Boston and from what we can gather he has been "grooming" her ever since. I'm so sorry, Em.' She looks it, too, though I know from experience Winter is a very fine actress. 'If it's any consolation, I think she resisted his advances for some time.'

'That makes me feel so much better.' The inflection in my voice betrays the lie. There is a spell of silence between us that drags on before I thrust the phone back into her hand. 'So where do we go from here?'

'As far as I'm concerned the plans haven't changed... In fact, we are already on our way. Welcome to the *Esprit d'Orleon III*. We arrive in France in approximately two hours. Then we set out to find your father. He is the only person who can answer all your questions and, hopefully, "defuse" the bomb.'

'Why did I have to wait for the "enemy" to tell me the truth?' I ask. 'How am I supposed to trust my father when he's the person responsible for rigging his own kid up like a walking fireworks display? This is crazy.

Let's tot up how many times he has let me down in the past and make an informed decision on who is the more trustworthy – him or Melrose.'

Her face adopts the same sympathetic expression. 'I know,' she says, touching my cheek. 'He regrets all this deceit... he really does. But the only way he felt he could keep his family safe was to disappear and that's what he did. Now, with things having taken such a serious turn and his enemies coming out of the woodwork, well, he knows he can't stay hidden any longer. Your anonymity has been compromised and he feels he has a personal obligation to protect you.'

'Only he isn't taking any personal risks, is he? Half the time he's floating around as a hologram while no doubt living a life of luxury in some secret location in France.'

Winter is distracted though. I sense she's no longer committed to the discussion and she proves me right by moving away and indicating I should follow.

'Where are we going?' I ask.

'On deck,' she replies. 'I can't get a signal down here.'

'I'm not a stowaway? I woke up in a bloody crate.'

'The captain knows all about you and was delighted to do us this service after I waved that envelope of money in his face. You were only in that crate so that I could avoid customs and any other interested parties. There were people everywhere keeping an eye out for you. I had to find a way past them.'

'You managed this on your own?'

'I had help of course,' she says. 'Those two lorry drivers in the café bundled you into the crate and had a forklift waiting around the back.'

'They were yours, too?'

I can't hide how impressed I am at the sheer audacity of the kidnap, or rescue mission depending who you believe. Winter always seems to be one or two steps ahead of me.

'Do you think we've finally lost them?' I ask.

'Fingers crossed.' She starts walking again then turns back as if having forgotten something. 'You're OK to climb these ladders? I expect you're still a bit woozy from the drugs.'

'I'll manage.'

I lever myself onto unsteady legs and stagger after her. I feel as if I've been hit by a truck. I watch her as she begins ascending, her long, crimson hair tied in a ponytail and swinging like a pendulum. I can imagine her slender, tanned legs beneath the police uniform working in perfect tandem to push her upwards and am surprised and acutely embarrassed when I realise my body is responding to my thoughts. I haven't felt this way since the early days of my relationship with Cherry. Since I began working long hours to keep a roof over our heads while diverting all my spare time to our daughter, there has been little room for meaningful sex, the odd fumbles in the dark few and far between and lacking the pace and urgency of those early days of our relationship. Not a surprise, I suppose, when you think we've been together since senior school.

Perhaps there is something in the drugs that causes my body to respond this way. Maybe they have the same "medicinal" properties like those of Viagra, the effect being enhanced by the adrenaline racing around my body. Whatever, I feel more alive than I have done for nigh on 30 years. Sharing this exhilarating adventure with this mysterious, intoxicating woman has sent the blood pounding to every corner of my body, the emotions exaggerated by the fact that my time on earth could run out at any moment.

'What's keeping you?' she asks, her head tilting back over her shoulder, and in that moment I know. I know she can understand my thoughts and feelings however much I try to disguise them behind a nondescript expression. It's as if there is some kind of telepathic link between us, messages flooding down the ladder like an electric current coursing through an invisible cable between our two minds.

Chemistry.

What is even more perplexing and astonishing in equal measure is that I can tell she feels the same way about me, harbouring similar desires and longings despite the fact I'm nearly old enough to be her father. She leans down and reaches out a hand. I grab it and move closer to her on the ladder.

'Not far now,' she says, looking deeply into my eyes, her face inches from mine. Then, breaking the moment, she scuttles up the remaining rungs, pulling me after her, and we arrive at a heavy, steel door which she pushes open. Suddenly we are out on deck, our cheeks flushed from the climb and the intimate thoughts that have passed between us.

'Aaaah, Mr Rabette,' says Professor Alexander Melrose. 'So glad you could join us.'

35

WHAT the fuck! AS I look in the direction of the voice, I see a figure dive behind a crate and hear a phut, phut sound – wooden chips leaping from the deck where my nemesis had been standing seconds earlier. Twisting, I see Winter adopting her best TV cop pose, down on one knee and holding the gun out in front of her with two hands, a silencer attached to the barrel. 'Stay away, Alex!' she shouts. 'He's ours now and you'll take him over my dead body.'

'Very probably!' replies Melrose, the voice distracted, as if he isn't totally committed to the conversation.

'He's planning something,' Winter hisses in my direction. 'Get down behind those containers while I check it out.'

'Is he on his own?' I ask.

'No, he isn't.' I swivel around in the direction of the new voice, its sneering tone as penetrating as a javelin to the guts. Two men stand there pointing machine guns in our direction. One is the CIA man I know as Franklin, but it's the other that shocks me more, the one whose words have made my skin crawl. Standing with one hand on his gun and the other on his hip is my work 'rival' Hayes.

'Well, what do we have here?' he says in his sniping manner. 'Old Emerson has been playing away, naughty boy. Who is this little vixen, eh? Didn't tell us about her when you were moaning about how taxing your life was being married with a teenage daughter. I'm not surprised. It must have been quite a juggling act trying to keep the family sweet and the fancy piece satisfied.'

Winter leaps in his direction, clawing for his neck like a lioness, but he smashes his hand across her cheek, sending her reeling across the deck. Instinctively I go to see if she's OK.

'Fancy you can get the better of me, bitch?' It's typical Hayes, firing off made-to-order insults in that catty manner of his. 'I don't think so. Oh, how sweet, your little pet poodle running to make sure you're all right.'

Before I can reach her a pink Doc Marten boot smashes into my ribs, sending teeth-jarring pain shooting through my kidneys.

'Naughty!' says Hayes. 'By the way, Rabette, you're out of a job as of today. Rufus Wagner doesn't take kindly to people missing interviews or having to explain their absence to police who have issued a UK-wide warrant for their arrest. You're all washed up, babe. Meet the new head of the Art Department.' He holds out his hand towards me, but I turn my head away.

'I'd say no hard feelings, but it seems there are,' he says. 'Don't want to shake? Too bad.'

He makes a slight head movement and Franklin approaches, his gun inches from Winter's head. 'Mr Rabette is being a real party-pooping, misery guts,' Hayes tells him. 'Maybe if he sees his girlfriend's brains blown all over this nice, shiny decking he won't be such a meanie.'

I instinctively crawl in his direction until one of those pink boots connects with my ear, sending me sprawling on my back. 'Oh, don't worry,' says Hayes. 'There's plenty of water so if we make a mess it will be easy to clean up afterwards.'

'Stop playing with them, Mr Hayes, they're not your toys.' Melrose emerges from his hiding place to interrupt my colleague's sadistic fun. Tossing his head and letting out a sigh of mock exasperation, Hayes backs away.

'Very well,' he says. 'I'm sure there'll be plenty of playtime later – on your feet, Rabette.'

Every inch of my body is aching, but I don't want to give Hayes the satisfaction of knowing the harm he has done. I grit my teeth and struggle upright. Next to me, Winter rises slowly, blood trickling down her face from a gash on her temple. She isn't letting it distract her as she keeps her eyes fixed firmly on the barrel of Franklin's weapon. Looking him in the face, she says, 'I should have known. You Americans always have a problem when it comes to picking sides.'

Riled, he takes his hand off his gun momentarily to backhand her across the face. The strike sends her reeling, prompting me to take a step forward only to fall flat on my face as Hayes sticks out a boot to obstruct my path. He laughs as if we are part of a bizarre circus double act. Send in the clowns.

'Enough, I said!' shouts Melrose. 'Tie them up. We need them both in good condition as a bargaining chip for the "Commander". This is all about the formula, not playing puerile games. Sometimes I wonder why I bother with you, Mr Hayes. You're so... uncouth.'

Hayes tosses his head to indicate he treats the remark as a personal affront. As he sulks, I see Franklin lean over and offer Winter his hand. Just at that moment, the ship's foghorn sounds, distracting his attention for a split second. It's the last mistake he'll ever make.

Reacting instantly, Winter sinks her teeth into his hand and pulls it towards her, aiming a perfectly directed kick between his legs. In the confusion neither Melrose nor Hayes know quite what to do, realising that if they fire off a volley they're likely to kill their own man.

As Franklin curses, Winter's eyes flash in my direction and I get the message, grabbing the barrel of the gun and turning it just as he presses the trigger. A staccato burst rat-tat-tats around the deck and Melrose's face takes on a puzzled expression in the brief second before his head detaches from its body, a victim of his colleague's wayward fire.

Hayes is too shocked to react at first, giving Winter and I time to wrestle the gun from Franklin's grasp and use his body to block my former colleague's line of fire. As Franklin falls forwards Winter perforates his guts with bullets. He keels over and behind him red blooms across Hayes's shirt. I watch in macabre fascination as his spiteful blood travels down his arms and pools in heavy clumps on the deck. His gun hangs limply at his side, his muscles severed by automatic gunfire.

'My Docs! You've ruined my lovely Docs!' he croaks. Indeed, large blobs of red have appeared on his pristine, patent-leather pink footwear. He sinks slowly to his knees then keels forward onto his face, the gun bouncing away from him on impact.

Another horn. This time it's coming from just off the starboard bow. I look over my shoulder to see a coastguard vessel closing in at a rate of knots. Tank is standing at the bow with a serious looking piece of military hardware in his hands.

Winter steps towards the guard rail and points the gun over the side. 'Stay away unless you want what your mate just got!' she bellows.

Tank doesn't move, just reaches back for the bullhorn being handed to him by a man dressed in the familiar white uniform of an officer of the British navy.

'Good to see you, Miss Winter,' he says jovially. 'I was worried we might be too late. We've only just found out Franklin is an impostor. The real CIA geezer turned up dead in an abandoned car at the long-term parking lot at Heathrow Airport. His throat had been cut, poor guy, and we're pretty sure this bloke did it. Is everyone OK? We had an idea he was heading in your direction.'

'I just hope you've plenty of body bags,' says Winter, 'though a dustpan and brush might be more appropriate in clearing this rubbish from the decks.'

'Damn!' says Tank, chuckling. 'Hey, Rabette, you OK, soldier? All in one piece?'

'No thanks to you,' I say rather churlishly. 'How could you be fooled by this bloke? He was going to kill us. It was only by luck that we're still here to tell the tale.'

'Sorry about that. I hold my hands up, he duped me. If it's any consolation, I'll probably lose my job over this. Your old man won't be happy.'

Despite everything I've been through, I feel a pang of sympathy. I know how he feels. Whatever the wrongs or rights of Tank's actions, I wouldn't want his mistake to cost him his livelihood. He has saved my life a couple of times, after all.

'I'm the one who should be sorry,' I say. 'I can't blame it all on you. I'll have a word with my father when I see him, try to straighten things out.'

'What happened to Melrose?' he asks.

'You could say he fell apart under pressure,' says Winter, winking at me.

'Permission to board?' asks Tank.

I look at her, still not sure who to trust. We are sitting ducks as things stand, but I have to believe in someone, sometime. I hear a buzzing coming from Winter's direction. She puts her hand in her pocket and pulls out the phone she'd used to show me the picture of my wife with Melrose. It shocks me back to reality.

Looking at the ID screen, she says, 'Talking of your father' and hands me the phone.

'Hello?'

'Are you OK, boy? We've only just heard the news about Franklin. Merde.'

'Tank's told us the full story.'

'He got to you OK? Thank God. You're in safe hands then.' I don't know how to answer, so let him talk some more. 'His real name is Lieutenant Peter Tancredi, by the way.'

'Sure you're not making that up, too? It seems to me no one is who they say they are. Melrose told me you're the bad guy in all this. He even has my wife...'

'Sorry,' says my father. 'I couldn't tell you. I'm afraid she's been spying on you for some time. She hooked up with Alexander while you were going through a rough patch. He's a pretty persuasive character. I'm afraid he struck when your wife was vulnerable and seduced her with, well let's be honest, he has plenty of cash at his disposal.'

As he says the words a feeling of helplessness and despair sweep over me. Cherry, my childhood sweetheart, the only true love of my life and the rock of our family, has betrayed Jamie and me. Everything I knew, believed and trusted in has been swept away in less than three days. Before I know it, the tears are flowing, and I press my hands to my face. Arms engulf me and moments later I'm crying into a curtain of long, crimson hair. I drop the phone to my side and weep uncontrollably.

'Come on,' whispers Winter, 'it's been a tough few days. You don't deserve this.'

She guides me on shaking legs to the side of the ship then lifts my face, her piercing green eyes focusing on mine. 'New beginnings, right?' she says.

I nod but can't find the words, a fresh wave of tears rolling down my cheeks. I'm crying for myself, for my memories of Cherry, for my beautiful daughter Jamie and for my old life that was nothing but a big, fat lie. I'm crying for my mother, who mourned my father so heavily I'm convinced it put her in an early grave, and for my father and the fact a normal life was stolen from him because of his genius, and I'm crying because I'm happy nestling in the arms of a beautiful young woman who really does seem to care.

Her hand on my chin, she raises my face and plants her lips on mine. Our mouths move together slowly at first, and I taste salt and peppermint and something indefinable that's sweet at first but has a bitter after-taste. The kiss becomes more forceful, quicker, her tongue darting into my mouth and, suddenly short of breath, I pull away.

She stares at me for one blissful moment then whispers, 'I'm sorry, Em. I love you, but you don't understand. It's something I had to do. For the greater good...'

For seconds my mind fights with the riddle she has set me. Then I feel a grinding in my guts, as if some kind of snake has penetrated my colon and writhes within, desperate for an escape route. I open my mouth to speak and a wave of nausea floods through me. My legs buckle but Winter holds me up.

No, not holds... lifts.

My feet scramble for purchase as I gulp in air and an acidic taste fills my mouth. A smell, like gasoline, leaks from my every pore as my back arches and I look over my shoulder at the cold, dark depths of the English Channel.

Instinctively I try to put my arms out to stop myself falling, but they're like concrete, solid and trapped to my sides. As I reach the point of no return an intense burning sensation races through my lungs and eats into my nervous system. I open my mouth in a silent scream and tumble backwards, the sea reaching up to devour me, and in those final moments the truth hits me like a sledgehammer; the final component to turn all the hidden elements inside me combustible has been transferred in a kiss.

I whisper my last word, the name of the ignition switch, the detonator, my executioner...

'Winter!'

36

'NURSE! Nurse! He's coming around! Sister: Over here! Quick. He made... you heard him... he made a sound. A, well, it sounded like he gasped, but I heard a word, I'm sure.'

'You think so? I mean, it's been almost a week. I know you're wishing for something, but it doesn't always work that way. Sometimes the ears and eyes can play tricks.'

'I know what I heard. I saw his lips move. He said, I don't know, it sounded like "Winter".'

'Well, what does that mean? We're well into summer. Perhaps it was just a release of gasses.'

'Does it have to mean anything?'

I recognise the voices: the sounds of heaven or the rhythms of hell?

A cool hand touches my forehead. I recognise it instantly even though it feels like I haven't experienced that touch in forever. Intense feelings sweep through me.

'Cherry?'

'See? I said I heard something! He did talk. Thank God. That's right, Em, darling. It's Cherry. Your wi... your ex-wife.'

Ex? She's divorced me already? Why bother? Her "boyfriend" was decapitated right in front of my eyes. Just before...

Wait. Where am I and how did I get here? Am I dead and is this some kind of waiting room for the afterlife? I'm reluctant to open my eyes, petrified I'll wake to discover I'm just a torso, limbs having been scattered to the oceans. Worse, maybe I'm just a head, being kept alive by wires and tubes and beeps from a machine.

I was a bomb. A human bomb. By rights there should be nothing left, no chance of survival unless my father's calculations were wrong... and he never gets his calculations wrong.

'I may be mistaken but I think he just said bomb.' This time it's a male voice, painfully familiar. There was a time when I used to hear it every day.

'He's confused, love,' says Cherry.

She calls him love? How many affairs is she having?

'That'll be the drugs.' A third voice, a woman's matter-of-fact assertion.

'You mean...'

'No one can consume that amount without suffering some adverse effects,' the medical professional explains. 'His brain is fried. Plus, he is still recovering from the accident. It's strange. Maybe in some ways the drugs that were slowly killing him have saved his life in this instance.'

'Shit!'

'You didn't know about the drug taking?'

'Well, of course I had a pretty good idea,' says Cherry. 'I just didn't want to think the worst, but I guess it was inevitable once he was on the slippery slope, especially with his condition.'

'Condition?' asks the doctor.

'He's on the spectrum. OCD. He hasn't been the same since... well, let's just say there have been some traumatic events in our lives.'

'Well, if you can give me a clue what we can expect, it may help his recovery programme,' says the hospital worker. 'We need to know what we're up against.'

'He's obsessed about doing things a certain way. There is a number, three. It dominates everything he does or did up until the last time I saw him which, you have to appreciate, was some time ago.'

'Hmm,' says the medical professional. 'That explains something. At the scene someone, a newspaper seller I believe, told the paramedics they'd seen him take three tablets. One is more than enough for most people and my impression when I was told was that it was a suicide attempt, but maybe that explanation is too simplistic. Perhaps this obsessive behaviour was to blame. What do you think?'

'I don't know,' says Cherry. 'If he's suicidal he's been feeling like that for the last 14 years and if he wanted to kill himself, I'm sure he would have managed it by now. He's pretty determined. I've often wondered what happened to him.'

'Che...Che...rry. Wha...?'

'Right, he's coming round. OK, nurses, let's be ready. No sudden shocks, right? If you could hang around, Mrs, um, Rabette? A familiar face might help him process everything a bit better.'

'It's Wagner now.'

What?

'Sorry... Mrs Wagner. Listen, it sounds like he's trying to speak to you. I'm sure he said your name. Hang on, he's opening...'

Bright lights, mysterious figures drifting in and out of a hazy fog, three ghosts hovering just out of reach. Smells of bleach or some other type of cleaner, ammonia based, mixed with boiled cabbage, making me gag. Someone coming closer. Cherry, but older. A great deal older. Grey hair, cut short, neat. Unlike my Cherry, the "free spirit" with the long, blond dreads. How long have I been out?

'Get him some water, quickly.' Someone else, a woman, issuing instructions. A plastic cup is put to my mouth. Insipid, luke-warm water trickles across my cracked lips, the cup held by a veined, ageing hand.

'Hey there, Rab buddy, you gave us quite a scare.' That voice in the background again. Out of place and time. I gather every little bit of energy I can muster and force the first full word from my lips.

'Wanker!' I shout.

37

'SEE? I knew I shouldn't have come,' says my boss Rufus Wagner. 'He's starting this again. He's going to kick off at any moment. Cherry, why are we doing this? It's like going back in time. Shit, I can't handle this – it was traumatic enough the last time. I'm out of here, he's all yours.'

'Oh, grow up, Rufus! He isn't my responsibility anymore.'

'Then why the hell are we even here? You're right. It's up to others to look after him now. Don't get caught in this web again, you know how it upsets you.'

'So, who is going to look out for him if we don't, wise guy?'

'Social services?'

The reply is greeted with silence and a strange feeling of smug satisfaction flows through me, helping to ease the pain coursing through every nerve and sinew.

'Pip,' I manage, deliberately using my pet name for my wife in the hope it might antagonise Rufus further. My throat is burning. 'Why bring him here?' I say the word "him" as if I've discovered dog shit on the sole of my shoe.

Cherry tuts loudly. 'Emerson, dear, me and Wags have come all this way to see you and have been waiting by your side constantly for days, so don't start now, please. The only reason we're here is that some do-gooder found my name and address among your possessions and decided to track me down. They were under the impression I was your next of kin and figured if you were dying, I had the right to know.'

'Still, why bring the perv?' I blurt out before I can stop myself. 'Don't let him near you he... wants to jump your bones.'

Someone in a uniform moves forward, pushing Cherry aside and putting her hand on my chest. 'I don't think he should be getting too excited,' says the medical professional. 'He's suffered immense trauma. The doctor has been called and will be here any moment.'

The room falls silent apart from an electronic bleeping from the equipment to which I'm hooked up. The distance between each bleep is getting shorter, the noise more frequent the more my anxiety grows. I have to say something, though. I can't just leave things as they are.

I push back against the bed, trying to raise myself on the pillow, the room taking solid form now, blurred lines coming into focus, angles and structures sharpening as I adjust my line of sight. I've moved barely a couple of inches, but sheer willpower enables me to pull away from the woman valiantly trying to do her job. 'He wants to sack me and ruin us!' I say.

'See! I told you he was a nutter,' counters Wagner, hiding behind Cherry in case I decide to lunge at him though I've barely the energy to draw breath. Once a coward always a coward, I think. Even so, his next words freeze me to the spot.

'I fired you over a decade ago, Rab, don't you remember? I did my best for you, but sympathy can only go so far. You were next to useless. You seldom turned up for work and when you did, you just weren't there mentally.' He jabs his finger against the side of his temple. 'Up here, you quit months earlier. Out of the kindness of my heart, and as a favour to your... to Cherry... I kept you on until we reached the tipping point. After that, I had no choice.'

'Rrrright,' I say, elongating the word to emphasise the fact I don't believe him. 'Watch him, Pip, he fancies you... always has done.' As I say it, though, an awful realisation starts nagging at my brain.

'Oh God...' she turns away.

'I'm afraid you'll have to wait outside now,' says the medical professional. 'The doctor is here.'

IT isn't until 36 hours later that I begin feeling human again, and wake after an afternoon nap to find Cherry alone at my bedside. She explains to me that I've been in a coma after a traffic accident and starts filling me in on other aspects of our life story which have eluded me until now. Each word strikes home like a dagger to my heart.

'You... married him?' I search her eyes for clues that this might be an elaborate joke. 'How does that work? How long have I been in a coma? Long enough for you to divorce me and walk down the aisle with him?'

'Oh, Em,' she says. 'Wags and I have been married FIVE YEARS! What did you expect? He was there when you weren't. When you hid away in that secret place where none of us could reach you. We tried, but it was no good. It's nothing to do with this recent coma. That's only lasted a little over five days. The truth is you walked out on me, not the other way around. It was our anniversary – Wags and I – when the hospital called to tell me you were here.'

My brain hurts as I grapple with this latest revelation. For a long time now I've been battling to divide fiction from fact, lies from truth. Something tells me this isn't part of the fantasy. It seems solid, undeniable. Then again, haven't the last few days all been part of some glorious charade – a game played out with smoke and mirrors?

'And what does Jamie make of her new "dad" eh?' I put it out there as a question and don't expect the response it provokes. Cherry's face crumples, she raises her hands to hide her anguish then bursts into waves of inconsolable tears.

'YOU really have lost the plot, haven't you?' says Rufus Wagner, turning up with two coffees in plastic cups to find Cherry disintegrating before his eyes. He gives me a disbelieving look as he puts the cups on a side table and nuzzles my wife's head into his shoulder.

She whispers something to him as I just stare in his direction, unsure of how to respond. 'You said that?' he demands, looking straight in my face, my wife tucked under his arm, her face turned away. 'To be frank, I'd have never thought it possible you could forget. Reminders must be around you every day.'

'What... what are you...?'

'Jamie, you callous bastard. Jamie. Your daughter. Your poor departed child.'

'No...' I say, trying to grasp what he is telling me, a joke in the poorest taste. A nurse has entered the room to take my blood pressure and looks anxiously between the two of us, realising the conversation has turned nasty. I feel a headache forming. There is a low hum in my ears and before I can identify where it's coming from it has developed into a high-pitched whine.

'Oh shit, Rufus... Look what you've done!' Cherry tears herself away from his embrace, races to my side and puts her slender red, nail-polished fingers to my lips. 'Shhhh!' she says, and I finally realise the piercing sound I can hear is coming from me. She strokes my arm under the hospital-issue blue patterned gown I'm wearing.

'It's all OK, all fine,' she says, planting a kiss on my forehead. 'There's nothing to worry about, Rab. We can talk it all through later, when you're better. I'll come back to see you in a few days... alone.' That last word is delivered with a pointed look at the man she claims is now her husband.

Out of the corner of my eye I see him toss his head as if to say, 'Why are you paying him all this attention? You're my wife now, not his', and I can imagine them continuing the row as they leave hospital. It's a scenario that cheers me up in a certain sadistic way and I fall silent, wallowing in my small victory.

As they walk out – apart, hands at their sides – I can't resist a smile before Wagner's words come back to me like a nagging itch I can't scratch.

There is something so preposterous about what he has said that a tiny voice in my head questions if it's a cruel prank to get back at me, or a truth too dark to contemplate.

Jamie. Your daughter. Your dear departed child.'

38

I'VE almost given up on Cherry when she returns in the middle of the afternoon, two days later. I feel much better now, having slept a great deal to restore my energy. In fact, I've even taken to walking the corridors of the hospital to build up my strength, wearing the plain old blue dressing gown and moccasin slippers my ex-wife left me on her previous visit.

It's shortly after my mid-afternoon cup of tea and biscuit when she pokes her head around the ward door and makes a beeline for me. She is alone just as promised and I feel a mixture of joy and trepidation, unsure I really want to hear what she has to say.

'All right?' she asks. 'You look better.'

I look around me. 'In hospital. No personal possessions. No clothes. My wife's left me for another man. I don't know what's happened to my daughter. In fact, no one's really explained to me what the hell is going on... Apart from that, yeah, everything's tickety-boo.'

'You always had a terrific line in sarcasm,' she says, smiling in spite of herself.

'I'm glad some of the old me still exists then because, quite frankly, I'm not sure who I am anymore.'

She ignores the moan, moving a few newspapers from the chair by the side of my bed and putting them on my chest of drawers. I've been scanning the national press to try to establish what's going on in this new world into which I've been plunged. There is no mention of gun battles on busy London streets, mad women riding around on horseback, trains being blown up, country houses coming under attack from jet fighters or people falling off ships in the middle of the English Channel. In fact, as far as it can be, the world seems pretty normal.

The only trouble seems confined to the Middle East as usual. At home, politicians have been caught massaging their expenses again and the more right-wing papers are accusing migrants of skulduggery in their efforts to 'invade' Britain. Not only that but a debate over whether Britain should leave the European Union is raging and a former Reality TV star has taken up residence in the White House.

There are few surprises on the sports pages either. My football team, Arsenal, are still reluctant to buy a decent centre back, England have just lost in a semi-final of a major tournament, Roger Federer is once again the man to beat at tennis and world athletics is entangled in a doping scandal.

Déjà vu.

It makes me question everything. Did I dream the whole business with my father, Department 3 and the European Plot or is a massive cover-up in operation? I know from personal experience how resourceful these organisations are.

'Can you walk?' Cherry asks, focusing my mind on the present.

'Walk?' I say. 'I've been a regular Usain Bolt around these parts.'

She laughs and taps me playfully on the arm. 'Funny! You know he's retired now and is giving football a go, don't you?'

'Who?'

'Usain Bolt, our Jamie's...' She stops mid-sentence. 'Come on, let's go and find a quiet corner of the canteen and I'll bring you up to speed as best I can. I don't want to do it here in case...'

She leaves the sentence hanging.

'In case, your nut job of a husband throws a wobbly,' I conclude.

'Something like that, yeah.' For once she doesn't correct me over the "husband" word.

'Not surprising though, is it?'

'That you've got yourself in such a state? No. I can understand how difficult it must be for you, trying to digest so much information after such a horrible accident. The docs say you have suffered severe amnesia and tell me that you had a brain seizure in the hours after the crash happened. On top of the nasty trauma to the head there are the drugs you took...'

'You believe them,' I say. 'You think I take drugs?'

'I can only go by what I'm told, that when the crash happened you were "tripping off your face". I'm sorry to be blunt, but I don't see what I have to say can do more harm than you've done to yourself already.'

'I would never do drugs and drive a car though, Pip, particularly with Jamie on board,' I protest. 'Yes, there's the medication for my condition, y'know? And I've been known to enjoy the odd beer...'

'Look, don't get worked up,' she says. 'You're still confused, and I think I can fill in the blanks. Let's leave any more discussion until we get to the canteen. OK?'

She retrieves my dressing gown from across the back of my other visitors' chair then holds it out for me. I push the covers back and ease my legs over the side of the bed, feeling slightly stiff. It's always like this at first, though. A few strides with the help of the frame they've given me and I know I'll be fine.

She holds my arm as I stand and slide my feet into the slippers. Pulling the walking frame out from the corner by the side of the bed with my free hand, I then twist it around. It's on wheels to make life easier.

'OK, let's go,' she says and leads the way past an old boy in the bed next to me who smiles and gives me the thumbs up. We'd talked earlier in the day; the poor fella having been rushed in after having a stroke at home. I can't imagine what it must be like to lose full control of your mind and your movements. He is impressed I'm up and about, as are the nurses. I guess they'd been getting used to seeing me flat out and were expecting me to remain in a vegetative state, perhaps forever. Pushing through the swing doors to the ward I then turn right only for Cherry to grab me by the arm.

'Where are you going?' she asks.

'Oh, sorry, I thought... It's just, I always go this way.'

'Not today,' she says. 'The canteen is in the other direction, back towards the entrance. It's quite big, really, and has plenty of nooks and crannies we can hide away in.'

I switch direction with her help, noticing for the first time the plaques on the wall which signpost various wards and departments, and wave my hand to allow Cherry to pass in front of me. I can't avoid focusing on the smooth swing of her hips in a tight-fitting beige skirt which stops just above the knee, revealing slender legs enclosed in sheer black tights. Has it really been more than five years since my marriage to this woman was dissolved? It feels like only yesterday that I said goodbye to her before heading out for the Tube and my job "interview".

She still looks remarkably good, though she has to be in her early 40s now. I feel anger rise within me as I imagine Randy Rufus patting her shapely behind, muttering "sweet" in that annoying way he does, like one of those un-PC cartoon characters we inherited from the States. In my mind's eye I can see them embracing as he removes her clothes and, damn, my fierce grip on the frame forces it to slide away from under me and my legs slip on the polished floor as I scramble to regain control. Cherry turns to see me hit the deck. Perfect.

'Fuck!'

'No need to curse, it'll be fine,' she says in her matter-of-fact manner, crouching down by my side. To my left is a communal area and I can see the host of a popular daytime TV quiz show smiling and making light-hearted banter with a guest. 'Let's just...'

'Wait!'

Cherry jumps back as if I've sunk my teeth into the proffered hand. 'Sorry!' she exclaims indignantly.

'No, it's not you. What's that doing there?'

'What do you mean, Rab? Are you talking about that poster? It's only a bloody advert!'

'Quick!' I say, making hand movements to indicate I need her to move out of my line of vision. 'Damn, I need a closer look. Can you help me?'

'OK, OK.' She says impatiently and puts her hand under my arms and lifts. Despite the fact I haven't eaten much recently and have shed a few pounds in hospital, I'm still a pretty big bloke. To her I must seem a dead weight but after a series of grunts and groans, and plenty of sighs on her part, I'm back on my feet. Pushing the frame to the doorway of the communal lounge I then enter to find a handful of people sitting around watching the screen. An elderly woman in the corner is sleeping, a thin line of spittle running from her open mouth to her shoulder. I wonder if that's the way I look these days when I'm out for the count and the thought worries me greatly. There is a sound like a set of bellows being gently squeezed, and soon afterwards a vague odour of slightly rotten eggs attacks my nostrils. Two younger men sitting a short way from the woman whisper to each other and snigger.

They shut up when I shoot them a withering look, switching their attention back to the television. Pushing on, I finally position myself in front of a cork board which takes up roughly half an insipid pastel-coloured wall.

'What's this?' I ask, pointing at one of the notices pinned to it.

Cherry looks over my shoulder. 'Jeez, Em, what's the fuss? It's just a bit of publicity for Colchester Zoo. They've got this fella called Rupert who's pretty famous, been there for years.'

I nod. I know Rupert intimately. We've met before.

'Did he escape recently?' I ask.

'I'm sure I have no idea,' she says. 'Still, I think I might have remembered seeing something about a rare white tiger going missing from one of the neighbourhood zoos.'

'Are you sure?' I'm becoming so insistent I feel all eyes in the room have turned their attention to me. 'The last time I left the house to catch the Tube to work it was all over the news, *"Tiger escapes from zoo"*. I don't know, maybe I've dreamt this last bit up, but it seems so real. I ended up in a barn and had to fight for my life to prevent this beast mauling me to death!'

Cherry's expression turns from confusion to despair. 'Oh my God,' she says. 'They warned me you might have suffered hallucinations from the drugs, or that there could be after-effects bought on by the coma, but there are so many things wrong with that statement I don't know where to start. You haven't worked for well over a decade as I've already told you and as for the Tube...' She shakes her head with pity, making me feel like a charity case.

'Look, the quicker we get to the canteen the better,' she says. 'Hopefully, what I have to say will stop this nonsense spinning around in your head.'

39

CHERRY sips coffee from a Styrofoam cup with the logo of a famous brand on the side. There's a glass of water in front of me but I haven't touched it, my eyes focusing intently on her as she gathers her thoughts.

'I need to give you a brief life history, Rab,' she says. 'Your entire memory has been scrambled by the terrible things that have happened to you. It's such a shame because I was hoping that, by now, you'd have recovered from the past and moved on with your life. I wanted you to retain the happy memories, sure, but was hoping you could let the others go because they were only causing you grief. If we'd been offered a pill enabling us to forget the last 14 years, I know I would have taken it and I suspect you would have, too.'

It seems a strange thing to say to a drug addict until I realise she isn't referring to hard narcotics. As I wait for her to continue, on the periphery of my vision I notice a hospital porter giving me a strange look as he passes our table. He pushes a wheelchair-bound patient towards the serving counter. Without warning, the man's presence produces such an electric charge in my brain that I reach into the pocket of my dressing gown, groping around desperately.

'What's wrong now, Rab? Do you need your painkillers? Christ, it's like you've seen a ghost!'

'A ghost. Yes!' I know I'm raising my voice but can't help it. 'What have you done with my gun? Where's the Glock? It was in the briefcase, then when we were on the boat...'

'What the hell are you talking about?' protests Cherry, my own fear reflected in her eyes. 'You haven't got a gun and never have had one.

You hate those things. In fact, you've always been against firearms of any description. Hell, you wouldn't even go on your mate's stag weekend because they were paintballing. What boat are you talking about? You hate sailing. And why are you looking daggers at that man? For God's sake, he's just a hospital porter and a very nice one at that. You're scaring me, Rab.'

'You know him?' I ask. 'So, what Winter told me was true. You are part of it all. That man over there tried to kill me.'

'Kill you? Jesus, Rab, he didn't try to kill you, he actually saved your life.'

'What?'

'He was the first to respond when you flat-lined. He heard the machine's alarm and summoned help. Luckily, the doctors were able to get your heart going again. By all accounts you were dead for a few seconds ... After they revived you the same man who sounded the alarm plonked you on a gurney and whisked you to the emergency ward. It was touch and go for a while.'

'You're lying,' I protest. 'You're playing tricks on me. That man tried to kill me while masquerading as a CIA agent called Franklin. He was on the boat before I went overboard. I thought he was dead, that Winter had killed him, but he must have survived somehow.'

Franklin looks at me now, a perplexed expression playing across his brow. He thinks he can fool me but I'm wise to his act.

'Am I supposed to know what you're talking about, Rab, because, honestly, honey, I haven't got a clue?'

She's playing her part so well the thought occurs to me that they probably gave her special training.

'That man's one of my father's most dangerous enemies. He wants to steal the blueprints, and you're helping him.'

'Your father?' she says. 'Your father died almost 30 years ago.'

'That's what he wants everyone to think. He faked his own...'

'Stop! Now!'

I've never seen Cherry so frightened. Her face is red, her eyes fixed on mine, imploring me to re-think what I'm saying.

'Your mother identified the body. It was a very upsetting day. He had a heart attack out of the blue... In the back garden. You were out there at the time, collecting conkers. If you don't remember maybe your mind is blocking it out because it was such a traumatic event in your life.'

'It wasn't like that,' I tell her. 'It was me who collapsed and my father ... there was a skiing accident only he wasn't involved. He staged his own death to escape the Female Cossack.'

'Female Cossack?' Her eyes open wide in alarm. 'Can you hear what you're saying? This is nothing short of madness. It's what all those drugs must have done to you down the years. What do the experts call it? Psychosis, I think. You poor, poor man.'

She covers my hand in hers, but I don't want her sympathy. She is acting her part well, the way she has been coached, probably by Melrose. Memories are flooding back, at the forefront of them the photograph on Winter's phone. 'You're protecting Franklin because you're having an affair with Alexander Melrose, his boss.'

'Stop it! Stop it! Stop it!' She is screaming, prompting other canteen users to stop what they are doing and cast worrying looks in our direction. I can tell they think I'm to blame for putting this poor damsel in distress, but they don't know the full story.

'I'm not stupid,' I shout, pushing myself to my feet and looking around the room, making eye contact with different people at different tables. 'I know what's happening here. You're all in on it, aren't you, every last one of you, intent on fooling me with this elaborate hospital charade? Melrose, your lover, was after the plans for the bomb – the one my father implanted inside me. I was getting away, heading for France on board a boat when Franklin over there turned up. Then, when I thought we were safe, Winter pushed me overboard and I...'

Stop. Mid-sentence. 'I exploded,' I mumble to myself. Lowering my head, I slowly start banging it against the table, softly first then harder and harder, trying to knock the pieces into place so I can work out what is really happening. Each time a version springs into my head and doesn't work I shout 'No'. Everyone around us can just hear this repetitive mantra...'No... no... no... no.'

Hands grab me and haul my head back and I summon all my strength to fight against my captors, but as I inflict blows on a couple, more and more people gather around me until my minimal reserves of energy are spent.

'Put him in the restraints.' I force my eyes open and see Franklin looking down on me, the image obscured by the trail of blood dissecting my face. He's lost the American accent, but in his job, I know he has to be a master of deception.

'Look, I'm sorry we've put you to all this trouble,' I hear Cherry say. 'My ex-husband is all jumbled up in his mind. He's suffered a serious head trauma, been in a coma and suffered seizures. I'm sure he'll be OK once he calms down. Thank you, though. Rab?'

I lift my head to look at her, the pain shooting across my forehead as I do so. 'You must behave, or these people are going to take you away and put you somewhere for your own safety. I have a very important thing I need to tell you which I'm hoping will clear all the confusion in your head.'

I nod weakly, my energy spent, the fight sucked out of me. The arms that have been restraining me slowly release the pressure and I'm able to turn my head. They're preparing to strap me onto a gurney and wheel me back to the ward. I notice for the first time a sign on the end of the stretcher on wheels that reads "Franklin and Co".

Hell. Maybe Cherry is telling me the truth. Could Franklin be the name of the company that manufactures the gurneys, not the orderly who was pushing it when I was first wheeled to the emergency room? I feel tears of frustration roll down my cheeks.

'Please, I think he'll be OK now,' says Cherry.

'Well, if you're sure, love,' says one of the men, who is wearing a blue uniform with some kind of badge at the shoulder. 'I'm hospital security and will be just over there if you need me. I have to warn you, though, if he starts up again, we'll probably have to sedate him and return him to the ward.'

'Thanks,' she says. 'I'll be sure to shout if I need you.'

I watch the man I thought was called Franklin walk away with three others and move my head from side to side to clear my mind. Cherry passes me a tissue and points to my forehead. 'You're bleeding,' she says.

I dab at the cut and wince.

'Now, if you don't want to spend the rest of your life in here or, in all likelihood, somewhere far less appealing where they look after the mentally impaired, I suggest you just sit there and listen for a moment while I tell you a story that might revive your memory,' says Cherry. 'We knew everything about each other once so all these allegations you're making about me are disconcerting, to say the least. If I still mean anything to you, then you will hear me out now.'

'I know,' I say. 'I thought I knew a lot of things until I got on that Tube.'

She falls silent, staring at me strangely, and an eerie feeling creeps like an irritating insect up my spine. 'Oh, Rab,' she says. 'Let's talk about the tube. The last time you boarded an Underground train for work was 14 years ago. Maybe if you had seen someone after that – a psychotherapist, like I wanted you to – we wouldn't be going through all this. But you were stubborn and refused, insisting it was all mumbo jumbo. I guess this is the result of a head full of negative thoughts being allowed to breed and fester over time.'

She moves towards me, putting her arm around the back of my head and bringing it down to her shoulder, like a mother comforting a distressed child. Only I'm not distressed, just angry. Angry at her, and Rufus, and Melrose, and Winter and most of all angry at my father... the man who has allowed this conspiracy to rage around me.

'OK,' she says, breathing out heavily. 'Looks like I'm going to have to relive the worst moments of my entire life all over again to help you. If it works, well I guess then it will be worth it.'

40

'LOOK, I want to correct some of the misconceptions you have for a start,' she says. 'It wasn't me who left you it was the other way around. You left me just after you decided to stop going to work, back at the start of 2006. You went away and my Emerson, the old Emerson, never came back. Oh, we weren't perfect before then, I grant you, but...'

'No,' I say. 'I don't believe that. It was that bloody Wagner who split us up, wasn't it? Talk about creative. He was always making up stories to pull the women. I guess Randy Rufus finally broke through your defences.'

'This is exactly what I mean,' says Cherry, stroking my hand. 'You're constructing an alternative history because you can't face the truth. You might not like to hear it, but Rufus was a great friend to me throughout this whole time and remained so after you left. We didn't get together, though, until I'd been on my own for three years and even then, it took another five years before we married. Your version is a myth but, wow, it makes me realise you can't have much respect for me as a person.'

Her remark stings and I don't know how to respond. One voice in my head tells me I've been much too harsh on her, the other says I should lay it on even thicker, punishing my ex-wife for her disloyalty. Then a thought occurs to me.

'He gave the job to Hayes, is that it?' I say. 'Rufus gave the job to Hayes after I was asked to reapply for it, and that's why I ended up out of work. I guess then he moved in and snapped you up when you were at your most vulnerable.'

'Hayes?' asks Cherry. 'Honestly, Rab, you've mentioned this person before, but I don't know who you're talking about, no one of that name ever worked with you. Plus, at no stage did you have to reapply for your own job... It's all a figment of your imagination.'

I try to spot the flaws in her argument but can't pin them down. 'Look, we're here for a reason,' she says, interrupting my inner debate. 'It seems harsh that I'm going to deliberately restore your worst memories, but the alternative doesn't bear thinking about. If this is what forgetting does to you, I need to shock you back to reality.'

From her pocket she produces a small black purse, a child's wallet, identical to the one I'd found in my pocket on my arrival at Liverpool Street. She hands it over and I pull back the zip tentatively before spilling the contents onto the table. There is a newspaper clipping folded up, a lapel pin, a silver nose stud and a familiar looking key ring. I turn it over in my hand and read the legend etched on it...

'You're not paranoid, everyone IS out to get you.'

It jolts a flashing memory in my head, and I reach automatically for the clipping. It looks faded and tattered and I open it carefully so as not to tear it, realising as I do so that it's from the free newspaper they used to hand to commuters on the Underground.

As I look at the pictures and start reading the article, small explosions of half-remembered nightmares bounce around inside my head. The more I read, the more the flashbacks come, one after another, promoting feelings of anguish, hopelessness and terror. The reaction they provoke is much stronger than can be translated by photographs and brief descriptive sentences inked out on newsprint.

Cherry speaks calmly as I read, never faltering, while the truth – the real truth – unfolds in front of me. With tears rolling down my face I'm finally prepared to admit there is an undeniable truth in what she is saying and wonder how I could have possibly managed to get everything so wrong.

Piece by piece the fractured remnants of my tortured soul slot into place as I reform the jigsaw puzzle in my mind to reveal a vision of living hell.

It's not simply a personal tale I'm relearning but a tragedy that plunged a whole city into grief, and as I look for my own starting point, I remember a conversation as I sat at the breakfast table one summer morning 14 years earlier.

41

7 July 2005

'COME on love, for God's sake, we're going to be late!'

I was greeted by the sound of pounding feet on the stairs before she appeared in front of me: my pride and joy. Jamie was munching on a piece of toast, melted butter and crumbs forming a glorious mess on her rosy cheeks. She had a trick of spreading happiness in the morning and I had no idea how she did it.

'Dad, chill!' she said. 'It's only just gone half past. Anyway, no one is going to be bothered about us being a bit late today. It's great news, isn't it? Can we go, Dad? I'm sure you can get tickets from work, you being in the "meeja" and all.'

She made quote marks in the air with her fingers, nails painted red, white and blue.

'What the hell are you on about?' I asked.

'Oh, come on, you know!' she said, giving me her best exasperated look. 'You're just teasing.'

'I haven't got a clue what you're talking about,' I said.

She flicked her shoulder-length blonde hair dramatically. 'You haven't listened to the news over the last two days at all?'

'No,' I said. 'I was very busy yesterday and myself and your mother were enjoying some quiet time this morning before you came charging down wittering on about some nonsense.'

'Not nonsense, Dad. I'm talking about the Olympics – we won!'

'What do you mean won? It doesn't start in Beijing for three years!'

'Noooo,' she said in a long, drawn-out voice, irritated by the doziness of her old man. I could see the frustration in her eyes, and it left me chuckling inside. I loved winding her up. 'It was the announcement yesterday for which city should stage the 2012 games and the Olympic committee chose London! It's going to be fantastic. Oh, pleeeeze say we can get tickets. I want to see Usain Bolt.'

Jamie was a promising young athlete. She'd done well for her school as a middle-distance runner and was also a leading light with the local pool's swimming team.

'Right, well, we'll have to see what we can do then. Now let's get this show on the road. The traffic...'

'You could do the journey in your sleep, Dad, you know that,' said Jamie. 'Granddad didn't call you Emerson for nothing. You're a master behind the wheel.'

Jamie knew how to flatter her old man. 'True, but what if, hell I don't know, there has been an accident, perhaps on the Lambeth Bridge or, well, anywhere to be honest. More to the point, the car's been a bit ropey lately. You never know.'

'Well, if we break down, you'll have the perfect excuse for turning up late, won't you? I'm sure Uncle Rufus will understand. Tell him, Mum!'

Cherry appeared in the kitchen doorway, still draped in her paisley dressing grown, holding a mug of something hot. 'Go on with you both,' she said. 'You know your father gets wound up about these things. Get your stuff and bugger off, please. I'll see you tonight. I'll order in.'

'Curry night, yippee!' said Jamie. She ran across and kissed her mum on the cheek, leaving a smudge of purplish/black lipstick in full view.

'Should you really be wearing that?' I asked. 'First, it's that damn nose ring, then the lipstick, and I haven't even got on to the nails...'

'Jeez, Dad, it's only college not military academy. You should see what the other kids look like. Maybe you would like me to get a tattoo on my neck, perhaps a nice rose or something, or a pierced tongue? Honestly, you're such an old fuddyduddy.'

I took a tissue from my pocket, spat on it and wiped the buttery mess from around her mouth. 'Uuurgh, Dad, that's gross!'

'Nothing wrong with it,' I said. 'My mother used to do it to me; better than going out with half your breakfast still around your chops. What would all those "lush" college boys say?'

'Oh, grow up!' she shouted. 'Talking of grannies, you're starting to act like an old person yourself.'

'Thanks very much,' I said. 'I don't hear you complaining when you're listening to my record collection.'

'That's because I make sure I've got these in when you're playing all that old-timers' stuff on the car stereo.' Jamie pointed to two small black orbs that fitted neatly inside her ears, almost invisible to the naked eye. Damn, she was crafty. I'd thought she was jigging along to That Petrol Emotion or the Charlatans. 'You mean...?'

'Yes, Dad, you can carry on listening to your wailing junk, it won't affect me because I've got my headphones in.'

'Wailing junk? Oh, you're talking about Nirvana now are you? I'll tell you, they were really big when...'

'When you were at university? Yawn. They've pulled it down now, haven't they? That old uni. I heard it was so old and decrepit it fell down by its own accord. The walls were stuck together with mud by the ancient tribes of... hey!'

I smiled. 'Sorry. Hand slipped!'

'Mum, he just smacked me on the bum! I should report him to Child-line.'

'Oh, come on, you deprived young lady. We really are going to be late.'

I ushered her to the door and turned to Cherry, giving her my questioning stare. 'Uncle Rufus?'

'Well, what's she supposed to call him?'

'I don't know, Uncle Perv?'

She patted me playfully on the cheek. 'Oh diddums. Is someone jealous?'

'Oh yeah, I wish I could leer at our models and make bizarre innuendos before rushing off to the toilets for a quick Tommy tank.'

'He doesn't, does he?' She looked genuinely shocked.

'I wouldn't be a bit surprised.'

'Well, he's always the perfect gentleman with me. Anyway, off you go, you were the one complaining about being late.'

She handed me my bag with the sketches for that week's centre spread. I'd been working on it overnight, the story of a good looking and highly successful British actress appearing in a bodice-ripping new Hollywood movie and rumoured to be bearing all. We had some nice racy pics to go with it. I expected Rufus Wagner to be pouring over them during morning conference, trying to decide her best 'angle'.

Cherry gave us a brief wave and disappeared back into the kitchen as I got into the driving seat and turned the key. The car didn't seem quite at its best at the moment and I knew it was long overdue a service.

'Hey, you like my new pin?' Jamie was wearing a small metal pendant above the pocket of her jacket. It featured three wavy lines under some sort of shape. She pointed to it.

'That's meant to be a swimmer and the wavy lines are the pool,' she said. 'It's an Olympic pin. One of the coaches handed us all one at practice last night. Cool, eh?'

'Very nice,' I said absent-mindedly as I reversed out of the driveway.

Traffic was particularly heavy that day. The road system south of the river was gridlocked and I had to get my daughter to college on the east side of the city. It was just fortunate that I was travelling in the same direction as her. Rufus had asked me to pick up a particular piece of artwork from a design studio near Aldgate, so I was happy to drop Jamie off and save her from jostling for position on London's overcrowded underground system at rush hour. Why the hell she'd picked an out-of-the-way place like Whitechapel to learn about marketing I had no idea. I was sure there were plenty of places nearer to home but for some reason she just liked the idea of it.

'It's the real East End!' she'd trumpeted when her mother and I had tried to talk her out of it because of the travelling. She was fascinated by it, her interest sprouting from watching a morose evening soap opera about "everyday Londoners" and then being sustained by dark tales of Jack the Ripper and the Kray twins.

'Me and Linda had a drink in the Blind Beggar the other day,' she told me as I moaned under my breath at the approaching queue caused by "temporary roadworks" on London Bridge. Nothing seemed to be moving.

'Hmm?' I said.

'The Blind Beggar, Dad, you know? Where the Krays were supposed to have gunned down that bloke Jack the Hat McVitie. It's a really big, dark traditional old boozer...have you been there?'

'What's it called – The Old Beggar? Nah.'

'Not the old beggar Dad, for God's sake, the Blind...'

'I know, I'm teasing!' I laugh. 'Anyway, you've got your facts wrong. Jack the Hat was killed at a party, not in a pub. The bloke shot in the Blind Beggar was called George Cornell and he worked for the Krays' rivals, The Richardsons. It's quite a story...'

Beeeeep! A car horn sounded behind me and I realised there was some space ahead and the temporary lights had turned green. I waved my hand to acknowledge the irate bloke in the car behind, though what I really wanted to do was flick a reverse victory sign in his direction.

Crawling across London Bridge and looking out at the giant mish-mash of buildings that made up London's architectural free-for-all I had to admit I did love my city. A short way from that strange office block that resembled a pickle you were thumped in the face by the past, the awe-inspiring Tower of London and the iconic bridge that dwarfed it. I could see it now as I looked off to my right before it disappeared behind a bank of shops. When the traffic ground to a halt again I looked right to where the London Monument stood a short way down a side street.

'Forget the Blind Beggar,' I said. 'You shouldn't just think about gang-sters but how tough ordinary Londoners are and all the things they've had to endure. Take the fire of London – that building over there was built to commemorate those who died in it.' I indicated the Monument. 'Do you remember we went up there once when you were a kid?'

I'd climbed the 311 stone steps of Sir Christopher Wren's 61-metre high Doric Column with Jamie in tow when she was quite a bit younger in an attempt to teach her more about the history of the city in which we lived. I could recall her moaning behind me as we made our way up, only to exhale in wonder as we reached the viewing platform at the top and took in the amazing vista laid out before us.

Reading from a guide book I'd told her how the fire had begun in a baker's house in Pudding Lane on Sunday, September 2, 1666, and wasn't brought under control until three days later after destroying the greater part of the city.

'We went up there?' she said.

I was surprised she didn't remember it, but I guess she was very young at the time.

'Yes, and you moaned all the way up,' I said. 'The fire destroyed or severely damaged thousands of houses, hundreds of streets, the city gates, public buildings, churches... even St Paul's Cathedral. Luckily not too many people lost their lives. What with that and the blitz I'm amazed we didn't pack our bags and leave years ago.'

'Leave London?' she said. 'You're kidding. This is where it all happens. Hey, there's a Tube station. Why don't you just let me out here and I'll get the train. These traffic jams are winding me up.'

'I'm sure it will ease soon,' I said. 'You've got bags to carry. I don't like the thought of you having to battle those grumbling commuters...'

'One day I'll have to do it, Dad,' she said. 'When I'm a top marketing executive for one of the big firms in the city.'

Somehow, I couldn't imagine her as Little Miss Corporate, but it was true she was growing up fast – 17 going on 23.

'Hell!' I exclaimed as we turned the corner and I saw the telltale red and white barriers blocking off Fenchurch Street. 'That's torn it. I was going to go up that way. It would only have taken us another few minutes and I could have dropped you at Tower Hill. It's only a couple of stops from there on the District Line.'

'Shall I get out then?'

'I've got a better idea,' I said. 'One of my friends showed me a good little place to park up here and it's just around the corner from Liverpool Street. You can get the Circle Line to Tower Hill and change for Whitechapel while I go one stop to Aldgate. Then I'll come back here, pick up the car and head on to Old Street. The traffic will hopefully have thinned out by then.'

I studied the clock on the dash. 8.35. I was still on some sort of schedule, though Wagner was expecting me in the office by ten. Looking back, the decision to dump the car would haunt me for the rest of my life.

42

I GLANCED at the large clock on the Liverpool Street concourse. 'It's 10 to 9,' I said, carrying Jamie's rucksack over my shoulder and my own portfolio bag in my right hand. 'Come on, here's the Circle Line. Oh hell, I've got to get a ticket.'

'Give me my bag dad and I'll go on,' said Jamie, holding out her hand. 'I've got my travel card and I really don't want to be late.'

'After all you were saying earlier about having built-in excuses and there being no need to rush?' I laughed. She gave me the mischievous grin that always melted my heart and I handed over her bag. Leaning in, she then gave me a peck on the cheek before I raced to join the queue for travel cards. After a brief wait, I reached the front, tapped the buttons, inserted my change and collected my ticket. Keen to catch up with Jamie, I pushed through the barriers and descended the escalator.

When I reached the platform it was heaving, and I looked at the board to see the next Circle line train travelling via Tower Hill would be arriving in two minutes.

'Dad! Dad!' I could hear my daughter's voice and looked around anxiously. She was waving from further up the platform but there was a huge barrier of humanity between us. Standing on the tips of my toes, I saw Jamie holding on to the arm of a blonde girl. They were smiling and chattering excitedly. She looked towards me and pointed, mouthing words in my direction. There was no way I could hear her above the hubbub, so shrugged my shoulders. Slowly, she repeated the words and I noted the excitement in her face and could lipread what she was saying. 'This ... is... Lin...da!'

Ahhh, the new best friend from college she'd told me so much about. I waved at them and Jamie beckoned me over, but I had no desire to make the other travellers grumpy by pushing past them. For once everyone seemed in such a good mood. All around there was talk about the greatest sporting event on earth coming to our city.

'It's OK!' I mouthed, putting my thumb in the air to indicate I was fine where I was. I made the universal sign for a phone call, suggesting she should ring me later. She nodded then turned back to her friend to resume their animated discussion, Jamie's arms flying left and right before she posed with one arm in the air, an imitation of her hero's famous lightning-bolt celebration.

I turned my attention to the train announcement board. There was a minute to go. The platform was still filling up, people jostling for position. A mixture of different smells invaded my senses, women's perfume, fast food, stale cigarette smoke and the oily odour of departed trains. I pushed forward to get a better sight of the approaching service, hoping I would be able to force my way into a carriage. I was only going one brief stop and to miss this train would cause another unwanted delay.

From my left I heard a screech as the underground train began pulling into the platform, slowing down on its approach, the deceleration accompanied by a teeth-jarring screech of brakes. Subconsciously I counted off the carriages, one then two and finally three as the train ground to a halt, a door conveniently sliding open in front of me. I clambered on, unsurprised that it was standing room only. Then, by a stroke of good fortune, a man in an expensive, electric blue suit awoke from his morning slumber. Realising he was about to miss his stop he leapt up and pushed against the crowd in an effort to reach the door. With his neatly groomed hair and refined clothing he reminded me of a spy from one of those big budget Hollywood blockbusters.

'Sorry!' he said, then 'Excuse me' as he pushed past me in a frantic rush for the exit, dropping something as he went. I bent down and picked up a key ring in the shape of a car – an Aston Martin.

'Hey!' I shouted, tapping him on the shoulder. He swivelled to face me, looking angry. 'Sorry but you dropped these,' I said. His expression immediately softened.

'Oh gosh, thanks, I really am most grateful,' he said. Then he was gone.

I jumped into the vacant seat, earning a rather disgruntled look from an elderly woman who had been making her way towards it in the other direction. Pretending not to notice, I put my head down and concentrated on my portfolio, peering inside as if something magical and fascinating rested within.

As a recorded voice announced the train's destination, I looked up to confirm I was on the right track, my eyes scrutinising the yellow Circle line map above the opposite window. *Liverpool Street, Aldgate, Tower Hill* ... Perfect. Below it, a scrawled piece of graffiti distracted me. What had once said "Hayes was here" had been itself defaced to read, "Hayes was queer."

Childish, but I chuckled. In my imagination I invented a broody graphic designer called "Hayes", who took great umbrage at the way his work had been defaced. In a bitchy voice I imagined him saying, 'which of you bastards changed it then? If I ever catch up with the homophobe responsible, I'll have them in front of an HR disciplinary committee, you see if I don't!'

The "shhhhh!" sound as the doors began to shut brought me back into the present and, with a rumble, the train moved off.

<h1 style="text-align:center">43</h1>

I TRIED to catch a glimpse of Jamie by looking through the glass partition to the carriage in front, but my view was blocked by bodies. The fact she'd found a friend from college was a comforting thought and it gave me a small thrill to think she was starting to forge her own way in the world. Shutting my eyes, I allowed myself to dream, imagining where my daughter might be in five, ten, 20 years' time...

WWWARRUMMMMPH!

I was catapulted back into the present as a loud, rushing sound assaulted my ears and the world was plunged into an eerie shade of orange and yellow. I smelt something burning, like that of damp wood thrown on an outdoor fire. At the exact same instant, wedding confetti filled the carriage, spiralling, twisting and turning as it reflected off the glow from up ahead.

It was as if time had been put on slow motion and, suddenly, I was being lifted like an astronaut floating amid a myriad of twinkling stars. Briefly I was transfixed, staring in wonder at the strange phenomenon, until the lights went out completely and I crashed to the floor, the carriage plunged into a darkness so dense I felt like I'd fallen through a black hole in space. An instant injection of pain shot through my body as I landed on a solid object. Reaching around I felt a cold, limp hand and withdrew my own as if I'd touched hot coals. The carriage was now eerily silent. I became aware of something trickling down my forehead and raised my hand, touching a sticky substance. Blood. It was strangely comforting because it meant I was alive.

From somewhere my ears detected a mewing sound, like the noise you might expect from a posse of starving cats, though I couldn't remember seeing any animals when I entered the carriage. As my brain tuned in, I realised the sound wasn't being created by furry creatures, rather it was the desperate whimpering of human beings. From among them came a hissing whisper.

'What is this? What is this?'

Another voice. Deeper, resigned, matter of fact. The one-word answer as simple as it was terrifying.

'Bomb'.

As I sought to digest this new information, I became aware of sharp needles penetrating my skin, thousands of them: pricking, pinching, tearing like torture by a thousand paper cuts. It wasn't confetti we had been bombarded with but millions of tiny shards of glass. Belatedly I cowered down, covering up to protect myself, though I could already sense liquid dribbling along my arms. My suit jacket was shredded, the left sleeve cut off at the elbow.

'Owww! Aaah! Oww!' The high-pitched, repetitive sounds emanated from my own mouth as my every sense was assaulted. Smoke stung my eyes, an oily, rancid smell like melted rubber and plastic filled my nostrils and there was a metallic, coppery taste in my mouth.

Slumping back, I exhaled loudly, seeking some respite from the pain in my back, only for another object to dig spitefully into my side. Putting my hands down to remove it, I realised this time it was someone's leg. For a moment I feared it might be detached from its owner until a low, guttural protest eased my fears. I twisted.

'Hey, man, are you OK?' I said.

'Hmmph!' I could barely make out the figure beside me, but he didn't seem in the best of health. Around me, others were moving, trying to get their bearings. Then the real screaming started, the choir of catastrophe growing as people belatedly realised the terrible predicament they were in.

'Jamie.' I whispered her name out loud. My daughter had been in the carriage ahead of us and my confused mind was convinced the explosion had come from that direction. The awful possibility dawned on me that she could be badly injured or simply just frightened to death. She would need her dad. If I had one duty on this earth, it was to protect my daughter from dangers such as this. I tried to clamber up, but my foot struck another foreign object, provoking a pitiful squeal like a pig might make when realising its fate in the queue for the slaughterhouse.

'Please!' a voice implored.

I bent down and touched cold flesh then involuntarily wretched as blackened soot found its way to my lungs.

'Please, my foot. I think it's... broken,' said a timid voice and I realised the figure that had been lying beside me on the floor was alive. In the distance I saw lights and heard shuffling feet.

'Look, the door,' said someone. 'It's gone. We need to get out of here. There could be another bomb.'

I moved towards the voice, but fingers clamped around my leg and stuck fast, like a limpet to a rock.

'Don't leave me... I don't want to die... please!' I looked down into terrified eyes peering out through a face mask of grime and blood.

'Help is on its way,' I said. 'I'm afraid I really need to find my daughter.'

'Please!'

Shit.

From somewhere a misty glow pierced the blackened carriage and I was able to take stock of the destruction. The seats were covered in rubble, there was glass everywhere, few of the windows were still intact and pieces of twisted metal hung from the ceiling. Bodies were slumped everywhere, some moving, others not. Among them ghostly grey figures headed slowly towards the exit like extras in a zombie movie.

'Come on!' I said, summoning all my energy to hoist my crippled fellow passenger in a fireman's lift. A sense of urgency drove me forward – if I could get him to the rescuers fast, I could then concentrate on finding Jamie.

'Down here, we've got survivors!' a voice shouted from outside and as I reached the entrance, arms lifted my burden from me and helped me down onto the track. Firemen and other first responders were directing the walking wounded back in the direction of Liverpool Street station. I tried moving against the flow but a burly man in a hi-vis jacket blocked my path.

'You have to go the other way, sir,' he said respectfully.

'Y...you don't understand,' I said. 'My... my daughter. Jamie!' The last word emerged as a shout in the vain hope she might hear me and come forward. I half expected her familiar voice to reply, 'Don't worry, Dad, I'm fine!' Instead, there was nothing but the mumbled instructions of the rescue workers.

I stood there for a long time, numb, facing the tide of human flotsam pushing past me in the opposite direction. Ahead, I saw a body hanging halfway out of carriage two, the one in which Jamie and her friend had travelled. I could tell from the tattered clothes it was a male, his clothes hanging limp and lifeless. A rescue worker reached him and tried to lift him from the train and what followed made me double up and wretch sooty bile into my hand. The torso came away cleanly and flopped silently to the floor of the underground tunnel, minus the rest of the body.

'Could be our bomber,' I heard one rescuer whisper to another.

'Jamie!' I shouted, my fear mounting. 'Jamie, come on, girl, it's your dad!'

Nothing.

As time progressed, bodies were loaded onto stretchers and transported past me in the ghostly artificial light. I tried to reach out and lift the blankets covering them, but other rescue workers pushed me back, clearing a passage through which the stretcher bearers could travel. Just as one poor soul was passing out of view I saw a hand flop down from beneath a blanket and suddenly my senses were on full alert. I turned and followed in a desperate attempt to confirm my suspicions.

The walk seemed to go on forever until finally we emerged into the lights of Liverpool Street station and I was engulfed by the sickening realisation that I had been right. A fist gripped my heart and I stood still, fighting for breath, unable to move forward even though I knew that was the way I needed to go.

The hand still hung loose, only moving involuntarily with the sway of the stretcher, and all I could do was stare in disbelief at the red, white and blue nails which had been painted with such pride in our house that morning.

44

I SAW so many shocking sights when I eventually emerged from London's depths into the glare of a busy Thursday morning.

People with blackened faces, their stunned expressions frozen in place by panic and dirt, wandered aimlessly around begging for water and shivering, their clothes having been torn from their bodies by the force of the explosion.

As I followed Jamie's stretcher, I became hemmed in by policemen erecting tape on the pavement to keep rubberneckers away from the area where the medical professionals were working. I heard a doctor, seconded from a conference at nearby offices, barking instructions and directing people to where they were most needed. My eyes watched him approach Jamie and lift the blanket from her body. I noted the grimace and realised the prognosis wasn't good.

'This one's priority 4,' he shouted gruffly to paramedics carrying the stretcher.

'OK, Dr Joel,' one of them responded and they immediately placed Jamie on the floor a few hundred yards from the ambulance before jogging back towards the station. A small, grey-haired woman in civilian clothes knelt beside Jamie's stretcher and I saw her grab the manicured hand and hold it tightly, whispering something under her breath.

I had to do something. Why wasn't my daughter being whisked away in an ambulance? Surely every second was vital if they were going to save her life. I moved forward until I was breasting the police tape. 'Hey! Hey!' I shouted to those on the other side of the cordon. 'Where is everyone going? Why are you leaving my daughter there? She should be on her way to hospital!'

'Too late, mate.'

A hand fell gently on my shoulder and I turned to see a burly man in military fatigues standing there. It took a moment for his words to register.

'Wh... what do...?' I was struggling to put words together in a coherent sentence. 'No, no, that's not right. It can't be. She was fine this morning, chatting away ten to the dozen as usual. She'll be fine, she just needs...'

I stopped, realising how stupid my words sounded, even to me. I was talking about a time BEFORE the bomb had ripped the heart out of the London Tube network; this morning, when we joked about the Olympics and music and my ability behind the wheel? It was all in the past, long before I took that fateful decision to abandon the car for the Tube.

'I heard that doctor say she's priority 4,' said the squaddie.

'Well, if she's a priority, that's got to be good, hasn't it?' I said.

'No, it means whatever they attempt, medically, the victim can't survive,' he replied. 'I heard it in Afghanistan when our tank was hit by an IED. The medics have to give priority to those that have a fighting chance of survival.'

He saw confusion on my face.

'Oh, you don't know what an IED is? Sorry. It's an Improvised Explosive Device – just like this one, I guess. The Taliban leave them at the roadside and if you hit one... kaboom! I saw mates carried away in body bags shortly after the medics had diagnosed them Priority 4: some of them had parts of their heads missing, limbs severed, one was cut in two...'

I leaned forward and grey bile poured from my mouth onto the pavement. Out of the corner of my eye I saw the luggage tag attached to his heavy-duty bag.

Sergeant Peter Tancredi.

'Sorry, mate, I didn't think.' He rubbed my back and I looked up at him, tears streaking my face. 'In my job you become kind of immune to the horror.'

'But that's my daughter,' I told him. 'She means everything in the world to me and it's my fault she's here.'

AFTER that I must have collapsed because when I awoke there were two paramedics at my side and the soldier had gone. I remember sitting on the floor watching a procession of bodies pass by, unsure whether any of them was dead or alive. I caught a glimpse of one person who had lost both legs at the knee. It was impossible to tell whether the torso belonged to a man or a woman, all the telling signs covered in a macabre facemask of soot and blood.

For a short time, I didn't know where I was or what was happening. Then it came back to me in a terrifying rush; Jamie, my beautiful daughter, my wonderful, talented young girl. I pushed myself up, ignoring the protests of the paramedics.

'Where is she?' I pleaded.

'Who's that, mate?'

'My daughter,' I said. 'She was just over there, lying on a stretcher.'

'Most of the injured have gone to hospital,' he said. 'Which facility your daughter was taken to, I couldn't say. Every medical centre in the London area has been warned to expect an influx of A&E patients from the four incidents.'

So there was still hope! Jamie might have survived. I was confused. 'Four?'

'Oh, sorry, sir, maybe you haven't heard,' he said. 'There were explosions on two other Underground lines. Hang on!'

We stood back and a man walked through with his arm around a woman. Her feet were coated in blood and dirt, her dress ripped at the bottom, her legs covered in grime. I caught a glimpse of the horrific burn marks that had deformed a face I imagined had once been full of character and life. One of the paramedics handed her something and helped her place it over her face. It was a mask to hide the burn marks and made her look like something out of a science fiction movie, a robot or alien.

Around her a phalanx of photographers gathered, snapping pictures. It was an image that was to appear on the TV news channels and newspaper front pages later, a single photograph to symbolise the full awful consequences of a random act of terror.

'We've heard there was an incident further along the Circle Line at Edgware Road and another on the Piccadilly Line at Russell Square,' said the medic. 'Then not long ago there were reports of a bus exploding in Tavistock Square. They're saying the death toll could be bigger than Lockerbie. The attacks were so well coordinated they think Al-Qaida could be responsible.'

Though I nodded, my mind was having trouble filtering the information. This was the centre of London, not Beirut, Kabul or Baghdad. How could terrorists be allowed to roam our streets in this way?

Once the paramedics had left, I stood amid the howling sirens, engulfed in despair. Family occasions whirred through my mind and it occurred to me suddenly that Cherry was completely unaware of our predicament. When we'd left the house that morning we were in the car and she would have no idea that we switched to the Underground. I needed to tell her what was going on and get her to ring around the local hospitals to see if she could find our daughter. I put my hand to my pocket, but my phone wasn't there.

45

Present Day

'I WAS on a break at school when they told me you were on the phone,' says Cherry. 'I thought you were calling to tell me you might be home late because of your doctor's appointment. Of course, we'd heard the news about the bombings and some staff were worried about loved ones who had travelled by public transport to central London that day. I was sure you were safe, though, because you were in the car.'

'I remember your reaction,' I say. 'You told me I was joking.'

'I know, stupid, but in that situation you just react before you put your brain in gear, I guess,' she says. 'It's the shock of it all, such a massive thing for the brain to absorb. I knew you wouldn't make a joke out of the misery of others – particularly something as shocking as an underground explosion. I just couldn't think of a scenario where you and Jamie would have ended up on the exact same train that was blown to smithereens by a bomb.'

'I was equally to blame,' I say. 'I was in shock too and couldn't communicate properly. As soon as I told you about Jamie, though, you leapt into action.'

'I rang every hospital in a ten-mile radius, but they were too busy to talk about individual cases,' says Cherry. 'In the end I thought I might have to get a taxi and travel around them but eventually the number for a helpline was flashed up on the news. I rang and pretty soon afterwards I got the news that our beautiful daughter hadn't survived the blast. When you came home that night, we were both in pieces and fell together in the hope that if we shared our agony, it somehow wouldn't be so painful. It was no good, though. You were wracked with guilt.'

'I couldn't help thinking that if we had left a bit earlier and avoided the worst of the traffic…'

'I know,' says Cherry. 'You were like a broken record. You kept saying, "She was in carriage 2. If she'd been with me in carriage 3, she would have been OK".'

Suddenly, the reason why I'm so obsessed with the Number 3 becomes abundantly clear. This isn't some mental fixation from my childhood but something far more recent. Another piece of the macabre puzzle falls into place.

'It's incredible really,' I say. 'Everyone in our carriage survived - every last one. If I'd made her stay with me, she would be alive today. Instead I let her race off on her own and she ended up being detached from me on the platform, caught up in conversation with her college friend.'

'There was nothing I could say to make you believe differently,' says Cherry. 'Eventually, I tired of trying, having run out of words. I kept telling you it wasn't your fault – that life was a series of random events and you couldn't really plan for them – but you were having none of it.'

'I thought you were saying that for my benefit and deep down you, too, blamed me for her death,' I say.

'Never,' she replies. 'I can honestly say with hand on heart I didn't think that. We were both in pain, though, and it became increasingly clear you were lost to me. I had to find other people to pour my heart out to because you were trapped in your own cell of grief and I couldn't break in.'

'I'm so sorry.'

'So am I,' she says, pausing to reflect on those painful discussions which followed Jamie's death.

'This idea that three was some kind of magic number was lodged in your head,' says Cherry. 'You started acting strangely, touching lamp-posts, cutting up the little pills you were given to cope with your depression, shutting and opening doors. It was both heartbreaking and frustrating to watch you. Then you went back to work less than a month after the incident. I insisted it was too soon, but you wouldn't listen, making the excuse that it had been three weeks, so it was the right time.'

She reaches out and holds my hand, her knuckles white as she applies more force than she realises. It has little effect on me because my whole body is numb as a result of our trip back in time.

'I rang Rufus at your work and let him know about your state of mind,' says Cherry. 'He promised to keep an eye on you. You couldn't settle back into the job though; you went missing at odd times and failed to respond to simple requests or complete everyday tasks. Rufus tried to cover for you but in the end the business was suffering. He was re-doing your work and it was leading to missed deadlines and all sorts of problems. Eventually, he ordered you to take sick leave. He thought you needed grief counselling, but this wound you up. Poor Rufus, he came to visit you whenever he could to check on your progress, but you accused him of failing to understand your predicament. You said he was only calling as an excuse to see me. You blocked him out and retreated into your shell.'

'This is all a blank to me,' I say. 'I recall the funeral and breaking down outside the crematorium, but little else.'

'It was maybe a couple of weeks after you had been sent home from work that you disappeared out of the door and didn't come back. I contacted the police, telling them I was worried about your health and feared you might do something stupid like take your own life. I told them a few places you possibly might be, but they checked and there was no sign of you.'

I shake my head. 'Did you find me? I'm sorry but I just don't remember any of this.'

'Yes,' she says. 'Eventually you turned up at some homeless shelter in a place called 3 Mills, out near Stratford. The police told me they'd been called there because you had caused a disturbance. Staff at the shelter had given you two pieces of toast and you were demanding three. When they said you would have to wait, you turned over tables and began ranting and raving.'

I feel waves of shame crashing over me as the blood races to my face. How embarrassing it must have been for everyone.

'The police told me you were OK, but you didn't want to come home,' Cherry continues. 'You were ashamed of yourself and said I would never forgive you for Jamie's death. I don't know, maybe I'd been giving off the wrong signals – perhaps in looking for a scapegoat I'd inadvertently apportioned some of the blame to you. Rufus drove me to the police station where you were being held and when they eventually released you, we had a massive row in the street. To be honest, I was surprised we weren't all arrested.'

'What was the argument about?'

'You said I didn't care anymore and refused to get in the car with us,' says Cherry. 'Then you accused Rufus of trying it on with me and taking advantage of our situation, even though he had carried on paying you through all your unexplained absences, insisting you would need the money. During that row you demanded a divorce. It really upset me. At the end of it all you punched Rufus, pushed me aside and ran off.'

I feel tears nestling in my eyelashes and as I try to wipe them away, they smudge on my cheek.

'You always hurt the one you love, isn't that the saying?' She pats my forearm.

'Sorry,' I mumble and squeeze her hand. 'Truly I am.'

She takes a deep breath, the emotion of the situation getting to her, too. After all, at one stage in our lives we had been so close and perhaps our heart-to-heart was reminding us of what we lost, besides our daughter, on 7/7.

'Rufus dropped me home and consoled me,' she says. 'In the following weeks, when I heard nothing from you, we became closer. Not that I'd given up on you, far from it. I made regular calls to the police and the shelter, but they said they hadn't seen you since that day. Finally, about a year later, the police called, saying you had overdosed on drugs and were in a bad way in the Royal London Hospital in Whitechapel. You kept ranting about how you wanted to die so that you could meet the bomber

– Shehzad Tanweer – and make his life a misery. You kept saying "he ran a fuckin' chip shop in Leeds, what the fuck was he doing in London" and I had no answer for you.'

It's another shocking revelation during a day full of home truths – how a boy who, at 22, was just a few years older than Jamie could have decided to sacrifice his life and destroy those of countless others.

'I visited you in hospital and couldn't even recognise you,' says Cherry. 'Your clothes stank and, well, your personality had completely changed. You were so full of hatred. I have to tell you that you were awful to me and left me in tears. They let me take you home and in one of your more lucid moments you told me you were ready to "let me go". I didn't know what you meant, so you spelt it out... you were divorcing me so that I could get on with my affair. However much I tried to tell you that it was all in your imagination you wouldn't have it. In the end I agreed. It was too damned exhausting to carry on the way things were, even though I loved you very much, and still do.'

'So how did we end up here?' I ask. There are still huge gaps in my memory. From what Cherry has told me all this took place at least six years ago, before she married Rufus.

'You sent me the divorce papers to sign and asked me to send them off,' she says. 'I didn't hear a thing about you for years after that. The decree absolute came through and you had disappeared off the face of the earth. After that Rufus and I became very close. It was as if the whole thing you wanted to prevent had worked the other way, forcing me into his arms. It seemed a natural progression to marry him, as he had been my rock through the whole business. To be honest, I had a horrible feeling you were dead.'

'When did you realise I wasn't?'

'When the phone call came through from an A&E doctor just over a week ago, telling me you had been involved in this terrible road traffic accident. I was told you were in a coma and it was touch and go whether you would live.'

'You came, though,' I say, smiling through the tears. 'After all I put you through, you still came. I may not sound it but I'm grateful. I can't tell you how much this is helping me, you just being here.'

'I only came because Rufus said it was OK. He's a good man, a really gentle, caring person. I'm sorry you feel the way you do about him.'

I sniff and wipe away a tear. I'm not in a position to concede that my replacement in Cherry's affections is everything I'm not – loyal, trustworthy and supportive. All that keeps going around in my head on a loop is one question: How did I manage to lose such a wonderful family and end up on this one-way path to self-destruction? My thoughts remind me of a question that still needs answering.

'Whose car was I driving when I had the accident?' I ask. 'I'd lost my job and everything dear to me. I can't imagine I could afford a car, yet I end up in this awful crash. Did I steal it when I was under the influence of drugs? And did my actions harm anyone else?'

'Oh,' says Cherry. 'Of course. We haven't had the chance to talk about it.'

I study her eyes for clues, afraid of what I'm about to learn. I envisage the police swooping in to drag me off to the cells the moment my recovery is complete.

'You weren't responsible for the accident, Em,' she says. 'You weren't even in a car. You were just an innocent bystander. Remember what I said about people getting caught up in circumstances beyond their control?'

I nod, but I'm confused. She expands on the story.

'I believe it happened like this,' she says. 'You were sleeping rough in a shop doorway in central London, somewhere near Piccadilly, when on the nearby main road, a car switched lanes suddenly and smashed into another one. The car that took the brunt of the impact spiralled out of control and mounted the pavement close to where you were lying.'

'Shit!' I say. 'What did I do?'

'Nothing. According to the nurse I spoke to you were out of it, totally oblivious to the danger, off your head on some substance or other. You certainly weren't capable of producing the instant reaction needed to get away unscathed. By a stroke of good fortune, the car avoided you. It collided with a store front and you were struck on the head by flying debris.'

I put a hand to my temple to feel the rough scab which extends some distance across it. 'You really had a lucky escape,' Cherry continues. 'According to your doctors, you had taken such a cocktail of drugs that they wondered if you had been trying to kill yourself. In the event, whatever you had taken may have saved your life because you were too far out of it to feel shock or suffer a heart attack, or whatever.'

The information opens a small window in my mind. 'Three pills,' I say.

'What?'

'I couldn't just take one – I had to take three.'

'That makes sense,' says Cherry. 'The docs said you had ingested enough bad stuff to tranquilise a horse. So, it wasn't a suicide attempt?'

I shrug. 'Don't think so.'

'Good, because if it was it failed miserably.' Cherry's face breaks into a melancholy smile. 'Instead, here you are, very much alive and kicking, so you're the lucky one and you have a second chance. You're certainly luckier than that poor man whose car crashed into the building. His daughter died from internal bleeding, while he followed later having severed an artery in his leg. They thought he would be OK but there were complications. Very sad.'

I study her sympathetic expression and feel pangs of remorse over how badly I've treated this caring woman. 'It was the paramedics attending the scene that found you unconscious and rushed you here,' she says. 'They told staff you had been mumbling about your daughter and asking if she was OK. It must have been a flashback you were having due to the drugs or the bump to the head. Anyway, when they searched your clothing, they found Jamie's old purse – that black one lying there. It's all you had to remember her by which is why you kept it, I guess. Inside was the Olympic swimming pin, her nose stud and that key ring you loved, you know, the one about being paranoid. There was also a slither of paper with my phone number on. It was the day after you'd been admitted that I got a phone call. They rang the number blind, not knowing to whom it belonged. When they told me about this patient who had been admitted in a grave condition and that they needed to find his next of kin, I guessed it was you. By the time I got here you had been in a coma for 24 hours and it was touch and go whether you'd live.'

46

'I CAN'T get over the fact you came, though,' I say, welling up again. 'Despite everything, you came. That's so nice of you after all I put you through and, well, please thank Rufus for me, too.'

'You can thank him yourself,' says Cherry. 'He's waiting outside.'

'Sure.' I can't say I'm looking forward to swallowing such a massive slice of humble pie in front of my wife's replacement lover, but I have to accept I've been wrong about him. Suddenly a thought occurs to me. 'Does he have a car?'

'Well, yes, I'm surprised he hasn't bored you about it,' says Cherry. 'It's new, his pride and joy. Why?'

'I need to see the crash scene.'

'Why on earth would you want to do that? It can only stir up bad memories and, anyway, I doubt there's any evidence left to help you work out what happened.'

'There are huge holes in my life I need to fill in and maybe it can help,' I say. 'If I don't straighten them out in my head, they'll nag at me forever. The visions I saw during my coma were extremely vivid, clear as day, and I find it difficult to believe they're figments of my imagination. I've already dug up a few things from the recesses of my mind which can help me get over this ordeal and return to a normal life... what if there's more?'

'How do you mean? What have you dug up?'

'There was a soldier in my dream – his name was Tank – and he helped me quite a lot. Looking back at the aftermath of the Liverpool Street bombing I can remember speaking to a soldier who filled in some of the gaps for me about what was happening. Unless my mind is playing tricks – and after what's happened, I guess there is a good chance it is – I think Tank and this soldier are one and the same person.'

'You need to be careful,' warns Cherry. 'Remember too much and there's a danger you'll be right back to square one.'

'Seriously? I think it's the other way around,' I say. 'While these stories and characters are imbedded in my brain, I can't let them go. If I can somehow get to the bottom of this, then it might relieve this anxiety I feel, the sense that I could be plunged back into this strange world I dreamed about at any second. Look at that business with the hospital porter...' I lower my voice and look around, but he is no longer in the canteen.

'Surely that was just down to the drugs you took,' says Cherry. 'They sent you crazy and you hallucinated. We don't want to trigger your addiction again, do we? Especially when it seems the one good thing to come from the coma is that it helped your system cleanse itself from the hold those things have over you.'

I shrug. 'Sure, but it's when you have a lack of answers that you tend to try to find them through drugs. If I can't clear things in my own mind, then I'm not sure how long it will take for me to fall off the wagon again.'

Cherry eyes me curiously and I detect an imperceptible shake of the head. 'Look,' I say. 'I've discovered that Franklin, the dangerous CIA officer in my dream, was nothing of the sort. It was the name I gave to a porter who helped me in hospital, because I caught sight of the gurney-makers name and associated it with him. That's a good thing, a positive I can deal with. Then there's the white tiger that attacked me – now I know it was just my imagination playing tricks on me after I caught a glimpse of that zoo poster, probably when they were wheeling me in here after the accident. I'm sorry, Cherry, I know you mean well but, with or without your help, I'm going to find my way there. Piccadilly you say?'

'Yeah, just around the corner.' I can see Cherry is wrestling with the conundrum in her own mind. Eventually she says, 'If Rufus agrees then fine, we'll go.'

I smile and squeeze her hand. 'Thanks,' I say.

BACK on the ward I ask one of the nurses where I can find my clothes.

'Oh, didn't they tell you?' she says. 'They were in a terrible state when they brought you in.'

'I know but...'

'The legs were torn right off, the arms ripped, they were filthy and no doubt teeming with parasites. As for the shoes, well, there weren't any. What we thought could be salvaged we put in a laundry bag and gave to your, umm, wife here for safe keeping.'

The woman has described the exact state my clothes were in during that period when I went on the run in my coma. Another piece slots into place.

'I need to wear them,' I say. 'Can't you see, it's the best way for someone to recognise me if they know me.'

'I'm sorry, Rab,' says Cherry. 'That's just not possible. I burnt them on a bonfire. I was worried about fleas and stuff and, quite honestly, there was no way you would be able to wear them again the state they were in. If I'd put them in the wash, they would have disintegrated. It was only dirt, blood and grime that held them together.'

'What am I supposed to wear then?' I protest. 'I can't walk the streets of London in this bloody hospital gown!'

'Look, don't worry, I've bought fresh clothes,' says Cherry. 'I've asked Rufus to bring them in for you from the car. Some of them belong to him and others were a bargain from one of our local charity shops.'

'You're joking!' I say. 'So now I'm a charity case?'

She looks at me and smiles and, for a brief moment, I see Jamie in there, her sweet nature and the dimple in the cheek they shared. It comforts me, bringing back a time when we were all so happy and, without warning, we burst into spontaneous laughter. It's an uplifting moment at a difficult time.

'I guess that's my answer,' I say, stifling the giggles for a second.

'I'm glad you can see the funny side,' says Cherry. 'It's a long time since we've been able to laugh.'

'I know.'

We fall silent, both of us considering the underlying pain behind those words. Cherry lowers herself down beside me and we perch on the edge of the hospital bed to wait. A couple of minutes later the door bangs open and Rufus materialises, a well-stocked bin liner in his hand. Immediately I stand, feeling awkward as if I was in the act of doing something I shouldn't have been. He nods at me.

'Rab.'

'Hey, Rufus.' I walk towards him until I'm about two feet away. I can see from his eyes that he is wary of what I'm about to do. 'Look,' I say, 'I just want to say I'm sorry for all the grief I've caused. I've spoken to Cherry about the whole business stretching back 14 years and it's now clear to me you're the good guy in all this. You have tried to help me and Cherry all the way down the line and all I've done is thrown it back in your face.'

'You were ill,' says Rufus. 'Your world had been torn apart and you had lost your beautiful daughter. I couldn't expect you to appreciate my motives at the time, Rab, but we go back a long way and I just wanted to help. If you're beginning to see that now, then I'm grateful and, really, it's been no trouble. For the record, I love Cherry very much.'

A lump forms in my throat as I realise I've lost her forever and must concede defeat for the good of all three of us.

'Sure,' I say.

'Look,' says Rufus. 'We don't want you to go back on the streets. This accident business has changed everything. We'd like you to come home with us. I'm not suggesting we live under the same roof but I've got a little flat in central London which I rent out as an Air bnb and I'm happy to let you have it until you get back on your feet. I haven't looked into it yet but perhaps you will be eligible for housing benefit and maybe there is a way you can get back into the graphic design business. Unfortunately, our mag closed a while back, but I have a couple more niche ones I concentrate on these days and there may be some freelance work available or casual shifts. First, though, you have to get better.'

The last thing I want is to feel indebted to this man or for Cherry to see me take his handout. It's one thing to thank him for his support and another to throw myself on his mercy. He looks at me as if he can read my thoughts.

'I know you're too proud to beg and I wouldn't ask that of you,' he says. 'Seriously, it would be doing me a favour if I could turn to you every now and again to help out. The flat could eventually be paid for out of your wages. Now, what's the plan? Cherry says you want to go on a magical mystery tour.'

I grab the bag of clothes and head for the shower room.

'Yeah,' I say. 'Thanks for these.'

47

TRAVELLING these strange yet familiar streets in Rufus Wagner's powerful and expensive BMW 3 Series, I look out of the window and muse at how the other half live. Though I can remember little of the years leading up to this moment, half-built memories flash through my mind as we pass the busy cafés, shops and landmarks of central London. Rufus keeps up an annoying and distracting commentary in the background as I sit silently in the passenger seat, searching for the clues which will piece my world back together.

'It does 0-60 in 4.2 seconds, not that I've had a chance to give it full poke,' he says. 'Cost me an absolute arm and a leg but Cherry didn't mind, love her, she knows what cars mean to me and, of course, you've got to spend your money on something if you haven't got kids. Do you like the colour? As a boy I always dreamed of driving a gold car and now, well, I had some money set aside and the Air bnb apartment has been a bit of a money spinner so here I...'

'Shut up!'

Rufus looks at me as if I've taken a dump on his plush, hand-stitched leather upholstery.

'Sorry,' I say. 'It's just, you know, I'm trying to concentrate. This area seems familiar. I think this was my old stamping ground when I was on the streets. I recognise the storefronts. I may have slept in some of them.'

'Sure, Rab,' says Rufus. 'It's me who should be sorry, rattling on about a 500-grand motor when you barely have a pot to piss in. I truly am upset that you ended up like this, mate. You were a pretty good designer back in the day. That's why I let you drive the bus sometimes.'

'What did you say?'

Rufus looks at me, his expression one of alarm. He thinks he may have upset me again but doesn't realise his words have prompted another flashback: one that has me sitting behind the wheel of a red London bus on the approach to Tower Bridge.

'Chill, Rab,' he says. 'It's just a silly phrase I inherited from my Yorkshire-born Granddad. When he put someone else in charge of the bakery while he nipped out for a pint, he'd tell them, "You're driving the bus".' He delivers the last phrase in an exaggerated northern accent. 'When I had to leave the office for any length of time, I had enough faith in you to tell you it was your turn to "Drive the bus".'

So that's it. My coma must have awakened something in my brain, a memory from those days working with Rufus at *Boys and Their Toys*.

'Thanks,' I say. 'You don't know how much it helps knowing that. Seriously. I really can't recall anything about back then and not much since Jamie died to be honest. I have a thin recollection of the office and, of course, I remember you but other than that, the last 14 years seem like a life lived by someone else. It probably sounds stupid to you.'

'Not at all. Fair play, you always...'

'Stop!'

Cherry leans forward from the backseat and I think for a moment she is attempting to prevent us tearing at each other's throats. However, Rufus turns the wheel to the left and pulls into the kerb and I realise my ex-wife has seen something relevant to my quest. Behind us a taxi driver sounds a long blast of his horn to let Rufus know he isn't happy at his failure to indicate.

'Bloody hell, Cher!' says our driver, turning to face his wife. 'What in God's name are you doing? You could have caused an accident.'

'We wouldn't be the first to have an accident here,' she points out, ignoring his complaints. 'I'm sure this is the spot. I asked one of the paramedics if he knew anyone who had attended the fatal car crash on the day you were brought in, and he introduced me to one of his mates. She told me it was on The Strand, close to Charing Cross station. Well, the station is just over there and, look, that shop front is under reconstruction. It must have suffered the brunt of the damage.'

She looks around animatedly, like a child searching for further clues in an Easter egg hunt.

'Ah ha!' she exclaims. 'There's a chemist, see, just as I was told there would be and, look, there's that well-known travel agency. Apparently, you were found slumped in the doorway of one of the company's branches. Putting everything together, this must be the place.'

'Sherlock Holmes strikes again,' says Rufus, a gleam in his eyes and sarcasm dripping from his voice. She ignores him.

'Recognise anything, Rab?'

I put my hand in the air to pause the conversation, open the door gingerly and step out onto the pavement. I'm overcome by an aura of trepidation. This may be where all the answers lie and I'm not sure how ready I am to face the truth. Rufus and Cherry fall in step behind me and, without the help of the walking frame I've needed until now, I set off tentatively in the direction my ex-wife has indicated.

My shuffling steps in borrowed, cheap trainers seem loud on the concrete, every move a challenge, underlining how much the accident has impacted on my body and how far I still have to go on the road to recovery. Already I feel exhausted but my determination to uncover the truth pushes me on. When I reach the travel agency window, I come to an abrupt halt, my mouth falling open, aghast at the vision in front of me.

Timidly, I put my hand out and run my fingers slowly down the window's surface as water mists my eyes and my heart beats loudly in my ears. I can see someone on the other side of the glass, someone who I've wiped from my memory until now. Long red hair shines in the bright sunlight as it cascades like a waterfall onto shoulders cocooned in a white, zip-up jacket. The slight blemish in her green eyes leaves no reason for doubt and I feel my soul crumple as I gaze at the person with whom I spent some of the most exhilarating days of my life.

'Winter,' I say.

In the reflection of the window I see Rufus mumbling to Cherry, who is tucked tightly underneath his arm. She gives him a quizzical look and a shrug in return before saying, 'What do you mean, Rab? It's the middle of flippin' June. I think you're a bit confused, love. Perhaps we should get you back to hospital.'

'No!' I say more forcefully than I intend as I welcome the tears tumbling freely down my cheeks. I'm powerless to stop them.

'Can't you see her? She's right there!' I say, addressing my comments to my two accomplices. 'What happened to you, my angel?'

Behind me Rufus is again whispering to my ex-wife. 'Who is he talking to? Does he mean the girl behind the desk? There's no one else in there, apart from a middle-aged man leafing through some of the brochures.'

He doesn't understand. No one can. Ours is a love affair beyond explanation.

'Rab, love? Come on.' Cherry tries again, tugging at my arm. 'Let's get you back. You're obviously worn out by all this. I should have known it was too soon. It's my fault.'

'That's Winter,' I say, pointing at the window.

'Oh my God!' I hear Rufus whisper. 'I think he's cracking up.'

Cherry ignores him, addressing her next comment to me.

'You mean the ski model?'

'Yes.'

'You know her?'

'Better than anyone,' I say.

'But you know her name isn't Winter, don't you? I mean, you do know that's just a cardboard cut-out advertising winter sport holidays? Look.' She points at the blemish in my soul mate's eye. 'She's just a photograph, there's even a bit of red eye.'

I brush angrily at the tears. 'Yes,' I manage to mutter. 'I can see that.'

The girl who infiltrated my dreams and accompanied me through the darkest depths of my coma, sharing with me the most weird and wonderful adventures of my mind, is nothing but a figment of my out-of-control imagination. For a long time before the accident, this striking girl was the first person to greet me in the morning and the last face I would see at night. She stood watching over me like a sentinel, her beaming smile probably the only friendly gesture I would experience as another day dawned on the streets.

Winter is Winter Sport, the company offering packages to the Tyrol, the Pyrenees and places as far away as Vermont and Chile. To acknowledge this simple truth only serves to open the fissures in my broken heart.

48

MY eyes scan the window display of the Go Explore travel agency and slowly but surely, I begin to complete the puzzle.

On a poster to Winter's left there is an ageing woman in a hat decorated with imitation fruit who is roaring encouragement as thoroughbred racehorses speed past. Underneath the picture of the person I know as the Female Cossack, a company is offering an exclusive, fun-packed Ladies' Day at Royal Ascot. Thankfully, the Cossack is another product of my coma.

Moving along to the next window I see alongside the words "Enjoy an action-packed adventure" a series of what we graphic designers call bomb-blasts exploding on either side of a train hurtling through the countryside. "Play at Poirot" one of them says, before going on to explain that, like the famous detective dreamt up by Agatha Christie, you can ride the Orient Express. "Solve a Gruesome Murder" the second bomb-blast implores, the words below inviting you to indulge in a 'Once-in-a-lifetime chance to act the part of a super sleuth and unmask a killer'. A third bomb-blast encourages the reader to 'Excite the little grey cells!'- a catchphrase synonymous with Hercule Poirot – and 'visit some of the most exciting cities in Europe'.

Moving along there is another poster saying 'Be treated like The King' which implores you to visit Elvis Pressley's famous home at Graceland on a week's trip to Memphis and New Orleans while a final display extols the many virtues of London itself. There is a picture taken from above of the iconic landmark Tower Bridge with an invitation to '*experience the spectacular Glass Floor across the high-level walkways when you visit Tower*

Bridge! This permanent feature offers visitors an incredible bird's eye view of London life from 42 metres above the River Thames. Look down to spy those famous red London buses...'

Spies. Buses. Another part of the jigsaw fits easily into place. I look more closely at the picture and spot a red bus heading south across the river and silently ponder whether an American CIA operative called Franklin might be on board, juggling with deadly grenades.

Next to this great offer is another, to spend a few hours in the company of the crown jewels and London's famous Beefeaters at the Tower of London. There is a selection of pictures accompanying the words, one of which shows the grounds of the Tower in November 2014 when artists Paul Cummins and Tom Piper installed 888,246 ceramic poppies to mark the 100th anniversary since the start of the First World War. Each poppy represented a British military fatality and I feel pain like a needle entering my arm as I recall the injuries I thought I'd suffered when I fell into those grounds. None of it happened, but it still seems raw and real to me. It's as if my body has developed a muscle memory for an incident concocted by my imagination.

Fingers softly touch my arm and I turn to see Cherry standing there, concern etched on her face. 'Are you OK, love?' she asks. I nod and search around me, as if I can find the words to answer her in other ads in the window.

'It's fine,' I say as I notice a section advertising days out in the UK. There's a picture of a stately home in Suffolk which features a maze as one of its main attractions, an invitation to take a helicopter ride above London, the chance to visit a local farm... the stories appear in front of me thick and fast, like pages being turned in a graphic novel.

Feeling spent, I finally turn away and am about to follow Cherry and Rufus back to the car when I notice something else in the periphery of my vision. A paper seller is shouting out today's headlines about the race for the Tory leadership following Prime Minister Theresa May's resignation. I recognise the seller; clear as day. It's the same character I spoke to at Liverpool Street Station while in my dream state, the bloke who called me 'Bunny'. As I walk towards him a sign in the window of the chemist shop next door catches my eye. It makes me involuntarily rub my stomach, having recalled the shooting pains that plagued me during my lost hours.

A cardboard display in the window is surrounded by stacks of pill bottles. The advertisement features a person in silhouette with brightly coloured circles spreading outwards from the abdomen region. '*Don't let stomach problems hold you back. If you suffer from irritable bowel syndrome, diarrhoea or simple tummy ache reach for Gastrozan. It will simply blow away your problems, enabling you to go about your normal day without rude interruptions.*'

Suddenly, I'm laughing out loud in the middle of a busy London street. A woman exits the chemist and stops to look at me, wondering if she should offer assistance. I turn to her and give her the brightest smile I can muster through the tears of sheer relief I'm shedding. 'I'm OK!' I tell her. 'I'm absolutely fine.'

She shakes her head in bewilderment, her expression suggesting she doesn't concur with my self-diagnosis.

Cherry comes running over. 'Rab, what is it? Are you OK?'

'Never felt better!' I say, trying to suppress my chuckles. 'See that poster?' I point at the chemist's window.

'Yeah, they're advertising pills for people with a dicky tummy – a simple over-the-counter remedy,' says Cherry. 'I'm not convinced they're much cop, but Rufus swears by them and claims they really sort him out after a night on the town. Why, love, do you think you need some? It's probably best if we tell your doctors you have a problem then they can prescribe what they think is fit for your condition. We don't want to mess...'

'My stomach's fine,' I say. 'You don't understand. In my dreams I had pains and when I looked down at my midriff, it was like there was a fire alight in my belly. It was actually glowing! Now I realise it was just because I had this advert in my head. Look at the coloured circles radiating out from the centre of that silhouette – just like I imagined was happening to me. It means I really am OK. There's no bomb...'

Cherry shakes her head as if I'm a troubled child describing an imaginary world she can't possibly comprehend.

'Bomb, Rab?' she says. 'You are funny. In what circumstances would you ever find yourself in close proximity to...'

She stops at once and puts her hand to her mouth. 'Oh my God,' she says. 'I'm so sorry.'

Right at the last moment she has remembered 7/7, Liverpool Street and the day we lost our Jamie forever. She reaches out and embraces me and the warmth of her hug feels really good. A mixture of happy and sad tears flow down my face, soaking the collar of her expensive-looking floral print jacket. I act quickly to assuage her feelings of guilt. 'It's OK,' I say. 'You didn't mean anything by it, I know. We both miss her so much.'

'Hey, can anyone join the love-in,' asks Rufus awkwardly. 'Seriously, I'm sorry to bother you but there's a traffic warden and if you leave your car around here too long, you're in danger of being clamped, or worse. I really don't want that lovely car towed away to some awful compound.'

'Sure,' I say as I prise myself from his wife. 'Sorry, Rufus, I just needed to borrow your wife for a second.'

To Cherry, I say, 'Thanks. I really don't deserve you. It would have been quite understandable if you had ignored the doctor's call about me and carried on with your life.'

'I couldn't do that,' she says. 'We have shared too much. I want you to know that in the really dark moments I'll always be there for you. Rufus is aware of that. We've had many conversations about it.'

'Thanks,' I say.

'Wait up, big boy,' she shouts and walks quickly off to catch up with her new husband. I feel genuinely pleased for her, now I'm over the early pangs of jealousy. Rufus seems a much better bloke than I ever considered him to be when he was my boss, and Cherry deserves to be happy after all the crap I've put her through. As I turn to follow her, I catch sight of a figure across the road which forces me into a double take. Then, as if someone has flicked a switch, everything changes again.

The man who has caught my eye is wearing tweeds that have seen better days, topping them off with a trilby hat. It's the chin that has really caught my eye though, more specifically the goatee attached to it which is inexplicably dyed purple.

'Melrose!' I whisper, gritting my teeth as I realise it's the person who for so long has been my nemesis.

49

'HEY, Melrose, you bastard!' I shout, hobbling past Rufus and Cherry before they are aware of what is happening. Tyres screech as a car stops abruptly, the driver stamping on the brakes to avoid a collision as I step out into the road. He winds the window down and shouts obscenities at me. Horns fill the lunchtime air, but I don't care. I'm too focused on my mission to worry about anything else.

The person I know as Alexander Melrose has spotted me and quickens his pace, barging past pedestrians on the pavement. These continuing pursuits of this elusive figure across busy streets are becoming a habit. 'Wait!' I shout, 'We need to talk.'

My words fail to make any impression on him, though, and when I finally reach the other side of the road, he seems to have disappeared into thin air. I curse under my breath and can hear the shouts of Cherry and Rufus above the noise of the midday traffic, which is slowly grinding back into action again.

'Rab! Rab! Come back. What's wrong? Where are you going?' says Cherry.

'Hey, mate, come on, we have to go!' shouts Rufus. 'I'll get a ticket. Stop larking about!'

My only concern is catching the man who has haunted my dreams. At last I know he is real. He exists. He isn't part of some shop-front window display, a faintly remembered character from my distant past or a member of the hospital staff. Here, in the heart of London, he's walking around as plain as day and when I shouted his name, he ran. He knows who I am, and he is desperate to avoid me.

Breaking into a trot, even though every step is agony, I touch a few street lampposts for luck: One, two, three... and as I approach the Charing Cross Underground station entrance on the corner of The Strand and Duncannon Street, I notice a man with a trilby hat pulled low over his head disappear into the bowels of the earth.

I reach the Tube sign and stop, feeling the anxiety build as I contemplate once again entering my own personal *Room 101*. This will never be over, though, unless I take the plunge. Forcing myself forward, with the assistance of the handrail I take the steps three at a time as I swallow back my fear and descend once again into the depths. When I reach the bottom, I look around in the hope of spotting him and, sure enough, there he is, pushing through one of the barriers.

Shit. I suddenly remember I don't have a penny on me. There are signs inviting you to top up your Oyster Card or touch and go with your credit card, but I can't recall how long ago it is since I possessed one of those. I have to think quickly or lose my quarry and any chance of uncovering the truth.

The sound of a baby crying interrupts my thoughts and I see a woman with a pushchair overloaded with shopping bags emerging through one of the wider gates that open in the opposite direction to the platforms. Without thinking, I push past her, knocking the pram and inciting the baby to more hysterics.

The woman scowls at me and swears under her breath while an Underground worker shouts, 'Hey! You can't do that!' I ignore them both and hurry on because up ahead I can see Melrose, bounding down the escalator towards the platforms of the Northern Line. I choose the left-hand side and descend the moving stairway three steps at a time, producing grumbles and groans from people I barge past on the way.

'Sorry,' I mouth to one lady who looks remarkably like my mother. 'I really am in a hurry, though.'

I'm gaining on Melrose rapidly. Good. I'm not sure how much longer my body is going to hold out before I hit the wall and crumple to the ground. Thankfully, something happens that gives me the advantage.

Melrose makes a misjudgement as he steps off the elevator and his feet slip from under him. His hat falls off as he hits the floor and skids along, only stopping when he collides with a wall. Disorientated and shaken by his ordeal, he begins to clamber up, but I reach the foot of the escalator and launch myself across, grabbing a handful of his coat. His arms flail about and he aims a kick at my knee, but I'm so driven by an inner resolve I won't let him go at any cost.

Grabbing hold of his swinging foot, I'm swiftly accosted by another staggering moment of *déjà vu*. He is wearing an expensive pair of Italian loafers; the exact shoes I was wearing the last time I caught the Tube – or was that just a mirage? They must have stuck in my mind from a previous encounter with this man. It appears he holds the key to everything.

'You're a bloody nutcase, mate,' he says, a glint of fear in his eyes.

'I want answers, Melrose, and you're gonna give them to me!'

'Who's Melrose?' he asks, squirming under my grip. 'You've got the wrong bloke. My name's Barry. Barry Ralston.'

'Don't play games with me, you bastard! What are you doing here? Are you watching me again?'

'Watching you?' His expression turns from fear to anger. 'Why the fuck would I watch you? Talk about mental.'

I push him in the direction of a passageway which leads out onto the platform and see a sign announcing we are on the Northern Line. The next train is due in one minute and its imminent arrival is announced by a rumbling sound coming from my left. Shit! It dawns on me that I'm back in the place that harbours my worst nightmares. My free hand begins to shake but I can't let Melrose see my fear.

'There he is!'

An Underground worker is pointing in my direction as he leads two transport police officers onto the platform. As they approach, there's a clattering sound and the train emerges from the tunnel. Pushing Melrose's arm up behind his back he responds with a grunt of pain. Unperturbed, I march him further along the platform, raising protests from fellow travellers about to board.

As the train stops and the doors slide open, I thrust Melrose inside, counting rapidly to three before jumping aboard after him. Through the window I can see our pursuers unsure of where we have gone, the Underground worker cussing his bad luck as the officers try to appease him. I force Melrose down into a seat, pushing his head low and ducking with him so we can't be seen.

'*This is a Northern Line train to High Barnet,*' says the automated announcement before another voice advises passengers they should push their way as far along the carriage as they can to make room for fellow travellers. I lift my head and through a gap between two standing passengers see the Tube worker on tiptoe, looking around. Eventually he shrugs his shoulders, mutters something and leaves the train, the police officers trudging in his slipstream.

There is a beeping sound, the doors close and I breathe a sigh of relief as the train begins to move. Then I turn to Melrose.

'So, what's the story eh?' I demand, grabbing his chin forcefully and turning his face towards me. 'If you don't know me like you claim, why the fuck did you run as soon as I shouted your name?'

'Cos you're a nutter, that's why.'

'So, you do know me, if you know I'm a "nutter"?'

'No, I...'

I punch him in the ribs, amazed at my own capacity for violence, having rarely resorted to physical aggression in my life before. 'Don't lie!' I say.

'OK, OK.'

He puts his hand in his pocket, but I grab him by the elbow. 'Woooah! No, you bloody don't,' I say. 'What have you got in there? A gun I suspect, if I know you as well as I think I do.'

He snorts contemptuously. 'Gun?' he says. 'Jeez, what planet are you from, you dopey fuck? I was just gonna show you how I know you.'

I'm confused but release him slowly.

'Let me get my sweeties,' he says, nervously scanning the carriage to make sure no other passengers are watching.

'You're kidding!'

'No, I'm not,' he says, his accent suddenly altering so the Cockney comes through. 'OK... yes, I admit it, I know you. Strewth, I can't believe you don't remember me; you must have taken a right bump on the bonce. Me name ain't Ralston, you was right about that. You were right in a way, but it's not Mr Melrose. It's Mel, Mel Rose, and until recently you were one of me best customers. I came back to see you the other day, but you wasn't at your normal place. A street pal of yours, some bloke who flogs papers on The Strand, referred to you as "Bunny Rabette" and told me you was in hospital. Well, I got worried, didn't I? Thought it might have been somethin' I sold you that put you there. When I saw you just now my first thought was you might be bringing the cops to me door. That's why I ran.'

'Prove it,' I say.

'OK, let me just get me product and...'

'Hold it. Take your hands away and I'll do it.'

'Let you get your hands on me stash? Not bloody likely. Do you think I'm a complete tool?'

I thump him in the ribs again and he cries out then moves his hands away from his pockets. I delve inside and pull out a clear plastic bag containing a few 'wraps' and about two dozen pills.

'See?' he says. 'They're your favourite, them. Don't you remember? Bit of Special K. Last time I seen you, you was crying out for them.'

I'm having flashbacks now... seeing the expensive loafers then peering up into bright sunlight, a figure above me, features hidden beneath a purple goatee and a hat. He's holding his hand out, three pills nestling in his palm. My supplier.

'After speaking to that paper seller, I figured you must have downed the damn lot in one go which was why you was taken away in an ambulance,' he says, licking his lips. 'That's suicidal, man. You're better now though, eh? If you meant to kill yourself, you failed. Never mind, there's plenty more where that came from.' He indicates the baggie.

'I'm skint,' I say.

'Hey, no sweat. As it's you and I probably owe you something by way of an apology I'll give 'em to you gratis. Here.' He snatches the baggie from me and his hand dips inside before pulling out three small, white spheres. 'Catch you later, maybe. I can't afford to hang around. Time is money and all that. Pushing me on this train, well, it's narrowed my selling window, ain't it?'

Looking at those pills in his hand my stomach flips and my skin radiates a cold sweat. It's as if my body no longer belongs to me.

'See,' he says. 'You know you want them and, of course, the sooner you partake, the quicker you can get back to that bird of yours. You know, the one you're always blabbin' on about...'

'Winter.'

'That her name? Sure. Whatever you say: Winter.'

Is my mind playing tricks again? Something doesn't seem right. How can I trust a drug dealer? Then again, how does he know about Winter?

'She exists?'

'Well, I'm only taking your word for it, of course. I've never met her but every time I come to see you, you won't stop talking about the love of your life, how you lost her but how this stuff allows you to find her again. You said you had a special relationship. I don't know, maybe it's all over, but perhaps there's still a chance. Swallow the pills from me lucky bag, take one of your magical trips and, who knows, maybe you'll rekindle that "special relationship".' The man's a walking cliché, making the inverted commas with his hands.

Goosebumps travel up my arms, fear and anticipation battling for control of my body as that familiar sensation takes over. I think of Cherry and Rufus anxiously waiting for me in the car, their promise of a new home, a new life, a new start. I think of the chance to work again, the golden opportunity to drag myself out of the gutter and form new relationships.

Then I see her outline, a silhouette, just out of reach, holding her hands out towards me, inviting me to move back towards her and fold myself into her loving embrace. The chance to see her again, to hold her, to love her... It's irresistible.

I reach out my hand.

50

'HEY, soldier! Hands off cocks, on with socks.'

I feel someone shaking me but don't want to open my eyes and emerge from the comfort sleep has brought me. The voice is insistent though, cajoling, ordering... It won't take no for an answer.

Peeling my encrusted eyelashes apart, I then peer out, the hazy figure in front of me gradually taking form. A shaved, bullet-shaped head confronts me, dark eyes fixed on mine. 'There he is. Thank God. I thought we'd lost you, Rabette. You feeling OK?'

I nod slowly. 'Tank, wha... what are you doing here? I thought...'

'There's your problem right there. Thinking. Never did anyone any good. You were going to say you thought I was a figment of your imagination, eh?' A smile cracks his face. 'That's what they wanted you to think. They injected you with something on that boat, I don't know what, but it was designed to make you forget, some kind of serum that wipes your memory. Fortunately, I was close at hand and able to pull you out of the drink. You remember, right?'

'Of course.'

I don't, but it seems logical. The last I can recall was over-balancing and falling over the side of that big container ship. I thought I was done for, a human bomb timed to explode. I'm amazed I've survived.

'Good. It looks like the medics have done their job.'

'We're back in London?' I cast my eyes around my surroundings. 'We're on the Underground. I thought we were heading for France.'

'Yeah,' he says. 'Well, change of plan, on The Commander's advice. Too dangerous to take you there, he thinks they were tracking you to find out his location. You probably don't remember, what with all them chemicals swimming around your system. They're designed to make you forget.'

'My father.'

'At least you remember that much. Listen, we got to act fast. Look!'

He points across the aisle at the grey metal section of the train that supports the seats and immediately a lump comes to my throat and panic grips me. How can this be? It's all starting again just at a time when I thought the whole episode was a glorious figment of my imagination. There, scrawled in black marker pen, are the three words that originally launched me on this adventure and, below them, three arrows pointing in one direction.

'*Run, Rabette, Run,*' the message reads.

I push myself to my feet and set off along the carriage, away from Tank. Familiar figures perch on the seats either side of me. There is Martin Aston in his electric blue designer suit, the Female Cossack in her fruity hat and the beggar who broke my nose when I refused to give him cash. I look more closely at him and realise he bears a striking resemblance to me, almost as if I attacked myself.

'Hey, Rabette!' shouts Tank. 'I got your back, remember. If any of these jokers make a move, I'll keep 'em occupied while you make your way down the train. Don't worry, she told me she'd wait, however long it took.'

I push on until I come to the familiar figure of the transport police-man, who nods at me and winks before opening the door between com-partments and stepping back so I can pass through. Looking through the window I note we are travelling through a station with no sign of stopping. My eyes focus on a giant electronic advertising board on the platform, the carriages of my train reflecting off it. I count back from the front... one... two...

Just two.

Clammy sweat gathers on my forehead and I'm about to turn back when one advert flips around to reveal another. *'Be brave, Rabette,'* it orders. *'They're just numbers. You've got this.'*

Taking a deep breath, I charge on, pushing past an array of fellow travellers who grumble and groan at the disturbance. I'm nearly at the front of the second carriage and feel light-headed, unsure of myself, even slightly delirious.

Then I see her, and all the clocks stop.

My breath catches in my throat as if the oxygen has been sucked from the room and I have to remind myself, 'In through the nose, out through the mouth'. In front of me a waterfall of long, red hair cascades down a slim back. The smell of intoxicating perfume fills my nostrils, reminding me of freshly cut flowers on a spring day, and those familiar stirrings rise deep within me. Reaching out a hand slowly in case this proves to be just another illusion, a trick of the light intended to create chaos with my senses, I feel the smooth leather of her jacket under my fingertips. Mesmerised and frozen in place like a statue, I watch the woman of my dreams flick her head to one side and slowly turn to face me.

Winter.

'Well you took your time, Em,' she says. 'Glad you could make it. I think my work is done here, and I have to say it's been a pleasure working with you. This is the end of the line for us. You don't need a babysitter anymore. It was never me you were looking for anyway, if we're being entirely truthful.'

Stepping promptly aside she stands stock still, a cardboard figure, and I realise the other passengers aren't moving either, the scene reminiscent of one an artist might capture on canvas.

The only movement I sense is that of my own blood racing to the centre of my being from every extremity of my body. As it reaches its target, my heart beats so fast I'm sure it's going to explode. Eyes misting over, I stare, speechless, at the figure standing there, as familiar to me as the face in the mirror. Now I know the mission's over, and I've won. I slide slowly to the ground as all my pain, my suffering and my anxiety is sucked away like air through a vacuum.

Peering down at me with a smile that could light up any room, my beautiful daughter Jamie says, 'Hello Dad.'

EPILOGUE

'HE looks strangely happy, doesn't he?' said the solid-looking police constable, studying the figure on the Underground station bench. Removing his hat, he proceeded to pat down wisps of thinning grey hair. 'I've been around a long time but can't say I've seen anything like this before.'

'It's probably just the effect of the gasses building up in the body,' said the female paramedic, pulling on protective gloves. 'I must admit, though, it's all pretty strange. Where do you think he got it from?'

'We had reports of a break-in at a travel agency on The Strand,' said the policeman. 'Apparently this beauty is the only thing that went missing. He must be a strong bugger. Apparently, he grabbed a heavy metal bin, smashed the window, grabbed her and brought her here for... well, I'm sure I don't know.' He shrugged his shoulders and gave her a meaningful look.

'Can't be all there,' he continued. 'I think he's a miss-per we were looking for. He'd just come out of a coma and left the Royal London with his ex-wife and her bloke yesterday morning. It was supposed to be a therapeutic day out, just a couple of hours before returning to hospital, but somehow, he broke away from them and disappeared. The ex-wife reported him missing and half an hour ago we got a call out from a station assistant.'

'You say he was in a coma?'

'Yeah, he was out of it for quite a few days, I'm told,' said the policeman. 'Apparently he was in a traffic accident around Charing Cross way. Really nasty, a bloke and his daughter were killed when their car was broadsided by a Jeep and this bloke was in the firing line but somehow survived. Maybe you worked it?'

'Not me,' said the female paramedic, taking a closer look at the figure on the bench. 'I think my partner might have, though... hey, Bill!'

A male paramedic walked across to join them.

'You worked the RTA at Charing Cross, two fatalities, Dad and daughter?'

'Terrible, Kate,' said Bill, looking at the figure on the bench. 'Hey, this guy's familiar. He had blood covering most of his face and was dressed in little more than rags but, yes, he was dossing down in a doorway and got hit by flying debris, poor lad. We got him to hospital, but it was touch and go if he'd survive.'

'Well, he did, but it looks like his nine lives just ran out,' said the PC.

'Right,' agreed Bill. 'Ah well. At least he didn't die in pain.'

'Who knows?' said the policeman.

'Well, he's smiling, ain't he?'

They all stood back and committed the scene to memory so that they could tell their loved ones about it over dinner that night. You needed a quirky sense of humour in their line of work, or you were likely to crack up completely. In the worst-case scenario you could end up like the dead man on the bench, his arm wrapped around the shoulders of a life-sized cardboard image of a red-haired woman in a white ski suit.

'Brrr, makes me feel cold,' said the paramedic called Kate. 'Like it's winter all over again.'

Bill dropped to his haunches in front of the corpse and shone a light into the eyes. 'Wish I was on what he's on, though,' he said. 'This geezer is definitely bloody smiling.'

'Shame we have to ruin his fun,' said Kate. 'Let's get him to the morgue.'

'What about the girlfriend?' asked the policeman.

'That's up to you,' said Kate. 'I don't know whether she is needed for evidence but if we take her, we'll only clutter up the ambulance. Otherwise, why not leave her here? She might give those stony-faced commuters a giggle when they arrive for another boring day at the office.'

Bill grabbed the figure and tried to move it. 'Bloody hell, he doesn't want to let go.'

'Rigour mortis,' said Kate.

Finally, he liberated the cardboard figure. 'Sorry, man,' he said apologetically to the corpse.

'Look, he's gone all miserable now,' said the policeman. 'You've separated him from his girlfriend, and I think you've broken his heart.'

The paramedics laughed as they watched the policeman carry the cardboard figure a short way down the platform, resting it against the sign informing people of the station's name.

'Well, young lady, this is as far as you go,' he said. 'Welcome to Old Street.'

THE END

About the Author

Nick Rippington is the award-winning author of suspense thrillers with twists and turns. His Boxer Boys trilogy - *Crossing The Whitewash, Spark Out* and *Dying Seconds* - is a series of UK gangland novels that has received high acclaim. A digital box set entitled *The Boxer Boys Collection* is available too. This is his fourth book and a departure from the norm in that it is a psychological thriller. "Alice in Wonderland meets James Bond" is how he describes it.

Nick lives in London with wife Liz and has two daughters, Jemma and Olivia. You can follow his progress on Facebook at *facebook.com/buckrippers*, on Twitter *@nickripp*, on Instagram *@nickrippingtonauthor* or on his website *www.theripperfile.com*

www.ingramcontent.com/pod-product-compliance
Lightning Source LLC
Chambersburg PA
CBHW021810110726
47902CB00006B/1727